OWNED

FAEBORNE BRIDES
BOOK 1

SIREN CROW

Released and Printed in the United States of America

First Edition e-book December 2022

First Edition paperback November 2024

Formatting Design by Vellum

ASIN: B09TWXHGMQ

Paperback ISBN(Amazon and Barnes & Noble version): 978-1-943773-68-8

❀ Formatted with Vellum

SIREN CROW

MYSTICAL WORLDS AND DELICIOUS MAYHEM

Thanks so much for taking the time to check out my book! I'm Siren and I write spicy, multicultural fantasy and paranormal romance. This debut series is a product of love and I've always wanted to write a series about brothers and elves, and Voila! The Faeborne Brides series was born!

This series will be a six-book series, so please consider signing up for my mailing list here to receive updates when each book will release. If mailing lists aren't your jam, you can always follow me on Amazon and Bookbub! Like my mailing list, they send updates on new releases and any preorders I put up. With either option, you'll never miss an update!

If you want to connect on social media, I'm *everywhere*! Through this link, you'll find a linktree where to find me! TikTok is where I'm the most active but I pop in other places every once in a while!

And last but not least, if you reach the end of this book and loved it, please consider leaving a review to convince others to read it too! Reviews, good and critical, help authors decide to move forward with a series and I *really* want you to meet these brothers! Of course, you're not obligated to, but the best is yet to come! You can so by clicking here.

CONTENT WARNINGS

This book explores dark themes. Please check the content warnings and proceed with caution.

Content warnings:

Death of a parent

Kidnapping

Mention of child abuse and abandonment

Explicit sex (including degradation, anal sex, and light spanking.)

Murder

Forced marriage

~This book is dedicated to all the women who never felt seen or heard...

May you all find your Aranzeiros

PROLOGUE

Aranzeiros

You are never your own being until your father passes. A hard truth I grew up believing and was about to learn if it carried any truth. Today I didn't have the pleasure of showing vulnerability, nor did my brothers, but it required strength to see my father on his deathbed before me. My father, King Tarron the Wise, had the will and the might to outlive us all. And here he was. An Elven male we viewed as having no weaknesses, killed by an accident. May the goddess help us all.

"He looks so peaceful. As if he's just dreaming," Vamir said. He was one of my younger brothers, and the one most heart-broken about our father's unfortunate fate.

Lianthore, the brother I had grown up with, was born second after me, and the only one of my younger brothers that had always carried our father's name and privilege. The Faebornes were the oldest and most prestigious family of all Esterbrooke, and you would have thought that would have made Lianthore and I unwilling to accept that our father had fathered other sons who could fight us for a share of our inheritances.

But for so long it was just the two of us, and being a Faeborne meant there was wealth and honor to go around. Our grandmother had always taught us the importance of family and getting to know them all, I didn't know where I would be if not for my six brothers. Today was only another cruel reminder that nothing was more essential than the bond of a family.

"I am grateful that I got the chance to know him. I used to think he was just an ordinary Elf. He would risk his safety just to spend time with me. I'm proud to be born of the mountains, but even prouder to have called him father. In my culture, esteemed males and females do not die. They are reborn as warriors and promised all of life's pleasures. Let us hope he is enjoying the afterlife luxuries," Zaos added, his light eyes wet from the tears he held back.

He was Elven on his father's side, as his mother was a Valkyrie and low-born. Truthfully, all of our mothers had been, but the luxury of being king is that father had his choice of any female he desired. Deities, dragons, nymphs, and monsters. If she was beautiful, he had to have her. Hence why he had fathered seven sons across every corner of the Fae Realm.

We had chosen to have a ceremonial funeral to mourn him in peace, but being that many loved him, the seven-day realm-wide period of mourning was a chance for all of his subjects to pay tribute. Dwarves, elves, shifters, and all fae adored King Tarron, something that made being the firstborn in our family more challenging. I bore the heavy weight of inheriting the throne, and while I had spent my whole life preparing for it, I had doubts that I could be the king my father was. Being a prince was much simpler, but I was born to follow in his footsteps, and there was no time for uncertainty.

"You always think you have so much time with someone and in the blink of an eye, they're just gone. Rest, father, and may you take your place amongst the ancestors that guide us." Ivaran softened, placing a light kiss against our father's dark cold hands.

My brother had had his share of losing people he loved and by now, he had reached a place to expect it. His heavy burdens for past mistakes made him reclusive to all with exceptions for us, but there was a permanent sadness in his golden stare that made me hope he would one day find peace. The lonely life that he lived in Castemont wasn't a life I wanted for *any* of my brothers. While it was too early to talk about wives and mates, I was briefly reminded of how Father had never remarried after his first wife passed.

I knew not much about her, and for his sake, no one outside of our grandmother ever asked him about her. So long as he produced heirs, he was not required to remarry after his first marriage.

Paying our final respects, in separate carriages, we rode to our summer home in BellaTerra, a region known for its fresh springs and lush forests. It was far out in the country and rather modest, just fifty rooms minus the servant quarters, but it was built on the uplands surrounded in evergreen foliage and no shortage of nearby waterfalls for when you wanted a quick swim. We nicknamed the manor The Crystal Star, named for how it glistened in the sun from a distance. It resembled a star in the sky, but for us, it was just a home away from home and served as the memory where our father would take us to bond whenever he brought in another one of his sons. There were so many memories here.

"Welcome home, my lords," Agnes said, lowering into a low curtsy. An older Faun, her furry legs were beginning to match the salt and pepper strands of her hair and even though she scolded me with a lifetime of slaps across the back of my hand for meddling in her kitchen, she was like a second grandmother, only warmer and more nurturing than any of us deserved. Not at *all* like our real grandmother.

"You will find all of your rooms cleaned and prepared for you. Except for you, Prince Aranzeiros. I was advised to prepare King Tarron's former chambers for you. Please let us know if everything is to your liking. We have prepared a ceremonial banquet in honor of your visit, and should it please you to visit the chapel before dinner, an altar has been assembled so that you may begin the first day of mourning of his greatness. Can I provide anything else, my lords?"

"No. That will be all," I said before she strolled away, her hooved feet clacking against the marble floors of the manor's lobby. The nostalgia stored in these lavish halls was enough to feel father's presence despite being gone. He was a part of us. A part of me. With my brothers and our blended ideas, I was going to be more legendary a king than my father ever could be.

***

Joining my brothers in the Great Hall, they took every seat minus the end, where my father always sat. It was finally sinking in that from now on, this would permanently be my place when I officially become king, ruler of Esterbrooke. I took my time getting to my seat as if quicksand had slowed my strides. It took everything not to feel like an impostor and even more not to let it get to my head that in a few weeks, I would become the most powerful fae of Esterbrooke. In Elven culture, while it was a first-born's birthright to become ruler, any of my brothers could have challenged me in a ceremonial battle for the throne should they see me unfit to lead. Today would not be that day.

"While the throne favors you, brother, I do not envy you." Ivaran spoke, easing the heavy tension in the room.

Soon after, the consumption of spirits and light jabs at one another eased our sadness. Laughter replaced the awkward silence as the servants finally saw it appropriate to serve the appetizers. Seasoned pheasants, hearty grains, and bright, colorful roots filled our plates. Meals fit for royalty. Dishes fit for a king. Cutting off a piece of tender meat, I reveled in the comfort that staff-prepared feasts brought me, and forced me to forget that I would only have weeks to enjoy last moments like this with my brothers.

Perhaps it was a tragedy that brought us back together after a long separation, but a taste of Esterbrooke's finest ale and exchange of old times was the one thing *good* about a day like today. To more moments like this.

Bringing each other up to date on our separate affairs, I learned that both Zaos and Ivaran, our father's third and fourth-born sons, were thriving in their controversial line of work. Both formally trained killers, Ivaran's area of expertise was bounty work, while Zaos was boastfully the world's greatest tracker. If anyone needed off-book solutions, they were the duo to see. Lianthore, my father's second son, was working hard on human/fae relations, something I had never taken an interest in, due to my indifference with humankind. I didn't share the curiosity of humans my brother inherited from my father. I only traveled to their world when I had to and personally, it had always taken several servant-prepared soaks to get the stench of the low-rent Human Realm off of my skin.

He was tactful and clever in ways I was never allowed to be, but with him by my side, I desired to see the world through his eyes. I only hoped I didn't have to spend the time he did in the Human Realm just to have an open mind about it.

Vamir, Tavnis, and Theoden were our youngest brothers, and because they were all born in the same year, we affectionately called them the triplets. They were still learning what it meant to be a Faeborne and so far, all they engaged in was what most young princes did with a legion of wealth and a powerful name.

I envied their freedom but enjoyed it when it had been my turn to be reckless. The next time we would see each other again would be at the next Council meeting. Something I found neither fun nor entertaining, but seeing how it was in a few weeks, I wouldn't be acting as just a prince anymore, but a prince regent since I could only be crowned king when I found a queen.

"The next council meeting..." I started, ignoring that it was improper to discuss such matters during realm-wide mourning, but I was curious if my brothers stood with me. They all had strong but conflicting opinions, all while two had their own ruling territories to govern. Most topics discussed with the Council affected both Fae and Human Realms. If we didn't have common ground on subjects, our decisions would affect our entire world, not just the larger territories that contributed to the vast majority of the infrastructure.

"Perhaps this is too soon to discuss the subject, but as my first act as Regent, it would humble me to have all of your support. Father, he wasn't a perfect male, and he didn't always see our visions. I promise that when I am king, all of your concerns, all of your wisdom, every idea will not go unheard." Six sets of eyes, ranging from soft gold to warm crimson, looked at me with collective concern and confusion.

Despite all of our dual heritages, we are all fortunate to present as Elven and bore enough resemblance to our father. Pointed ears and wild stares made us unmistakably brothers, but it was times like this I wished we shared a mental bond. It would be easier to be in their heads and know what they were thinking. Thankfully, Zaos spoke first, easing whatever doubts I had about fealty and lack of support.

"You will always have our support. In times such as this, we cannot afford to look weak or disloyal. I think I speak for everyone when I say it is an honor to carry the Faeborne name. And being a Faeborne means we all have our parts to play. I will see that no one brings shame to our legacy," Zaos added and being the maddest and most vicious one of us all, I was certain that was a promise he intended to keep.

To my surprise, Lianthore spoke next, reminding me why he had always been my closest brother. Even when I was getting ahead of myself, he can make me see reason. He was my anchor, and I was his guide. Here, he found little importance in discussing business matters while we are supposed to be spending this time as a family. Goddess knows when we would get together like this again. I prayed for a wedding because even *I* couldn't deal with another funeral.

"Perhaps this discussion serves a greater purpose at a later time, but I would much rather have it *after* we've mourned King Tarron. Let us grieve, brother. Let us preserve his memory without the talk of duties and protocol. Our father isn't even in the ground yet. Yes, you are to become king. But before you are king, you are our brother. And with that, there is no need to question where our loyalties lie."

CHAPTER ONE

Aranzeiros

A loud banging at my chamber door filled me with murderous rage and anger. Not only was I asleep, but it had also been the first night in a week I'd woken up dreamless, which was much preferred to the nightmares that plagued me. Upon the news of my father's death, someone had better have a *very* good reason to wake me in the middle of a peaceful night. Gathering my robe, I marched to the door to see a quivering Raina, I believe her name was. She was a servant Pixie new to staff, and this trip had been my first time meeting her. Perhaps it wasn't the *best* time to voice my frustration.

"Your Highness. I'm sorry to have troubled you at this hour. It's just... it's just..." she stuttered. Lifting her chin upward to meet my gaze, her violet-tinged irises had nearly disappeared in the darkness of her pupils. And rightfully so. There was no guide on how her new king would react.

"Raina, is it? Take a breath. Exhale. What is it you wanted to tell me?" I asked, sensing her fear easing up, knowing I had no plans to harm her.

"Your Highness. As I was saying, I'm sorry to have troubled

you. This summon comes from His Highness, Prince Lianthore. He requests your presence in the West Wing cabinet. He marked his claim urgent," she said with another curtsy. My brothers and I had a history of pranks and tomfoolery amongst these walls, especially concerning each other. If this was a joke, I was going to rip his heart right out. He may have been the last of the Dragons, but I had five other brothers. I could live without one.

"Thank you, Raina," I said, permitting her to head back to her quarters. As I made my way down the grand flooring, exotic tapestries, and antique relics of our ancestry, I could hear a collection of voices from afar in the West Wing cabinet. Father had always used it as a study, but it doubled as a refuge for lounging and lighting the rarest cigars. Entering the room, I accounted for all Faeborne brothers, wearing the same miserable expression I was certain to be wearing.

"You... look like you've gotten sleep," Theoden said, his tired emerald gaze eyeing me head to toe as he poured a glass of Scotch into a shallow glass.

"No thanks to Lianthore," I spat, plopping down on the space of the couch between Vamir and Zaos. Lianthore stood near the fireplace, watching the flames dance and glow, something he had always done being the child of the last known Dragon line. The flames had always called to him, the way darkness had always spoken to me. It was his source of comfort, finding solutions to unanswered questions with just one flick of the flames. If he was seeking guidance in the embers, it was clear he had a lot on his mind.

"Well, brother, we are all here. No need to keep us in suspense when there's sleep to be had," Ivaran grunted, his long gray hair pulled back and out of his fierce gold eyes. Lianthore turned, finally making his way toward us with a sternness that told me none of us were going to like what he had to say.

"I was going to wait to tell you all this. But we are all his sons. I figured you had the right to know," Lianthore explained.

"Oh, just get on with it. No one has time for your dramatics and prefaces," Zaos spat, his impatience getting the better of him. It was true. No one set up a story quite like Lianthore. If we had been well rested, we'd entertain it, but six sleep-deprived Elves were not here for theatrics.

"Father's death was no accident," Lianthore said, the shared exhaustion and annoyance replaced by shock and anger. I blacked out, hearing my brother's outrage but unable to voice my own. We were supposed to be mourning him. I needed an explanation.

"There was something I did not trust about the Human Realm's lab reports. With trusted Intel, I outsourced and conducted my own autopsy. It appears as though it was an assassination. One the humans tried to cover up in fear that we would retaliate."

"Well, of course, we will retaliate." Zaos stood circling in the armchair that hosted Tavnis. Like me, Zaos had no love for humans, so if he had an excuse to kill one, I was ready to join the witch hunt.

Lianthore had the patience and tolerance to work with them. For decades, he had led EsterBrooke's military forces and was the head liaison in charge of fae/human relations. He had resources and spies situated across the globe because, while he worked diligently to bridge the gap between our two worlds, he had just as much trust for them as I did. If he brought this to our attention, not even halfway through our realm-wide mourning, everything he discovered had to have been true. Lianthore was a stickler for tradition.

"Why? Tell me why the Dark War peace treaty continues to serve us. They started wars over our land. They started wars over our resources, and now, as a final fuck you, they know who murdered our father. Perhaps even took part in it," Zaos continued in a fit of rage, only for Lianthore to interrupt.

"I have not confirmed their involvement. Only that his cause of death was concealed. Whoever killed him knows of our vulnerability to iron. The explosion was not the cause of his death. It was the iron shards left behind that no human hospital was advanced enough to check for." It wasn't public knowledge that the fae suffered life-altering effects should our bodies be exposed to iron.

In small amounts, it was lethal. So in larger quantities, even shards could bring forth an untimely death. This wasn't just some amateur. This was someone who had intel on the Fae Realm beyond the Veil.

"I don't need a confirmation. Someone has to pay for our father's death," Zaos roared. "If we do nothing, they will think us weak!"

"Why don't we just withdraw our support? Hundreds of countries rely on our natural resources. Imagine how their governments, their infrastructure, and their leaders would collapse if we agreed to stop helping them," Theoden said, naïve to the dirty game of politics and the devastation an act like that would cause. I had spent my life learning why the Dark War peace treaty was established, and why it was important to keep the peace despite my hatred for humans.

"You forget why we need peace with the humans." I finally spoke after witnessing my brothers go back and forth about what we should or should not do. "The humans, they host the prison to the Arcane Sorcerer." The Arcane Sorcerer was a myth, a legend, and a devastation to the world that we knew.

It was famine. It was death. The destruction of both fae and humans. During the Dark Ages, no Elven prison could contain it, as it drew its power from the life and the creatures around our mystical homeland. It was before any of our times but how Father spoke of it, if something like that returned, this time, there might not be a way to stop it.

Seven hundred years ago, humans provided aid to help build a fortress. One that their low-level technological advancements were able to succeed at. In exchange, they asked for resources to save their otherwise dying land. As much as it pained me, we needed the treaty. Even if we planned to hold them accountable for King Tarron's death.

"The Arcane Sorcerer," Ivaran grunted. "Something neither of us has ever seen. An old Dwarves' tale they tell rebellious fledglings to get them to obey their parents. A thousandth-year-old treaty, for a thousandth-year-old fable. For all we know, they could be guarding nothing. Cutting ties to humans and strengthening the Veil should be our biggest concern," Ivaran concluded. It appeared as though half of my brothers agreed.

"As much as I'd like to consider that, I am to be king, and it is my call. The Dark Wars treaty is part of our father's legacy. We don't have to like his decision. But if he deemed it necessary, I choose to honor that his judgment wasn't based on an old Dwarves' tale. If it's as bad as history tells it, it doesn't affect just the Human Realm, but the Fae Realm, too. I, for one, am not willing to gamble fae lives," I said with finality and in a rare occurrence, my brothers chose not to argue.

Tavnis, one of my youngest brothers, raised a finger to get everyone's attention, having been silent for the bulk of the conversation.

"So it appears that the talk of the peace treaty is adjourned, but I wonder if I have to be the one to remind you all of a discussion that serves greater importance. Aranzeiros is only the *acting* prince regent. To be officially crowned, he must wed. How long do you think the Council will find clauses and loopholes to undermine any decision he makes while he is dragging his feet to marry?" Tavnis finished. *Blast!* You couldn't solve one problem without another one presenting its dreary head.

"This will be an unpopular opinion," Lianthore started, our gazes directed toward him. He was the intellect, the strategist, the wisdom. And as of tonight, the only one of us that had kept a level head.

"It is fact. To be recognized as the *true* king of Esterbrooke, our brother must take a bride. Marriage doesn't open just keys to the kingdom. Our future queen will serve as another vote on the fae side of the Council. After an extensive investigation, I uncovered this holds true for all of us who wed. As you know, the fae members of the Council have never matched the number of human members. The more elected officials we add on our side, the more they pack on theirs. The exception would be our wives. A fact that Father failed to mention in all of his reign."

Zaos brought his hands together in a clap, his gaze panning the room with his next proposal. "Then it is settled. We shall host a gathering. Perhaps even a gala. Extend the invite to all eligible highborn fae and simply have our pick. We will all be wed by the end of the season," Zaos boasted.

Lianthore pinched the space between his eyes, frustration and hesitancy etched into his calculating expression.

"That's just it. I'd considered that, but the harsh reality of choosing women born of the Fae Realm would only result in suspicion. My counterargument is that we all take..." He hesitated, as he shielded his face with his large fingers. "*Human brides.*"

His suggestion caused an uproar amongst males who were already agitated. I hadn't even known I was capable of such vile profanities, curses leaving my lips like a mother tongue. What he was proposing was not only abhorrent, it was unthinkable. *Human wives for highborn fae?* Next thing you know, he'll be suggesting we design our own wardrobe, or prepare our own meals. Judging by the broken coffee table, I wasn't the only one who thought his idea was ridiculous.

"You are all not seeing the bigger picture," Lianthore continued, his plan laced with absurdity. "Should we choose human wives, ones with a stake in both realms, it will give the impression that we are fair. That we are just. Investing stakes in both worlds. If anything we will appear more... *progressive*," he said, hesitating on that last word. "Ivaran has the most experience in choosing a human mate. Let him be the first to convince you of its benefits."

If there was one topic we tried to avoid, it was the matter of Ivaran's past marriage. He barely even liked humans, but the hold that woman had on him had made him forget his disgust. Unfortunately, like King Tarron, her fate had reached a tragic end. We almost lost him from the suffering his heartbreak cost him. She had been his one true love, and he hadn't been the same since the accident.

"It's not just humans, it's the *right* human. There will be this enchantment, rendering your willpower feeble. This compulsion you cannot fight. You'll know when it happens because you won't be in control of your actions. You will want to claim her. You will want to ravish her. You will want to *own* her. No relationship with female fae compares," Ivaran grated.

In the early scrolls, there was a history of Elven folk that engaged in ritualistic abduction to find human partners. More than a millennium ago, such a practice had been discouraged due to the Veil and closing of the Fae Realm borders.

"I must warn you all. It could take years to find a mate, decades even. I'm in full support of you bringing back Elven traditions, but I'm afraid I would not choose that for myself a second time," he said, lowering his head and offering no other words for the remainder of the night. This lucrative idea Lianthore had, as much as I hated the idea of marrying a lowly human, wives *typically* voted in favor of their husbands. Now there was just one problem. How did we honor tradition and obtain spouses without starting a war?

CHAPTER TWO

Aranzeiros

The Council met in Nobledane, a portal access point that led directly into the Earth Realm's historic city of Washington, DC. A link between worlds as most entry points into the Fae Realm were just that, entry points. What made Nobledane different was that it served as a refuge city for many humans recently discovering their hidden fae heritage and the fae that were from small towns looking for a fresh start in a bustling city full of work and opportunity. It's been said that the city was built in the image of a deciduous forest, its beauty, and marvel, making it one of the more successful multicultural cities as a bridge to both worlds.

A glittering skyline of unique skyscrapers made its architectural structure a wonder to see with your own eyes. However, outside the Council meetings, I didn't make a habit of exploring the veritable treasures the city offered.

As the carriage approached the Qrictenvale Citadel, I reminded myself to keep a level head and an ounce of civility. Being that this was my first meeting as acting regent, it had been decided by my brothers and I, that these humans had to know their place. Joined by Ivaran and Zaos flanked at my sides, we marched through the walkway and found ourselves in the lobby that had changed since our last visit.

A swarm full of uniformed safeguards replaced the two to three typically standard guards, with a slew of metal detectors, scanners, and conveyor belts adding to their heightened security. Lianthore wasn't in a good mood. Usually able to fake civility better than all of us, it appeared he had been arguing with the guards blocking his—along with my other brothers'—entry. Given their point of the conversation as we approached, they had been quarreling for a while.

"But why do we have to surrender our weapons? They have permitted us to bear them for decades. You still haven't explained why all of this is necessary."

"Your Highness, it is just standard procedure now. No surrender, no entry. I'm just doing my job," the guard replied. I stepped in, recognizing that fire in his eyes when he was just moments from incinerating something to mere ashes.

In most cases, I rather liked when Lianthore was this close to the edge. He spent a lifetime controlling his rage, something that fueled his power to summon the flames, but in this case, that poor halfling deserved to return to their family. After all, we had just lost someone close to us.

"Brother, she's just doing her job. They are to be returned, correct?" I asked the guard in question. With an enthusiastic nod and desperation in her eyes, Lianthore took a frustrated breath and surrendered his blade.

"That has to be handled with care and delicacy. It has been in my family for centuries and it is not to be treated like some novelty keychain," he shot back. With a grab of his shoulder, I used methods from our childhood to calm him.

"It's fine. She will handle it. Now adjust your temper before you burn through your suit," I insisted, watching his fiery pupils dull down to their usual soft crimson.

"Your Highness, please don't make this harder than it has to be," another guard lamented as when he went to relieve Ivaran of his sword, he was met with a beastly growl as Ivaran cornered him to one of the check-in tables. Without another word, he handed him his weapon and joined the many of us on the other side of the metal detectors.

"This is absurd. Where was all this security concern when King Tarron died on foreign land?" he grated as we waited for Zaos to relieve himself of what looked to be ten or more concealed weapons from underneath his armor. "This is all unnecessary," he said with a wave of his hands and a snarl on his lip.

Now we just waited for Vamir, Tavnis, and Theoden, who characteristically always found themselves flirting with anyone and everyone. This time, Theoden insisted on being *thoroughly* searched while Tavnis wasted three minutes inviting a guard to their next concert. Never one to impede on their mating missions, I finally intervened because this needed to be moved along.

"You three, come! Save the charm and courting for another time. We're on a tight schedule," I demanded, and they reluctantly joined the rest of us as we paraded to the main conference room where council meetings were routinely held.

"You didn't really turn in *all* your weapons, did you?" I asked the moment we were out of earshot. To my astonishment, each one of them pulled out at least two undetectable weapons, small and hidden in fancy compartments or disguised as something common.

"You think we would let you go in there without some sort of protection? With the failure of father's guard, you will be the last king to perish by fault of a human," Vamir insisted.

"Your little wooing sessions made us late for an important meeting and with how I see things unraveling, it would have been helpful to have that extra minute."

The Council comprised of sixteen humans and was supposed to be the same on the fae end. With the recent death of our father and the fact that all my brothers were unwed, we only seated just five other elected Fae officials, bringing us to twelve members to their sixteen.

President Lunaya represented the Mountain clans, Princess Harpy for the Forest clans, and Viscount of Cornia, Lord Wivern represented the Winged Elm clans. They were always the easiest to deal with, or rather, easier to pay off for them to align with my father's agenda.

Lady and Lord Zappa Wolt from the Demyn clans, on the other hand, were always the wildcards. Demyns had their own way of life in Chudivishte, where my brother Ivaran was from. They did not need money or materialistic things. All they wanted was a chance to represent their community in the Council. Many of them hated Elves as much as humans did, and it was my father's biggest regret not mending the alliance between the other fae.

"Nice of you all to join us, sons of King Tarron. I assume your clocks work the same as ours do," Councilman Hamilton remarked in his usual passive tone. He was an ordinary man, ill-favored with a bloated face and a middling height that would never be mistaken for tall.

Why he was appointed to the Majority Leader of the human half of the Council had been unclear to me, but fortunately, as the prince regent, more information that my father desperately tried to hide would be made available to me. Faking a smile, I found a seat at the impressively large round table.

"We apologize for our tardiness. We weren't expecting the added security that aided in our delayed entry. Is that all new?" I asked, masking my disdain for him with fake interest and courtesy.

This time, Councilman Bourdelon spoke. He was one of the few humans my father considered a staunch ally. They had worked with one another for decades, but because of my disinterest in getting to know my father's human allies, I had never warmed up to him.

He had a certain thing about him that seemed earnest enough. My father didn't consider many of his acquaintances friends, but *this* man had visited the capital Arisnoto and stayed at Regalhelm Palace as a guest on many occasions. I had planned to make my own alliances so I wasn't sold on the idea that he had to be my first one.

"Why yes, it was decided after we lost King Tarron to unpredictable circumstances. We wanted to ensure everyone's peace and safety. I'd also like to say I believe I speak for us all when I offer my prayers and condolences. King Tarron was not only a good friend but a useful ally. Your father always aligned with the Human Realm's mutual shared values. He will be greatly missed." In most instances, I wish I could be more like my father. Smiling in people's faces. Pretending there was peace and unity amidst chaos and contempt for one another. Humans, they were so good at it. The deception. The broken promises, and the false sense of hope our support gave their world to escape extinction. To call King Tarron a friend, and then cover up his murder, was why I clung so close to my stubborn but *loyal* brothers. Who needed enemies with friendships like these?

"Your words are very kind, Councilman, but prayers are just as empty as excuses. Brother, do you mind sharing with the rest of the Council, your findings?" I requested, and he confirmed with a nod. Lianthore stood to pass manila envelopes to the remaining twenty-one members.

"In these envelopes, you will find the autopsy and confirmed death reports, as well as retracted statements and testimonies confirming the former king's death was no accident. We have spent the last two centuries reconstructing the Veil, the magic that shields us from the Human Realm, and with it, our worlds have known a semblance of peace as agreed upon following the Dark Wars clause."

One by one envelopes opened, the collection of expressions around a table a mix of shame, disgust, and embarrassment. Even those that didn't align with Tarron's politics still cherished fae lives, and while the information was still being processed, they had felt the impact. The one responsible for murdering our father knew of a fae's weakness, despite fae existence not being public knowledge. If one would be so bold as to kill a king, it meant no one was safe.

"Is this...is this all true?" Zappa Wolt from the Demyn clan, questioned the humans across from us.

"This was supposed to be sealed. No one was supposed to have access to this information," Councilman Hamilton argued.

"So, you do not dispute it?" Lianthore asked as a result of his unjustified response.

"The cover-up is just the beginning of this scandal. Elven, Demyn, Winged Clans, and all fae, this disgrace affects us all. We must right this wrong. You cannot kill us, and then turn around and ask the Fae Realm for resources. This is a declaration of war," Lianthore challenged, his eyes returning to that fiery dancing crimson I took the morning talking him down from. This time, if he became a little flame happy, I was thrilled to say I would not intervene.

"And you agree with this Prince Aranzeiros—"

"That's *King* Aranzeiros to you," I interrupted as his thin lips curved into a half grin.

"You are not King yet."

"Oh, but I will be. Let's see if I am as agreeable as you found my father to be when your nation crumbles after another recession, which is predicted to happen in the next year. Our generosity has been a privilege, and frankly, the way you're testing my patience, I'm running out of reasons to continue being charitable."

Before the Veil, the Elven Realm spread across seventy-five percent of the world's nations. Now we barely made up half. For centuries, humans have had a say in making decisions that affected our people and claims to our land. All because of that damn prison. Someone had to pay for this crime against our kind. Hands slammed down on the table, as my brother Zaos stood to his feet, unmeasurable watts of electricity stirring in his ferocious blue eyes.

"I have had enough of this back and forth. You are all pushing us into a corner. Holding our land's ransom and withholding secrets of the former king's death. Tell me there would not be outrage if it were us instead, conquering your lands, murdering your useless leaders, and kidnapping your women. We would be at war right now. And we would not be granted the dignity or the honor that my brother so graciously offers you," Zaos raged, waving his finger at the now stunned human members of the council.

"He's right," Princess Harpy humbly agreed, giving me a moment to consider the clever solutions that sprung from my brother's anger.

"If this had happened to a human leader, there would be no in-between. We'd be preparing for war," she finished, causing the room to erupt in indistinguishable chatter about how this situation would be handled. In the chaos, it came to me. Didn't the fae of the past engage in a ritualistic abduction to secure human spouses? A thing of the past, the former queen worked viciously to encourage the males in our family to solely marry Elven females of high-born families. So any choice we had to choose a different path was ripped away by burying certain traditions. Now that it was my time to be king, it would only be right to honor our ancestors by bringing back our sacred customs.

"Do you have any brothers, Councilman Hamilton?" I asked as the quarrel came to a calm.

"I beg your pardon?" Councilman Hamilton replied.

"Brothers? Do you have any?" I asked again, his gaze distancing, trying to figure out how this related to the subject.

"No, Your Highness. I do not."

"See now, I pity anyone that doesn't have any brothers, or any siblings really. Do you know what the gift of having so many brothers is?" I pointed, as he shrugged and brought his salt-and-pepper brows to the center of his face.

"My brother has helped me see the possibility of things I had not even considered. Unknowingly offering solutions to problems that would help those on both sides. Now, this whole cover-up is unforgivable, and not the way I wanted my reign to begin. However, I will reach an agreement that risks no human casualties. This is good for you. No dead humans." Sixteen human faces went expressionless, trying to find the catch.

"And what would we have to provide on our end to reach said peaceful agreement?" Councilman Bourdelon asked. I leaned back in my chair, my head tilting to the side.

"My brothers and I need wives. The Human Realm has plenty. When the time comes when we must choose a partner, you agree that no harm will come to us or any other born of the fae should they also take human wives. And yes, we need that in writing. We shall deem it the Earth/Esterbrooke Accords."

From the looks on their dimwitted faces, it did not surprise me when Councilman Hamilton followed up without considering the downsides to said agreement. Because in claiming wives, our culture varied from the human tradition of getting on one knee and asking one's permission to marry.

"Well, we don't see the harm in you choosing human wives. We will not stop you from consenting human women agreeing to marry you. This isn't the sixteenth century."

Forming my hands into a steeple, I explained that there would be no consent needed in regard to claiming brides.

"I'm afraid you misunderstand me, Councilman. For fae, we take part in a ritualistic practice that allows us to *abduct* our brides. We do not need their consent to claim them, meaning that many of them will not go willingly. Which is why we need it in writing," I clarified. His eyes widened, looking amongst the seven of us, mouth agape and lost for words. It took another human female council member at his side to break the silence.

"What you're suggesting sounds a lot like human trafficking. This isn't just coming into our home, and as respect for us, doing as humans do. How do you expect us to agree to kidnapping innocent women?"

I didn't care about having respect for them. I only cared about leveling the playing field. Even one hundred thousand human lives would never make up for the life of our esteemed father. But one chance to tip the power scale would be quite the start.

"Know that your custom to kidnap women is prehistoric and barbaric," Councilman Hamilton retorted.

With a point of my finger, I turned in my chair.

"You know, I find it astounding how a country that built its wealth and infrastructure off of similar practices wants to lecture me on barbaric customs. Let me remind you that the Fae Realm has supplied weapons for your wars for centuries. If we have the power to provide artilleries across nations, imagine what we could solicit for ourselves," I said as a warning.

Mustering up a last bout of confidence, Councilman Hamilton finally found the words to speak. "Is that a threat, Your Highness?"

Reducing the room to darkness, I waited as Lianthore's flames bathed the room with just enough light to confirm the fear in their eyes.

"A threat, Councilman Hamilton, it is not. If I were to threaten you, believe me, you wouldn't be standing long enough for you to cry for help. But I'm afraid that *those* are my terms." I added with a clasp of my hands.

"Well, I suppose to protect the many, we must sacrifice the few," he confirmed. And from that day forth, the Earth/Esterbrooke Accords became protected by law.

CHAPTER THREE

Paige

Deep Breath, Paige. You can do this. I went through this every morning coming home from my night job. Living on the second floor right across from my landlady wouldn't have been a big deal if I hadn't owed so much back rent. Avoiding the squeaky steps was the easiest part, but it was always the loose floorboards leading up to my apartment that always did me in. It's like she didn't fix it on purpose. Like clockwork, her crimson-colored door flung open, and out came a robe-clad woman with rollers adorning her net-covered hair.

"Miss Paige, where's my rent? Back and forth, you try to avoid me, and I've given you more time than I give most people. We even talked about breaking it up. But how can we come to some kind of agreement if you don't talk to me?"

Truthfully, she had given me enough time. She was probably the most pleasant landlady I'd ever had. But in the City, where she lived for over thirty-five years, the neighborhood was becoming more and more gentrified. I knew she could get twice, maybe even three times as much, from some twenty-year-old student from Maine whose parents were paying their rent.

Even *I* wasn't originally from here. Fort Scott, Kansas, to be exact. But after a really nasty breakup, I knew New York City was going to be my fresh start.

What New York lacked in people skills and hospitality, it made up for it with its diversity and cultural experience. Before moving here, I never met another Black person who wasn't American like me. Now I met all types of Black folk, including my landlord who was from Kingston, Jamaica.

"Ms. Robins, I swear I haven't been trying to avoid you. It's just I started this overnight job at a warehouse to get a little caught up. I got sued by a huge credit card company and now they're garnishing my wages. They take my money before I can even spend it."

My ex-boyfriend back home had opened all these accounts in my name. All the faith and trust I had in him to make things right dissipated when I learned he was just using me to start a future with someone else. I was from a small town and everyone talked, but the fact that he'd been cheating on me with some girl that was barely twenty had been the last straw.

I'd found him in the act in a bed we both shared. Having parents that threw me out the second I turned eighteen, leaving Kansas was the best thing I've ever done for myself. I just wished I would have researched how expensive New York was to live in. Even a rat hole of an apartment like mine was nearly fourteen hundred a month and that was before utilities and groceries.

"If you just give me one more month, I can get caught up and give you everything I owe you. My boss at the diner promised to give me more shifts, and I make more there since I make all my tips in cash," I pleaded, only to have her gaze falter, rising again to meet mine, her lips pursing into a thin line.

"Miss Paige, I can give you two weeks to give me half. I feel like that's more than fair. I don't want to evict you, but I want someone more reliable. Someone I don't have to time running into just to get my money. This will be the last time I ask you and if I don't see a check for fifteen hundred by the end of two weeks, I hope you understand that I have bills to pay. I know you work hard, child, you're barely home. But maybe the city is too much for you," she said with a pat on my shoulder and then headed back to her apartment.

Maybe she was right, but I refused to give up on myself. I deserved to live a life without stress. I deserved everything I wanted in life. My goals weren't even lucrative. I just wanted a safe place to live, a decent job, and maybe a man who valued me as a partner. So far I had neither, but at thirty-seven my life was far from over. It was just beginning. I was going to come up with that money. Even if I had to work myself into the ground to do it.

After a short sleep, a quick shower, and a fight with a scrunchie to secure my thick coily curls into a pineapple, I was on the first 4 train to the diner I worked at in Brooklyn. The thing I loved about New York was the entertainment you witnessed in just a twenty-minute ride. Living in the City, I could never predict how a day would start. From the kids who showed off their dance moves from car to car, to the swooners who serenaded you with their self-trained vocals.

Spontaneous things like that didn't happen in my small home-town, and if I could help it I was never going back.

***

The quick walk from my train stop made me arrive just in time for my ten 'o'clock shift. Walking into work was like walking into hell with every tasty temptation right at your fingertips. Between the warm smell of freshly made pastries, Uncle Lou's signature blueberry cheesecake, slices of his famous bacon, and maple bourbon pie, it was a wonder I could stay at my comfort weight.

Everything was always so good, it never surprised me that this place was constantly packed and always looking for help. Before my move, I'd worked as a waitress to help put me through nursing school. That hadn't panned out, but it gave me the experience I needed to keep up with a place as busy as Lou's Diner.

It was one of the few landmarks that have survived gentrification here, and because of that, regulars lined up like Friday night basketball games back at home. I couldn't complain. The tips were always incredible and every bit helped. Slipping on my apron, I made my way back out of the backroom to attend to my section after relieving my coworker Stacy, mentally preparing myself to wait on Mr. Todd.

He was an older gentleman and much friendlier than I'd like to admit. But he was a regular, and I was never one to turn down his ten-dollar tips for small orders. His skin was a warm brown, just a shade or two darker than mine, and he always wore this fedora that made him look like he was still stuck in his era.

"Morning, Mr. Todd. You getting your regular today?" Being predictable, I didn't even bother taking out my notepad.

"Yeah, give me what I usually get. But throw in some of those raspberry Danishes I like so much. I know you ain't gonna listen to me, but there's this one spot I'd love to take you, even more flavors than Uncle Lou's. A young lady like you in a big city, needs a strong man like me to protect you. But pretty ladies, like you always want the knuckleheads. One thing a knucklehead can't do is pay a bill," he bragged, but like the many times he put the offer out there, I just had to laugh.

Pretty girl wasn't something I spent my whole life hearing. *Chile*, it wasn't even something I heard a lot now. I had accepted the fact that I was more of a plain Jane than a knockout, but one thing I knew was that I wasn't ugly. I just wished men my age looked past looks and saw me for the amazing woman I was. So far, it hasn't happened yet, but I had faith that one day the man of my dreams would just walk in here and whisk me away like some cheesy eighties romance novel. Which reminded me, I needed to upgrade my romance game.

"Listen, Mr. Todd, why don't I just get your sandwich and Danish, and I'll do the worrying about who I need to protect me," I said, back-stepping my way through the bustling crowd to prevent his creepy eyes from checking out my ass. I poured him a large cup of coffee as my coworker Jenny snapped her fingers and gestured for me to turn up the volume on the restaurant's retro TV.

"Turn it up, Paige. I want to hear what they're talking about," she said, squealing like it was Sadé announcing a farewell concert. I suppose the man on the screen was as *equally* famous. You couldn't turn on any news station without seeing one or more of the famous Faeborne brothers after their billionaire father passed away a few months ago.

Aranzeiros Faeborne. Born into the wealthiest family known to men, he had been fortunate to be on the lucky side when it came to good looks and was in no hurry to shed his most eligible bachelor of New York title anytime soon.

I always found it interesting that the late Tarron Faeborne, a gorgeous silver fox Black man, had adopted sons of different races. Before his untimely death, he was still one of the most beautiful men on the planet and could have any woman of his choosing to have his babies, even in his seventies.

Instead, he had taken in seven handsome strays who, with the right name and resources, conquered every industry this country relied on. Military, hospitality, casinos, you name it. There wasn't a person alive that didn't know the famous Faebornes. I'm sure one of them could run for president with their charm and looks alone. That's how influential and powerful they were.

"Ugh! They're all so handsome. But there's something about that eldest son that makes me want to abuse my vibrator until the shit just stops working," Jenny said, knowing damn well she didn't need an excuse to pull out her old faithful. Like me, she was single in this big city so damn near every attractive man activated her divine inner goddess.

"Looks like the country's biggest playboy is here to complete some kind of weapons contract with the Security of Defense. The man's a real-life Iron Man. Wonder what else is cooking in that brain for him to take over his father's company so soon after he passed."

Faeborne Industries cornered the weapons market, specializing in heavy artillery and creating weapons of mass destruction. He wasn't discriminatory either. Any country that had the resources supplied their armies with Faeborne weapons. To be that in demand, they probably had every continent in their pockets.

"Long as he stays *fione*. I'll give him a reason to raise his weapon," Jenny joked, and even I had to admit it was funny.

"Girl, you are too much sometimes. Not everything you're thinking has to be said." I laughed. Back home, you kept thoughts like that to yourself, but he really was fine. A well-trimmed beard, expensive style, and dark piercing eyes that could impregnate you from just a single stare.

Men like him didn't exist in my world, and he probably went through women like bulldozers. Unwed and the eldest of his brothers, it was clear he had options. I probably couldn't get a man like that to look at me unless I was doing his dry cleaning. Which was why it was helpful to have a creative imagination. In my dreams I could have any man I wanted and with my one night off, I was going to bust out one of my go-to toys with him as my muse.

"I feel safer knowing people like the Faebornes are aiding in our country's defenses. Now that's patriotism," a middle-aged white woman from across me added. As the cook called my order up, I almost didn't hear the rant one of our regulars had in opposition to the famous brothers. He never ordered much, just a coffee and eggs sometimes, but mostly he'd always been friendly. He was not a fan.

"I guess I'm the only one who thinks they're absolute garbage.

I mean, look at them. Just another family of one-percenters who think they own the world. All people like them do is buy every person in power and push their crooked agendas." He took a sip of his coffee, jealousy clouding his usual crystal blue eyes. Jack, I think his name was.

"It'll just be a matter of time before these Faebornes," he spat their name out like a curse. "Spread the entire world with their sickness. Someday, I hope people learn the truth about them."

Chile, I knew everyone was entitled to their own opinions, but hating on people you didn't know was just a waste of energy. Those wealthy people didn't spend a minute of their days thinking about regular people. They were out living their best lives, and that was how I was trying to live mine. Sure, the brothers were entitled. Who knows? They probably even had shit personalities, but that didn't take away the fact the eldest brother was a force to be reckoned with. What I wouldn't give to be on the other side of those full sensual lips.

CHAPTER FOUR

Aranzeiros

Curse the wretched obsession Tarron Faeborne had with humans. "Your Highness, we are approaching five miles out. We should reach the base at thirteen hundred hours, give or take."

"No rush," I replied, straightening my back against the luxury cushion. "My visit is rather unexpected, but I appreciate the update," I added, waning my attention from the pilot to the choppy clash of blades spinning above us.

Lianthore's Royal Guard had been gracious enough to loan out one of their more elegant helicopter crafts to ensure my comfort. It was expected of me as prince regent, but even comfort couldn't prepare me for an impromptu meeting with a most reluctant and unlikely ally. Weapon contracting was my stamp on the human world, but they meant very little without a military to use them.

That's where Lianthore came in, considering he had established many of the useful relationships we had with human leaders and the military for nearly three decades. When I didn't have to deal with humans, I preferred not to.

I would have very well left this trip to my younger yet more capable brother Lianthore had I felt my message would ring clearer without my presence. However, I had to remind myself that he had his own responsibilities, and this well-oiled machine my brothers and I ran, only worked when the burden of the Faeborne name was shared. It was a challenge to ignore the smell of fuel, metal, and gun oil, but the tilt and sway of the helicopter more than reminded me I wasn't here for fun.

"We are reaching the landing zone, Prince Aranzeiros," the pilot said over her speaker, prompting me to secure myself on the rare occasion there was a rough landing.

Normally, if I interacted with humans, it was for supplying their weapons and giving demonstrations on how they worked. This visit, however, required a much more pressing matter. It involved speaking with the chairman of the Joint Chiefs of Staff, the United States' highest-ranking officer.

As the pilot prepared for landing, it reminded me why I preferred airplanes to helicopters as that pressure of being pushed downward caused that stomach-in-your-throat sensation that I would have rather much avoided.

General Lenrick, along with a few of his skilled and trusted men, approached the loading dock moments after we landed, matching my appearance with preparedness. "To what do I owe the pleasure—" General Lenrick spoke, but not before cutting himself off at the sight of me and not Prince Lianthore.

"Your Highness." He uncomfortably bowed, signaling for his men to follow suit. "King Aranzeiros," he started. "We humbly ask what prompted your visit?"

A light gesture prompted them to their feet, leaving me face-to-face with the General himself. "So quick get to the point. You haven't even invited me in for drinks yet."

"With all due respect, Your Highness, I have a base to manage, a staff to—"

"See, that's where you mistook me for an Elf who cares," I interrupted, a sinister smile shaping across my lips. "A more hospitable reply would start with, '*Come to my office. Let's see what I can do about this visit.*"

General Lenrick's expression spoke louder than words, given the irritation forming amongst the signs of age near his eyes. He was probably used to being the smartest and most powerful man in the room. Must have been humbling to have his men witness there was someone more powerful than him.

"Would you like to join me in my office?" He spoke through a tight jaw.

"I would love to," I chimed.

General Lenrick led the way, as he announced his departure from us and his men. I followed Lenrick through big white doors that led to the location's base of operations.

"Don't worry, this won't be long. You just need to relay a message to your boss for me," I clarified as we arrived at his office, and soon after, he offered me his finest scotch.

"I have to give it to you humans. As far as ale and wine go, Esterbrooke has gotten you beat. But no one distills a rich, dry Scotch quite like you." I drank it down, admiring the framed military regalia on his desk.

While he masked it, my impromptu visit made Lenrick at a constant unease. From the moment we reached his office, he just would not sit. The man had grit, surely. Most humans I met would shiver in their boots at the thought of having to speak with me one-on-one. As a son of Faeborne, we were not always as reasonable as Tarron Faeborne had been and many of our reputations preceded us. I take it General Lenrick had seen his share of less than agreeable Elves.

"Telling me why you're here would make this dance a lot easier." He crossed his arms, revealing pale white arm hair that matched the hair on his head. He was pale for a human, my guess in his late fifties, with calming blue eyes that screamed authority to the right people.

"Straight to the point, aye?" I finished my scotch and got straight to it. "Melissa Harlot." I spoke with cold, dry disinterest.

"What about her?"

"I want to know *why* she's not only national news, but I see your boss..." I struggled to find the proper word. "Parading on about how he will do *everything* in his power to get her home safe—"

"No argument there. The President is an idiot," he said, holding his hands out in front, defensively. "But that girl caused a national panic—"

"I've been made aware." I smiled sarcastically. "But right now, all I need on your end is for her to be forgotten."

Arguably, there wasn't much I understood about the woman's role in the human world. Theoden, Vamir, and Tavnis on many occasions had poorly attempted to educate me on how and what a "socialite", "reality star" or "internet famous" person was and where they stood within human societal groups, but apparently, Melissa Harlot had been all three. Her disappearance needed to be as far away from public news as possible.

"You humans have explained yourselves out of wars, famine, genocide. Surely you can handle deading the coverage of a disappearing woman."

Our accords between fae and men have always been clear; once put into place, Elven folk honored their roots of claiming human mates.

Perhaps I'd been naïve thinking most Elven folk thought like I did and could never imagine wanting to share a meal with a human, let alone fuck one. There'd been a great underestimation of how many humans would fall victim to this ritual, but humans had agreed to it.

Unfortunately, to keep my place as king, I too would have to partake in the tradition. As one can see, it was not on the top of my list of things to do. "Her family is going to want to know something."

"Is it compensation? Because if that's all it'd take to make this go away, you could lead with that next time," I dismissed, assuring I could handle any dowry.

"All the family wants to know is if she's dead," he said, like he wasn't sure he wanted the answer.

"If it puts you at ease, we don't force ourselves on them or end their lives. They're claimed and decide for themselves if they wish to stay. That being said, she mated with a member of the royal guard. So naturally, she is well taken care of. That's all you need to convince your boss." I stood to my feet.

"I have to protect my people, but I imagine you must protect yours. Maybe my people have become careless with their attempts to claim mates. I will send out a realm-wide decree that in the future, captive partners could be more discreet. But on your end, making sure I never need to come back here should be at the top of your to-do list. Am I making myself clear?"

***

"You're late," Ivaran scoffed at the far end of the table in the main conference room.

Faeborne Enterprises was the world's largest conglomerate corporation. Stock, military, weapons, airlines, if the human world needed it, you can bet we dominated that industry.

To humans, we looked like the richest family on Earth. Politically, it looked like we ruled the world.

"Nonsense. The lot of you are just early," I deflected, hoping my brothers would have taken my tardiness as a sign.

"You stated that after father's death, if you didn't pick a human bride, we will be forced to do it for you," Tavnis said, kicking his feet on the conference table, revealing his designer cowboy boots.

"I've waited this long. What would another hour be?" I took

my spot at the head of the table, not expecting what was about to come next. "Where's Theoden?"

At the sound of his name, he fell from thin air and onto the center of the table. I don't think he had any intention of taking an actual seat. "What did I miss?"

Lianthore stood, his stalking frame pacing across the room, the tension in his gait a constant reminder of my weekly nightmare. "You'll be best to remember, we all agreed to entrust ourselves with bringing every one of us to task, should we drag our feet when it's time to secure a bride. With too much to lose, if one won't do so willingly, force would be a last resort. Even for you, brother."

"*Force* is such a strong word," I interrupted. "I prefer encourage or lightly suggest—"

"We do not have time for your childish games, Aranzeiros." Zaos banged his fist on the table, his violent blue eyes flaring. "The council wishes for you to waste your limited time just for the chance to challenge your throne."

"Easy for you to say. You're not the first of us who has to marry one of them," I defended, dismissing him with an eye roll.

"As we've mentioned before, brother. We wish to support you in every way that secures all of our positions in the court. So long as it requires a path to a human bride in the next two weeks." Lianthore arrogantly smiled, finally choosing to sit in the chair next to mine.

"Any more time, you risk the Council growing more influential, and since Father did not secure that your throne or our positions could not be challenged, that burden now falls to you. I reckon it's time to put your brothers, your people, and our legacy before your pride."

The one time I truly hated my brothers was when they were calling me out on my shit. For times like war, all of them being my equal was necessary. But not so pleasant when they were telling me things I didn't want to hear.

"Fine." I waved a dismissive hand. "Bring on the potential... candidates," almost choking on the last word.

Sitting lotus-style, Theoden conjured the imagery of close to one hundred human women, a visible technology, or in his case, an illusion for all of us to see.

"As you can see, there are twice as many potential brides as last time," Theoden smirked, believing that I would be grateful to have a look at more human females to choose from.

"Eliminate her, her, her, and her." I swiped away the definite no's, forcing each remaining image to grow against the naked air.

"What about her?" Tavnis chimed in, but seemed more eager for himself than for me. "The information in her database reads that she's of good stock, the lineage of a European Baron—"

"That's too notable," I interrupted. "If I don't have a choice, I want someone highborn but not commonly known. A person whose captivity won't make headlines. Daughter of a Lord at the lowest."

"What about this one? Hair a combination of flaxen and fire. Buxom like you like them—" Theoden winked.

"That is what *you* prefer, brother. Aranzeiros has his own tastes," Tavnis challenged.

"Eliminate the first ten and the bottom row of seven," I stated, and by now I was bored. We were down to seven potentials. Fairly attractive if rounded ears were your thing. Regal enough to satisfy lust, but not well-known enough to create a national panic.

"What do you think, Ivaran?" I asked, hoping he might have a suggestion that could make choosing easier. He had been the only one without an opinion. I imagined it was because of his memories.

"I think that they'll die. So, if you're worried about having to be with one, it won't be for long. Just pick one already. Secure the throne like you were meant to and stop hosting these time-consuming meetups," he grumbled before standing to his tall, hulky frame of six feet and eight inches, slinking out of the conference room.

"Who's going to volunteer this time?" I asked, hoping for a show of hands. Ivaran sat through these for support, but every time I was dragged in and forced to consider brides, I imagine it reminded him he was once, willingly, in love with a human.

While it was never my goal to torture him, I'd waited until there was no time left to consider marriage. With only two weeks to consider it, I remembered why we made this pact. If we hadn't, I would've lost everything most important to me. My connection to everything father had built.

"I'll go," both Zaos and Vamir volunteered. Zaos had more experience fighting Ivaran when he had gone too far, but Vamir convinced Zaos that this time he could handle him alone.

"He may need a rough hand and if he gets too out of control, I could just drown him," Vamir joked, but we all knew of Ivaran's fear of water in his berserker form.

Vamir disappeared into the hallways to find our isolated brother, and soon it would be time to conclude our meeting. "So, these seven, two weeks from now, one of these women will be the future Queen of Esterbrooke." Theoden jovially smiled, enhancing each profile to make each digital picture stand out.

"It's not like I have a choice," trying hard not to show my sense of defeat. "I made you all a promise that I—"

The room was suddenly silent. I'd known words were leaving my mouth, but somehow, I couldn't focus on finishing my sentences. I couldn't focus on anything. That *smell*.

"Aranzeiros!" Lianthore shook me, his ruby gaze a fixation of worry and fear I hadn't seen in his eyes for some time.

Rubbing the space above my brow, it took a second for me to focus long enough to notice Vamir and Ivaran had returned. "Why are you yelling?" I barked, bewildered by why they were all shouting at me.

"You don't remember?" Lianthore looked to our brothers,

confusion shared among them. "We've been screaming at you for over thirty minutes. You didn't even flinch when Zaos punched you in the face."

I had to thank my little brother for that display of affection now that the pain was setting in. "No, all I remember was being distracted. By a smell, I don't know. I've never felt that way before."

The room parted for Ivaran as he looked into my eyes, searching for what, I did not know. "How did you feel in the moment?" he questioned, the faint smell returning, forcing me to my feet to sniff the premises like a madman. "Just to be clear, none of you smell that?" I asked, looking under the table, just to be sure.

"What's wrong with him?" Lianthore directed toward Ivaran.

"You'll see," Ivaran chided.

Suddenly, an unknown aroma overwhelmed my senses. Sometimes it was faint, then seconds later it would hit me like a jab. I couldn't even focus. What had we been discussing?

"So, none of you smell that?"

"Smell what?" Zaos snapped, his eyes blinking with bafflement.

"Ivaran, Aranzeiros looks high. Are we sure he's not with fever?" Lianthore asked, my patience wearing thin at the state of my condition.

"No. But it's possible that the list of brides won't be necessary."

"It's like a combination. Of nectar. Or earth...*skin*," I said, taking off my suit jacket to ensure it wasn't coming from me. "Pheromones. It's like fucking...are you telling me you don't smell that?" I shouted, frustrated that they all looked at me like I was seeing things.

It was like I had no control but all the control at the same time.

"Perhaps this has been a lot so close to when you're expected to wed," Lianthore said, trying to calm me with a consoling pat on the shoulder.

With whatever came over me, I wasn't myself. Normally I wouldn't just grab Lianthore by the collar, but the urge to grab something, take something, just came over me. "You're telling me you cannot smell that and it's not driving you completely mad?"

"Get off him," Zaos interrupted, pushing me hard against the table. "What has come over you?"

"I'm..." stammering to find the right words. "I apologize. I don't know." The air in the room was being ripped away from me as I scrambled to get to my feet.

"This happens at first," Ivaran offered, an attempt to explain my symptoms. "Most times, your emotions mask it, like anger or frustration. You'll always try to fight it, thinking you're stronger than the compulsion—"

"Are you sure?" Zaos asked, with a sudden surge of interest.

"Look at how crazed he looks. I couldn't be *more* sure." Ivaran crossed his arms across his chest, as they all watched in amazement at me wildly sniffing the air.

"Oh Goddess, it smells...it smells like..." I closed my eyes to better focus, taking one long breath to make sense of what I was feeling.

"It smells like *mine*."

CHAPTER FIVE

Aranzeiros

Nothing had ever smelled so compelling, so delectable. I had to drop everything to know where it was coming from. I was being summoned and did not know where that road would take me, but I could start by following the breadcrumbs leading me there.

Rushing out of the Faeborne Enterprises building, my driver Vestan, met me to open my door. "Where to, Your Highness?" he asked, lowering his face to the back window.

"I am uncertain. But I am going to need you to follow my instruction carefully," I noted, explaining that I may not make sense, but that there was a method to the madness.

"Take a left here," I suggested, instantly regretting the decision, as the smell grew fainter. The trail went distant, so the euphoric scent had to be in the opposite direction. We rectified that mistake by turning the car around.

"A right," I demanded, sniffing the air like an Elf in heat, basking in the scent heightening in this direction. Never had I ever been under a spell so powerful, a desire growing so strong the closer we came in contact with the source.

It became increasingly difficult to concentrate, and I was not sure that I would be much help guiding Vestan for long if we didn't find it soon.

"Stop!" The wheels of the limousine screeched forward, forcing me to hit my head on the vehicle's ceiling.

Whatever it was, it was coming close to where we had parked. Before Vestan could open the door for me, my impatience grew thin, and I was already outside on my feet, investigating.

I was conscious. My legs were in motion, but I had next to no control over my body. Eyeing the eatery up and down, the location was a strange place. I half expected a coveted high-rise or a luxury condo. Imagine my shock that what stood before me was a place I wouldn't be caught dead in, as it was *so* beneath me. My body shivered in disgust at the thought of going inside.

Lou's Diner the sign read, blinking in and out and in need of an electrician. Was what I was meant to find in a place like this? I almost turned back, until that captivating, spellbinding scent intensified that I hadn't even noticed my nails digging painfully into my palm. Without further hesitation, my feet propelled me forward through the glass door entrance, as three little bells chimed above my head in a bird-like melody.

The conflicting onslaught of smells nearly overwhelmed me, as I tried to focus only on the earthbound scent that brought me here. Amongst the lowborn chatter, I scanned the diner, not finding a semblance of anything worthy of my time.

"Order up on table ten," a line cook yelled from the back, likely from a kitchen that was only meant for employees. There was nothing special about this place. Why did my instincts lead me here?

Finding my footing, the place was so small that one step in either direction felt like walking out of the store, driving me to a point of frustration. Nothing explicitly pointed to why I was here.

"Order up on table eight!"

"All right, all right. I'm coming." The employees-only door swung open, and like that, time stood still before me.

My heart pounded in my chest like it was moments away from ripping straight through my skin. A woman dangling a tray of food in one hand, and a tray of drinks in the other, faking a cheery smile as she approached the table. Was it my senses? Was it her beauty? For the first time in my life, I couldn't think of a single thing to say.

"How are you liking the sweet potato fries?" She beamed, and in an instant, I was drawn to something I never thought possible.

A smile. A human smile.

She was...beautiful. Her warm brown skin reminded me of every forest that I had ever loved, as if her skin had grown to be the best of friends with the sun. Most human females looked the same to me, but there was no way I would ever confuse her for another, not when her beauty was a perfect marriage of features. Tightly wound coils complimented her sweet, gamine face, but I needed a closer look. I had planned to memorize everything about what made her so unique.

"I'm gonna go refill some of the ketchup bottles for the tables," my mystery woman announced to her fellow wait staff, walking right by me and exposing me to the strength of her essence.

My impulses propelled me forward before I had even discovered what I was doing. When the employees-only door shut in my face, it was then that I knew I needed to amplify my connection to the Veil, just so I could get a better look at her in private.

When fae crossed over to the realm of man, we had a useful gift that allowed us to mask our appearance or presence from unsuspecting humans. Some of us hid our features and blended in with humans and when it wasn't necessary to share our lineage, many of us hid from humans altogether, with our connection to this magic we universally referred to as the Veil.

Humans born with gifts could see past it but thankfully they didn't makeup enough of the population to start a worldwide outing of the fae. Then there were halflings, humans with significant amounts of fae ancestry, who were either knowledgeable about our world or unaware.

Most of the time, halflings convinced themselves their eyes did not see what was right in front of them, and that was convenient for us all. Never having used my magic this way, the doors that hid her from me, suddenly felt heavy and foreign. Pushing through, a gust of her fragrance rendered me senseless all over again as she rushed past me through another set of doors.

From a distance, I watched as her ample hips swayed side to side, securing her apron around her back. Was my fated human a commoner? I had been so focused on her essence that I failed to recognize that this was her place of employment.

She pulled several condiment bottles from a tall shelf and laid them down on the nearby countertop, filling every container to the top before closing them.

This was my opportunity. I needed to take her in. Needed to be certain that this wasn't some trick of my senses in attempts to fool me into choosing anyone other than the seven candidates I agreed upon for my brothers.

Slithering behind her, I enveloped her body, and she jerked around, startled to discover that her human eyes decided she was alone in here. Her breathing increased, and she hummed to herself to ease her anxiety. I should have stopped myself, but I had no control over my actions. I leaned into the crook of her neck, her scent this close, mollifying every ounce of willpower I ever had. For goddess' sake, I was trembling. My heart thrummed wildly against my ribcage, my lips finally finding the words, lost to her enchantment.

"You're *mine*," I growled, perhaps a bit too close to her ear.

This time, I was certain she heard something, prompting me

to back away from her as she ran her fingers through the air, expecting to touch something. The look on her face was pure confusion. If I had hesitated for just a moment, she would have surely felt my presence watching her.

She turned around, prancing over to a spice container on the backroom's counter. She poured a smidge of salt onto her palm and tossed it over her shoulder and grabbed three condiment bottles, quickly galloping out of the pantry space, refusing to look back.

Everything I thought I knew about myself felt like a lie. I lived with the constant notion that I could never fall for a human and yet, I had fallen victim to her sorcery without even knowing her name. I finally understood the compulsion that drove Ivaran to his first human mate. Now that I saw her, there wasn't a chance I was leaving without her.

***

"Hey, what's a man got to do to get a cup of coffee around here?" I yelled in a New York cadence to disguise my noble accent.

"How would you like it?" A server approached my table, but running out of patience, I cut her off.

"No, not you! The one with the curly hair," I said, pointing to the astonishing beauty helping another table. The waitress excused herself and approached my mystery human with my request for her service.

My fated mate shot her fellow server a look of annoyance, like she couldn't believe a person could be so entitled. She then dismissed her colleague, left her current table with a warm departure, and with a dose of controlled anger, poured a cup of coffee.

"How do you normally like it?" she asked, her back to me as she refused to meet my gaze.

"Black. One sugar," I stated as my eyes raked whatever figure I could make out through her uniform. I had to leave most of her to my imagination, but her sizable hips and ample backside sated enough of my curiosity.

There was no doubt that what hid underneath would satisfy me once she was mine. Until then, I would settle for a look in my direction.

Handing me my coffee, I fought the impulse that longed to reach out and grab her hand, just at a chance to feel her skin on mine. "Anything else?" Again refusing to even look me in the eye.

"Your name to start," I replied, with a slow, secret smile forming on my lips.

"Why would you want to know that?"

"So I can know what to call you *other* than beautiful."

Her temperament wasn't like most humans. From my brother's stories, our unearthly charms easily manipulated them. Even an Elven female would have been on her knees, begging to suck my cock after a similar exchange. My fated mate was going to be more of an obstacle than I initially intended. And yet...it only made my call to her stronger.

"I'll tell you mine, if you tell me yours," I singsong.

"Fine." She grumbled her annoyance, so instead, I volunteered to go first.

"My name is Aranzeiros. Aranzeiros Faeborne." The same look of irritation flashed along her face as she fixed her gaze to meet mine, her mouth dropping and her eyes doubling when she discovered I wasn't lying.

"Holy fuck, you're Aranzeiros Faeborne." Her voice screeched at the sound of my name.

"Now you have me at a disadvantage because you know my name, but I have yet to learn yours."

Bringing her hand to her forehead, she profusely apologized, her anxiety endearing. "I wasn't intentionally trying to be rude. I just thought that maybe you were trying to be an asshole, and I'm having one of the worst days possible."

"No need to apologize. I'm sure you deal with men like me every day." There weren't many men like me. I wasn't even a man, and frankly, no man could compete with a Faeborne male.

"But you could make it up to me by telling me your name," I crooned, a smug smile forming on my lips. With her eyes on me, her posture relaxed, retiring from the big tough girl act. She was slowly letting her guard down.

"I'm sorry, it's Paige. Paige Anderson. Forgive me, I'm just so nervous because I ain't—I mean, I've never met someone famous before," she corrected.

"I would hardly call myself *famous*."

"Oh, please! You and all y'all Faeborne brothers are on the TV all the time. That's not including magazine covers, even when you're not looking for them. If that ain't—I mean isn't famous, then I don't know what is."

"Coming from a well-known family certainly has its challenges, but here I'm just an average patron," I said, learning how easy it was to lie through my teeth and blend in like a commoner.

"Can I get you anything else?" Nervously, she pulled out her notepad and pen, dedicated to keeping the conversation going.

"Why don't you take care of that table I stole your attention from, and then when you come back I can have you all to myself."

"Please tell me you're joking. You're not hitting on me, are you?" she said, rubbing the smudged condiment on her face away with a napkin. "I swear, this is just a terrible day for me. I usually look ten times better. It's just, I have two jobs."

"Trust me, you don't have to worry about the way you look," I said as her worried gaze relaxed. "What you should be worried about is when you get off."

"And why is that?" she asked, accompanied by a nervous laugh.

"Because that's when I plan to take you out. That is, if you're interested." I waited, eager and anxious about what she might say.

"I wish I could. I leave here in about twenty minutes, but I have a second job and only have a two-hour window to get to and from, between the subway and catching a Lyft the rest of the way."

"How about this? After you get off, why don't you share a meal with me? I'll see to it you arrive at your second job on time. But I'll ask again, are you interested?" Craning her neck back, a look of misbelief distorted her features.

"Like I'd turn a Faeborne down!" she blurted.

"Well, I have to say I'm flattered." I laughed. "But that doesn't answer my question." Her expression softened, a sense of satisfaction flashing across her autumnal stare.

"You may be rich, but I can still play hard to get."

"That you can," I flirted back, resisting every impulse to pull her onto a table and shove my face between her legs.

"If you don't mind waiting, secure a booth. I won't be long," she replied, lustful thoughts flooding my mind at the sight of her walking away. Perhaps one couldn't see it now, but I knew there was the confidence of a ruler hiding deep within her framework.

She was mysterious and guileless, but most of all, ladylike. All the things I wanted in a mate, and in a queen. While interest in the female sex had never been an obstacle for me, she lived for the challenge and I welcomed the chase. Little did she know that once I caught up to her, there would be no refusing of my proposal.

***

Twenty minutes flew by like seconds as the time had come when she met me with two plates of food at my reserved booth.

"What's this?" I gestured toward my plate of food.

"It's a BLT and pie." She beamed, before admitting the challenging transition she experienced moving from the Midwest to New York.

"They got just about everything here in the city, but couldn't grill a set of ribs to save their lives," she explained before offering me half of her sandwich and accepting my polite refusal.

"So you're new to New York?" That had to explain why I never sensed her here before. Since establishing ties in the Human Realm, New York had been my stomping ground. I would have never ignored her compelling aroma. The fact that she had lived halfway across the country made much more sense.

"I just needed a change of scenery. Small-town girl problems, I guess." So she wasn't from a place that would draw attention? This kept getting better and better.

Sliding the dessert plate in my direction, she blessed me with a sweet smile that made me question if she was a witch. Surely she had to know the compulsion her presence had over me. No one should have this kind of power.

"I think you should at least try the pie. It's not as good as something from my neck of the woods, but it's the best lemon pie I've had in New York."

"If I eat the pie, will you do something for me?" I loosened my clenched fist, containing my urge to reach for her hand. Her skin was crying for me to touch her. Even this brief encounter was proving to be difficult not to surrender to my nature.

"That depends on what it is." She offered a warm, shy smile.

"Promise me I'll see you again. This brief stolen time will not work for me, as pleasant as it is."

"Why are you in such a rush to get to know me all of a sudden?" she questioned, her eyes smiling with curiosity.

"Because I don't play games. I see something I like, I take it. So, imagine what I'll risk for something I *need*." I reached in to dip her finger in the custard, just to have an excuse to lick it off. She jerked back, her posture tense as if she was not used to being worshipped. That was all about to change.

"You're so fresh," she flirted and bit back a smile.

"I am about to change your life."

"You barely know me." She laughed, visibly confused.

"And you," I started, before wetting my lips. "Are the most beautiful human being I've ever laid eyes on. When should I pick you up tomorrow?" I inquired, knowing that I had no plans of waiting, but eager to hear her answer.

"Seven, I guess," she answered in a shaky tone.

"Should I bring flowers for your mother? Expect an over-bearing father?" I asked to survey how much family would miss her.

"Don't be silly. I live alone. Plus, don't you remember me telling you I'm not from here? Most of the family I even still talk to is back in Kansas. And even that's a short list." This had to be a sign. She was beautiful, coy, and in a place where most wouldn't notice her gone.

"That's perfect."

"What's perfect?"

"You mean other than you? Just the fact that no one would miss you. It makes it so much easier to do what I am about to do..." I stood to my feet, her wide-eyed curiosity shifting into a state of confusion when I ripped her from her seat at the booth and threw her over my shoulder.

"What the hell are you doing?" she questioned, her tone riddled with fear and anger.

"I'm fulfilling my obligation as Prince Regent of Esterbrooke." And gone was her sweet demeanor, only to be replaced with a hysterical madwoman hell-bent on fighting me off.

"You're crazy! Put me down, NOW!" It was finally setting in when we exited the diner's door that this was not a prank, a game, or a foolish lapse in judgment.

"Someone help me! He's trying to hurt me," she screamed at a sightless audience of people walking by.

"They can't see you. All that kicking, and all that battering, I'm afraid, will go unnoticed," I explained, wading through the mob of bystanders who fell victim to the Veil's influence.

"Please, don't do this! I don't know what you want from me, but I don't have it." She cried as Vestan opened the door and she thrashed and kicked, her unanswered screams growing louder and more frantic. She howled, pleading for her life as she called out to her human god. Only she didn't know her life wasn't coming to an end. It was entering into a new beginning.

CHAPTER SIX

Paige

How could I be so stupid? This man, this crazy, psychopathic, and *dangerous* man, was going to take me someplace and kill me.

Why would I ever think someone like him would be interested in me?

You heard the cautionary tales about women letting their guards down and letting handsome men trick them into gaining their trust. But you never in a million years think it could be you. I wasn't some naïve jogger who chose the nighttime in a questionable area to pound the pavement. I wasn't even the girl who trusted dating men on dating apps.

So why *me*?

He laid me down in the backseat, the constricting rope around my limbs growing tighter every time I moved. I don't even know where he got the rope from. One minute I was over his shoulder screaming for help, the next I was tied up without him taking a break to bind me.

Did I black out? Did I lose time? All I can remember is us being back at that diner and me ignoring my better judgment that a man like this could never be interested in me. Unless he was married or batshit crazy, which judging by my current situation, I'd go with the latter.

I squirmed and struggled, even trying to scream one last time, but like the constraints constricting my movement, my mouth had been sealed shut with something I had never even seen him put over my mouth.

Tears trailed down my face in rapid streams, recognizing that this might be my last day on earth, and that's when I heard it. His once heavily accented New York speech transformed into a soothing, regal tone.

"There is something about your crying that is leaving me vexed. The binding was to limit your movement. You presented as high-strung and it was more for my convenience, as nothing irritates me more than one's resistance."

Blinking back tears as my vision cleared, he stood there crouched beside me, his eyes the epitome of pitch-black darkness. For a second, he almost looked sorry for me. But then I reminded myself that he'd just kidnapped me and with no way of moving, I had a zero chance of survival. His look of pity could have easily resulted from thinking I wasn't much of a challenge.

"I wish to untie you if it helps with the insistent crying, but it is only under the impression that you *behave*. The instant you break my trust, the binding goes back on," he threatened. His accent was more English now, posh and refined the way you'd expect someone from the royal family to sound. Or maybe he was just getting into character. Anything to absolve himself of the hurt he'd planned to inflict on me.

"Will you do as I say, Paige Anderson?" he paraphrased, and desperate for any chance of a way out of this, I nodded my answer. He sat back in the seat across from me, ridding himself of his trench coat and a rake of his dark hair.

"Ah yes, where were we?" With a wave of his fingers, he forced me upright, the constraints and gag dissolving as if they were never there. Did fear have me *thinking* my ass was tied up? The man had barely even touched me. With the cross of his legs, he stared at me, anticipating what I did next.

"Better?" he asked as if he only adjusted my seatbelt and not just abducted me. I nodded my head, grateful that I hadn't dropped my tote in the scuffle, but his eyes never left me. My chest tightened with fear when his once-hard mouth curved into a sinister smirk.

"I have waited my whole life for you, Paige Anderson," he said, his eyes narrowed as he interlocked his fingers together, eyeing me intently.

"I am not a believer of fate or destiny. I've always been taught to stay true to the path I was set to take. Very rarely have I steered away from what's been expected of me. But you, you are the winding road one takes instead of the path of least resistance. To call me a non-believer of fate would be a figment of fabrication." A figment of what? What the hell was this man talking about?

"I'm not sure what you want from me," I said, fighting back tears. "I have no money. I'm just a woman who is trying to live her life in peace."

There was something in the way he stared at me. One part intrigued, another part annoyed. Now that I had an up-close chance to look at him, it was hard to tell if there was a difference in color from his irises to his pupils. I'd never seen eyes that dark on a man before, and frankly, did not want them to be the last set I ever saw.

Perhaps they were beautiful in an '*I fuck serial killers*' sort of way. But as ethereal as they were, they were home to a man who was both frightening and powerful and had the resources to make sure no one ever found me.

Reaching in my tote, my spirits leapt at the feel of a familiar cylinder-shaped tube of pepper spray I bought in case anyone robbed me on the way to my night job. I observed each window in the back of the limousine, in the instance the safety locks were on and I'd have to kick through to escape.

"Just tell me. Is it your plan to kill me?" I said, mustering up a decent performance that had him right where I wanted him. He let out a bored sigh, his eyes rolling back in his head at his evident annoyance.

"What is it with you humans and your foolish questions? If I wanted you dead, you would be dead. By my hands, no less. No, Paige Anderson. I have *other* intentions for you."

Now he was just freaking me out. There were a lot worse fates than death, and I was on borrowed time coming up with an escape plan. When he invited me to sit down next to him, I'd only have a second to react before he realized what I planned to do.

Taking a deep breath, I took my purse with me and made my way over to his side, a sizable distance in the instance that he tried to grab me. As I turned to face him, his eyes, those shadow black orbs watched me viciously like a predator seconds away from pouncing on his next meal.

I didn't like it one bit. But I especially didn't like the sudden bite to his lip when he attempted to close the distance between us. With an uncharacteristic quickness, I pulled out my pepper spray and aimed it toward his eyes, expecting him to cower in pain.

Instead, his night gaze widened, brows furrowing with his mouth, baring his white teeth like an angry animal. Grabbing my shoulders with an inhumane strength, he tossed me back to the other side of the limo, and once again my body went immobile, as if the seats grew vines and held me hostage to the vehicle.

"Please don't hurt me," I pleaded, watching him dump my bag of all its contents as he cradled my concealed weapon.

"Silly human. Your earthly repellents do not affect a creature like me. And seeing how you are incapable of following just *one* request, you... will not move...until we reach...our destination."

He spat out the words as he tossed both my phone and mace out the window. Now no one was going to find me. But what did he mean by a *creature* like him? Perhaps I was going to find out sooner than I wanted.

"Please, let me go, Mr. Faeborne. I promise I won't speak a word of this to anyone. Not the media. Not law enforcement. Not anyone. Just please don't kill me. I promise I'll do anything if you just let me go."

With a handkerchief, he wiped the excess chemical away from his eyes. His gaze met mine and his once furious tone returned to his scarily calm one.

"I keep trying to convince myself that you're just jesting. Unless marriage is a means of death to you and your human world, then no, I do not plan to kill you."

That was the *second* time he called me human, as if he was something different entirely. He looked human. He sure as hell talked like a human. Could non-humans even speak Queen's English? I couldn't help thinking that he was trying to tell me something. Like he was not of this world.

"My human world? What the fuck are you talking about?" And that's when I saw it. His face, the one I thought to be a human face, had changed before my very eyes. It wasn't as if he looked different. No. Those shadowy black eyes still peered into me like a hawk on a hunt. And his skin, pale and porcelain, contrasted against his trim dark beard, appearing even more beautiful and enchanting.

The tailored pinstripe suit I'd sworn he'd been wearing appeared more like an expensive costume, a custom regalia fit for an important man of status. But it was his ears pointing in the corners and laying perfectly pinned on his beautiful head that gave him an unearthly distinction from me.

"You finally see me as I am," he said, and I'm sure my face said it all in one wide-eyed glare. My eyes had to have been playing tricks on me. Maybe he'd given me something that made me hallucinate.

The limo we once rode in now appeared to be a spacious carriage, decked out and modern, like the ones you read about in fairy tales. With a sharp slide to the window, my captor advised me to take a look outside, and when I did, I regretted it.

There was nothing familiar about this place. Dank and dark terrain made home to a barren wasteland, as if malice possessed the trees and darkness had conquered the atmosphere. Even the roads looked infected with disease and famine, mist rising from the ground like the scene of a cursed graveyard. There wasn't anywhere on this earth that looked like this. Not even in a nightmare.

"Wha...What are you?" I turned to face him, his devilish beauty eyeing me with wonder and fascination, like he wanted to devour me. Wait a minute. Did he say marriage?

"I...am something only a privileged few are aware of. The collective term we use here in my realm, is fae. But more specifically, I am an Elf. And you are to be my bride." The carriage took an abrupt stop as the otherworldly being's eyes widened before sticking his head out the window.

"What is it? Why have we stopped?" he scolded, and I looked outside to find some answers. A roadblock had caused hundreds of service and luxury carriages to be jammed in a sea of traffic.

Even if there was another way, it would be further on a path much spookier than this one, and judging by the lengthy wait, no one had plans to head in that direction. He turned back, gaze focused on me, and with a flick of his wrist, my magical chains loosened.

"Well, it's not like you can go anywhere. Not unless you wish to find yourself lost and afraid," he admitted, giving me a chance to stretch out my arms, as I took advantage of circling my wrist and ankles.

"You keep saying that I'm to be your bride. I barely even know you. I'm three seconds away from not *wanting* to know you. How the fuck do you go from 'let-me-take-you-out' to 'you-are-to-be-my-bride?' FYI, you abducting me isn't exactly helping."

It was clear this man, this creature or whatever he was, was out of his duck-plucking mind.

If this was how one showed interest in someone they liked, I hated to see what he did to someone he loathed.

"I do not have to know you to marry you," he argued, prompting me to cross my arms over my chest and snap my neck.

"Well, ain't no *way* I'm marrying you." With genuine confusion etched in his otherworldly features, he sat back in his chair, helping himself to a shot of brandy stashed in the minibar in the middle of the carriage.

"And why not?"

"Because I don't want to! People don't do things like this in the real world."

"Well, I am not a person. I am fae. And whether you accept it, we are a far journey away from your dreadful Human Realm. The scenery makes a vast improvement the further one travels into Esterbrooke. And as far as your consent, Paige Anderson, I do not need your permission to take you as my bride. You are in my territory now, and you will do as I say."

The hell I was! The forceful tone in his voice was the motivation I needed to tell him what was and what would not happen. I never tolerated one second of a man, fae, or whatever he was, barking orders at me like I was a damn dog. And it didn't matter how frighteningly good-looking he was. Today would not be the day I started.

"My permission? Boy, if you don't take me back to my job right now, I'm going to kick, I'm going to scream and I'm going to make your life a living hell until you release me," I demanded, forcing him to sit up and put his glass on the table beside him before he dissolved into a dark shadow materializing on my side of the carriage.

With his arm snaked around my neck, his hand shielded my mouth from screams or cries. Maybe he wasn't trying to kill me, but he had no reservations about putting his hands on me.

"You listen here! You are in no way, shape, or position to demand anything from me! I, for one, would have loved to have finished the evening we initially planned because we have a long way ahead of us. But seeing as though you have an innate need to be difficult, I'd rather you not speak at all. I can remain here all day and not grow fatigued, so you only have yourself to blame." He chastised, his hold around my neck impossible to break free of.

A muffled ring broke the silence of the carriage and with his free hand, he reached inside his pocket to answer. Only it wasn't a phone but a pocket watch, or at least that's what I thought it was until the image staring back at him replaced the ringing of the mirror. A booming, distinct voice filled the carriage, differing from my captor's swanky accent.

"Is this a good time, brother?" he asked from the other side, for which my abductor boasted that there had never been a more perfect time.

I bided my time. Waiting for the moment he was riddled with distraction, as my teeth sunk hard into his palm. He swore, his grip loosening, as he dropped his pocket mirror on the carriage floor to tend to his wound.

Not wasting a second, I opened the carriage door, leaping out onto the ground in an ungraceful tumble. I didn't care if I was filthy, broke a wrist, or got lost. I'd rather be anywhere than with him. I took off into the woods and it wasn't lost on me that the last words exchanged between Aranzeiros and his driver were indications that I didn't stand a chance. But even *that* outcome was better than the alternative.

"Sire, shall I retrieve her for you?"

"No," Aranzeiros spat. "Let her take her chances in the Netherspark. Only then will she see that she needs me."

That's where he was wrong. I didn't need anyone, and I was going to make it out of this wasteland...Even if it was the last thing I did.

CHAPTER SEVEN

Aranzeiros

Darkness and shadows were old acquaintances, especially in the Netherspark. There were many paths to Esterbrooke's capital, Arisnoto, but I took this route in the vein that my future bride *would* run. Regrettably, my instincts were right.

"Would you like for me to pull over someplace, Your Highness?"

"No. We'll likely be here for hours, and I may not have hours if she's as useless as humans in the Earth Realm," I said, darting out of the carriage before Vestan could fetch the door.

"Sire, where are you off to? Surely once she sees how dangerous it is, she'll return," he contested.

"If she hasn't gotten herself killed first. I need her. As soon as I can, I will be back," I warned as I conjured the darkness and disappeared in the shadows. Shadow travel was an unrivaled skill, an ability that was just as much art as it was science. Everything cast a shadow and in the Netherspark, darkness was everywhere. I simply drew from that power and let it engulf me.

The darkness was a part of me. Even despite my grandmother Aranzales the White's need to suppress it. She had been the last sitting queen of Esterbrooke and, like every woman that inherited the Faeborne name, was a host for the coveted power of the Light, a direct opposite of my power.

Through perseverance, I harnessed my gift, accepting that it was the source of my greatness. Through the shadows, I moved like the wind, and while I wasn't as skilled a tracker as my younger brother Zaos, the gloom had always guided me where I needed to be.

Her scent was fresh, proving she wasn't far, but her fear was driving me into a frenzy with the primal need to hunt. It was like before when I couldn't control myself and threw her over my shoulder. Most couldn't see with their eyes closed, but when you were the son of darkness, it extended my reach.

The outcry of wailing leaves made it hard to pinpoint her, but in the distance, I sensed her. The image was blurry, but she had bludgeoned a creature with a rock. Her fear had subsided, adrenaline becoming her biggest ally in navigating the forest. Perhaps she was not as useless as I had originally thought.

Picking through a patch of weeds and fungi, tears fell from her eyes in thick streams. She looked up, a flashing light giving her a flash sense of hope as she followed it, begging for help. It appeared as though she encountered others and was most likely heading into a labyrinth of tricks. There was a danger lurking in these woods and with Paige Anderson's bad luck, I wasn't the scariest thing that skulked in the woods.

The Netherspark was home to many creatures that did not mesh well in respected society. Hosting every vagabond, bandit, and vandal, it was the roughest part of the Fae Realm, no matter which entry point. With no interest in conforming to educated civilization, many prowled in the trenches hoping for something as sinfully delectable as a human to come their way. The trees squelched and howled in anguish, making it a challenge to decipher the voices in the distance.

"No, please! You don't have to do this," a feminine cry echoed nearby, and I made haste in that direction. The taunting and laughing of threats to fuck this human to death fueled my rage.

The moment I saw Paige Anderson's torn blouse, I drew from the nearby dark energy, bending it into the shape of a scythe that cleared the line of trees before me, as well as an unlucky Demyn whose body still twitched as its head rolled over to my booted feet.

A group of outlawed fae, a mixture of sorts, charged toward me. A rouge Elf, a Minotaur, three Ogres came at me with their worst, but my eyes only fixated on two Orcs that seemed mildly passive compared to the bulk of their party.

Paige laid there in a pool of her own terror, not looking thrilled to see me. I took off my dress coat, offering it to her to shield her soiled top, then I turned to the offenders, a flash of recognition in many of their eyes as they lowered to their knees and bowed before their future king.

"We meant no harm, Prince Regent of Esterbrooke," the rogue Elf spoke first. "We had only assumed 'twas a stray that was not claimed."

"I don't care what you assumed. I want to know which one of you lowly creatures put your filthy, worthless hands on my future wife," I howled. Surprising me not that fear overcame them with silence. When no one would come forward, I gave them one last chance to confess their wrongs, knowing one would break to save their own life.

"If none of you confess, you all die," I roared. "Is there not one brave soul among you?" I paced between the lot of them, watching the few of them willing to look me in the eye, trembling on their knees.

"What an intriguing, pitiful band of weaklings. Where has that boldness that someone so willingly displayed when they threatened to fuck my fated human to death?" My temples throbbing with rage.

"Please." An Orc, having had a much closer look, was very

much a child. Larger than most Fae Realm creatures, but a child, no less.

"My sister and I weren't a part of this. We were only with them because it's hard to survive out here on your own. We lost our parents and didn't have anywhere else to turn to," the older child pleaded. Bending down to Paige's level, I questioned her to corroborate their story and was pleased to learn that what they said had matched up.

"Well, someone needs to be made an example of." My voice lowered to a whisper as I pulled at the darkness that bleed from their shadows and shaped them into pointed planks. All at once, I commanded the spears through the back of their necks, a red storm of blood coating the ground like a Pagan sacrifice.

Some of their deaths were instant, others weren't so lucky, but the children remained there on their knees paralyzed with fear, as tears streamed down their faces at the presence of death. Orcs came from a line of construction workers and rarely were they victims of impoverishment.

If two children were out here fending for themselves, they likely had no one. Being burdened with being the eldest brother of my family, I could not bear to see any of my brothers suffer. I tore off one of my cufflinks, knowing it was worth more than most could spend in a lifetime, and threw it at the younger female Orc.

"Take that and sell it. It's worth more than enough wages to set the two of you up for the next coming years. And you, get your sister out of the Netherspark."

"Oh, thank you, Prince Aranzeiros. We will not forget your act of mercy," the older brother cried, guiding his sister into the Netherspark to an alternative portal point. Trekking back to my intended, I expected her to move but by the look of her pallor complexion, she was unwell.

"Paige!" Violently I shook her, worry gnawing at my core until her dead eyes struggled to open. Dried-up bile stained the sides of her chin as I forced her to sit up to gauge how badly she was hurt.

"Paige, if you can hear me, tell me what's wrong. Did any of them violate you?" I inquired, struggling to get the last question out.

She clawed at my chest with next to no strength, a wasted effort because of her ailment, until I pieced together that she wasn't trying to harm me. She was pointing at my throat.

"You ate something?" I asked, and she gurgled sounds I translated as yes. "If I ask yes or no questions, can you confirm to me what it might be?"

Gurg. The only sound she could make with what I could only guess was a closed throat. Was it red? Was it blue? Did it have a pointed shape? Using the power of elimination I come to learn that what she consumed was Demyn's fern, a weed mages used for beast traps but fortunately not fatal.

"Good news. You'll live, but you will be out of it for a while. For fae, it feels like a war on your insides, so I can only imagine what it's like for you." I hoisted her up in my arms, wading through the trail of corpses I left with the summon of dark matter.

"I'm afraid that what you feel now won't even be the worst of it." I stroked her hair, disappointed that the impurity had already caused her to pass out and curse me with another dilemma. I would only have two weeks to bond with Paige before we officially wed, and it was likely she wouldn't be well for the courting period. This is what I had feared. I would be marrying a stranger.

At record speed, I arrived back at the traffic point. The carriage had not gone far, making it easier to find. With Paige in my arms, Vestan met me outside, opening the door so that I could secure my beloved inside. If only I had reached her sooner, she would not be clinging to life and plagued with sickness. I had learned the hard way that I would do whatever it took to keep her safe. No man, creature, or beast would make me break that silent promise.

"Will you require restraints, Your Highness?" he asked as I examined Paige's lifeless body, then took a seat on the opposite side.

"That won't be necessary. As you can see, she won't be going anywhere."

CHAPTER EIGHT

Paige

Terrifying screams. The stench of death. Soreness in my wrists. Replaying the last few days in my head, I feared what more harm would come to me if I spent another day here. I dreamt of my own bed, but I lacked the strength to leave this one. My escape plan hadn't been well thought out but often I wonder which was worse, being kidnapped or being rescued by my abductor?

My recovery had been slow and I could barely keep anything down, except for liquids, but the times I blinked in and out of consciousness, I'd always found some stranger, nursing me back to health.

I moved to New York to start over. Now I'm seeing that it had been the worst decision I ever made. If I had stayed in Fort Scott, Kansas, I would have never met Aranzeiros and I wouldn't be the object of his sick desire. I was his captive, his prisoner. People didn't cage someone they planned to treat well.

Wherever I was, the residence had been well-staffed. I never saw the same face twice, but perhaps that was a ploy to keep me from recognizing and implicating accomplices. Whomever these people were, they were one hundred percent in on keeping me his trapped bird.

Judging from my last breakaway, winging it was not my expertise. If I planned to escape, I didn't just need to know where I was. I needed to know my captor.

Shadows from underneath the door forced my head down to pretend to be sleeping. If it was an attendant, they would just leave whatever food or clothes they had for me on the nightstand. Only, the visitor didn't leave. And something about their footsteps was off. The attendants were always in a hurry, but this one was in no rush. Graceful, collected and remarkably composed.

"I know that you're awake." A calm, penetrating voice echoed across the room. It was Aranzeiros himself.

I turned around in the bed to find him slowly pacing back and forth. There was something...different about him this time. The way he was dressed looked straight out of a fantasy romance. Like before, gone was his designer suit for a costume that was far more regal.

A dress coat, maybe? A cape? When I found a way out of here, I'd google the difference. Silver embellishments lined the details of his dark formal wear, making his dark eyes against his pale skin appear as though they glittered.

"How did you know I was recovering?"

"Your attendants made claims that your behavior changed. That you move trays from the nightstand to the vanity. I wanted to view your well-being for myself," he explained.

"There would be no need to check on my well-being if you hadn't ripped me from my job and taken me here." In my mind, I was completely rational, but my eruption made me sound hysterical.

"You would not be here if you had just listened to my explanation as to why I took you."

Now that he was just a few feet away, I took in his features, lingering on the most distinct thing about him. In the carriage, I wasn't sure if he'd just drugged me, but now that I was conscious, I was sure his ears were pointed in the corners and his skin was hauntingly pale. Outside of that, he looked like a normal human, or at least normal by New York's standards. There, I had seen everything.

"You're studying my ears?" he asked, catching me in the act. Was it that obvious?

"Why are they pointed?"

"We've gone over this before. I am of Fae lineage, Elven to be exact. We do not have those rounded ears you consider standard." He crossed his arms, offended.

"So you're an Elf? Like, J.R.R. Tolkien or World of Wizarding Elf?"

"You say such strange things," he said with an unpleasant scowl souring his face. Did I say such strange things? Perhaps I could make things simpler by getting straight to the point.

"Why am I here? Like really? And don't give me any of that I don't follow human laws bullshit!"

"All right. You wish to know why you're here. Because you are fated to me."

"Fated to *what*?"

"How do I put this simply? It is Elven custom to be entranced by human mates. Abduction has been a recently restored practice. I did not believe it until I saw you. My instincts compelled me until I finally gave in," he admitted without an ounce of guilt.

"I just had to have you, and after all that has happened, I don't have time to do things the traditional way." Who knew abducting a woman and making them your captive was a part of anyone's tradition?

"You couldn't have just grabbed Ariana Grande or Angela Bassett?" I mocked with a roll of my eyes.

"I do not know those humans," he said with squinted eyes, the sarcasm lost on him. "But it would not matter if I did because they do not call to me."

"Have you ever tried dating apps?"

"Paige, I'm sure this is a lot to process. In a sane world, we would have had a courting period and would have had weeks to bond with one another. But I fear I have run out of time."

"Are you listening to yourself? I feel like I'm in a twilight zone," I said, pulling at my hair in hopes the promise of pain woke me up from this nightmare.

"Paige Anderson, our meeting didn't come by mere chance." He sighed, struggling with the last words.

"Esterbrooke is your new home now. And I am Esterbrooke's prince regent. Many humans are ignorant of fae existence, but your politicians are not, and I have struck a deal with them. I am to claim a human bride and because the goddess wills it, fate has decided it will be you."

"Are you kidding me? You can't just kidnap humans and force them to marry you," I argued.

"Well, the alternative are fae who abduct humans solely to fuck them. Would you rather I had done that?" he snarled.

"We must wed before I am to be crowned king. A kingdom without a king leaves the Faeborne name...vulnerable," he said, almost unwillingly. "There is too much to lose and far too much to gain with the joining of this union."

"What do I stand to gain from this?" I scoffed. Aranzeiros leaned in close to my face, rendering me still to stare into deep, shadowy eyes.

"What every maiden would feel honored to have. My obsession."

CHAPTER NINE

Paige

Those unnervingly shadowy eyes were going to haunt me. Overcoming that penetrating, unblinking stare was going to be the biggest challenge I would face. Oddly, they could have been scary. They were as cold as they were malevolent. A dangerously dark, but addictively tempting risk.

Finding the strength to look away from his inky black gaze invoked a wave of both fear and arousal, making it wise to devise a plan to find a way out of this place the second I was able. I let an adequate amount of time pass before I pulled back the covers to prepare for a look around my prison. There must have been a letter opener, a pair of scissors, anything that could pass as a weapon.

The room he moved me to was modest but spacious, with a collection of extravagant furniture, elegant drapes, and remnants of a mystical woodland that made the room feel like it was alive. I tested the floorboards, flipped over the mattresses, and ransacked every small compartment I could find, but the only thing I found were dressers filled with robes, long sleep gowns, and too many vials of fragrance no normal woman in their lifetime would ever own.

Someone came with food every day from what I could remember. Perhaps a knife could go missing and I'd finally have a real shot. I wasn't much of a fighter, but I *was* a survivor, and people always underestimated what a person was capable of in survival mode.

My only disadvantage was that I didn't know my environment. That bit me in the ass during my first attempt at fleeing. If I wanted to make it out of here, I'd have to have the patience to learn my surroundings.

A brisk breeze cloaked the air and had me running to the closet, suddenly grateful for the luxurious robes. Deciding that knowing more about where I was being kept was crucial to making my next move, I contemplated my two options.

I could either head through the door that everyone came through or look outside the balcony. I took one deep breath before choosing option number two, expecting a world of nightmares and terror with menacing creatures lurking about.

Instead, my mouth hung open, blown away by its fairy-tale splendor. The world beyond was like nothing I had ever seen. What stood before me was magical, thriving. Gone was the eternal darkness replaced with an arboraceous metropolis that felt both modern and ancient under an iridescent skyline. Part futuristic and part mythical forest. It felt like I'd woken up in a dream.

My first mistake was misjudging how long of a way down my prison was. This place was enormous. Scanning the sights from all sides, I wasn't even sure what to call a place this vast. This building would swallow NYC up for breakfast and perhaps even take Los Angeles with it. Now that he had taken me to the place where he had the advantage, escaping here wouldn't be as easy.

Try the door, Paige. What have you got to lose? That's what I kept telling myself as my unsteady hands rested on a doorknob for what felt like forever. Fear twisted in my gut, wondering what lie on the other side, but even more so at the idea that it could have very well been locked. *Come on girl, you can do this.* Whatever was out there couldn't be worse than this.

"Here she is. She's awake this time." Before I dared to try the door, a half-dozen people entered the room, each with something different and useful in their arms.

A brown-skinned woman with long blue hair and bright eyes instructed all the women to their respective duties. She was a short woman, nearly as short as a child, but her presence more than made up for it. I guessed she wasn't Elven, but I didn't know enough about this world to assume which race she came from. Like everyone else in the room, she was hauntingly beautiful and spoke with a thick Scottish-adjacent brogue.

"Easy. The water's still hot." The female fae addressed another woman that shared her skin tone but was clearly Elven. With what seemed like the power of her mind, she hauled a bathtub into the room.

"Let's get you out of these clothes before it gets cold," the lead fae commanded as she stood on a stool, tearing away at my clothes.

"What are you doing? Get away from me!" I cried, but with her inhumane strength, she held me in place while the rest of the women forced me into the bathtub.

"I'm sorry for being so rough with you, darling. But the prince regent has his orders and we must get you sorted for tonight." Back and forth, the women scrubbed at my skin, plucked at my stray hairs, and combed through my curls. The strange thing about it was that it didn't hurt when they did, and with hair as thick and as frizzy as mine, it was clear they had a case of magic to aid in their effort.

"Why are you doing this?"

"Because it is our duty to tend to you, lass. The future queen of Esterbrooke ain't expected to bathe herself," the leader said.

"But I am not a queen! Seriously, stop!" I yelled, and for the first time since they entered the room, everyone ceased their actions.

"Milady, let me explain something to you. Perhaps you're not queen *yet*, but you will be. And it makes all our jobs extremely difficult when you tell us to stop working midway into the work. We're trained to do whatever you tell us to, so if you tell us to stop, we'll remain here until you give us the word to proceed. But I'd like to remind you that while you were ill for a fortnight, it was *us* who tended to you." Or, it could have just been that I was, I don't know, unconscious for two weeks, but okay, go off!

"So what Aranzeiros told me was the truth? He's an actual king?" I asked, doing my best to cover my unmentionables with the bubbles at the water's surface.

"His Highness, the Prince is currently acting prince regent since the death of his father. He won't become king until he marries you," she replied.

"Oh, I can't believe we get to bath and attend to a queen. We're going to be the envy of all the servants at the Summer Palace," a dark-skinned Elven woman exclaimed, her loose curls peeking out of her maid's bonnet. Was she bragging about serving me? Maybe Aranzeiros was to be a king.

"Are you really a human? No fae blood at all?" another woman asked me. This one was olive complected with flaxen hair that looked too pale to be real.

"As far as I know, yeah," I said, backing away from her. Apparently, Elven women had no regard for personal space.

"How did you meet the prince?" she asked, wistfully draping her arms on the side of the tub, not caring at all if the sleeves of her uniform got wet.

"You're joking, right? The man abducted me." Hoping that would garner me some sympathy. Instead, it did the exact opposite.

"Oh, how romantic," she beamed, rushing to fetch me a towel as the others helped me out of the bath and helped me dry off.

"I need you to take off your towel, darling. We need an accurate measurement of your bust, waist, and hips," the leader requested.

"Why can't you just give me a simple change of clothes and I'll dress myself? Surely that would eliminate the need for such an invasive process?"

"Invasive? Lass, get used to people seeing you naked, because a queen rarely ever dresses herself. It's just a body, everyone has one," she retorted, bullying me into letting the towel hit the floor.

Wrapping measuring tape around my bust, the swoon-a-holic Elf radiated. "I can see why the prince regent likes you."

"Always a sucker for the buxom ones," the leader continued. Okay, just talk about my body like I'm not even there. Having several people dress you was both humbling and necessary. I could never put on a dress this elaborate myself, which was unfortunate because then it meant I'd need help to get out of it, too. Why couldn't I just wear what they were wearing? Light, comfortable, and easier to run in!

"I'm sure one of you told me, but what is this glorious occasion for?"

"The prince has requested his future queen's presence for dinner. Since you weren't in the best of health, the prince regent has lost time in getting to know you." Aranzeiros had mentioned that but truthfully, he had said a lot of things that went over my head in a fit of anger. I wanted nothing more than to get as far away from him, but strangely, I wanted to see the look on his face when I did it.

"Don't you have a dress that's a little lighter?" I complained. "Also, it would be helpful to know your name, so I'm not just barking orders like I have no home training." Her ethereal face grimaced, almost as if I had offended her.

"Neither one of us is your seamstress or permanent staff. I'm the head maid of the west wing and once you are wed, they will bring you to the royal quarters, which is on the east wing. Maybe it's better if you don't know my name since you might not be seeing me again. But the goddess willed it and I struck a deal with His Highness the Prince to let me and my girls serve the future queen just once. So, it has been an honor," she humbly admitted.

Working in service my whole life, I never thought I'd live to see the day at someone serving *me* being considered an honor. This entire experience meant something to her, and here I was, being a total nightmare. Maybe I could be a little nicer.

"You've been a delight. I'd still like to know your name, even if only to thank you." Her face creased into a sudden smile, her spirit wildly contagious.

"My name's Silvine. Silvine Strongbark."

"Well, it's nice to meet you, Silvine Strongbark." Another fae female helped me into a chair and styled my hair, solidifying my past thoughts of having magical hands, because I was tender headed and when I did my hair, I didn't feel this relaxed. It almost made me forget how much I hated the dress I was wearing.

Sure, it was pretty, and I had never worn something this fancy before, but it seemed deliberate that the dress he chose was cut to make me appear more alluring and inviting. Knowing that it would give Aranzeiros the satisfaction of drinking in my curves made me want to tear the dress to shreds.

We argued back and forth about my shoes. They insisted on heels and I just wanted the ballet flats. Running in a dress was going to be hard enough, with flats at least I wouldn't trip or fall. A loud knock at the door made me cut my eyes to the person entering. The being was tall, well-dressed, and remarkably handsome. He presented as East Asian and one look at his pointed ears let me know he, like my captor, was an Elf.

"The forthcoming queen, I presume?" He spoke formally in a monotone voice. "I was instructed to present this pre-wedding gift to the one they call Paige Anderson." Unsure of what to say, my next words came out shaky.

"Okay?"

"May I?" he asked, gesturing the necklace toward my neck as I answered him back with a nod. With a careful hand, he lifted my coily curls in the back and placed it around my neck. It was an old necklace, likely kept in the family for who knows how long.

Its presence sent tingles across my skin resulting in the tiny hairs along my arm to rise. There was this level of unease that I couldn't quite put my finger on, or perhaps I didn't have the language for how something as simple as a necklace could make me feel...different.

"He has left this for you as well," he said, handing me a small letter. "I've had a word with the kitchen, and they inform me that dinner should be served shortly. There will be an escort to send for you shortly."

All at once, the mob dissipated, leaving me with nothing but uncomfortable silence and the sounds of my grumbling stomach. I held the letter in my hands, debating whether I would open the damn thing.

The seal comprised of black shimmery wax that instantly reminded me of my captor's glittering dark stare. Everything about the recent chain of events left me infuriated and in contrast, withdrawn and guarded. I was angry that I was taken against my will, but I couldn't risk bringing attention to the fact that I had no plans to stay.

What if something in the letter fueled the fire in me I was learning only Aranzeiros could ignite? Or what if it contained details that would change my mind about what was happening to me? One thing for sure, was that boredom and hunger rarely had good outcomes, so to feed my curiosity, I broke the seal and read.

My dearest Paige Anderson,

It brings me both immense joy and deep gratitude to finally see you doing well. I pray that you humbly accept this token of a queen's legacy as a bridal gift for the marriage that is to come. My family heirloom has been passed down amongst generations of queens. Because of our uniquely blended union, I believe it will suit you well. It would be an honor if you wore it to our first dinner to commemorate our recent engagement.

Out of frustration, I attempted to rip the letter to pieces before reading the rest of it, but the damn thing wouldn't budge. What kind of paper was indestructible? I huffed, deciding to continue with the rest of the letter.

There, we will have more time to properly speak and prepare for our upcoming nuptials.
Sincerely yours,
Aranzeiros Faeborne of Esterbrooke

Now I didn't just want to escape. I wanted to stick a fork in his thigh and watch him squirm. How dare he impose something on me I didn't ask for? I had had it with men coming into my life and trying to control everything around me. The only thing that changed after reading that letter was deciding whether to run or kill him. Besides, it's not like they could force me to marry a dead man.

CHAPTER TEN

Aranzeiros

"Which one of these says *let's start over?*" I asked Lexium, my chamberlain, as he held up two tunics to my chest in two calm shades of grey. Without a courting period, every free moment of the day was spent planning and anticipating the royal wedding, so I thought it might be useful to learn more about my bride in the short time leading up to our big day.

I could see why father never remarried. The exhaustive preparations that accompanied weddings were something I would not take part in a second time. Especially given the less-than-admirable start between Paige Anderson and I.

"Both dress shirts favor you, but you insisted on being more... welcoming." In other words, common.

"I would go with the silk," he said, and I confirmed with a nod. One tailor helped me into the tunic, while another reached for my trench coat. However, Lexium insisted on me passing on it with the accusation that it made me appear too regal.

My goal was to make an ally tonight and the only way of accomplishing that was to show her I could relate to her. Taking one last look in the mirror, I appeared about as common as I was ever going to look and surprised no one when I rejected all the counsel to *at least* wear jewelry.

"Lexium, see that the kitchen and dining staff arrange for dinner to be served in the east tower. The one that has the best view of the stars. The main hall feels a tad grandiose for a first dinner and I am sure she would appreciate the change in scenery.

Do insist that the decorators don't go overboard with the details. I want it to feel...homelier. It might be something the future queen might prefer, considering her background. This Paige Anderson, she is so hard to win over. First, she runs, then she finds herself ill. It is so draining how much I have to try with her."

It was no secret that the Faeborne line was highly exalted, and with that came competitively good looks that few fae males could compete with. I could walk into any home in Esterbrooke and watch daughters, even mothers, fight over the chance to bed me first.

Meanwhile, this one I could barely get to smile at me. That is, of course after I took her as my captive.

"Your Highness, you could always juggle the idea of taking a second wife, or perhaps even a third. King Tarron was known to have five lovers at a time. Surely, any female would see the honor to be second to your fated mate."

Zylina, a servant pixie stylist, was putting the last finishing touches on my signature coif as she ran one last comb through my hair before joy traveled across her bright brown face in the form of a smile.

"Yes, *lovers.* Not wives." As mouthy and disobedient as this human is, I am not sure I'd burden myself with a second. Besides, she will give in to me, eventually. "That reminds me. Send for my intended. I wish to escort her myself to the east tower before we're summoned for dinner as she has not yet ventured the palace."

"As you wish, Your Highness," he said with a swift bow.

Following my instructions, he made his way toward the door but was blocked by two guards storming the entrance, a restless Paige Anderson in his thoughtless grasp causing my nostrils to flare and my eyes to center on a threat that shouldn't have laid a hand on my wife-to-be.

"Sorry to disturb you, Your Highness, but we caught this one trying to slip past us in the courtyard."

"Get off of me," Paige Anderson cried, struggling but failing to match the strength of an Elven guard. I rushed over to the guard, the darkness leaving my fingertips in the form of black threads of living shadows.

Like a cobra, I guided the strings of nightfall around his neck, letting the rage inside me take over. The darkness was a living thing, something that could corrupt a weaker being. However, I was no weakling and my ability to control it was a testament to my true power.

"Her name is Paige Anderson, and that is no way to handle your future queen." True that she was my captive, but no one, and I meant no one was permitted to touch her in that way. Had we been so long without a queen that suddenly the palace staff have forgotten their places?

In the struggle, Paige fell to the ground, the darkness inside of me lifting the guard several meters into the air. He clawed at my black wire, begging for mercy, as his face purpled under my savage assault. With a clench of my fists, the life in his eyes dimmed and his motions ceased, until finally, I released him, letting his large, stiff body descend to the floor.

"Well, don't all volunteer at once. Clean this up. And make sure you use lavender-infused cleaning agents. The last thing I need is for my dressing room to reek of death," I said, wiping my hands of any residue left behind from the conjuring.

I bent down to where Paige had crawled, extending my hand out for her to take. Soft brown eyes stared back at me, silently debating if I was someone to trust. I acknowledge we had gotten off on the wrong start, but at the end of the evening, I prayed we would be done with all of this.

"It is all right. Take my hand," I insisted and with a better act of judgment, she did as I asked. As I helped her stand to her feet, I was reminded of how small she was, barely reaching my neck in stature. But there was no forgetting her scent and regarded beauty. To be in her presence again when she was herself and healthy was truly a treasure. For a second time since we met, I knew what it felt like to activate the need to protect her.

"I apologize for my outburst. The plan was to send for you, but it appears that you have already found your way to me." Her guarded expression was hard to read. If there was fear there, she was becoming blissfully skilled at masking it. Her scent however, was neutral, like her expression, and her mouth stayed closed, likely uncertain whether or not it was permissible to speak.

"It would please me if you joined me for a late dinner. The staff is preparing something you might find...*familiar*. In the meantime, I would like it if you would accompany me on a brief tour of Regalhelm Palace," I said with a light kiss on the back of her hand. Her posture straightened as she fixed her earthly gaze to meet mine.

"That depends. Will I suffer the same fate as that guard if I refuse?" she said, her guile returning. Releasing her hand, I clasped mine together, trying to keep my depraving and lustful longings to myself. The craving, the pining, just touching her was enough to send me into a rage of conquering her. And to think, we hadn't even had our first proper conversation yet.

"Now Paige Anderson, when will you learn I would never *willfully* bring harm to you? You seem to believe that what I'm offering you is captivity. It is the exact opposite. I've been trying to explain that to you for days now, but you decide to be stubborn. You and I, we are not savages. This is our last real chance to learn about one another before we are to be wed. What can be the harm in that?"

With a feisty roll of her eyes, she crossed her arms in front of her chest and forcibly brushed past me, waiting at the room's entrance. "Well, it's not like I have a choice. I might as well get this over with." With a signal of my hand, the palace staff cleared the room, leaving Paige Anderson and me alone to talk in private.

The gold embellishments on her dark gown left her warm brown shoulders bare, the neckline swelling at her ample breasts, and my grandmother's necklace adding elegant and feminine touches to her otherwise naked décolletage. Closing the distance between us, I stood before her, bold and unyielding.

"Listen to me, Paige Anderson. You may be the future queen of Esterbrooke, but I want you to know something. If you ever speak to me in that condescending tone in front of servants again, I will personally see to it that you are punished in all ways imaginable." She swallowed a gulp and took a deep breath before speaking her next words.

"What happened to all that stuff about you saying no one will bring harm to me?" she questioned, invoking a series of laughs from me. How silly of her to assume that I was talking about pain. There was more than one way to torture a woman. And she would find out soon enough.

"I am your king and I will do what I want with you. Am I making myself clear?"

"Crystal!" she seethed and surprised me when she took my hand when I reached out for hers, as a sinister side of me wished for defiance. Inflicting punishment was always a satisfying reward. She didn't know what I was capable of, but I was more than eager to let her learn the hard way.

"Now, shall we?"

CHAPTER ELEVEN

Paige

"So, Miss Paige Anderson. What are the wonders that come with your mysterious nature?" the Shadow Prince asked, his posh accent scarily calm.

A quick walk led us straight to the vestibule of Regalhelm, a splendor in itself, considering that with my arrival, I hadn't walked through the door on my own accord. Even with my desire to leave, there was something so enchanting about this place.

Sights like majestic moving artwork, mystical Gothic architecture with clinging and twining vines along staircases, nature-touched pillars, and even more extravagant chandeliers. I had never been to a place that felt so alive. Almost like one big greenhouse, but majestic and fit only for a family of fancy titles.

Even the polished limestone floors felt like a crime to walk on. Every room we passed gave further proof that this man had wealth beyond the typical one percent of my world. More than once, we'd circled back to the sights my gaze lingered on, as I wasn't free from admiring his residence like a wide-eyed tourist.

"Trust me, I'm *far* from mysterious. Just a waitress with bad luck. Long story short, I am nobody." I said, eyeing the many creatures that passed us who never failed to acknowledge their prince regent on their way to complete their daily duties.

"Nonsense. There is always *something* to know about everyone. Why don't you start by telling me about your family? It is customary to provide the bride's family with a sizable dowry following the ritualistic abduction. But my brothers—who never have a problem finding *anyone*—are having issues locating yours. Perhaps you can assist, or point me in the right direction?" he ended with a smug expression.

I learned from my folks that when push came to shove; I was on my own. My dad was a grifter. My mom, a con artist. It was their life mission to not only tell me I wasn't a priority but to treat me like I wasn't as well. If it hadn't been for the welfare benefits they got from having me, they would have gladly let me fall into the foster system. Some people weren't fit to be parents, and it's taken me over twenty years of self-love and undoing the damage they left me in to accept that I deserved more.

"Let me stop you right there," I said, palm spread as he stopped to face me. "My parents don't deserve a dime of your money. Hell, they probably wouldn't even recognize me if my face were on the back of a milk carton. Save yourself the trouble and stop looking, okay?" The fire in my tone left a sadness in his eyes. A look of pity that I wish I could unsee.

The contrast between his skin and hair brought attention to how pale his skin was, and even though he was far from ghostly, I'm sure he could even enchant the snow. It made his twilight eyes glitter, despite the lack of light reflecting from them. Though looking at him was hard to do, looking *away* from him was even harder.

"Very well. There must be something that you wish to share about yourself before I am to become your husband. Surely that makes me entitled to more than just your name and birthplace."

I shook my head in unison with me pinching between my brows. I didn't mean for that exasperated sigh to follow, but with his arrogance and lack of understanding of why it wouldn't be my choice to stay here, it was looking like I had to *explain* that I was just a normal person with a normal job living a normal life. Not some Elven noble of an unknown fantasy realm.

"Look, you sadistic prince. There's nothing important to know about me. Maybe you just made a mistake by kidnapping me. Do you want to know the most exciting thing that's ever happened to me? Moving to New York!" I said, with a little too much fire to burn out.

"But even *that* was something you took away from me," I fumed, hands balled into fists, trying to keep my beating heart composed.

Despite his power and privilege, he was a calm creature, which was what made the next thing he said to me even more frightening. "I think I preferred you when you were sleeping and suffering," he said with a next to no emotion in his eyes.

"And you should watch the way you speak to me. In a matter of seconds, I could force you to your knees and watch you choke on my cock," towering eerily close to me. If he could hear how fast my heart was beating, he would have steered clear, because this fist-sized instrument of beating muscle was bound to hurt someone as furious as it was throbbing in my chest.

"The reality is, I could do it right here, and no one would say a word. No one will question my actions. No one will come to your aid. And you know why that is, Paige Anderson?" he asked with a scary calmness. I huffed, knowing the answer, but not in a rush to give him the pleasure.

"Because..." I said, against gritted teeth. "You are to be king."

Which prompted a nod and an arrogant furrow to his brow. "Precisely. So, I advise you to reassess that attitude before I exercise my right to give you a lesson in manners."

Inhaling deep, I convinced myself that if I was going to get through this; I was going to have to play his game and fake interest to stay in one piece.

"Why don't you begin by telling me about yourself? I don't know *this* world's version of you and I don't think there's anything I could say that would pique someone of your caliber," trying to flatter him.

He hadn't expressed amusement, or any emotion for that matter. He just looked to the side and carried on with a stoic, "Very well," as we continued along the corridors.

"I was born Aranzeiros Faeborne, first son to King Tarron, ruler of all fae, and the only child to Rayvana, a dark star Nymph, dweller of the skies. While both fae, their union was uncommon. Even if you are unfamiliar with our world, the first thing you will learn is that Elves—especially those of royal lineage, prefer to keep their bloodlines Elven. When I reached the stage of juvenile, I learned the hard way, why."

In his words, Elves possessed many abilities. Magic was in his family's blood, the most common being the ability to manipulate elements. While I kept my expression neutral, it was fascinating to learn that he could have inherited several unique abilities from his lineage of being a Faeborne.

Only, his story took a dark turn as his abilities developed into a power most creatures feared. Something that could counter the light magic every queen of Esterbrooke was forced to bear each generation.

"It was small at first. To start, I could only manipulate shadows. I remember when my brother Lianthore, was an infant, I was thrilled to become an older brother," which seemed to be the only thing to garner a non-malicious smile out of him.

"I would perform these intricate puppet shows for him, unable to explain why the shadows would take on shapes and sizes my small hands weren't even capable of forming yet," he admitted at first, he thought he was a disappointment for not inheriting his father's affinity for controlling storms or the Paleforce's affinity of manipulating earth and stone from his grandmother.

He had become something never seen before in the Elven race

of fae. An Elf with dark magic. "As my powers grew, I learned it was not only shadows I controlled, but Darkness itself. Dark magic had been outlawed for a thousand years. And here I was, this child who was just born with the ability. No one believed that I'd ever be able to control it. But it's where I proved them wrong."

The part of his story took a disparaging turn when he spoke of his grandmother, a pure Elven royal who despised her grandsons, all because they were different. I, for one, could relate to that.

"Goddess, rest her soul. She hated us all. Thought of us as impure, but it was me she feared the most. One day, his darkness will consume the world, my dearest grandmother would always say. Never failing to remind my father that whom he chose to love would one day be his greatest demise. Be it in the form of heirs, or the destruction of everything he knew and loved. Though it was inevitable, it pained her to know that I would one day replace my father."

His admittance made me clutch the necklace he gave me in my palm. The note that came with it, told me the necklace had belonged to his grandmother. He didn't deserve it, but I felt pity for him at that moment.

Being feared by someone that's supposed to love you and still feeling an obligation to preserve her legacy. It made me wonder why he gave it to me in the first place. Who wanted a constant reminder of a family member that hated you?

Mustering up some courage to speak, I asked when we might reach our final destination, the East Tower. He surprised me by saying we'd finally made it, forcing me to stop and take the sight in.

Examining the night sky, I had to admit; it was probably the best view of the city from any other place in the palace. My eyes confirmed what my ears could only speculate, as festive lights and candles decorated every other crenellation. Whenever I heard the hustle and bustle of staff behind my door, it was clear they were responsible for creating this wonder.

A part of me hated that it added to the ambiance of a well-prepared dinner table. The kitchen staff must have gone through a lot of trouble to get tables, chairs, and food up here. Even though I'd never admit it, it looked nice.

"The kitchen staff informed me that they found it...*challenging*, fulfilling the dietary needs that you requested. I took the liberty of having them commission a cook from your home state to make something comforting and familiar. I hope it pleases you," he said, holding out my chair for me, seeing that I was seated before he sat across.

As I lifted the plate cover, this time I couldn't hide the joy and excitement that caused my mouth to drop and my eyes to widen in unison. In front of me was a plate of Kansas staples. Deep fried ribs, baked mac and cheese, and a side of baked beans.

It had been so long since I'd had fried ribs Kansas-style. As much as I tried to find a substitute in New York, it never came close to the real thing. "It looks good," I downplayed, masking my joy in a shrug of disinterest.

But all it took was a hefty bite to break the mask I'd been wearing, unable to resist the pleasure and warmth that surged through, as I shut my eyes and basked in the aromatic smell. Its crispy, savory taste, transports me to a place of pure bliss. Gosh, I missed this stuff.

When I opened my eyes, Aranzeiros was eating it *all* wrong. You were supposed to eat ribs with your hands, but given his royal background, he had chosen the proper knife and fork route to slice away at its crispy goodness.

If I weren't trying to mask my true feelings, I would have found it hilarious. Did he expect me to eat like that? *Chile*, I hoped not.

As he brought a morsel to his lips, his face soured, prompting him to reach for a napkin. "Is it supposed to be this greasy?" This time I did laugh, but quickly thought against it when he peered up at me with a raise of his eyebrow.

"Actually, if you eat it with your hands, you might get more meat off it," offering to show him. "See? Like this," taking a pair of ribs in my hands and bringing it to my mouth to rip off a portion with my teeth.

At first, I thought he was just going to stare at me and eye me with a look of disgust. Instead, he followed my instruction, tearing away at the tender meat with his near-perfect teeth. Wiping away the excess sauce left on his fingers with a handkerchief made me feel like a complete savage for licking my fingers until they were damn near clean.

"What's wrong? Too unsophisticated for you?" I taunted.

A nonchalant shrug followed. "Perhaps, but the same could be said about you. And we both know how that went."

If he was trying to wipe that smug look off my face, it worked. I hadn't needed another reminder that he had kidnapped me.

"I see you're wearing the necklace I gave you. It looks becoming on you," he said, taking another bite of his food. A spoonful of mac and cheese this time, which he didn't comment or complain about. No one could resist soul food style baked mac and cheese.

"I don't understand why you wanted me to have it. From you sharing about your former relationship, it doesn't sound like you and your grandmother got along," I said, taking a huge swig of wine that I couldn't decide whether it was more sweet or fruity. I would have to be careful because if I drank too much, the intoxication would creep up on me, and I wouldn't know it until it was too late.

"We got along fine enough," his fist growing noticeably tighter on his fork. "She just didn't care for me. Not in the way she cared for her own son," as he reached to wipe his mouth with his handkerchief. His grandmother was a chink in his armor, but I wasn't sure I cared enough to ask why.

"We all had our differences, but the one thing we all could agree on was family. Legacy. And that no being is anything without those. That necklace is a part of that legacy. A part of *her* legacy. Do not be fooled by its appearance. It is the physical embodiment of pure light secured in precious metal. I know little about it, but I know that it can only be found in the Fae Realm. We have passed it down to every generation of queen that sits on the throne. For you, it will take on a different meaning, as I am the son of darkness," he admitted.

"I made a promise that only a woman fit to wear it would be its next owner. Now that I've gotten to speak with you, I am ever more certain that that woman is you," he ended, finishing his mac and cheese in a mouthwatering bite.

With liquor in me and familiar food shifting my mood to something more amicable and pleasant, I was ready to give in and talk, but first I needed answers.

"You keep telling me I'm the one. That I'm to be your queen. But not once have you told me why? Why, out of seven billion people on the planet, did you choose my life to disrupt? There's no doubt you have access to gorgeous actresses and models. It wouldn't even surprise me if you had a roster of eligible princesses lined up, *willing* to sign their soul away just for a chance to be next to you," emphasizing my point with my hands.

"So enough with the ambiguity. Why not someone else? Why did it have to be me—" as he surprised me when he slammed the table, not even waiting to see if I would finish that sentence.

With a menacing presence, he stalked over to me from his side of the table. "You make it seem like I had a choice," he said in a controlled state of rage. "Paige Anderson, from the moment you entered my life, you have been nothing but a thorn in my spine. An irritation that infuriates me to the point of revulsion. Yet I am tortured by the power your existence has over me."

By now, I could feel his breath on my skin, an unwelcome surge of excitement coursing through me. His nearness made my senses spin, and at that moment, it would have been simpler had I just given in to him.

This was his playground. There would be no rule not enforced by him. I could give in and make things easier, but the smarter half of my brain just couldn't give in. I couldn't see how any healthy relationships in their infancy could form this way, no matter how attractive my said captor was.

Dusting a stray curl out of my eyes, his dark and unfathomable gaze was stripping away all of my free will, but I had to be strong. I had to stay alive, and I planned to do whatever it took.

"You do not understand what it is like to have *no* control over your actions. From the moment I caught your scent, I followed, unable to find peace until it led me to its source. Even in your low-born attire, all I saw was you. And now..." He hesitated, like he was about to regret what was about to follow.

"All I ever see is you. I will not rest until you share this burden." His finger tenderly traced the line of my cheekbone and jaw. I should have stopped him as that finger found its way caressing the flesh of my collarbone, lingering far too long to be an accident.

Without thinking, I grabbed the closest thing to my right hand, a jagged-teeth dinner knife, and held it up to his pale throat. Watching his once-tight expression ease into a smug smile, I couldn't help thinking that this was far from the reaction I was trying to garner. I wanted to wipe that smile off his face.

"You are more interesting than you let on, human. And *that* is why it has to be you."

With a flick of his finger, the knife flew out of my hand and landed far out of my eye's reach. I backed away to the tower's edge, as he cautiously followed, keeping a good, long distance this time.

"What makes you think I would ever willingly be with you? Maybe you can force me to marry you, but there will be no love.

Is that what you dream of? A marriage without love?" I asked curiously.

Condescendingly, he rolled his eyes as he clasped his hands behind his back, pacing in a way where his frame still hugged the table. "You humans and your whimsical perception of love. We royals do not marry for love. We marry for power. We marry to forge dynasties to strengthen alliances. Marrying for love makes one weak," as he leaned in close to my face, ending his point in a sinister whisper that would have been sexier in another circumstance, but all I kept pondering was, whether I could manage another try at the knife.

"But marry for *need*. Marry for *mutual* gain. That in itself reveals one's true ambitions. You will learn, Paige Anderson, that when it comes to love, I may not be what you want, but I will be what you need. And in the game of negotiation, need is a far more useful bargaining chip than the concept of love."

CHAPTER TWELVE

Aranzeiros

This is your moment, son. Everything you've been preparing for has led you to this.

Father had never said those words, but his voice was singed into my musing, disturbing my level of peace. I was lucky to have my brother Lianthore here with me to distract me from myself.

"Are we allowing Father's words to be in our heads, again?" Lianthore guessed, lighting his dart with flame, just before he set it flying toward the dartboard.

"No," telling the truth in a different way. Technically, they were *my* words. I just heard them in Tarron's voice. "But I am having doubts about my upcoming nuptials."

I raised both my arms so that my tailor could ensure they didn't miss a spot in designing the perfect regalia for my wedding. "Should we go with the black? It is a favorite of yours," Patrov, my royal tailor, suggested, too lazy to consider a different color.

"What's there to be worried about? Has father not prepared you for this? Has this not been his lifelong dream, finally fulfilled in his golden child?" Lianthore taunted, though I know it was just in jest. Tarron was an excellent king, but he'd never been perfect when it came to being a father.

It was not lost on me, that even with all the mixed feelings I held toward father, he'd been a much more present father to me than he'd ever been to Lianthore.

"It is far from duty that has me in such a stupor," as I insisted that Patrov change my garb to royal blue.

"Leave us," Lianthore commanded, emptying the room, leaving us alone. "What is really the matter, brother?" as his ruby eyes burned, concentrated on me.

The center of the city's cathedral provided a pleasant distraction, ringing two, sometimes three times every half hour, reminding the common folk that today would be like no other day.

"I think I'm managing, but I'm sure I'm not over father's death."

"That's all right. None of us really are. Not even Ivaran, no matter what he says."

"Despite my...enthusiasm, a part of me wishes it would not have been under these circumstances. I knew I would always be king. But all the excitement of today makes me wish he could have seen it. For all of us." Squeezing Lianthore's shoulder, hoping it provided comfort.

"I miss him, too, and believe me when I say we are working diligently to find his killer. But I'm also glad that he's not here. *Relieved* even. I knew Tarron the king, and I knew Tarron the father. But I knew you *before* you were a king. And I still know you before becoming a father. I knew you as a brother. I knew you as a mentor. I know you as a friend. If anyone deserves this, I'd say it was you." Lianthore took me into an embrace, and my emotions got the best of me.

"Not my little brother, growing wise on me overnight," trying to use humor to ease away my tears and tension. Truth be told, he was the only brother I'd let witness my uncertainty. He knew I wasn't all-knowing and that despite the practice, this transition would still be hard for me.

Lifting the former king's crown to try it on for the first time, I pivoted toward my younger brother. I gathered my hands in back and asked, "How do I look?"

Lianthore joined me at my side, as I inspected myself in front of the mirror, he smiled. "Like Father. But more like you."

***

Without a moment's notice, the doors of the saloon—where I was determined to stay to keep my mind focused and free from stress. But when it came to my brothers, none of that mattered.

"Thought you could hide from us, brother." Zaos boisterously held his arms out at both sides. "On the biggest day of your life?" His wild eyes taunting.

Tavnis, one of our youngest brothers, boasted about finding the ale mugs. "We will toast! As today, our eldest brother not only secures his throne, but our positions on the court as well," Tavnis spoke through shady eyes.

"And since you will finally be king, this calls for song," Theoden and Vamir both ignoring my pleas, encouraging my brothers to join them and sing.

Ohhhhhhhhh........

All across the great blue skies and just beyond the seas,

Is home to such a just wise king and magical is he...

He rules his realm with an iron fist, his subjects reach past the silver mist

He hunts the girl who drives him mad and claims her as his queen

I hated the song; Lianthore and I should have never taught it to them. But despite not being raised Elven, they took pride in embracing their Elven ways. Even though my brothers had lineages and power sources inherited from their mothers, our place in Esterbrooke would always be Elven.

"Nothing like an impromptu claiming to calm the nerves." Zaos hit me in the chest. "We were sure that you would pick from the nobles, but natured called. My question is, what is it like?"

From Lianthore's account, Zaos' mind was slowly changing when it came to claiming a bride. Zaos had always shared my sentiment on humans, so it came as a great surprise to him to learn that I was not only excited to wed, but had claimed a human on my own. Most of my brothers gathered around, all except for Ivaran, as I gave them my account of what transpired.

"You all remember that day? Nothing about me was in control. Every pulse, nerve, and impulse led me to my mate." Wanting to leave some mystery, so that they could imagine on their own what theirs might be like.

"No wonder you're looking forward to it. I admit, I still have my reservations. But now I am salivating at the mouth, impatiently waiting on Lianthore to get his over with."

"Says the Elf who lost ten grand, assuming our eldest brother wouldn't go through with it," Theoden slyly interrupted.

"You bet against me?" I asked with enthusiastic confusion.

"Well, you are your father's son," Zaos mordantly remarked. "Besides, can you blame me? You were always firstborn, but always the last of us to break out of your normal. Need I remind you how much arm-twisting it took for you to finally make your mark on the Human Realm?" He stood, playfully mocking me.

"I will have you know that I've secured our places and found my fated mate, all while being devilishly more handsome than the six of you. You're welcome—" The room was bursting with rambunctious laughter. I didn't even have time to defend myself as Lianthore and Vamir violently rough-housed me to a chaise lounge.

"So, what is this human called?" Zaos challenged.

"You won't understand it."

"Come on. The woman is to be our future sister. Surely, she

would not have something too complicated. She's human." Vamir shrugged.

"Brother, even you could make something as simple as sharing a name so complicated? Just tell us what she is called."

With a slight hesitation, I swallowed my breath, shrugging despite my certainty. "She is called Paige Anderson."

A brief bout of quiet crept across the room, as if they were expecting something grander to follow. "Page? Like a page in a book?" Zaos asked, confused.

"I believe that there is an I in there. I will have to ask her to double-check."

Zaos laughed, nearly spilling over his mug. "Humans with their strange names. Is her father called Ander? And why is her surname Anderson? She is no man."

"I'm still working through the semantics of how names work in the Human Realm." Scratching my beard, agreeing with him.

"I pray I find an Alfhild or a Kelda. Now that would be a name worthy of the son of a Valkyrie and Elf," Zaos boasted.

Theoden, with his mischievous smile and fiery red hair, asked what everyone wanted to know. "The real question of the day is, is she beautiful?"

Beautiful didn't even describe her outward appearance, and I was typically better at describing what I liked. Paige's beauty was so otherworldly, I was often at a loss for words.

"Never mind that. What I want to know is if she's feisty?" Tavnis interrupted before I could even get my first answer out.

"Does she have a sister—"

"I can only answer one question at a time. To your first, beautiful she is. Feisty? Irritably so. Lastly, as many of you are already aware, she has little family she is willing to claim."

"What made you sure she was the one?" Vamir asked, a strange, almost childlike wonder in his expression that contrasted his enormous frame.

"She's already tried to kill me twice." Which seemed to leave my brothers with either envy or pride that my fated mate had a fire in her.

"It is even a romantic partnership if she doesn't try to kill you?" Zaos boldly interrupted. "Half the reason I breathe life today stems from the many times my mother tried to kill Father. 'Tis the nature of a Valkyrie," he bragged.

"Have you decided what you plan to give her during the offering?" Lianthore directed his question toward me. Even though we all had different traditions on our maternal sides, since I was to have an Elven ceremony, I was expected to perform an offering to the future consort.

All of us were. An offering was a tradition royal siblings took part in, to make their future brother or sister by marriage feel welcome. Father too had a sister, but losing her at such a young age, he didn't have the privilege of participating in such a tradition. It almost made me feel lucky. Losing a parent is hard, but losing someone so close to you...it's like losing a family member and a friend at the same time.

It might have been one of the many reasons Tarron had been so private about his life. As we still grieved his death, I fear he died, with us never really knowing him.

Back to Esterbrooke, all of my brothers valiantly bragged about their planned offerings, putting me to shame that I did not know what I planned to offer. "I'm still considering," was my only rebuttal.

"You needn't worry about your bride not receiving a warm welcome," Lianthore toasted. "Not even Ivaran can ruin a night like this."

Ivaran, who until now had been isolating himself in the corner with his mug of ale, wasn't always this anti-social, but when he was in the company of us all, he didn't always deem it necessary to add to conversations.

He would never admit favoritism, but he was closest to Zaos, mainly due to their shared bloodlust. Despite Elven culture being the hardest for him to assimilate into, he'd been the first of us to mate with a fated human, but because of the outcome, he preferred to keep to himself.

Weddings were hard for him, so I knew it was a big ask of him to be in attendance. Since he was born a Demyn, and could only be claimed by Father once he proved he wasn't pure destruction, sizeable crowds would always be a gamble for him. But I had faith that, like all my brothers, he could master his own destiny.

"Have her keep her distance when necessary," Ivaran retorted, a low rumble in his tone.

"Now that I've answered all your questions," I started, trying to hold in my laughter. "I have a few of my own." Knowing I would have to pay for my close-mindedness in the past.

"This may sound indecent." I was unable to curb my laughing halfway through. "But for those of you who have actually *bedded* a human female, is there anything I should know? Mechanics? Anatomy? Will I run into any issues when we consummate this marriage?" Embarrassed that I even had to ask.

"I will take this one," Lianthore volunteered, grateful to him since he had the most experience of being intimate with humans. "Mostly, anatomy is the same. You have to be gentler with humans, as they do tend to be tighter, in the worst ways." He lifted his drink, damn near bragging.

"Human men are a grab bag of sizes and lengths, so they are not always expecting our endowment. Half of them won't be able to handle it. But the ones that are willing, rather enjoy having to accommodate us."

"You think her scent drives you mad when she's still? Wait until you become one. It will be like edging on the brink of insanity." Ivaran sneered. "You will constantly be at war with being responsible, or being inside of her."

I had to hand it to Ivaran. Despite his youth, this was more his expertise. Knowledge of human women was one thing, fated mates were another altogether. "While we are all having a grand time, would any of you mind if Ivaran and I had the room for a moment?"

I had certain questions that I didn't want to get the brothers that had lacked the experience, to be overcome with obsession, especially if they weren't next in line. With no objection, five of my brothers respectfully stepped out, admitting they had matters in a ceremony to attend to.

Not that we were alone, I forced him out of his corner. "Brother." Patting him on the shoulder, praying I didn't ask the wrong thing that might bring up his trauma. "I apologize in advance if I sound forward, but this topic is delicate. It is only you who has the experience over any of us."

"I know," he scoffed, backing away, wearing a confusing combination of pain and a smile. "I fear that I won't be able to offer you much. But I knew I would have to guide you if and when it happened."

I hesitated, making sure once more that this wasn't too much for him. "Are you sure you are in a good place to answer my questions?"

Ivaran blinked hard, and I knew he fought hard trying to combat his grief. "I will try to be. Because it's you. I know that at times, it seems as if I don't care. But I'm happy for you. Happy that you get to feel the bond you only get once in a lifetime." He smiled, and I'm sure he thought of warm memories of his late wife.

"And I am grateful that you have a power you can control, so you never have to experience the loss that I have," he spoke, shame in his voice.

"You *can* control it. I promise you that." Reminding him, he's come a long way since we first experienced his berserker shift in battle.

"*Sometimes,*" he shamefully admitted. "But not when it mattered most, brother." Faking a smile, insisting I ask him what I'd like to know.

"How do I make her *happy*?" I found myself juggling with emotions unfamiliar to me.

"This I do not believe you need my help with—"

"I do," I interrupted. "I'm not ashamed to admit that I don't know where to start in achieving her happiness."

Ivaran took a deep breath, meeting his piercing golden stare to mine. "Aranzeiros, when destiny chooses two erroneously fit people together, there will always be pushback. But you don't attract a human that's not attracted to you. Or perhaps their attraction to you grows. But in time, her joy, her pleasure, her pain. To give and take those things away will be all that you'll want." He shifted, eyes glassed over.

"When your bodies join, it will become worse, at least for you. You will long for her laugh. Yearn for her smile. Ache for her touch." His voice suddenly soothing, almost poetic. "Soon, her happiness will be like breathing. Your actions will match your feelings, and when they don't, it will tear you up inside. Love will humble you."

"Goddess, Father did not prepare me for any of this," I interrupted.

"He prepared you more than us," he boldly stated, reminding me of how little of Tarron my brother received in comparison to me.

"You will find your own ways to express your love, but be prepared to put in effort. Elven maidens are moved by status. Human women are moved by humility. And flowers." He nonchalantly shrugged.

"Outside of nature?" I asked confused.

"They rip them from the ground." He used his hands for emphasis. "Cut the stems. And then watch them die in a pot of water. It's barbaric, but they find it endearing."

"Is that really all there is? Without hindsight, it's as if I've done those things and we are still not quite there. We still struggle to relate to one another," I humbly admitted.

"Brother, take it from someone who knows and loves you. Not everyone is susceptive to your charm. But one who is yours will learn. I promise it will be like no experience in our world or theirs." He smiled warmly, a gesture uncommon for him.

"Now make haste and get this thing over with. You know, more than anyone, that I don't do well with crowds." He winked.

"Consider me grateful that you're making an exception."

"I'm morally obligated to make exceptions for my king." He could hardly say without bursting out in laughter. Despite preparing for others to refer to me as their new king, I admit there was an everlasting cringe at the sound of my brothers referring to me that way.

"That will be enough of that *My King*, nonsense. When I am ordained, it will be my first task to officially ban either of you from the use of the phrase, *My King*."

"Whatever you say." Ivaran faux bowed for extra emphasis. "My King."

CHAPTER THIRTEEN

Paige

And I thought that last night was bad. Try spending a morning being woken up at the crack of dawn to prepare for a wedding I didn't even want.

Between the final fittings, three hired staff were sent to do my makeup, as they brought an expert in from the Earth Realm to perfect my signature curls. One appeared to stay just to keep the others company.

It was exhausting having so many people dote on me, which only got worse by the end of the day. Several women in court served as my bridesmaid party. Mostly Elven and wealthy, from prestigious families, and boy were they beautiful. It was a wonder Aranzeiros hadn't chosen any of *them* to be his wife.

"Oh, Lady Paige. Would you look at yourself? You're finally beginning to look like a queen. The prince will be so happy when he joins you in the offering," an Elven girl with deep mahogany skin and ginger hair as bright as flames, said with a clap of her hands.

With all the primping and pampering, I hadn't had time to look at myself, so when another female Elf insisted on pulling me to the full-length mirror, I didn't argue. I didn't recognize the woman looking back at me. The liner on my eyes brought out my inner seductress. The rouge that adorned my cheeks made me look healthy and vibrant. Last, my full lips were muted, a neutral yet polished color that brought attention to my mouth but looked far from boring. Amazed didn't even cover it.

For once in my life, I looked the way I felt. Beautiful. I didn't even know I could look like this. "It's as if your necklace matches your dress perfectly," another said, this one a tawny-skinned Elf and with the looks of it, hosting naturally lavender-colored hair.

I touched the necklace the prince regent gifted me, cradling it in my palm, recalling my mother's last words to me. *"You better be good at things, because being pretty isn't one of them."* If only she could see me now.

The dress was figure-hugging, a deep sapphire blue that was reminiscent of the night sky on a captivating, full moon. The starburst sparkles hand-sewn in its design, resembled constellations, making the dress appear like a work of art, as much as an outfit. The princess neckline made me the envy of every woman in the room.

"I've never worn a dress this epic before. Will people know that I'm the bride if I'm not wearing white?" A question that caused all five members of the court to gasp in horror, as they clutched their chests like I said something wrong.

"White? To an Elven wedding? White is our color of mourning. Why in the goddess would anyone wear colors of mourning to a royal wedding?" One faux fainted, Jeweliana I think her name was.

"That is what they do in the mountains. Just tasteless," another said. If I recall correctly, her name was Rukshana, but I wasn't entirely sure.

"I'm sure if you were to wear it, it would be nothing short of amazing." Correcting herself, a reminder that their pleasantries were hard to distinguish. Not that they weren't nice, but it was hard to tell if that kindness was out of obligation to their prince regent.

"The rich blue is a stunning choice, Your Grace. In fact, I believe it was the prince regent himself who chose it," she said, causing me to curl my lip in disdain. I hated any thought of him molding me into his ideal bride and if I wasn't so desperate to see this day through, I would have gladly thrown a hissy fit and tossed the dress to the floor.

"To be wedding Prince Aranzeiros. Oh...how lucky you are. When I was a part of his mistress line, most days I couldn't even walk straight. He is quite the lover," said another lady-in-waiting, this one a blonde, with light brown skin and hooded eyes, her admittance causing my mouth to drop to the floor.

"*You* were a part of his harem?" I asked the blonde as she guided me back to the chair to rest my feet.

"Why, yes, Your Grace, we all were. That's what they brought many of us to court to do," she said unabashedly. So not only was I being forced into a marriage with a man who kidnapped me, he was a known, unashamed, adulterer. Just great.

"So, *all of you* have had sex with the Prince Regent," I asked, unsure as to why I cared but eager to know.

"He and his many brothers," she clarified. "I can attest to all but one, that their appetites require full-time...maintenance. But it is all good fun, for they are all superb," she ended with a gleam to her eyes, as if she were just talking about her love of ice cream.

The redhead snapped her fingers to one of the makeup artists, signaling for them to address an issue with my eye makeup. Only, there was nothing wrong with my makeup, just lines of worry. Hearing how easily these Faeborne brothers passed around women, would they expect me to do the same?

"What plagues you, Your Grace?" the redhead asked.

"This is just overwhelming. Where I'm from men, don't have harems. Or at least they weren't supposed to."

"Is that all that worries you? Might I inform you that the line of mistresses is only for *unwed* princes. Once they are wed, all their sexual demands are expected of his wife. Does that provide comfort? One forgets you are human at times, Your Grace. I know how inanely monogamous your culture can be," she said, ending in a curtsy.

"Yes, but Her Grace is his fated mate," the lavender-haired Elf chimed, her gloved hands gently gripping my bare shoulders. "You will be hard-pressed to get him interested in another. Forgive me, Lady Paige, but that is why I will never seek refuge in the Earth Realm. The last thing I need is to be so smitten that I uncharacteristically demand and threaten him should he refuse to bed me and sire my children."

The rest of the women lowered to the floor by my feet, their multitude of jewel-tone dresses hugging the rich carpets. I wonder if this was all they did all day. Gossip, look pretty, and attend weddings and galas. What a peaceful life that was.

With a wave of her hand, the blonde Elf continued, "It's so easy for the male Elves. You human women, many of you are light enough to just grab and go. One baroness in my old court mated, and she practically had to drug her human to get him here. And get this? He didn't want to leave his wife and children," she chastised, proving the women were just as psychopathic as the men. My ass had to get out of here.

"Corra knows all about the Earth Realm and fated mates. She's the proud result of one and now finds herself in the king's court," she sing-songed.

The female in question had chestnut brown hair piled elegantly on top of her head in a sophisticated chiffon. Her eyes, a deep shade of green, reminded me of the fields I used to play in when I was a kid. Unsure why I didn't notice it until now, her eyes weren't as sharp as the rest of the Elven woman.

"You're only half fae." Not knowing where my boldness came from. So up close, she had an aura about her, both modest and heavenly, like an angel in an old painting. It's not that she didn't look human, she just looked out of this world.

"You flatter me, my future queen." Accepting that as a compliment. I had so many questions. What was she doing here? Was she widely accepted? I had too many questions to settle on one.

"If you don't mind me asking, where are you from in the Earth Realm?" Noticing her slight drawl. I was no expert, but I suspected Southern roots, but I couldn't pinpoint it.

"If it pleases you to know, I'm honored that you ask. I am from a small parish in Baton Rouge, Louisiana." She smiled warmly.

"What made you come here?" Preparing myself for a tale. Her story was honest. A woman from a prestigious rich family. One that only knew deception, scandal, and cover-ups, but most of all, were consumed by greed and power. I couldn't exactly relate, but I knew what it was like growing up in a family you felt you never belonged in.

Her family had hidden her fae heritage from her, so when she discovered others like her, she decided the Fae Realm was where she'd rather be. That's where we differed; I couldn't wait until I was able to plan my escape.

"There are things I regret, like leaving my son." Her tone softened as she looked down at her gloved hands and pulled at the fingers.

"But my family denied me the right to take him, in fear that I'd raise him here. The only thing that comforts me was that he was well taken care of and loved. My father and brother loved that boy." Her warm smile replaced her once sad frown.

"How old is he now?" I asked with great interest. Her emerald gaze met mine, her crimson pout pursing to one side.

"I'm afraid I don't know. Time moves much differently here. For a halfling, I'm afraid I don't look as old as I am." I didn't bother asking how old she was because she looked incredible and no number would take away from that. Maybe there was a time when I cared about how others judged women as we got older, but I, for one, wasn't afraid of aging. I was just happy to be alive.

Reaching out for my hands, her sharp stare locked with mine. "I know it does not seem like it now, but you'll learn to love it here. Perhaps it is not the life that you have chosen for yourself. But the Faeborne princes are good fae. Prince Aranzeiros chose you. Your life will only change for the better."

As lovely as her prediction was, my only intention after becoming queen was to use my power to hightail it back to where things made sense. I don't care how good of fae these people were. I refused for this to be my future. All the guards and staff the prince regent advised to keep a close eye on me, wouldn't be able to tell me shit once we were married.

Aranzeiros and I weren't lovers, or even friends. Hell, I didn't even like him enough to consider him my enemy. If pretending to go through with this would save my life, all I had to do was survive today.

***

Soon, I was collected and escorted by a fleet of the Royal Guards. All the roads in the street were closed off from the palace to the chapel, an endless sea of creatures, hundreds of thousands, watching me as I walked down a long aisle red-carpet stretching miles long.

Some whistled, while others applauded. Many whispers remarked on my beauty and wedding dress choice. I had never had so many eyes on me before, especially so many that weren't considered human. All I could do was take a deep breath and pray that I didn't slip on this long train. Luckily, I had handmaidens for that, but a lot could happen when you were nervous and had no desire to reach the end of that podium.

As I walked up the steps of the outside chapel, they led me to a large platform decorated with intricate flower arrangements and exquisite banners swinging high above our heads. There was a bishop of some kind. They may have called it something different here.

With a tall hat and a long matching gown, he held a book in his hand and gestured for me to face the steps. A rich booming voice accompanied loud cries of orchestrated horns, over what sounded like an intercom, as it announced the house of Faeborne.

I'd probably seen them on TV once or twice, but as the aisles came alive with movement, six of the most beautiful people I had ever seen in person stalked the runway, a sight beyond belief.

The regalia they wore didn't match in the slightest. It was as if the cultures they resembled matched the attire they adorned. I had never seen them beyond the Veil, as some of them were severe looking, but it didn't take away from their ethereal-ness. Bright Eyes, sharp features, and hawkish stares, formed a tight line below the staircase, a sizable distance from me but close enough to where I noticed the first one stepping forward.

"I am Prince Lianthore. Duke of Xiángyún and second son of King Tarron. It is with high esteem we welcome you into the house of Faeborne. It has been decades since we have blessed the Fae Realm with a crowned queen, and I am certain that if you are of my brother's choosing, you are worthy of such a title."

He inched closer, a sword emerging from casted flames, as he planted the blade in the space between us, ending his action in a bow. It was only then I noticed the soft crimson of his eyes.

They made him nearly as pale as Aranzeiros, but his broader nose and epicanthal fold were just the beginning of their phenotypical differences. He was handsome in a different way, with a light mustache accompanied by a soul patch, compared to Aranzeiros' full beard. But the biggest difference was his eyes. They looked like they were dancing. They looked like they were on fire.

"This is why I offer you my wisdom. May my counsel serve you well, as you find your place in our family." With that, the sword lit up in flames, forcing me to jerk back in fear that it would burn me, only for it to transform into the shape of a dragon.

Impressive.

Preparing myself for the younger brother, who was as tall as Lianthore, only instead of a perfectly combed coif, he wore his long hair, with an intricate detail that resembled ropes. I almost didn't notice that half of his hair was loose because from the moment he locked eyes with me, I was distracted by the large scar on his face that only complimented his strikingly tormented blue eyes. In the Human Realm, he resembled a Viking, a culture dead for a millennium.

"I am Prince Zaos. Duke of Vetrarfjall," he started, lifting his hands out to match the raspy voice that carried across the chapel. "To my newest sister, it is my privilege to serve you. And on this glorious day, I offer you my loyalty. So you may know honor, and the unbreakable bond that blends our two families." as he took a knee, his eyes glowed, the sword he held emitting a surge of lightning. Instead of fearing the gift, I welcomed it, preparing to receive something similar from the next brother.

The third one advanced forward, almost too effortlessly for someone his size. He was so tall, maybe the tallest of them all, that I swear I could hear his weight with each step. At a six-foot-eight minimum, his frame was wide and built, contrasted by his messy pewter hair and eerie wolf-like gold eyes. Expecting him to sound fearsome, I was taken aback by his low, soft-spoken, yet brooding voice.

"I am Prince Ivaran, and I exude pride for my brother on this day." He bowed his head, but it did little to reduce his height. "For today, my brother becomes king, and in turn, we gain a sister." He kneeled, as the others had, but just when I thought it was over, he slammed his fist against the ground, as the broken earth traveled beneath me, forming a throne of stone.

"Show off," the brother with the scar over his eye jovially whispered to his brothers, proving that even in a smile, there was madness to his appearance.

"I give you my strength, so that no foreign hand, human or fae will harm you in your reign." I rewarded each of their offerings with a round of applause, continuing until each brother pledged to me their fealty. Not once in my life had anyone looked at me in the way they did now. Even though it was in a familial way, something was empowering about being made to feel adored, important, seen.

Another orchestra of horns bellowed amongst the crowd, announcing the king's arrival. Through the red paved carpet, he marched gracefully up the steps, his brothers parting their formation, allowing a clearer path to me.

He was different today. His gleaming dark eyes beamed with pride, complimented by his blue and gold ceremonial regalia, adding flair to his towering frame. He would be the last person the word angelic could work for, but then again, dark angels existed too. This moment marked the one time I looked at him without fear.

He was always handsome, whether or not I admitted it, only he was delectably so, that I almost forgot that I couldn't stand him. As he approached, wearing an expression of glass to hide the exhilaration that he had won, his eyes finally regarded me and...

I liked the way he looked at me.

"Lady Paige, will you stand for me, please?" he lightly demanded, my judgment fighting the urge not to obey him. He was about to taunt me, I just knew it. Reiterate that I was his wife now and that he owned me. If I wanted his trust, I would have to do as he asked. I could survive one more day being at his mercy.

"To my beloved Paige." His words halted, so that he could take my hand in his and in its place, leave a kiss. "Our journey has not been the seamless arrangement I hoped for. I also know that our challenges will not end today. But your presence has granted me the honor of calling myself king. In the eyes of many, it would be unthinkable for a king to bow to someone he deems lower than him. As a king is taught to bow to no man," as before I could stop him, he dropped to one knee, a sight leaving many mouths agape.

"And yet, you are no man. Fate has chosen you as my queen. You have made me whole, so as a token of my gratitude, I offer you, my humility. From this day forward, you will be my equal in all ways. I will cherish you, open myself to you, and please you. But in return, I ask for your guidance. Be my light, in dark times we may face together. With this ring, I solemnly swear to worship you. But most of all, I promise to love you."

The ring bearer handed him the ring, a dazzling circle adorned in the fashion of intricate vines and leaves made up of mithril metal and an alexandrite center stone. Slipping it onto my finger, he stood to his full height again, stealing the air from me with just a simple stare.

From there, the coronation flew by in a blur and before I knew it, we were whisked away to an open-top carriage ride that put us on display for all of Arisnoto to see.

It didn't take long before we were back at Regalhelm, celebrating in the palace's opulent and massive throne room. Lustrous braziers hung from each of the twelve marble columns, bathing the room in warm yellows and dancing oranges. From our plush thrones, we watched as others drank and mingled, taking in sights of the many, celebrating this occasion.

The lyrical harps and flutes courtesy of the live music forced strangers to make acquaintance with the dance floor in the form of foxtrots and waltzes. Not far from us, his brothers with drinks in their hands, laughed and shared stories of past memories and old wagers. They looked close and happy, that I wondered if they made Aranzeiros a different person when they were around.

Taking one last scan of the room, I had never seen so much high-couture fashion in one place. Displayed by a montage of different races that made up the fae, it was like the Met Gala only this time; I was the guest of honor. While I was busy surveying the room, the menacing Elf couldn't take his dazzling, dark gaze off of me.

"Have you been watching me the whole time?"

"Yes." Catching me off guard that he didn't deny it. "It is challenging not to peer at you without obsessive interest."

Why did he have to say things like that? I needed to hate him, not blush. "Did you hear what I said, my queen?" It took the warmth of a spotlight pointed in our direction for me to realize he had said something.

"No." Flustered that my mind went someplace else, so quickly.

"Then I will repeat myself." He held out his hand, instructing me to take it. "We are to partake in the first dance."

My nerves flared, and nearly everything I ate this morning plummeted to the pit of my stomach. He held out his hand to take, as rushes of uncertainty and reluctance must have been clear on my face. "Do not worry," he whispered.

"I haven't been taught any dance steps." He led me toward the center of the room, our attendees parting the crowd to make way for us.

"There wasn't time," he whispered, taking my waist in one hand, my outstretched hand in his other. "But if you trust me, you will see you're in expert hands."

My first attempts at following his lead were a series of missteps that dredged up my self-doubt and fear of being judged. "I can't—"

"You can and you will," He interrupted, forcing me back in my effort to pull away. "I will not let you fail." He let go of my hand, so he could tilt my chin up to face him, locking me into that obsidian stare.

As he guided my body to move to the song, against my better judgment, I trusted him this time. Instead of fight his lead, I worked with it, allowing him to turn me when necessary, and not appear startled any time an unexpected lift swept me off the ground.

Despite all eyes being on me, Aranzeiros was my only focus. In the short time we'd shared space, I had only admired his beauty once without pushback, when I was naïve and grateful to catch the attention of someone so prominent.

Once I could predict the lifts, dare I say, I was actually having fun. I had never been much of a dancer, but as his powerful arms brought me up into the air, the train of my dress skimmed the floor in magical sweeps, as he synced our every movement to the music.

The moment my feet met the ground, Aranzeiros linked our arms, forming an intricate chain that we maintained as we danced in a rhythmic circle.

"You adapt nicely," he said, just low enough for my ears to hear.

I laughed. "Just trying not to look ridiculous."

"Paige, you could never look ridiculous. Not to me. Not to anyone. You are a queen, and you deserve the world. And I intend to give that to you." With another captivating lift, I was a prisoner once again to his hypnotizing stare.

This morning, my mind was made up. I would find a way home, even if it killed me. But when I looked into his nearly black eyes, I found truth in the words he said. Even if I wasn't a queen, I still deserved the world.

What would I even go back to if I found a way out? "I must warn you, my queen, it is customary to join each other in a kiss to conclude our first dance. However, if you are not comfortable with that, we do not have to."

In the Earth Realm, it was something you did right after sharing your vows. Bracing myself for it, no such thing happened. Now I had to make a choice. If I had any shot at getting out of here, he couldn't have any doubts that I was all in.

"Who would I be to break tradition?" I assured, allowing him to guide me through one last elaborate turn, before the song came to an end. Facing one another, Aranzeiros pulled me in close and lifted my chin in his other hand. He studied my features closely, almost to the point of discomfort, as I placed my hand on his chest and I rose to meet his mouth.

At first, his lips were petal soft, a contrast to his well-groomed facial hair. He opened his mouth to mine, gliding his tongue gently past my lips, in a fashion gentler than I assumed he was capable of.

But as seconds passed, the intensity changed his kiss. My energy was waning as if I had become severely weaker the more of me he took. To claim the sensation wasn't an addiction would be a lie, but for as good as it felt, my body felt like a prisoner. Unable to move, unable to fight back. Was this his darkness? Or was this something else?

All I know was when he finally pulled away, he had to catch me in his arms, otherwise, I would have lost my balance.

"It appears my queen has fallen." His smile was menacing but smug.

Not wanting him to have the last word, I mustered up the confidence to reply, "I may be your wife, but I won't be that easy."

CHAPTER FOURTEEN

Aranzeiros

My chamberlain was prompt, knowing tonight I would require special care. I was used to him getting me out of my clothes for the night in my *own* bedroom, but I was presumptuous in assuming the night had gone decent, or at least well enough for us to require the use of our marriage bed.

While most marriages could take their time, Paige and I didn't have the privilege before becoming husband and wife. After the coronation, much of what Paige owned would be moved to her new chambers, but it was my hope that she might join me before she became accustomed to her own accommodations.

"Have you heard word from the Queen's attendant before you arrived?"

"Yes, Your Majesty," Lexium answered, holding my wedding attire on his forearm.

"And what of the Queen's temperament?" It was wishful thinking to believe she might come to our wedding bed without a fight, but if she'd been unruly post the reception, I wanted to know what I'd be dealing with.

"Silvine, her temporary chambermaid, speaks that she is overcome with...angst," Lexium did his best to find the proper word. "But that is to be expected so soon after the ceremony."

I predicted as much. From my limited understanding, humans experienced such complex emotions. It has been both a journey and a conquest to understand the many. The promise of duty, loyalty, and humility were amongst the many things I had promised to her in my vows. But I would be a fool to assume her love would be instant.

This wouldn't be a human-love marriage for her, but I could still give her everything she's ever dreamed of. All that would take is for her to trust me. Whatever happened tonight would likely set the tone for what our future would look like.

The door opened, forcing both of our attention on the visitor. It was Paige, the newly crowned queen, dressed down in a sleep robe, wearing her fear in her body language. It was obvious she assumed tonight would go a certain way, so it was my duty to assure her she had choices.

"I bid you good night, Your Majesty." Lexium bowed, before excusing himself. Paige hadn't left her spot at the foot of the door, making our vast distance even more noticeable.

"They moved my stuff into another room, I'm being told." Her voice started confidently but nervously broke toward the end.

"Yes, they did. I hope that you find our marriage chambers as comfortable as the chambers they brought you to recover in," I answered in a matter-of-fact tone, careful to keep my step steady and less threatening.

Attempting to erase some of the distance between us, she sensed my intentions, her body tensing as she took a few steps behind her, to match every step I'd taken toward her.

"You're afraid. What do you think will happen tonight?" Ignoring her comfort, so I could gently caress her face. Was this fear? Or was it something else? Because she smelled incredible.

"I've never been alone with you before," she said, with short-ness of breath.

"You have. Many times," I assured her.

"But never as your wife. I'm sure that has expectations." As if she expected some vicious attempt by force. Ruining her had always been at the top of my priority list, but from her cowardly stature, I could tell we had two definitions of what that might entail.

"It does."

Nearly choking on a gulp, she broke my gaze, staring nervously at her feet. "So, it won't matter if I don't want to?" she asked, tone defeated.

"Paige, I understand you find my traditions strange. I was required to marry, so I knew this marriage would be a political one as much a..." I lost my train of thought.

I couldn't say love marriage. She and I may never fall in love how *humans* do. She was fated to me, so in my eyes, that meant she was mine and I would struggle to exist without her.

"Duty is something you don't always want to do, but you do it because it needs to be done. A good deal may invalidate this union if we never consummate it. I would be lying if at some point I didn't expect us to lie together. But with that being said, I don't want to take your choice away. I want you in all the ways a husband should want his wife. But I want you to want to as well."

The shared curious look gave me a false sense of security, as her attempt to walk further into the room prompted me to stop her by the wrist, desperate to know. "*Do* you want to?"

"Aranzeiros, I know nothing about you. A part of me is still afraid of you." She hesitated. "It would be a while before I even allow myself to trust you in that way."

It wasn't the answer I was looking for, but I would have to accept it. "Fair enough." Letting go of her wrist to prove I wasn't trying to contest her choice.

"Inevitably, our marriage will have to be consummated to

legitimize a human-fae union. But it doesn't have to be tonight." Her doe eyes followed me as my legs carried me past the bed and toward the balcony.

"Should you require rest, I shall not disturb you." I bowed, masking the rejection shifting through me that my night hadn't gone as planned.

Here, the veranda of this room hosted a lovely view of the eastern city lights. Creatures were still celebrating my night, and here I was spending it alone.

The night air was cool, a draft blowing in that was far from unkind. Taking a deep breath, I wondered if kings before me experienced nights like this. Where you felt more alone, even in the presence of your intended.

Perhaps I should consider myself lucky; there had been no attempt to kill me, despite the opportunity. Just as I was about to close the balcony door, I realized my bedmate hadn't given me a chance. Assuming that I would spend my company alone, I wasn't sure of what to make of Paige joining me.

This wasn't some game-changing moment, as she still kept a respectable distance. I doubt she planned to say anything until I burdened her with what was on my mind.

"My entire life has been preparing for this night. Sometimes, I wish I had been born second. There would have been responsibility, but there would have been choices. Everything in my life has been a part of some divine plan. No one really wants to be king, yet someone has to take on the role." I turned to her, knowing I was about to bear a part of myself neither was ready to hear.

"I've been given so much to mitigate the fact that I never had a choice. I've never felt I had a right to want anything because I was given everything." Clasping my hands behind my back, choosing to gaze at the city's sights.

"So, I've never wanted anything. Until you." Her silence could have been a sign of her sympathy or pity. With her I would never truly know.

"You're the only thing about my life I got to choose. I hope that one day, you and I might become the masters of compromise, instead of what we are in *this* moment." My words, whether they reached her, I would never know. She exited the balcony not long after, and with it, the door behind her.

CHAPTER FIFTEEN

Aranzeiros

While patience wasn't one of my strongest points, I waited for as long as I could before I joined her in bed. Her discomfort was the last thing I wanted, so I thought it best to give her an hour or two to ease her anxiety.

Having done everything but sleep in a bed, sleeping next to someone would be a first for me. I would have to remind my brothers—especially given that Ivaran certainly hadn't—that sleeping next to someone you're fated to, even when you've done little to stir their unease, would give you nightmares.

Granted, our situation wasn't easy, but when she was uncomfortable, her smell affected me in more ways than just uncontrollable lust. Perhaps it would have been less affliction on my part if her anxiety had tailored to things *she* feared. But no, in all her agitation, my dreams were tailored to mine.

Light.

My body shot up in a panic before I could assess that I wasn't in any immediate danger. Having frightened Paige, she crawled even further away from me, balling the comforter close to her chest as if she expected me to snatch it away.

"Do you plan on doing that the *entire* night? Or just to where we both don't get sleep?" I asked, trying but failing to hide the wrath in my tone.

"I'm sorry," she apologized, surprised when I ripped myself from the bed. There was no way I would let her witness me shaking, in a state of distress caused by a dream about light.

"I realize you're still adjusting," I said, making sure my robe had stayed securely over my shoulders.

"We are both adjusting. But your moods, they affect me now. It is one thing to not know peace when I am awake. But I am not even free from you in my dreams." Rubbing my palm from my forehead to beard, wondering how long—assuming we ever got along—this period would continue for us.

"Are you okay?" she asked sympathetically.

"Would you prefer I call my steward to have someone in the kitchen prepare you some tea?" Ignoring her question. "It does wonders for fae. It would be bound to knock a human out." Praying she took me on my offer.

"I don't think that would help." Her head plopped onto the pillow, discouraged.

"You slept adequately over the last few days. One can only assume the difference is me." I was unsure of what action to take, or words to say.

"How many *people* have you had in this bed?" Paige sat up, revealing what was likely one of her biggest concerns.

"*People?*" I asked, unsure.

"Lovers," she clarified.

"This palace has been in the Faeborne line for close to three thousand years. One can only assume that plenty of lovers have shared this bed."

"That didn't answer my question," she scoffed.

"That's because I'm not sure I understand the question. If you are asking have *I* ever made love in this bed, I would not have the privilege. It is meant only for kings or queens. Even if I had become king through a technicality as my father had, I would never bring a lover into a space meant for my wife."

"Right? Like your harem of my bridesmaids." She turned over, rolling her eyes, and I detected envy and sarcasm in her voice and scent.

"Paige Anderson, they were very kind to you." Doing my best not to raise my voice.

"You must not be used to being in awkward situations. And you can stop calling me Paige Anderson. I never knew that I could get so sick of my own name." She scoffed. I tilted my head in confusion.

"I apologize. That was the way you had introduced yourself. I assumed that was what you preferred. But what about today was awkward for you?"

"Aranzeiros, I'm not sure you know this, but human men, while they desire female harems, it is far from an everyday occurrence. And they *definitely* don't meet each other moments before they meet your wife." Now I was sure I could sense jealousy or some form of it. I'd have to remember that smell in the future.

"How am I to know what is common? I have never been common. I apologize if their presence brought out insecurity in you, but here in Esterbrooke, it is customary for a prince or princess regent to celebrate their new beginnings with those who have made their lives comfortable beforehand. It's an honor for them to be included. Especially given their services are no longer needed."

Paige set up in bed, hair disheveled and wild. "I'm just curious. Were those women *all* the people you were entitled to? "

"Are you asking because you want to know, or are you asking to fuel your animosity toward me?" She assured me it was the former, but her scent told me she was lying.

"I've had a rotation of about forty-five Elven maidens over two decades. I consider that quite modest considering my time before that..." I struggled to find the words.

"Let's just say, for my privilege and age, I could have done worse."

It was my choice not to scare her by sharing I had a certain talent, one that makes it a challenge to be with a single maiden. Now that my body wasn't in a constant state of trepidation, I could relax and bask in the honor that Paige and I were sharing a civil conversation.

"Since we're sharing, would it be rude of me to ask about your history with past partners?"

She laughed and I could swear there was a hint of mordancy riddled in her tone. "Well, it's not forty-five."

"I wouldn't judge." Assuring her there wasn't a number that could surprise me.

"It's three," she said, slapping her hands against her clothed thighs. When she hadn't clarified what she meant, I followed up with a question of my own.

"Three *what*? Dozen? Hundred?"

"Just three." Throwing up three fingers for emphasis.

"Three lovers in total?" I asked, convinced I hadn't heard her right.

"Yeah."

"*Why?*" I questioned, unable to hide my repugnance. Were humans really that conservative and deprived of intimacy?

"It's not exactly easy to have as many partners when you're not a man or a soon-to-be king. Human women are cultured to look at sex more personally than men. When you choose a partner, you're sold on a fairy tale that that person is going to be yours forever. By the time you're thirty-seven, you realize it's rare when it's forever. All it does is feel good. And sometimes, it can't even do that," she admitted, defeated.

Sensing both her shame and willingness to share, I didn't want to upset her or make her feel inadequate for her lack of experience. "Sometimes, I forget how young you actually are." Rubbing the frustration from my face, as she unconvincingly attempted to convince me that thirty-seven in human years wasn't technically old, but it wouldn't be young either.

"That argument might have more success with someone who isn't enjoying their third century on the realm," I joked, relieved that she laughed too.

"That, I won't argue on you with." Pointing a finger toward me for emphasis.

"While still on the subject, there is something I will argue with you about the matter. You mentioned that on occasions where you've made love, it doesn't always feel good. Why are you sharing yourself with partners who don't make your pleasure their priority?"

"Easy for you to say." Finally drawing the covers from her body. "A man will come every time—"

"I am not a man." Frustrated that she kept referring to me that way. "And there is no lovemaking—at least regarding what pleases me—where a maiden does not come. Every. Time."

I edged back on the bed, taking her willing mood as an invitation. "It is as if I can't stop. One will never be enough. Three will never be enough. Six thousand will never be enough. There are times when I feel I've been put on this realm, with the sole purpose of pleasing a maiden. Even over my birth rite of becoming king," I seduced.

For the first time since our pillow talk started, she seemed to be lost for words. She could do nothing but stare, her body language betraying her scent.

"I fear if I share something with you, it will only drive us further apart. And I have enjoyed this exchange," I said, my voice louder than a whisper, but lower than my usual speech.

"What is that?" Unable to hide that she was curious.

"It takes me time. To shift through the scent you give off based on your emotions—"

"You can smell my emotions?" she interrupted.

"Yes. It is both my gift and curse when it comes to you. It is

why I can tell when you are anxious. Afraid. Fatigue. Frustrated."
I watched her eyes dance, hoping I wouldn't say what she would
later ask me to confirm.

"What scent do I give off now?" she asked curiously.

"I do not believe you would be honest if I told you." I backed
away, noticing her move an inch closer to the center of the
mattress.

"If you can tell anyway, what would be the point of lying?" she
admitted, one of the first times we could agree on something.

"You smell much like the time we first met. Curiosity. Attraction. Desire. Lust." Assuming it would make her draw away from
me. If anything, my suspicions were true.

"That is when you smell the sweetest to me. It is taking all my
restraint to resist what my body feels entitled to," I whispered,
surprised by her inching so close to my face.

"You told me that this marriage could be challenged if we
never planned to consummate?" she asked as a question.

"I did. Though I would do everything in my power—"

"What if we just got the consummation over with?" she
interrupted.

"Paige, I have wanted nothing more than to legitimize this
union. But it is also not a checklist act to get rid of."

"So, you don't want to?" she said, biting her lip. There was an
ulterior motive here, but what it was, I did not yet know.

"I have never kept my intentions to myself. You've denied me
many times. If you want it now, you'll have to beg for it."

"I don't intend on begging for sex from someone I didn't even
have a *choice* in marrying—" she started, but as my hand made its
way underneath her chemise, rubbing the fabric leading to her
greatest treasure, as the threat of ripping my hand away, her
reflexes forced me back, prompting a helpless, "Please don't stop."

As I worked my starving fingers against her sex, I almost
didn't notice her trying to pull my robe down my shoulders.
Snatching my hand and body from such a willing participant I

would likely regret, but I wasn't ready to show her—or rather, I didn't trust her not to pity me, if she saw my scars.

"What is your problem?" she rightfully protested.

"If we are to consummate this marriage, we will do so on my terms. You will sit back and I will please you. Am I making myself clear?"

Confused, she shot a look of revulsion before admitting she was just trying to touch me and wasn't sure what the big deal was.

The truth was, there was no big deal. It was vanity at best, insecurity at worst. She had never seen me as anything but perfect. For now, I didn't want the sight of my back to destroy that illusion.

"If I'm barely allowed to touch you, I have a quip of my own," she stated boldly. "If all this marriage is, is for politics...I would prefer you not kiss me on the lips."

That would be hard for me. We had only had the privilege of sharing a single kiss and even then, I wouldn't have stopped until she asked me to. My body wasn't patient enough to ask if this request was temporary or something to expect for the entirety of our matrimony, but in this moment of weakness, wanting to have her body in every possible way, I reluctantly answered, "Agreed. So long as I have consent to kiss everywhere else."

I positioned her back to me, admiring and kissing the skin that was so opposite to mine. So smooth, even, and without blemish. Her temperament changed, and despite the recent tension between us, she cooed, melting at the act of being touched.

"Mmm...You smell so sweet," I whispered, easing down the fabric from her shoulders, tracing kisses all over her swan-like neck. "I bet you'll taste even better."

Paige may not have been good at admitting her desires, but her scent couldn't lie. Now that I had her so close, so willing, even the slightest trace to her shoulders welcomed me with wisps of breath and a racing heart.

"Look at you," I whispered, drawing kisses against her goose-bumped skin. "Falling apart for me and I haven't even done anything yet."

Her shivering back felt cool against my lips, and I almost lost myself in the obsession that was her skin. It had the allure of satin, specially woven to invite my touch. She was the perfect shade of brown that made my colorless skin appear dull.

I thought I could handle the sight of her naked breasts, but I had spent so much time admiring her pore-less back, this feral need came over me, the moment I turned her around. Her flowing flesh and hungry curves made me wild and one-track-minded. Kneading and suckling, my mouth was compelled to worship her breasts, despite her having a whole body I would need to attend to.

Her eyes met mine, with her left nipple settled between my lips, and the other settled between my pinched fingers. This was my fated mate. Of course, we would enjoy each other. *Eventually*. She would never find a better lover for this body than me.

Gentle kisses snaked down her neck as my hands eagerly roamed and traced the contours of her body. Every time my lips touched her skin, it was a promise of what to feel. An expectation of what was to come.

"All this time, I believed you were truly afraid of me." Snatching my mouth from her breast, following the trail made by her soft stomach.

"I don't think that the fear you feel is just you being afraid of me. I think you fear that I'm the darkness you're afraid to admit consumes you." Changing things up, so she couldn't predict what I'd do next, I crept up to meet her eye level, indulging my curiosity.

A human's rounded ears had never been a source of intrigue for me, but I wanted to know everything about her body, and I intended on keeping my promise about kissing her everywhere. It felt strange at first, but bizarrely erotic.

Nuzzling against her, I reveled in the fact she shuddered at me nibbling her earlobe. "You don't have to admit it, but I will. Your very essence consumes me. Every part of you, I want to take and make my own. My mind becomes thoughtless, my logic becomes mindless, consumed and replaced by you. Kissing your body. Making every inch yearn and tortured, so that you may know what one ounce of you does to me." Kissing my way back down, to my original target.

"My hands want to touch you. My mouth wants to kiss and bite you. My tongue wants to show you why it's better at tasting you than the words could ever make you feel."

"Aranzeiros, what are you waiting for?" The tormented whisper left her lips.

"I'm waiting for you to *beg* me," I replied in a menacing whisper.

"Please, Aranzeiros, fuck me like you own me!"

With that command, I ripped open her undergarments, diving between her brown thighs to taste the result of all my teasing. "There's more than one way to kiss your lips." I smiled sinisterly before kissing her soaking folds and slipping my tongue between them.

"You taste as sweet as I thought you would." Kissing her inner thighs, so that I could gauge her reaction. The way she tasted was an understatement. She was sweet, like ripe cherries and wine. Or maybe because she was fated to me, her pussy was made to taste like something I would never want to stop eating.

She caressed her breasts in conjunction with my tasting, making her hand the envy of my tongue. That would not do, as I reached out and grabbed the other breast, to ensure they were both well played with.

"Oh fuck. Aranzeiros, that feels so fucking good." Gracing me with her beautiful eyes, she lifted her head to observe my face buried between her legs. With her hitching breath and eyes violently pressed closed to process her pleasure, I watched her become undone over something so simple. Just wait until she reached the next peak.

Arching into me, I happily drank from her candied well, drowning in her taste, tongue lapping to make her reach that release. "I'm about to come." A guttural moan escaped the back of her throat as she squirmed and thrashed until her feminine cry came to a sound-shattering scream.

"Okay, okay, I'm done," she innocently cooed, assuming that once she reached her plateau, it would be time to move on.

"Well, I'm not," I challenged, right before I dove between her legs once more, more aware of all her triggers, this time around. Locking my arms around her hips, my tongue circled and swirled, taking time to switch between sucking and flicking her clit, letting that tension build until there was nothing her body could do but release.

"Fuck baby, this is fucking torture," she moaned, peering down at me helplessly through her big, trusting eyes. She had never referred to me in a term of endearment before. I had to fight against my cheeks getting warm to finish the job. Even though it wasn't an ideal moniker, I craved she might refer to me in that way again.

Keeping at a pace that was likely to drive her insane, she held the back of my head down for the sake of her own selfish pleasure and allowed me the privilege of feeling those sensual contractions once more. Her cries weren't as coherent as before, but her body tensed and thrashed in a way that couldn't be compared with another feeling.

"Okay, okay, that's enough." She squirmed underneath me, trying to escape her blissful cage.

"I told you, no number would ever be enough before I'm done with you." Wiping down my beard of her sweetness.

"No wonder you needed so many mistresses," she joked, before stating that she needed a break before we moved forward. That option just gave me a better chance to truly worship her body. Kissing and kneading her thighs, caressing and biting her ass. There was plenty of fun to be had in the anticipation of sex. It brought me peace exploring her brown skin, inch by inch.

"I think I'm ready," she later bashfully admitted, biting her lower lip.

Before now, the only one free from all clothing was her. Now that we were both prepared to lose ourselves in one another, I stepped out of my pants of leisure, revealing a cock ready for lovemaking.

"Wow, um, you're bigger than I thought," she said, allowing me to push her back to the mattress. "No wonder you wanted me as wet as possible."

Finally finding the confidence to take the robe off of my back, knowing she wouldn't be able to easily see. "That had nothing to do with fucking you and everything to do with your pleasure."

Hovering over her, she seemed nervous and tried to put her arms around my back, but my instinct just forced her wrists back to the mattress.

"You're so defensive." Her voice cracking between a coo and irritated bark, as my cock slid and milked itself in the arousal visible outside of her pussy. "I was just trying to hold you."

Instead of reaching for my back this time, she reached for the back of my neck, and it made me realize how experienced I was at pleasing, but at how poor I was at connecting. Elven women could handle lovemaking any which way; or maybe I had just never made love to a maiden who was interested in a connection.

Every intention I had to ruin my delicate wife was replaced with wanting it to last forever. "I've never been with someone as big as you. I don't think that it'll fit." She shuddered, watching our bodies meeting but never truly connecting.

"Trust me," I whispered. "It'll fit," was the only warning I gave before positioning myself right into her entrance.

Something happened at that moment. I couldn't even explain it, as few words could describe the way it felt to drive inside her welcoming walls. There was an initial pressure that came with the first thrusts as you both commit, but I had never been so delirious just being inside someone.

"You're so fucking tight, Paige." Ill-prepared for how velvety soft and warm she would feel. "Mmm. You feel like nothing I've ever felt before." Slowly rocking into her, careful not to go fast, too soon.

"I can be gentle for you," I whispered, watching her face switch between pleasure and pain. "Teach me how to be gentle for you," whispering again, as I bit the top of her ear.

"Holy shit, you're so fucking big," she said through gritted teeth.

"Tell me if I'm hurting you."

"I just didn't know I could feel so...filled," she ended with an exhausted laugh.

"How does it feel?"

"Like I'm in excellent hands." She smiled, insisting that after some vigorous but patient rocking back and forth, she could take a little more.

Careful to increase my thrust strength in stages, the rhythm that we became accustomed to, seemed to allow her pussy to accommodate me faster. My body started demanding deep, intentional strokes inside her.

"See, it's like our bodies were made for each other." Gritting against the immense waves of pleasure her tight little pussy provided.

It wasn't long before I was pressed up against her, skin-to-skin, cock buried as deep in her pussy as it would allow, her fingers digging deep into the back of my neck, beckoning me to stay in that position for as long as possible.

Whether it was pure curiosity or proximity, she bit my ear, forcing me to learn that I had next to *no* control when it came to driving faster inside her. She wasn't aware how much biting and sucking my earlobe made it a challenge to focus on more than my release.

Having no time to prepare for it, my cock emptied into her, centering all of my lust, need, desire and malehood in one spot. Her delicate walls tickled and teased, lighting every sense I had on fire. I would have to answer for this humbling experience; it wasn't like me at all.

"I've never come that quickly." Resting my face in the crook of her neck.

"I guess there's a first time for everything," she joked, prompting me to wake up my well-worked hips.

"Okay, you're still thrusting?" she said, confused, wiping the sweat off my forehead.

"Nonsense. It takes me at least three or four more times before my cock is not hard anymore."

"Um, good to know." Her voice breaking despite her thighs having never been so accepting.

"Fucking always feels so delicious once you've already come inside someone." Smiling at her face morphing from a state of confusion to one of pleasure once I matched the rhythm she'd become accustomed to.

"Oh my god," she started with a short of breath, tugging at the nape of my neck. "Is this you all the time?"

"This is me. *All the time*," I growled.

There was little for her to do but just accept the pleasure. The sensation of fingernails digging into my neck mixed with her feminine cries, excited me. "I'm about to fucking come again," she whimpered, her violent spasms tightening all over me, encompassing me in her euphoric embrace.

In a time like this, I wish I could bask in her kisses. It's the one time a kiss would have been appropriate. But I respected her wishes and opted to kiss her neck instead, as her body grew limp and weak.

Now was the perfect time to switch up my routine, moving

her body so that we met in a spooning position as I entered her at another angle. "Okay, this is a lot," she huffed, exhausted.

"I just want to make you come until you fall asleep. Now that I'm fucking you, I've learned that I *love* fucking you." Using her hip as an anchor to thrust in deep.

"Maybe *one* more time," she accepted, both reluctant and enthusiastic at the same time. "I barely recovered from the third one."

"From my experience, a maiden can always handle one more." Opening her thigh to me so I could access her every inch. She wrapped the arm she wasn't leaning on awkwardly around my neck, but I was pleased that she even *wanted* to look me in the eye as we made love.

Our shared expressions of pained agony made it that much more intense. No maiden could ever make me this weak, as I thrust into her without abandon.

No maiden had ever seen me this vulnerable during sex. No maiden *could* make me this vulnerable during sex. "Fuck, I think I'm close," she cried, biting her lower lip.

"I think I'm about to join you." Our joint cries of passion echoed and fought against the ambiance of the room. Kissing the pleasure-drenched salty-sweet flavor of her neck and back drove me wilder than one could imagine, that dare I say, I was moments away from convincing her to go again.

"You're amazing." Finally feeling the weight of her own exhaustion. Her skin still felt soft under my lips, and if she had let me, nothing would have stopped me from making her come one last time.

"I want to make you come again." Taking another chance.

"Aranzeiros, I *cannot* handle you making me come again," she whispered as I pushed her face closer to mine.

"You sure?" I half smiled, kissing her on the chin.

"I'm pretty fucking sure."

Letting go of her face, I reached for my sleeping trousers,

quick to drape my naked shoulder once again in a dress robe. "At least we'll finally get that rest neither of us was getting," I joked, unaware that through my efforts, a light snore could already be heard from her side of the bed.

Kissing her shoulders and back, I draped the cover over her bare frame, but not before noticing the stream of brilliant sequence coating her pussy lips with translucent glitter.

Unable to turn my eyes away from this rare human beauty, if this was what sex with humans was like, I envied every single fae who could get past their disdain for humans. Or maybe this was just a trait of my *human*, but I would never find out. I didn't want an alternative. No woman had ever felt so good, so perfect. And here she laid physically spent and covered in me. This was about to be an interesting union.

CHAPTER SIXTEEN

Paige

"Mmm..." I moaned, hoping to take one more inch of that glorious dick. Hovering over me, Aranzeiros ripped through me, working through every fiber, muscle, and wall as he leaned into his skill.

"This is me fucking you like I own you. Imagine how it'll feel when I actually do—"

"*Shit!*" I shot up, mystified that a dream could wake me up better than any alarm. Last night, I gave in to my desires. Last night, I shared my body with my captor.

Guilt or shame was among the first things I thought I'd feel, but outside of the typical soreness, I was more...confused? Being alone with Aranzeiros hadn't been what I thought it would be. While it was overwhelming at the moment, he had been the only partner who had cared about my pleasure during sex.

Growing up, I was taught sex was just for men; something that *happened* to you, so if you had fun doing it, you were lucky. This put my exes—who I'm sure purposely went down on me *wrong* so I wouldn't ask for it, to shame. There were some awkward times when Aranzeiros showed hostility toward me, but it was only when I would try to touch him.

He had experience pleasing women...maidens? But I don't think he had ever been vulnerable before. He may not even have been as vulnerable as he could be, but he promised to make things memorable for me, and I'm not ashamed to admit that he didn't disappoint.

Last night was just to make sure no one questioned the legitimacy of our marriage, something I gave a lot of thought about before I gave in. I kept thinking if I wanted out of here, wouldn't I have a better chance at it, if I was his *actual* queen?

My strategy had to be different; I was no longer in a realm of men, so I was going to have to learn how to manipulate Elven folk in a way I never had with humans. If I thought escape was possible, wouldn't it be easier if I had a husband who let his guard down?

Or, at least, that was my thinking process when I fucked him. Use the only weapon I had against him. So why was this strange part of me disappointed when I didn't wake up next to him?

"I can be gentle for you."

"Teach me how to be gentle for you."

His tender words wouldn't leave my head. Hugging my legs close, I remember how ill-prepared I'd been, experiencing his unexpected level of care. I was prepared to hate him until I could be free of him, but now I wasn't sure what I wanted to do.

He hadn't violated my body, but the same couldn't be said for my mind.

Ripping the comforter away from my naked frame, it took now to remember we hadn't used protection. Didn't he come inside me like three times? What if Elven cum was more potent? What if Elven cum got you pregnant ten times faster? What if—

"What the fuck?" The trail of dried-up glitter between my legs interrupted my chain of thought. There was a long mirror close to the balcony door, but before I could investigate, a knock at the door prompted me to rush to find my lost robe.

"Your Majesty, we have been waiting to prepare you for over an hour. Should we just come back?" a voice on the other side of the door spoke.

"Over an hour?" I mumbled to myself, curious to know how to tell time around here when all the watches looked like digital sundials.

"Just a minute," I yelled, convinced I could still investigate what Aranzeiros had left behind after such an active night. Unbeknownst to me, my staff took that *just a minute* literally, as I was crouched awkwardly against the wall inspecting my nether regions when I noticed the door swung halfway open.

"Wait, don't come—" I said, in an agitated scream. Only, it would have been normal had it just been a scream. It could have been a trick of the light, but that wouldn't have explained the hole that burst through the bedroom door.

The only explanation was that it had come from *me*. But it couldn't have come from me. Even though I felt the warmth radiating from my fingertips, even though I witnessed the light blast a hole in the entrance, all I kept thinking was...that didn't just happen.

"We'll just give you a few minutes." A friendly face poked her head through the hole and smiled before backing away.

Bringing my hands out in front of me, I tried my best to re-summon that trick of the light. Nothing.

Punching the air, I looked like a fool trying to get back a light I wasn't even sure came from me. *Someone* had put a hole through that wall. Tightening my robe against me, I went to investigate, learning the hole was still warm from the blast. So many things were changing about me. Was this all because I gave myself to Aranzeiros?

***

"I'm so glad you could finally join us," Aranzeiros sarcastically flirted as I walked into the main hall, three hours past our scheduled rising time.

"You could have woken me up." Hoping he'd hear the bite in my tone.

"Where would have been the fun in that?" he said, as he closed the distance between us, filling me in on what I had missed in his absence.

Since it was only my first day as queen, the only thing expected of me was to meet with the court painter, Lycana, the creature responsible for painting the portraits of all the royal family members.

"She's already done my first portrait as King. I promise it'll be the fastest you've ever posed for a portrait." As if I had *ever* posed for a portrait. When Aranzeiros guided me in front of him, there was no point in hiding that my heart raced faster than any horse could, when he put his arms around my waist.

"What is the point of portraits again?"

"My queen, you flatter me with your demureness. Don't you know?" He bent down, arching himself so that I could see his smile. "You and I have left a mark in history. You are the first human bride in the Faeborne legacy. Future generations will want to know of King Aranzeiros and his human Queen Paige." His tone was jovial and sarcastic, and I swear he intended to make me laugh. To his surprise, it did.

"Is there no way you might commit to a different pose?" the court painter interrupted, suggesting that we looked too stiff and disconnected. "This will be your defining portrait until you decide to produce heirs," she exclaimed, her nasal-y accent dominant.

"Heirs?" I looked back at Aranzeiros, expecting him to correct her. Instead, he lifted me off my feet, forcing me to hold him close in a warmly affectionate, yet wildly tame embrace.

"Perfect! It is reminiscent of a claiming. This I could work with," Lycana confirmed, using her renowned hands to work at the canvas.

"To answer your question, sometime in the future, yes. Heirs cement any legacy. But rest assured, they don't have to come tomorrow. I can tell from your scent alone, they are the furthest from your mind," he assured.

Heirs *were* furthest from my mind. Children made situations harder to leave. If I started a family with Aranzeiros...that would make things complicated. I'd always wanted to be a mother, but I didn't want to do it on my own. Nearly every man I'd been with before wanted me to roll the dice and have their children before even considering the prospects of marriage. It took a village to raise children, and since I had next to no support system, it had taken hard decisions to walk away. Yet, here I was, wondering what our kids might look like.

"You appear nervous," he whispered, squeezing the bottom of my thigh.

"It's just weird to think about kids with someone not human." But Aranzeiros assured me that Elves and Dwarves came as close to humans than any other race in Esterbrooke.

"So, these *hypothetical* children. Would they look like you or me?" Now I was curious.

"Elven blood is fairly strong, so I imagine more like me." He turned to me, not the least bit tired of posing for the picture.

"I don't know. Black blood is pretty strong, too," I countered.

"I do not understand." He spoke through squinted eyes.

"You would think you'd know that since you're adopted." I smiled.

"Adopted?" Aranzeiros asked, confused. "Oh, you mean how we are perceived in the Human Realm? That is just a tale we tell humans. Tarron Faeborne is not our adoptive father." Before I knew it, Lycana was announcing the completion of her master-piece. But I was going to need Aranzeiros to explain a few things.

***

Staring profusely at the portrait of King Tarron would not change what I was looking at, but I could see it with my own eyes and still couldn't believe it. "So, this creature is your DNA?"

"Fae don't have DNA. We are not made up of the same science as humans. I don't believe it is the same, but we have a term for everything that makes up what we are. Magical Ancestral Lineage, or MAL for short," he explained, though it didn't curb my confusion.

"So, this creature is your MAL?"

"Paige, I've told you a dozen times, yes." He was clearly annoyed.

"Boy, that creature is Black," I said, aggressively pointing at the picture.

"His skin is darker, yes, which is common from where his MAL is from, but you have to remember, I also have a Dark Star Nymph for a mother, so no one could predict how I would come out. I present as Elven, so that's how I identify, but fae do not define our race by skin color."

Aranzeiros later explained that in Esterbrooke, culture was more important than race, as all his brothers came from different backgrounds based on their maternal lineage. Mountain born, forest dweller, none of those terms would make sense until I saw it for myself, but comparing it to my Midwestern background made it easier to follow. He still didn't understand how humans referred to ourselves as different races when we were all the same thing, but he admitted he never consider the Human Realm a permanent place of residence, so didn't care either way.

"Before you, I couldn't tell *any* of you apart," he nonchalantly admitted, as we casually passed by a portrait of a white-haired woman, light brown skin and a severe scowl on her face. His jaw tightened, and his fist balled up so tight, you could see his palm turn red from him pressing his fingernails so hard into it.

"Paige." He faked a smile, holding out his hands like a red carpet. "Meet the queen I was named after." Forcing me to examine her appearance harder to see if I could find any similarities.

This female Elf was pretty, but in a prestigious, I-think-I'm-better-than-you type of way. If this was Tarron's mother, in my world, maybe they could have passed for family members, but their phenotypes threw me off.

Where Tarron was light-skinned, possibly even biracial looking by human standards, Aranzales was fairer, but visibly non-white. She had a nose that was elongated and overly prominent, but it made her more ethereal, especially against her striking grey eyes. Aranzeiros was good at faking it, but his mood changed whenever she was mentioned. I couldn't help thinking that maybe she abused him.

"Every effort to bridge the gap between man and fae was because of Tarron. If it had been up to my dear maternal grandsire, you may not be standing here." His fingers delicately brushed the frame of the portrait, lost in his train of thought.

"Why don't you show me something else?" I pulled at his wrist, trying to distract him from the memories dredging up. "I'm sure there are other worthwhile hallways or rooms you haven't shown me yet." Hoping he caught the hint.

Within seconds, Aranzeiros was backing me into a study, hunger in his eyes. My feet had left the ground before I could object to it, as Aranzeiros secured my frame on the closest desktop. He leaned in to kiss my mouth but thought against it based on our agreement. He did, however, find his lips a new home, on my neck.

That little stipulation wasn't because I didn't like Aranzeiros' kiss; it was actually the opposite. But after our first kiss, my body experienced a physical draining I wasn't sure I could explain. It was as if he could kiss anywhere *but* my mouth and I'd be fine. Having sex with him proved that. Until I knew what it was, it wasn't wise to allow that kind of strain to affect me. Especially given the fact I debated staying once I had a plausible way to return home.

"I was sure you would have smothered me in my sleep," he said, kissing and panting against the skin of my collarbone. "Imagine my surprise to sense that last night may be one of many." Kneading my breasts through the fabric of my dress.

"I thought about it," I joked, pressing his mouth closer to the breast he'd released from my dress. "But you're too heavy. What would I have told our chamberlains?" He rushed to reach underneath all my layers to find my panties.

Not for nothing, but these dresses were hard as hell to get in and out of. There had to be a better way to attempt a mid-day quickie. The dress was so complicated; we didn't even get the chance to. "King Aranzeiros, your mid-day meeting is here. Should I tell them to meet you in the Stateroom?" a device on his wrist called out.

"Dammit, I have to take that." I fought disappointment when he backed away. Pressing my breasts back in my dress, I climbed off the desk, careful not to trip. If my clothes had been more accessible, I would have at least gotten to enjoy Aranzeiros' special company at some point before bed.

"I have to know, now that I'm a queen, is it tacky to request things?" The question sparking his curiosity.

"During your onboarding, you will notice you have far more creatures attending to you until you put in a request for a permanent staff. Nothing you ask of them will ever be too much."

"How about new dresses?" I spread out my attire's long skirt.

"Your dresses look ravishing on you—"

"My *dresses* are hard to navigate in. They take thirty minutes to get into, and I feel like I'm lifting weights every time I have to pick up the dress and walk up a staircase," I said, voicing my concerns. Not to mention I can't even fit in a ten-minute rushed encounter.

"I have some prior engagements to attend to, and I apologize in advance that I will not be joining you tonight—"

"You won't be joining me?" I interrupted.

"I'm afraid I will be hosting the Marquis of Bravisha and the Baron of Lozramore, hoping to garner an alliance. They do not get along well, and it is in Esterbrooke's best interest to secure them as allies. Unfortunately, it requires the use of the royal apartments in Vidine, as they host the diverse activities required to keep my guests entertained."

"Sounds official." Pretending I wouldn't be lonely without his presence.

"It will not be a leisure trip, but may be necessary when the time comes. But I promise, once I am done with that, I will see to it we get you some new dresses."

CHAPTER SEVENTEEN

Paige

Days passed before I got another glimpse of Aranzeiros. I was getting used to expecting him more in passing than actually spending time with him. The time he spent fulfilling his duties were things he did long before I got here. I just wish I had more to do that didn't appear as if I were waiting for him (which I was).

The only routine I got used to was getting up once daylight hit and being prepared by chambermaids. Sadly, even that was a challenge, as they rotated between each other so much, it made it hard to get to know them, despite learning all of their names. I ate by myself, explored the palace grounds by myself, and you'd think with all that isolation, it'd give me ample time to find a way out of here. It was safe to say that a part of Aranzeiros still didn't trust me because when I did venture too far from the designated places, you could bet a guard was watching me to ensure I stayed put.

My mind was craving some kind of mutual exchange, a conversation, and not just one asking what entrees I'd like today. On my way to breakfast, recognizing a familiar face, I was compelled to end her duties for the day, just so I might have someone to share a meal with.

"Silvine, right?" I asked once we were seated against the garden behind the palace.

"Yes, Your Majesty." She unnecessarily bowed, despite sitting down.

"How has your day been?" Desperately seeking chatter outside of my routine. Silvine looked to the guards around, aware of some royal etiquette I wasn't accustomed to, so her body language showed she was choosing her words carefully.

"Well. I am behind, but I will manage."

"I'm sure that's because of me." Shamefully tearing away at my bread.

"'Tis a privilege to have an audience with the queen. It would be an insult if I turned such down." Silvine's blue locs were tied up today, making her hair appear as a mini-crown. It fit the angelic aesthetic of her round, cherub face that I almost wanted to pinch her cheeks, but knew that would be infantilizing.

"Do you think we could ditch these guards and talk human to Elf?" I leaned in, hoping she had some insight into how. Whispering back to me that she would take care of it, she hopped off her seat, and had them bend down to meet her four-foot-five frame. Without argument, they disappeared.

"What did you say to them?"

"It would be best if you don't know. But we only have a window of five minutes before they return." As I finished whatever food I could manage, and followed her around the winding labyrinth of vertical hedges.

"Thank you for taking the time to eat with me. It means a lot to me, even though I know you're only doing it because you feel you have to." Trying to keep up with her pace. For someone short, she sure was fast.

"I don't have to do anything. You've been kind, Your Majesty.

I've served the palace for close to three decades, and you're one of the few to remember my name. Not that I expect it. It is just...nice."

"Silvine is too pretty not to say out loud. Plus, I grew up as poor and working class. I'm a couple of weeks in, and I'm afraid to admit to anyone, I have no idea what I'm doing. There are times I wish I could go back to being poor again," I admitted, as she found a way back into the palace through a passageway meant for the staff.

"I can't imagine Your Majesty ever being amongst the common folk." Silvine turned to laugh with me, and before we knew it, we were in the below guard quarters of Regalhelm, the chambers where all the servants lived.

"It's not much, but this time around, it's quiet," she offered to give me a tour. It was more space than I'd ever had, but I'd be careful not to say that. I wasn't sure how working-class fae viewed their situation, and the last thing I'd want to do was offend anyone.

"It's perfect. At least I don't feel alone."

"*You* feel alone?" She sounded surprised, as I sat on the floor of her room.

"Sometimes. *Most* times. I think I'm still not sure whether I like it here, and with Aranzeiros being the sole reason I'm here in the first place, barely seeing him makes me ask whether or not it's worth it."

Silvine sat on her bed, her worn-in boots dangling off the edge. "I don't serve Aranzeiros. Most of my duties center on housekeeping for guests."

Tearing at my cuticle, it was too much to admit, but I didn't think I'd ever say it out loud, so I took my chances admitting my insecurities. "He says I'm *fated* to him, but I'm not always convinced he likes me very much."

"Why do you say that?"

"He finds time to do everything else but be around me, mind you, I didn't *ask* to be here. And the one time we...*you know?*" Trying to be classy about it. "He was aggressive at first. I'm convinced because I tried to touch him, it made him very standoffish."

That admittance made Silvine's once curious features cower like she knew something she wasn't supposed to know.

"Did I say something wrong?"

"Did you try to touch his back?" she asked with caution.

"Yeah, maybe." When I thought about it, he wouldn't take his robe off unless my back was to the mattress. I tried two times to wrap my arms around him, only for him to hold me down and demand I let him work. Now that I think of it, every position, everything he did was so I couldn't see his back. It was only when I caressed the back of his neck that he trusted me not to explore further.

"I think you should give the king some grace, Your Majesty. I haven't served the palace long enough to see or hear anything with my own eyes or ears. But creatures talk. He could be a lot crueler due to his upbringing."

Every time I thought of Aranzales, I couldn't help thinking she must have done something to him. I'd have to be careful who and how I asked, but unless he'd confirm it himself, there was a wall of his I couldn't climb.

***

"What are you doing down here?" Aranzeiros' accent strangely striking in his confusion. Perhaps it was inappropriate, but I was so grateful to have someone to talk to, I hadn't realized how much time had gone by getting to know someone outside of him.

I jumped up from the floor, attempting to introduce him to Silvine, as she greeted him in a curtsy, choosing not to look him in the eye. "How did you know I was down here?"

"Everyone has been looking for you. It's easy for me to find you because...you know why." I hadn't seen him face-to-face in so long, I was beginning to assume his sense of smell didn't work anymore.

"Did you need something from me?" I asked, nervously clutching my hands together in front.

"I sent a message for you at lunch. Did you not receive it?"

"Tis my fault, Your Majesty. The Queen asked if I could keep her company in your absence. Had it not been for my carelessness, she would have rightfully received your message," she conveyed with an additional bow.

"It's really all my fault," I interceded. "I asked this of her. I was considering promoting her to the queen's royal staff coordinator."

"You were?" Surprising even her.

I wanted someone who I could confide in, but most of all, I wanted someone easy to talk to. Spending just a few hours with her, we weren't all that different regarding upbringing. We both grew up in rural small towns, we both had parents we had to survive and neither of us had ever been told we meant something to someone. Until now.

"Very well," Aranzeiros dismissed. "We'll see to it her belongings are moved to the staff bedrooms, but in the meantime, I require your presence."

Aranzeiros seemed like he couldn't wait to be as far from the servant's quarters as possible, but I'd honestly never felt more welcome than spending time down there. It's almost as if when I'm having fun, *suddenly*, he has time for me.

"I take it you will at some point have a permanent staff this week?" Not slowing down his stride, but allowing me to catch up. Today, he wore an indigo kaftan with brocade embroidery to match his regal stature.

"What is this about?" Picking my dress up in an effort to keep up with his stride. "Am I in trouble or something?"

"Why would you think that you're in trouble?" His brows furrowed. "It has taken me days to confirm with her capricious schedule, but as promised, I have hired a seamstress for your dresses." He opened a dressing room door for me, revealing an eccentrically dressed, dark-skinned woman. Fae? I wasn't sure, she could clearly pass for both.

"Meet Navarria DeMorte, the most sought designer in Esterbrooke."

"And the Human Realm, for that matter," Navarria boldly interrupted, pushing down her sunglasses. "You should see my shows during Paris Fashion Week." Now that she mentioned it, her accent sounded French-adjacent. Like it derived from a French-speaking country but wasn't quite.

"Anyway, I'm halfling, so I know what Fae like, but most of all, I know what humans like," pointing a plastic ruler in my direction, snapping her fingers at the two assistants, pleased to hand her measuring tape and fabric.

"First, I will need your measurements—"

"Bust, forty-two. Waist, twenty-eight. High hip, thirty-four and hip, thirty-eight," Aranzeiros cut in before I could be measured. "Trust me, I've studied her well." He winked in Navarria's direction.

"Now that we have that out of the way." Navarria twitched her hips, though I wasn't sure if it was because that was her normal walk or if her dress was too tight. "What is your vision? What do you crave for your queen's wear?"

Shrugging, I wasn't sure my answer would satisfy her. "Something every day would be nice. Comfort above everything."

As if she were waiting for me to say something else, she hesitated, not intending to sound rude when she asked, *"That's it?"*

"I believe she means to say she wants elegant and regal, but she wants it to be breathable. Curve accentuating—" *Now he knows I didn't say that.*

"But most of all, inclusive to not just balls, galas, and evening wear. Sporting wear, and nighttime wear. Her frame isn't hard to dress. She just needs a place to start," Aranzeiros ended gracefully.

"Well, take your clothes off, so I can dress you," Navarria spat out impatiently. Her assistants rushed to each side to take off my dress, but even though Aranzeiros had already seen me naked, having an audience of three other unknown female fae still made me sheepish to take my clothes off in front of strangers.

Covering my modesty with my hands, Navarria slapped them away, draping a fabric over my skin that barely covered anything. With a snap of a finger, right before my eyes, it changed into a form-fitted dress that covered my entire frame. "How about this?"

Picking up the tail of the cream-colored frock, while it was lighter, I'd still find it a challenge keeping up with the pace of a someone as tall as Aranzeiros. "The detail's nice." Trying not to hide my disappointment.

"The color looks like a wedding dress from the forties—"

"So, then, different color?" Navarria interrupted, snapping her fingers as it had transformed into a crimson red frock.

Navarria was assertive, but it was obvious she preferred the design better than me. She snatched off the fabric, giving me little time to cover myself, and draped on a new cloth with a similar result. We must have gone through half a dozen dresses, and I had to turn down corsets, boob windows, and anything that made me more self-conscious than confident.

"You are very picky." Pointing her ruler back at me. "Humans are never this picky. But, I should expect nothing less from a queen." We went through endless more options, and none of them appeared to impress me. Most of all, none of them seemed to impress Aranzeiros.

"What about this?" She conjured a midnight blue dress onto my frame. It was the first choice that had a slit on the side, complemented by a shimmery veil. It was the first time I felt comfortable.

"I like this one." I twirled. "Can we go for some more like this?"

"It pleases me that you *finally* fancy something I have offered." *She knows she didn't have to sound that condescending.* "But I want to make sure your king approves as well. He has been quiet during this ordeal, and I wish to make sure that it also compliments his tastes."

He had said little up until now, so I assumed fashion wasn't his expertise. "I wonder if I can have a moment to speak with the queen? I want to be sure of something before I give my answer."

"But of course," Navarria exclaimed, confused when Aranzeiros led me behind a room separator in the corner of the dressing room. "Shhh..." Bringing his finger to his mouth, expecting silence to follow the command.

Like a few days prior, he lifted my dress, but unlike the last time, he found his way in with ease. Despite missing his touch, I wasn't sure what his plans were, especially given that he had ordered no one to exit the room. By the time he disappeared under my dress, I had seconds to prepare for Aranzeiros' tongue, finding its way to wake my sleeping, neglected nerves.

The collection of whimpers that escaped my lips were unavoidable, as my body adjusted to him. He wasn't eating my pussy to warm me up. This fae was eating my pussy with the intention to make me come. "Mmm..." Fighting the sound trying to escape, as I grit my teeth against his rapid laps and hums.

Did this creature's jaw ever get tired? I could barely keep myself upright, before he was pushing me against the wall, lifting my thigh onto his shoulder so that he could gain better access. Silent gasps were all I could manage, keeping his head into place from beneath the fabric, as his flattened tongue swirled and slushed, forcing an all-out eruption between my legs.

My walls cried, my muscles tightened, and all I could do was surrender to the handiwork of my husband's tongue.

I was a quivering mess by the time he reappeared from underneath the fabric, wiping off his beard of any traces of me. I never knew what he was thinking any time we would lock eyes, but like times in the past, I couldn't look away. Not until he was done.

Without saying a word, he walked from behind the room divider, and in an eerily jovial tone, said, "This dress seems perfect."

"Excellent!" Navarria clapped. "I will stay true to this design and adjust to ensure the perfect wardrobe. You will be the center of every stage. Even as a human." *She could have left that last part out.*

"I will leave you maidens to your devices. Surely this type of thing doesn't require the audience of a king." Aranzeiros politely bowed.

"You're not staying?" I clasped my hands together, assuming we'd at least have dinner together.

"I'm afraid not."

"But I'll see you tonight, right?"

Aranzeiros took my hands, and I knew nothing satisfying would leave his lips. "I fear that, like the rest of the week, you won't be seeing much of me for a while. Both of us require rest, and with my schedule, it wouldn't be fair to you to wait up for me."

At that, I snatched my hands away, but he didn't even notice how upset his answer made me. He just gestured for me to meet him at the threshold of the door so he could speak to me privately. "I would ask you to join me, but I had plans to reveal you during the royal tour, so that anyone who's anyone could all meet you at once."

I knew little about royal tours, but what I knew, is I would be sleeping alone. *Again.* "I understand." I was trying to give him grace, but he was making it hard. It was like, he wanted me hooked, just so I'd question whether I should run.

"Paige. Look at me." He took my chin in his hand to force me to look up at him. "When the entire realm knows you, our times together will not be so infrequent. I promise, when it comes time for the official royal tour, and we are finally alone. You will *see* how much I've missed you."

CHAPTER EIGHTEEN

Paige

"That should do it," Silvine said, as her worry lines transformed into relief. I took Aranzeiros' advice and looked into hiring my *own* staff. Silvine, the Elf-gnome I'd gotten to know, was now responsible for choosing staff for me. While her title was that of a coordinator, I likened her to more of an advisor, as she was integral to how I survived this long with little guidance.

"Everything from your chambermaid to your personal daytime and evening cook are ready to start as soon as tomorrow. You already have your dressmaker, which is to be considered the best of the realm," she cooed, as I had Navarria throw in a month's worth of custom frocks for Silvine so she could have a brand-new wardrobe. She was sporting a beautiful ice-blue kaftan that made her glittery blue strands pop. Not to mention it brought out the golden brown in her hue and, even more so, her feline-hazel eyes.

"I feel so weird hiring someone to make my bed for me every morning," I said, plopping down onto a nearby lounge.

"Half the time, I'm barely using it." Painfully aware that the past few days I had slept in it alone.

"You can always retire to your own quarters, Your Highness."

"Ya know, Silvine, when we're alone, you can just call me Paige. I know it's not protocol, but I would love it if someone outside of my husband just called me by my name," I interrupted before I had noticed what she said.

"And what do you mean by my *own* quarters?" I perked up. "Is this not my bedroom?" Asking for clarification.

"Your Highness...Paige," she corrected. "Technically, this is your room. Especially when you and your king require time for... intimate engagements." Exerting every effort to be tasteful.

"But members of the royal families have separate quarters, something many find quite necessary," she explained. With that revelation, I had her lead me to my actual room, wondering why none of this had been explained to me since becoming queen.

She had been correct. The Queen's quarters were twice the size of the first room I stayed in and it was much more elaborate. I barely needed one room, and now I was being told my room was triple the size of my last apartment. What the hell was I going to do with all this space?

Silvine sashayed over to the room's walk-in closet, home to what looked like every dress Navarria had made for me so far. There were also some neatly folded sportswear and rows upon rows of designer shoes.

"Every dress commissioned for you, any requests you have made, are stored here. As you can see, many of the crown jewels you will be required to wear may not always be readily accessible, but the most endearing pieces are kept with the Queen's wardrobe." Her arms presenting them as if she were a game show presenter.

"Is it to your liking..." She hesitated. "Paige?"

Surveying the walk-in closet, a wave of uncertainty overtook my senses.

"To be honest, I'm not sure *what's* to my liking anymore. It's like, I can't get used to everything, by the time that it changes," I said, massaging my forehead. As grateful as I was for this new life, a small part of me still clung to my old normal. Easily accessible. Easy to navigate. Just *easy*. I tried to look at things with a half-glass-full mentality, but at times, I felt like an imposter.

"Ah, there you are. I've been looking all over for you," Aranzeiros' tall frame joined us inside the closet. He wore a loose black blouse with fitted trousers that made him look delectable, but it was his tall black boots that helped his muscular thighs look well-worked. I think I just enjoyed seeing him in something other than his formal king attire. We hadn't seen each other much after the visit from Navarria, so I wasn't too proud to admit I was sick of waking up alone, craving his touch.

Silvine's posture straightened as she greeted the king in a curtsy. He turned to me, tracing a pale finger across my face, as he reached in to kiss me on the forehead.

"Silvine, would you mind if I had a moment of the Queen's time?" Her hazel eyes softened, nodding as she excused herself.

Finally, I was gifted with the embrace of powerful arms, wrapping around me from behind, as a light yet teasing kiss snaked down the length of my neck. Even kisses felt like torture after not getting any for days.

"Your scent of arousal is a pleasant welcome." He gathered the front leg of my gown, fondling my breasts through the fabric, his teeth gently nibbling the top of my ear. "I love it when I can sense that you want me. The ache is like food to my soul."

At this point, he could have ripped my dress off and had me every which way. I wanted to feel human again and not a figure-head of some unexplored land. He didn't act on his lust for long, as he released his once possessive hands to get back to his original reason for seeking me.

"This fated mates predicament is both a gift and a curse. I came in here with every intention of informing you what was to come in the next few days, but your scent made me lose my train of thought."

Slipping the loose strings of his blouse between my fingers, I seductively smiled—or at least I thought I did—putting it out there, that there was time to make up for it. "I mean, we *could* always take a few minutes. Just in case neither of us manages to reach that marriage bed of ours." And by us, I meant him. I was in that marriage bed every damn night, praying tonight would be the night.

He straightened his posture, and it was clear he was now in King mode, a time when everything came second to his duties.

"I promised to make up for our lack of quality time. Unfortunately, we have put off the Royal Tour long enough. Everything was so rushed, in a perfect realm, we would have done it as soon as we wed. It's the only way to prepare you for what's to come and how to conduct yourself as queen." As Aranzeiros paced back and forth, a crew of chamber maids greeted him with their proper curtsies. I don't know why they felt the need to pack me endless amounts of clothes, but they had a schedule and they were sticking to it.

"What is the point of the tour other than us being seen together? It felt like all of Esterbrooke showed up to our wedding," I asked unknowingly. I had seen princes and princesses getting bombarded with coverage after getting married, but it felt like a waste of time and resources.

Half the time they were visiting countries they helped destroy. I knew nothing of the Fae Realm's politics, but even less about whether my husband's family caused any devastation to its people. If I could skip it altogether, I would.

Judging by Aranzeiros' complacent expression, I probably wouldn't get my way. "Come, let us finish this conversation on the way to the dining hall. Our first stop is a half day's travel, and if you've had a morning like mine, you will need nourishment."

Not long after, they pulled our seats out for us at the breakfast table and my husband began his explanation with a brief history lesson.

"As you are aware, we now have subjects," he spoke, managing to speak without sounding like he had a mouthful of food. "It may not appear this way at first, since the realm is still making up their minds about you, whether or not you're well perceived, you are now *everyone's* queen. Even those who may not marvel at the idea of a human consort," he wiped his mouth with a napkin, as I was doing my best trying not to stress myself out.

All I could do to curb my nerves was mix the contents of what passed as a parfait in the Human Realm, gobbling it up to cure my hunger pangs.

"You smell different all of a sudden." His face suddenly soured, instantly making me anxious.

"My wish is not to upset you. I only wish to prepare you that it may take longer for a human to gain the trust of the fae."

"We wouldn't want to disappoint the people," I said in jest.

"We don't say, people. In the presence of fae, I think you should use the term creatures. Most fae prefer the term creature, being, fae. But just to be safe, fae is always the safest term."

"Okay, creatures. I'm not used to creatures distancing themselves from personhood is all. And I'm especially not good at getting people to like me."

"Paige, I have no doubts that despite everything being so new, you will be the queen I know you can be."

"And what kind of Queen is that? A quiet and submissive one?" I accidentally said under my breath. There was an immediate pang of regret, given that Aranzeiros cleared the dining hall just so he could speak freely.

With a stern, crossed-arm look, Aranzeiros leaned against the banquet table and stared at me for longer than felt comfortable, before asking. "What makes you believe I intend for you to be quiet or submissive beyond a bedroom?"

"It just came out. I didn't mean it." Even though I kind of did.

"Since your transition here, when have you ever had to submit to someone?" It felt like a trick question, considering that despite the fact this place was growing on me, kidnapping me, forcing me to marry, and keeping me from leaving, all felt pretty standard submitting-against-my-will type actions.

"I guess it feels like I'm submitting all the time." I clumsily dropped my soiled spoon on the table.

"You *guess?*" he asked, genuinely confused.

"Just because I'm a queen doesn't mean I'm always in control. Especially around you. Even when you're not around, indirectly, it feels like I'm waiting on you. If that's not submission, I don't know what is."

Aranzeiros gathered his fingers to delicately clutch my chin, forcing me to look him in the eye. "Paige Faeborne, you are no longer an ordinary human. Whether you choose to see it, I will not always be able to convince you. But I expect you to behave as if you've known never known a day without power. Your power is not secondary just because you are a queen consort. It is equal to that of mine. I'm sure humans shape your definition of submission. But no, you have not submitted to me. You consented to consummate this marriage, but outside of it being expertly aggressive lovemaking. That's all it was. Lovemaking. Should you ever submit to me, trust me, you would know it. There would be no *guessing.*"

He walked back over to his side of the table, finishing his salted meats and cheese. "I am but a patient king. I understand I have not earned that type of devotion from you, but know that where we are now, you have not submitted to me. You have just chosen not to exercise your power. It matters not whether you *feel* like a queen, you are one. It's best you start acting like it."

***

Green wasn't my color, but I was advised to keep my attire as close to the colors of Earth as I could when meeting with the common folk. Anything red would have washed out my complexion but anything too close to my hue would have made me feel naked. When it was between green and gold, I opted for the curve-hugging, deep moss dress.

It would be a long journey there, and while I wanted to opt for comfort, I was sick of spending nights with nothing but my hand to get me off. As important as I was being told this trip was, I craved that alone time Aranzeiros promised he'd give me. My scent usually did it for me, but I hated that Aranzeiros had a cheat sheet for when I was horny and then did nothing about it.

It was like I was constantly throwing myself at him without even trying. Aranzeiros' behavior was confusing, but maybe it was normal for Elven males to not be as one-track-minded as human men. Sometimes I wish he *was* as simple as wearing a low-cut top and never being able to do anything but think about sex.

Even with my shittiest partners, I could at least count on them to beg me for *bad* sex once a day. How did I have a husband that claimed he couldn't even concentrate when I was in a room with him but could go days without so much as walking past my bedroom?

Mixed signals probably weren't the right term, but I witnessed that his duty often greatly outweighed his desires. If I was going to survive a week of people judging me for being human, I was going to need some serious, *expertly aggressive lovemaking* to get me through it. But I'd be damned if I lost this game of chicken.

By the time I was led to the outside carriage, Aranzeiros eyed me down to the point of discomfort, as he had me seconds away from hopping in this carriage before someone opened the door for me.

"What?"

"You look lovely." He spoke it as fact, almost like it wasn't a compliment. When the coach creature opened the door, Aranzeiros helped me inside, sitting in the opposite space of the carriage.

There was an awkward bout of silence as the carriage took off.

But what made it more unsettling was how Aranzeiros could sit there in total silence and just stare at me.

"Is there anything I should avoid when expected to greet the public?" I asked, trying to alter the atmosphere of the carriage.

"You are so beautiful. Sometimes I can hardly believe that you are mine." He spoke calmly, like he hadn't even heard my last question.

"Thank you?" If he really felt that way, why wasn't he showing me by tearing off this dress and ravishing me?

"And yes, there are several things I would avoid dealing with the public. But there will be grace given considering your background."

It wouldn't be until the next day, as our arrival time would be far into the evening but Aranzeiros tried his best to educate me on all the different races of creatures I would encounter.

It wasn't expected of everyone to respect the differences in etiquette, but as a monarch, there were ways I had to show my respect and vice versa. "One of the greatest takeaways to you becoming queen is we will see how well the Council responds to humans who aren't halflings living in Esterbrooke. Before our realms became divided, humans and fae shared land. Not always peacefully, but those of the land knew how to command respect."

"When did you all stop sharing space?"

"Much before my time. Sometime between the thirteenth century in your time. Many of the reasons Elves outlawed our traditional practices were because it would only result in *more* humans, so some fae have never seen a human in real life." Understandable. It wasn't very neighborly to kick humans out and then capture them for mates.

"What was the last Queen like?" taking advantage of having his full attention.

"Aranzales was—"

"No, I meant your *father's* wife. Didn't you say a king couldn't take the throne without a mate?" I was sure I didn't hear that wrong.

Aranzeiros was silent for a moment. It made me think he had no intention of answering the question. "As far as I was told, it is a sensitive subject. Tarron rarely talked about his past directly, but my grandmother would discuss it in passing when she didn't think anyone was listening. As far as I know, his wife died during childbirth before she ever got to be announced to the world. He wed her in secret. My guess was she wasn't from a family that my grandmother approved of."

Something didn't add up to me. Even when Tarron faked his lineage in the Human Realm, there had been no mention that he had a child before Aranzeiros. "If King Tarron's wife died during childbirth, what happened to the baby?"

"If I am not mistaken, the child was stillborn. Since it was likely the outcome Aranzales would have preferred, it is a subject everyone chose not to speak of. I'm afraid I don't know more." Since Tarron had fulfilled his requirements for matrimony, they didn't expect it of him to marry again. "Father had a *type* for the unattainable fae," he admitted, and it seemed like the first time since bringing him up that he seemed embarrassed by his actions.

"But that's not important. What is, is that we may encounter council members during this trip. Mainly the fae council members, but I suspect they'll have their guard up until they know your hand."

"Whenever you mention the Council, I get a little lost. Remind me why they matter again."

"The court comprises of royals and nobles, which you are now a part of. But there are members of both fae and humans that speak for their own interests. We meet nearly three times a year, maintaining that our alliances and arrangements are consistently being upheld."

The concept of the court and council had always been referred to in passing, so it was a relief to have someone explain it to me.

"It was why I couldn't push back the Royal Tour any longer. You need to experience how to deal with creatures not like you. There is no better way to prepare you for your first council meeting than through a royal tour."

"Will a human voice be welcome?"

"Yes, and no. You have not been alive longer than some people have served the Council, so your voice will be new and assumed to be naïve. You will receive pushback on both sides because, for now, you will be unpredictable."

According to Aranzeiros, the court always struggled to get the votes to pass things or prevent unfavorable outcomes, but with their brides packing the court, they could increase their numbers without ringing the alarm.

"What if I don't vote the same way as you?" Who's to say I'd agree with everything on the side that I served?

"No one expects you to blindly vote complimentary of your husband. But given that our interests are the same, it would be wise to consider the actions of your decisions. You need not worry about that today. Today, all you need to worry about is making sure you eat well and get a full night's rest. Tomorrow will be filled with too much for you to earn a break."

***

I thought I had seen so much in my short time in Esterbrooke, but traveling outside of Regalhelm taught me something could still surprise me at the promise of unfamiliar sights. And sights to see, they were.

We reached our destination before the day got too dark, so I had a better image of what Springmage looked like when its lobby was filled with patrons. It was resting place for nobles and royalty, a strange combination of a resort and a colony, but boy was I in for a surprise for all the creatures.

In Arisnoto, I hadn't met many creatures who didn't appear

human-like. It was rude to stare where I was from, so I had to keep my attention on anything but the looming eight-foot minotaur's clicking hooves, as Aranzeiros lightly introduced us, before they walked and talked about politics.

I had prepared myself for pixies, brownies, gnomes, dwarves, and orcs. But there were so many races, and even sub-species within those races, that I would have to get used to some creatures walking on all fours. In fact, many were now.

"I must take my leave of you. My wife and I have had a long trip and we have a busy schedule ahead of us."

"Of course, King Aranzeiros. I just couldn't resist the urge to discuss our upcoming get-together a month from now. And I had yet to be introduced to your beautiful human bride," the charming minotaur flirted.

"She is beautiful, isn't she?" Aranzeiros arrogantly smiled. I was sure that they had said something else, objectifying even, but for as much as I should've been used to Aranzeiros' constant words of affirmation, it was a strange concept to hear creatures discussing me like a trophy wife. I was convinced that didn't happen for women like me.

Women who weren't unattractive but were far from the traditional beauty standard. I was torn between being powerful and not quite feeling so yet. I prayed this royal tour gave me the experience where I didn't flinch every time I was paid a compliment.

Forcing my mind to think about something else, as the lobby of Springmage seemed like it went on forever. Apparently, resorts like this were all on ground level, as the rooms were like castle apartments. It took us an hour just to reach the king's suite.

"Don't forget to have your floating lady-in-waiting go over your itinerary for the morning. The day will feel long, but it should be fun once we arrive at the traditional hunting event. A handful of my brothers plan to attend, so there will be several familiar faces."

"Your brothers?" I asked nervously. I had only met them at the wedding and even then, they were intimidating. "Which ones, if you don't mind me asking?"

"It is hard to say. Ivaran is sure not to be in attendance because... that's Ivaran. Lianthore and Zaos have quite the responsibility, so despite them RSVPing, I don't expect them to honor it."

Counting in my head, there were three brothers left. "That leaves Vamir, Theoden, and Tavnis," mumbling under my breath. "And they're your younger brothers?" I asked to confirm.

"Correct, though they have been on this realm for over one hundred and eighty-five years. By Elven standards, they are reaching adulthood, but because of their maternal sides, they may appear more mature. Don't let their looks fool you, they hardly take anything seriously." He cringed.

That helped a little. The first three were the most serious and intimidating anyway, and maybe without the pressure of juggling between the six, I'd have a better chance at connecting to them.

Aranzeiros didn't play around when it came to his brothers. If I could impress either of them, perhaps that would show Aranzeiros how hard I was trying at becoming a Faeborne.

"This is your suite. My room is further down the hall. Should you need anything—"

"So, our rooms are separate?" I asked, offended. Here I thought, after days of barely seeing each other, that we were trying to change things. Nothing changed since the palace.

"Not unlike the palace." He sounded confused. "Is that a problem?"

"No," I lied. "I guess I just thought this trip would be different. I've hardly seen you at all in the last few days. It makes it hard to get to know someone."

"I was told humans required space. If that is not the case—"

"It's fine." Burying my disappointment. "I'm just confused. It's hard to look in love in front of strangers when I see you once a week."

Aranzeiros stalked close to my room door, stopping before he got too close. "What an impression that would make. What could be more terrifying than a king and queen who are actually in love."

"I guess I should check in with my lady-in-waiting." Trying to hide the defeat in my voice, choosing to end the conversation before I put any more cards on the table.

CHAPTER NINETEEN

Paige

I didn't know how many wardrobe changes I could take in a single morning. From the time that I rose, they fit me for a new outfit in *every* town. I expected the crowds to be unwelcoming to a human queen, but many greeted me with curiosity and intrigue. Sure, there were a few creatures that weren't always warm, but in contrast, a lot of them were kind.

No one ever pretended I wasn't there. No one ever ignored my attempts at joining them in tour scheduled activities. It was quite the culture shock especially given that in my old world, I wasn't used to people being so gracious. Connecting with creatures, listening to their stories, and indulging in young children's fascination with a human outsider. This might have been the one thing I was good at since taking on this role. From helping communities to build a new school for their districts, to sharing an ale with a host of local Orcs, it wasn't the scary moment I was making it out to be in my head.

Aranzeiros occasionally would throw in a subtle, "You're doing better than I thought. Keep proving me wrong." And if I hadn't been exhausted churning butter on a dairy farm for optics, I could have gone an hour or two more. Next up we were scheduled for a royal hunting match, and since it was a tradition for a queen consort to take part, I couldn't avoid it. It surprised me to learn that Aranzeiros had other family but that many of his extended family while noble, weren't always royal.

"That is Lord Zorrien Steeleborne. He and my father share blood on both their mother's sides. Though not very close, they are second cousins." Aranzeiros pointed out a kingly salt-and-pepper-haired male with dark skin and a sexy beard. In the Human Realm, he would have been Black, but with pointed ears and an unearthly allure, it was not hard to clock him as Elven.

"Is there a reason the two are not close?" I asked, my eyes lingering because the Elf was *fione*.

"Sadly, it may have stemmed from a light feud we might inherit. They hail from the equatorial region of Esterbrooke. For as long as I've been alive, Lord Zorrien has sought his region's independence, while my father has fought to keep Esterbrooke unified," he said as he led me to a tent serving as a temporary armory. I looked forward to hearing more about that, but his attention wandered to a group in the corner, his face lighting up with cheer and glee.

"Ah, little brothers. It appears as though it's becoming quite the challenge to bask in you all at once. It is a fine day indeed." They shared hugs and playful teasing as brothers did, but I laughed at the thought of his herculean-sized brother ever being considered *little*. The one with waist-long hair and mysterious hooded eyes was the first to approach me. He was one of two of Aranzeiros's brothers that weren't pale-skinned. With sharp cheekbones, tan skin, and a rock star western style, he looked like an indigenous prince.

"Paige Faeborne, formerly known as Paige Anderson. It is an honor to make my queen's acquaintance," he purred, reminding me he had gifted me his courage during the ceremony.

"Tavnis, right?" I smiled, hoping I didn't mix him up.

"Your human has an excellent memory," he replied, his smile infectious and downright seductive. He was wearing this top that he wore barely buttoned, so his chiseled, firm chest and sculpted abs were on full display. By height measurements, he was closer to Aranzeiros, but he had this youthful mischievousness about him. Especially the longer I stared into his eyes.

"Eh, eh," Aranzeiros interjected. "Do not glare into my brother's eyes too long. He bears the gift of charm spell. He'll have you eating out the palm of his hand with lavish demands." Woo, I'm glad he told me. I *knew* I had felt something.

"My brother takes the joy out of everything. I would have only gotten you to tell me things that might serve useful in a roast. Goddess knows how I live to torment my older brother," he said with a tuck of his glossy black hair behind his ear.

"I'm guessing charm spell is some kind of hypnosis?" I questioned, as he explained it was more of an influence than control, and that the skill worked best on humans, but especially women.

It was hard to forget Aranzeiros's second-largest brother, Vamir. He was a toasted light brown, the darkest of all his brothers, with stormy grey eyes that appeared ferocious on a face so gentle. He sported a thick beard that screamed mountain man, and his 6'5" muscular frame was both intimidating and manly. His hair hung down his back in long, beachy waves and I was learning he didn't need a reason to go shirtless to show off an impressive collection of tribal tattoos.

"Prince Vamir?" I guessed, hoping I guessed right.

"It is good to see you again, sister." He spoke in an Oceanic accent. I was ashamed to admit that I'd never met anyone from Australia, New Zealand, or any other country that had Polynesian natives. If I had to take a guess, this brother was from the part of the realm surrounded by Oceania. He kissed my hand, my thoughts shifting back to when, for a wedding gift, he gifted me his protection.

"And Prince Theoden?" A guess taken through the power of

elimination. He was one of the few of my husband's brothers that didn't have dark hair, and his thick beard added to his numinous ruggedness. His style was part highlander, part rockstar, rocking a kilt, a leather jacket, and a Scottish-style bunnet without looking out of place. His ginger hair spilled across his head in long loose curls and he spoke with a masculine brogue, making me assume that where he was born was somewhere close to the British Isles.

Either way, he took off his bunnet and bent a knee, a reminder that he had gifted me his empathy, as he was sure that I would need it in years to come.

"There ain't no missing me," Theoden joked as I felt a tap on my shoulder, jumping out of my skin at another version of Theoden, real or an illusion, I didn't know. I had to remember Aranzeiros had told me his power focused on projections, but I'm sure there was more where that came from. Like Aranzeiros, there always was.

Once I got over the awkward introductions, it was time to choose a weapon.

"Oh no, Paige Faeborne, formerly known as Paige Anderson. You might be better off picking a weapon more balanced and catered to you," Tavnis warned as he offered to take it off my hands. It was a crossbow and nothing fancy. You could probably find something more elaborate at Walmart.

"I'm sure I can handle a crossbow," I challenged. "I've been handling them since I was eight."

"My brother Tavnis means no harm, but you are delicate and small. Might I interest you in something more standard? The bow and arrow is a fine choice. For us Elves, you can't go wrong with a bow and arrow," Vamir intercepted.

"Are you assuming I can't handle a crossbow because I'm a woman?" I accused.

"On the contrary, my queen. Females in our world make the finest hunters. It's likely because humans can't aim for shit." Theoden laughed. "This won't be your regular game, lass. We'll be hunting fauna you've never seen before. Faster, too. I reckon the lot of us will struggle," he countered.

Granted, I didn't know how to prepare for something I'd never seen before, but I would not let someone convince me I couldn't handle a crossbow. I had experience hunting rabbits and had even put down a bobcat or two that was gunning for my ex-neighbor's cat.

"I'll take my chances." I smiled, gripping the bow and leaving the tent to see how much practice I'd need after a few short months in the city. There were plenty of spots for practice on the training grounds, and while I wasn't one to show off, there was no reason for me to hit a stationary target.

Aiming for high in the trees, I watched for movement on the branches, as I waited for the right moment, and took my shot. I hadn't even noticed Aranzeiros had been watching me. When I went to examine my target, a wild rabbit-like mammal had met the end of my arrow.

Theoden removed the arrow and inspected it. "Well, it's not very big, but it's clean through the eyes. Where did you say you learned this from?" I hadn't said, but suddenly I was embarrassed about why I knew how to hunt.

"Just being from a rural town in the Midwest," I explained, hoping no one pushed me further. Tavnis was the only brother to have a vast knowledge of US regions, and my guess from his accent was that he had lived there, too.

"Let us pray to the goddess that Lianthore does not drag his feet to wed. I, for one, can not wait to be married." Tavnis swooned.

"Technically, you bed humans all the time?" Theoden shrugged, running a palm through his thick bed of curls.

"Yes, but imagine what it would be like to be married to one," Tavnis concluded, wide-eyed, grinning with joy.

While it would have been nice to get proper introductions to everyone in our hunting group out of the way, especially given that many had arrived late, we all agreed to get started so we didn't lose light. Fae were used to hunting at night, but my human eyes were not.

"Don't mind me if I take a head start." Tavnis winked before disappearing into a blur. "Wait, I forgot my bow." He blinked back, my eyes too slow to register his speed. I wonder what he was mixed with on his mom's side to move fast like the wind.

"Well, since neither of us is gifted with the speed of a trickster deity, the lot of us will require steeds for the hunt," Aranzeiros started. "Paige will ride with me and—"

"I can ride a horse on my own. Unless you think I can't do *that*, either?" Aranzeiros gave me an unreadable look.

"I'd prefer if you rode with me," he muttered.

"Come on. Let the missus ride her own mare. I wish to see how she *rides*. It's not as if she intends to soar away into the sunset and leave you a jilted groom," Vamir joked, but I could tell by the look on Aranzeiros's face that it was *exactly* what he thought I would do.

Aranzeiros and I had spent little personal time together, so I knew he didn't trust me. It wasn't like it was my fault. One minute, he gave me space, and the next, it was like he wanted me on lock and key.

"I think I'll take my own horse, thank you," I said, dismissing his offer.

"So, Paige Faeborne, formerly known as Paige Anderson—" Tavnis blinked to the side of my horse as he held up an animal that was a cross between a red panda and a monkey with a bow between its eyes. I would never get used to him creeping up on me.

"You know, *Paige* is just fine, Tavnis. As long as I'm allowed to call you Tavnis," I said, growing tired of them chanting my full name. That was a trait Aranzeiros and his brothers shared.

"It is fine." He laughed. "It is just names are so important, both here and in my ancestral land in the Earth Realm. I forget that this world is new to you and I only wish to make you feel at ease and welcomed, Queen Sister," he said with a pet to my horse.

"If you don't mind me asking, where do the portals close to your ancestral land lead to?" He disappeared, then reappeared right next to me, making me jump at the suddenness of it.

"Much of my ancestral land spreads across the West in your country. It is the area you refer to as New Mexico, Oklahoma, Colorado, Wyoming, and Montana," he flirted.

"So, we were practically neighbors," I said, feeling silly that I couldn't stop smiling in his presence.

"My brother tells us you are from Kansas. I visit that area quite a lot. If I had known maidens as fair as you were native, I would have spent far more time there in search of a fated mate."

"Boy, stop!" I teased, because if he kept going on like that, I may just have to find a new husband.

"We used to be spread further but have lost much of our land to—" He stopped mid-sentence with claims that were more appropriate for another day. But I can only assume that what he'd meant to say, was that they had lost their land to humans and he didn't want to offend me.

Vamir yelled commands in a language I didn't understand as he rode his horse close to mine and sandwiched me between him and Theoden.

"Sister, I hope you don't find me rude. I was just asking him whether there had been signs of any fauna. I know your kind find it rude to speak more than one language in the presence of others," Vamir finished. And by my kind, I'm sure he'd meant human.

"Not offended, I just wasn't aware you all had an official language. No one so far has spoken to me in anything but what humans call English," I said, confused.

"We have over forty official languages in Esterbrooke. We speak those and all of our brothers' languages." Vamir beamed.

"Wait, so y'all all speak Lianthore's language?" I asked, interested. Without wasting a minute, they showed their efforts by carrying on a conversation that sounded a lot like Mandarin.

"And Ivaran's?" With a change in pitch, they switched to a Slavic-sounding dialect.

"I feel so unaccomplished. You all seem so talented."

"Do not fret, little sister. By the confidence in his strut and the glow to your cheeks, it is evident that the only language you are required to know is love. Humans make the finest lovers. It is something about the way you moan and receive pleasure. I can only guess it heightens with the one you are fated with," Vamir stated.

They were all so innocently candid, it was hard to be offended by otherworldly charm.

Looking back, I eyed Aranzeiros to the back of the group having words with a noblewoman. He looked to be in the worst of moods, which I can only assume was because I refused to ride with him.

"I only know English, but I suppose if it's customary to learn more, I would try." My tone was laced with insecurity.

"You will need to learn more than languages if you intend to compete with our grandmother's legacy," Vamir said before I explained how this wasn't a competition for me.

"You must forgive us, Paige. *Everything* is a competition for us," Theoden joked.

"But we will do you the honor of treating this like a game. Just don't expect us to go easy on you, Sister," Vamir added, his horse lifting and neighing before he steered it to take off into the maze-like wilderness.

"I hate to break it to you, but we've all gotten an unfair advantage. The magical link that bonds us to this land. That doesn't mean you won't do well, sister. It just means we'll do better." Theoden winked, his hazel eyes sparkling every time the sun hit them. That brought me to my next question.

"Hey, Theoden. I was wondering, is it common or even heard

of for humans to summon magic?" His ginger brows shot up in a troubling way as he rode up beside me.

"It's not something humans should even entertain. Most humans lack the understanding and humility to wield magic. Because, mostly, they haven't given up something to earn that power. It's not something I'd go around asking just anyone. So, for your safety, my Queen, I ask that you please not mention this topic again if you're not around those you trust. I would hate to lose the only person capable of pacifying my older brother," he joked.

That reminded me. I hadn't been able to re-summon the light, but perhaps it was good that it hadn't reemerged. I didn't even want the power, and I sure as hell wasn't giving up anything to have abilities I didn't completely understand.

Amidst my daydreaming, Theoden whistled to our party, signaling his plan to inspect the opposite direction Vamir rode off to. I, on the other hand, adhered to the path ahead of me, basking in the fact that I'd never been to this part of the forest.

Everything around me was so vibrant and colorful. Majestic purple leaves, cerulean blue roots, and animated emerald green bushes made up the plant life, as trees glowed with a mystical air that hinted at their old age. It was the complete opposite of the forest I'd seen when I arrived, and truly it was a sight to be seen.

In my peripheral, I spotted movement from something fast, but not fast enough to escape my sight. I hopped off my horse, intending to sneak up on it. With tough, charcoal-gray skin and tusks well past its wet snout, the animal resembled a cross of a boar and a baby hippo.

As cute as it looked, I didn't want to be on the other end of those tusks, so with stealth and caution, I made myself scarce to follow it. After a rigorous twenty minutes of ducking and dodging, the fauna finally stopped at a small waterhole, exiting as quickly as it entered to snack on a small fish from its exploits. I raised my crossbow, aiming toward the round, fleshier part of its torso before being surprised by a hand over my mouth and a powerful arm around my waist.

"Shhh." Even without turning around, I knew it was Aranzeiros. Who else could transform me into a panicky mess with one touch?

"You are aiming in the wrong direction," he whispered, redirecting my shot to its head instead of its body. "The skin on its body is too difficult to pierce. With those creatures, you must aim for the head where its flesh is the thinnest," he added in another purr. Only now, I had no interest in making the shot altogether. His creamy low voice in my ear and possessive grip on my body had made sure of that.

With reckless aim, I released an arrow, missing the animal's head by an inch as it took off into a thick brush of bushes. Certain that I could catch up to it, I struggled myself free of his embrace, and with his horse, I took off after it.

The crafty creature soared a respectful distance ahead of me. So fast, it was almost hard to keep up. Still, I persisted, following it into a clearing that led to a vast open meadow. The horse galloped, fierce and triumphant, and it wasn't long before I forgot what I was chasing.

Reveling in the vast land that awaited me, the open field felt like freedom for the very first time. As the steed put distance between me and my party, the thought occurred that this was my chance to do anything. To go anywhere. To go home.

Could I be happy if I found a way out of here? There were certainly things I missed about home. Experiences I would never have again should I fully accept my new life. Truthfully, I hadn't fully come to terms that this was my life now.

The one thing I was certain of was that the King of Shadows was growing on me. I cared about him. I treasured his feelings. I valued his aspirations and, aside from his need to control, I loved the way he made me feel.

For the dozen of undesirable traits he possessed, he had a

million more favoring ones that eased my trauma into the possibility of receiving the love I deserved. But there was so much attached to this life. Was it the freedom that he promised or the bondage I feared?

I should just know the answer, but in all honesty, I didn't.

With a gentle tug of the horse's bridle, I brought the horse to a stop. In front of me stood my old life. Boring, and struggling, but free to make my own choices. Behind me led to wealth. A found family and in time, a marriage that *could* someday grow into love.

I was at a crossroads and with no one to guide me, I took a deep breath in the hope I wouldn't regret what I did next. With a quick steer of my steed's direction, I turned back and rode back into the forest where I left Aranzeiros.

As for now, I would choose a life with him.

***

When my husband refused a ride back to the party, I suspected he sensed my long absence had been an effort to run. Every question had been met with one-word responses. Every attempt at conversation redirected him to a chance to speak to his brothers instead.

Even when I tried to reach for his hand, there was no warm tangle of affection. Just a limp hand that wanted nothing to do with me. I almost let our ride back to the resort continue on in unbearable silence. But I just couldn't take it anymore. Enough was enough.

"Aranzeiros, you've been quiet and distant all day. Is there something bothering you?" I asked as he fixed his gaze on me. His usual arrogant stare was withdrawn and indifferent, as if he were looking through me and not at me.

"You tell me." His voice was a shred of a whisper, something I found to be far more frightening than rage.

Releasing one exasperated sigh, I pinched the space between my brows as I adjusted on my side of the carriage. "Aranzeiros, I'm trying. It's just you're so confusing. I thought that by being your fated mate, I would always know where I stood with you. But one minute you're methodical. Focused on nothing but being a king, which I completely understand. But the next minute you're all over me like a dog in heat. I just never know what to expect from you. What makes it worse are the times we don't see each other. You test me, and you test me, and you test me. I don't know if I'm passing or failing."

He leaned up interlocking his fingers, as the life returned to his onyx eyes. "I test you because I want you to stand your ground. You think an outsider will handle you with the delicacy that *I* do? You, Paige, are going to have to build a thicker skin because if simple things like me taking my duty to the realm seriously as king bothers you, you won't be prepared for what the future has in store." He seethed.

"There you go with the gaslighting. You say that we're the same, equal. But then you speak to me like that."

"Then challenge me!" he interrupted. "And not just when you have an audience. You see yourself as easy and compromising, but truthfully, you are neither. All while being indecisive and divergent. I have been exceedingly patient with you. Doing everything in my power to make your stay comfortable. Giving you all the things a female could want. Trying to make you happy."

I released a deep breath, followed by a theatrical groan. "Yeah, but I didn't ask for any of those things. Spending time with your brothers, they didn't assume things about me, they asked me. I know you've been on this planet a whole three hundred years longer than me, but you don't know what's better for me than *I* do. Don't assume, just ask." He leaned back in his chair, peering out the window one last time.

"Did you try to run today?" he asked, with this look on his face that said "Oh, don't look surprised."

"Yes," I hissed, lowering my gaze to my hands. He must have sensed my plan to run, which explained why he had been so distant when I came back.

"Do you know how ridiculous that would have made me look, Paige?" he said through gritted teeth. But I was sick of playing by his rules. If a queen was what he wanted, a queen was what he was going to get.

"Do you think I care about making you look ridiculous? I'm my own person. I'm my own woman, and you're going to stop treating me like a pet you snap your fingers at, expecting me to follow! Do you know why I came back? Because for some dumb reason, I'm completely infatuated with you. I wish I knew why. I wish I wasn't such a fucking cliché. But the second I got far enough, you were the only reason I rode back. Not this lifestyle, not this title. So, you better start treating me like the queen you want me to be. That means checking in on me *every* day. I'm human. I need *daily* hugs and kisses. And no more assuming things about me. I don't care if you have to buy a dozen of those couple card games to find the right questions. Put more time and effort into getting to know me. "I huffed," suddenly feeling out of breath.

Looking into his hawkish dark eyes, there was no hint of what he thought about my outburst. I wasn't even sure I wasn't getting through to him. Assuming he'd lash out, he managed to keep his typically calm, collected demeanor.

"You know my grandparents, Aranzales and Nieven, tolerated one another. Finding neither love nor understanding outside the constraints of their arranged marriage. He was insufferable, and she was bitter because of it. And then there was my father, Tarron. He and all his trysts were an act of convenience. Perhaps there was respect, but there was no genuine bond. No actual future. I don't want the only times you tolerate me to be when we share a bed." He paused, the suspense building for what was yet to come.

"I will honor your request of me. I did not realize I gave you this much doubt in our marriage so soon after we'd wed. Too often, I forget that I have a human wife who has human needs and human customs. The stage you humans call the honeymoon phase does not exist in fae culture. For you see, how I feel for you is how I'll always feel for you. There is no adjusting or falling out of desire. At times, this is why, for me, it is easy to go without you. Nothing will alter the prison your presence has over me. I will try to be more accommodating. And congratulations." I cocked an eyebrow, confused what caused his congratulatory wish.

"Why are you congratulating me?"

"Because today was the first time the pretender *sounded* like a queen. I wish to see more of this, Paige. Do let her out more."

CHAPTER TWENTY

Paige

A series of late-night knocking left me stumbling out of bed and racing to the door. Struggling with the heavy weight of the handle, my sleep-induced eyes widened at the presence of my fully clothed husband standing at the door's threshold.

"Is there something wrong? Nighttime visits aren't exactly common for us." Not that I was complaining. Here was my other-worldly husband, and even in my fatigue, I could admit he looked most striking in the darkness of night.

"There is nothing wrong, Paige. I wish for you to accompany me somewhere."

I yawned. "This late at night?"

Aranzeiros took a deep inhale, followed by a release of his collected breath. "Our destination looks far more pleasing in the darkest of hours. But I will honor your desire, should you wish to return to bed."

Looking back at my comfortable, *luxurious* mattress, I hated that it called to me, assuring me that if I gave it my attention, there would be no doubt I'd fall back asleep within seconds. But it was clear Aranzeiros wanted to talk, so as tempting as it was, sleep would have to wait.

"Sure, let me slip on some clothes," I said, attempting to head toward my room's closet. The force of his strength pulled me into a forceful embrace, as hints of the scent of evergreen and amber held me hostage.

He hesitated, unsure of where to redirect his mouth, as I braced myself for his kiss, only for his lips to meet my forehead, in an enduring kiss to the temple. Tilting my chin up to meet his gaze, and in an endearing tone asked, "It is well past midnight. Does this count toward your daily hugs and kisses?"

***

By horse, we rolled past territory lines into another maze-like forest. Only our surroundings weren't as welcoming. It reminded me of the forest that we detoured when we first arrived. The NetherSpark, he called it. All I knew was I never wanted to be caught there alone.

"Where are we?" I asked, taking his hand as he helped me off the horse.

"I can smell your fear," he replied, avoiding my question.

"I'm just not sure I like forests in Esterbrooke." Hugging my arms, trying to muster up some courage.

"Not all forests are built like the NetherSpark." He matched his pace to mine.

"Those lacking fae blood, through which portal, it matters not, will always be led to the NetherSpark. This ensures that they lose their minds or they never live long enough to reveal our world to their own. My main reason for requesting such a route was to ensure that if you attempted to escape, you would regret it," he admitted dryly.

"Let me assure you that there are no other forests like the Nether-

Spark." He gave me a brief history of its possible origins. It was an old fae's tale, that the very first Demyn—a race of fae humans akin to beasts or monsters—poisoned every oak, letting her blood soak the soil, and that her scream carried so that it would echo for all eternity.

"Do you believe in all that?" I asked, and he admitted that while possible, it sounded outlandish.

"I used to. Until I met my brother Ivaran. I can't imagine the Queen of monsters mating with Tarron Faeborne if any of that were true." Not to mention, she was from a place *far* from other fae. My guess was, it was a convenient story that humans made up, back when there were no borders between realms.

Upon asking how many other queens existed in the Fae Realm, Aranzeiros assured that the Queen of monsters was only a nickname. One that was given so long ago by humans, and it became a challenge to shake a term existing long before his birth.

Having nothing but the cool night air and crunching branches underneath our feet, I couldn't sit in silence for too long. "Aranzeiros, you still haven't told me why you brought me here."

Aranzeiros let out a breath of frustration, leading me to believe he was annoyed. "Paige, since becoming my wife, I've done a combination of controlling your whereabouts, to giving you things I *thought* would please a woman in your position. Being married to you shows that I still have so much to learn."

He turned to me, his dark glassy stare rendering me still and useless, my legs freezing until he looked away. "I have never been taught to listen. I have only been taught to act. It is the one thing I envy about everyone else.

Many times, more than I have asked to be, I have always been in the mentor role. But never in the privilege of having one. Everything I know, I've had to learn on my own. It is why, so far, I have expressed love the way I do. Love in your world is achieved through understanding and similar values. Yet, love in my world is earned through loyalty. Perhaps even other things that don't sound like love at all. I want to love you, in the way that you're used to, but I'm ashamed that I don't know how."

It was hard to admit for a *regular* person you didn't know something, so I can't imagine how hard it was for Aranzeiros to admit we had two different love languages. The only time I'd ever seen him so vulnerable was when we first made love, but this was the first time I'd seen tears well in his eyes.

"Everything I care about leaves. One day, I suspect you will too." He turned his back to me so that I couldn't see him wiping tears from his eyes.

"I realize I can't keep you. Not when I can not predict if and when you take your chance to return to your former home. I want you to be able to survive without me, so what happened to you in the NetherSpark never happens to you again." Ending with a runaway queen was better than a dead one.

He once told me, in Esterbrooke, he would make his presence in my life a necessity. Now that he was letting go of that idea, a part of me couldn't wrap my head around why I was so disappointed.

Pulling back a lush canopy of misleading leaves, the wondrous sight before me explained why it was a better sight at night. Much of the flora gleamed against the offset darkness, as if it were making a special trail for anyone who followed.

Glowing vines snaked down lengthy trees, as many of them curled around tree trunks, while others wrapped around a well nearby, in suffocating loops. If even half the forests in Esterbrooke looked like this, no wonder the fae stayed so close to them.

"Foraging appears to be a talent for you. Perhaps it is time you learned how to differentiate flora that harm and flora that can heal." By heal, I assumed he meant many things, not just in that literal sense. Knowing the environment would've helped prevent being poisoned during my first two weeks in Esterbrooke.

Aranzeiros went over the basics, distinguishing between some of the easier herbs, roots, and tubers, forcing me to unlearn all I remembered from the Human Realm about what was edible versus what could harm me.

He appeared so humble, crouching down, pulling out a fern from its root, and pointing out what to look for. "See this textured skin?" Waiting until he received my nod as confirmation.

"You can soak this in the water and use it as a bandage if your wound is not severe. Avoid placing it on the textured side. Since it has a numbing effect, it makes all the difference if you don't have access to a healer."

"There are healers in Esterbrooke?" I asked, never sure if fae had things like medical school or doctors. Apparently, in the Fae Realm, magic and medicine were one and the same.

"There are different types of healers, stretched across cultures. None of them compared to the type of healer my grandmother was. Not that she was very good at it. At least not when it came to me," he spoke blankly, and even though he wouldn't say it, I was sure if he wasn't abused, he wasn't used to being healed by her either.

"Did she hurt you?" I placed my hand on his shoulder, surprised he didn't react like other times when mentioning her.

"It matters not whether she hurt me. My respect for her is infinite. She made sacrifices for this family even my father would not make. She was not *born* a Faeborne, but she was worthy of the name more than any of us," he admitted, with no love in his tone.

As someone who'd also married to earn the name, I wondered if that kind of loyalty and sacrifice would be something expected of me.

"If I'm being honest, you and Aranzales have a lot in common." His expression was calm and stoic. "Both of you are headstrong, stubborn and at all given times, wanting to have nothing to do with me." He attempted a dry joke that I didn't find funny.

"That's not true," I defended.

"You could have fooled me."

"Aranzeiros, I told you how I felt. Don't think that I don't notice how the sparkle in your eyes lights up when I tell you I enjoy being around you. You get off on me *telling* you, but I respond better to your *attention*. I want to like you. I want to love you. But if you listened as much as you acted, I think we could get to a place we'd both want to be." Aranzeiros came to a stand, wiping his soiled hands in the nearby well.

"I fear that even if I tried, you would be resistant, regardless of the outcome."

"Aranzeiros, I'm sure this is hard to believe, but I am not as headstrong as you think I am."

"You're right." He wiped his wet hands on his trousers. "That is hard to believe."

Fighting my embarrassment, I shared more of my past. "Before you, I was a bit of a pushover."

Having been bullied by my parents, bosses, and romantic partners, by the time my last relationship ended, I was fed up. I knew I didn't deserve to be a punching bag my entire life. I just hadn't known that development would lead me to Aranzeiros.

"You see me so much different from my own kind. I'm secure in myself, but I would be lying if I said I wasn't used to being passed over for the prettier girl. The only reason I'm not a pushover with you is because you make me feel like I can demand those things from you. Instead of making me feel like I should be lucky that you want me," I admitted, sheepishly.

There was an uncomfortable silence, at least for me, as Aranzeiros processed that information. "Thank you for sharing that with me." He grabbed my wrist, preventing me from putting distance between us.

"I know that the Human Realm is your place of birth, but you make it sound so horrible. And not just because it's a filthy, destitute place, devoid of any actual class or culture."

With no warning, Aranzeiros delicately caressed his fingers

across my chin, forcing me to get lost in his words of affirmation and deep-set eyes. "But because I can never live in a world *permanently*, where you weren't the most beautiful woman in the world." Aranzeiros released his grip and gaze, ending with how much it pained him that he has failed to be a good husband.

"You're not *terrible*," I said, pulling at his wrist so he could turn back to face me. "We just need work-life balance. I know we have duties. But we have duties to each other too. Isn't that how marriage works?" Grateful that his woe-some demeanor was warming up.

As if reading each other's cues, not being able to fight the urge, we leaned into one another, preparing ourselves for an impromptu kiss.

Aranzeiros and I exposing things about ourselves made me forget that fateful liplock at our wedding and how much of an energy-drained wreck I'd become after our first dance. No matter how good his lips felt, I was weaker than normal, unable to resist, but unable to fight.

Any attempt at nudging away only made him hungrier, because he could smell that I wanted him, but he was too distracted to notice anything else. I couldn't communicate how exhausted I was, despite wanting nothing more than for him to make me feel like the woman he couldn't resist enough to kidnap.

For reasons unknown, my necklace heated against my skin, and before I could stop it, a blinding light rushed out of my fingers, forcing Aranzeiros back.

"What in the blazes was that?" The only other time I'd seen that ferocious look in Aranzeiros' eyes, was when he woke up from a nightmare he claimed that I caused. Before I could answer, he aggressively grabbed me, silently accusing me of things I had not yet done.

"Have you been keeping things from me?"

"No, Aranzeiros. I swear, this has only ever happened once—"

"Tell me the other time it happened," he spat with impatience.

"It was the morning after we married and I—I was confused."

"Humans are not supposed to practice magic." His anger clear, as it replaced his once vulnerable state with insatiable rage.

"Aranzeiros, please." I fought against my tears. "You're scaring me. I didn't do it on purpose. It's just that something happens to me when you kiss me. I swear, I'm not lying to you."

Aranzeiros eased his grip on me, and I tried to gather myself and stop myself from crying. He had never looked so angry with me, and it was the first time I thought he'd actually hurt me.

"I believe you." His voice was calm but still suspicious. "And I'm sorry that I scared you." He took me into his arms to comfort me.

"Paige, I care for you deeply. I did not intend to accuse you of things that have not yet been done. But magic is dangerous. Even for fae. A majority of my anger is because, once magic touches you, it can destroy you from the inside. That would not be a fate I would choose for you."

"I didn't mean to." Trying to sniff away my runny nose. "Many people have already told me what happens to humans who practice magic. I was just hoping it'd never happen again."

"You don't know what triggered this in you?"

"No!" I interrupted.

"Light magic should have been lost when Aranzales died. The only remnant close to light was..." As with that statement, it was as if a light switch had turned on in Aranzeiros' head.

When he reached for my necklace, I had every reason to assume he intended to strangle me, so when his hand grabbed the necklace, searing pain stopped him and he violently snatched his hand away.

"Baby, I'm sorry, I don't know what's happening." I ran to put one of his lessons to work, dipping the kelp in the water from the well to wrap around the burn mark left by the necklace.

I could tell by his heavy breathing and trembling lips that this brought up terrible memories for him, as I held him close, trying to calm him through his episode.

"It's okay, baby." Bathing his face in kisses, my poor attempts to calm him. "You take care of me all the time. Now let me take care of you."

The fear and shame made him hold me tighter, as through his shirt, I could feel the texture of his uneven skin. Whatever had happened to him, happened so long ago, he'd pushed it down so much that the emotions were finally coming out.

"Does that feel better?" I kissed the top of his head, trailing kisses down his face, trying to get him to smile. He loosened his grip, allowing the opportunity to take his injured hand and kiss it, hoping the gesture alone would make him feel better.

Before I could stop it, light poured from my fingers, as Aranzeiros' instinct was to snatch his hand away, but when he didn't, I wondered why he appeared so short of breath.

"Are you okay, baby?"

Aranzeiros removed the makeshift bandage, revealing that where there once was a severe burn, now looked completely healed. "Did I do something wrong?" His silence frightened me.

"No, it's just...I've only ever been harmed by light, never healed by it. It's a fresh change of pace." Aranzeiros forced himself to his feet, leaning over the surface of a well-maintained well nearby.

"Is that what it feels like when our lips meet?" Aggressively turning to me.

"I don't know what it's like for you."

"Shortness of breath, in the moment significantly weaker?"

"I guess." I shrugged.

"At least I know where a queen's power comes from now." He then reminded that the Paleforce's inherited magical gifts were commonly associated with manipulating Earth, his grandmother's family house. "At least I know why she was so afraid of me."

Not wanting to bring up his trauma, I had to know. I was the current owner of the necklace, and if this was going to happen every time he kissed me, I needed to know how to take it off. "Why was she afraid of you?"

"Because her power—your power. It directly opposes mine. I was far from her favorite grandson, so anything attached to her, only sought to hurt me. She was the last to be the bearer of that necklace, so some of her essence must still live inside it."

"Okay?" I said as a question, not wanting to convey that I understood.

"Heirlooms hold meaning in the Fae Realm. Almost like guidance. It's not as explicit as having a teacher, but sometimes items can hold knowledge from past owners. As if they silently speak to you, even when you hear no voices."

"But what does that *mean?*"

"It means that the necklace is bonding to you. And it cares not whether you're human. I think you're stuck with it." My thoughts piecing together that maybe that's why I couldn't take it off.

"When I officially decided to take a human bride, Aranzales died not long after. Unlike Tarron, it was her time. Imagine my surprise, when at her deathbed, she asked to see me, insisting that my human wife be gifted the necklace and not another female family member."

Maybe she hated humans and wanted his fated mate to suffer. I didn't know her personally, so I'd never get the chance to ask. "This is a development that requires sensitivity. Until we know more, perhaps we should keep this between ourselves."

"Is it possible to get rid of it or strip the magic from me?"

"I fear it is too late for that. Your only option moving forward is learning how to control it." I didn't like the sound of that.

"Maybe you could teach me like you're doing with the foraging?" I asked, hoping he could offer more insight.

"Your power is beyond me." I tried to step toward him, and it surprised me that he took a step back. The power of light must have done a number on him.

"I don't even want it if you're just going to be afraid of me."

"I do not *fear* my own wife," he interrupted, loosening his once-balled fists. "I just...I have not had positive experiences with the last person I knew with that ability. It will take some time getting used to, is all."

"I'm not like her." Erasing some of the space between us.

"I don't want to harm anybody. Especially not you." Praying he didn't step away as I moved closer into his space. You could tell in his posture that he was trying to brace himself, as I stepped onto the tips of my feet and slowly leaned in for a kiss. His lips were light at first, almost like he was holding back, waiting for something to happen.

The necklace's stone grew warm against my skin, as I felt his intruding darkness engulf me, only it didn't feel malevolent, or invading like before.

Maybe he was right about the last owner's essence being attached to it. Maybe it was trying to protect me until I accepted it was mine.

I no longer saw Aranzeiros as a threat, so instead of being overwhelmed by him, I just felt him. His shadow, his darkness. But most of all, him. Tonight, marked the first of many for us, as we bonded over more than just our mutual lust.

"How did that feel?" I asked, pulling away.

"Overwhelming. But in a pleasant way. Light and pleasant have never been in the same sentence for me," he joked under his breath.

"I should get you back. I'm sure by now you're tired and beyond the usual," he said, nervously balling and unballing his hands into fists until I reached in and slipped my fingers through his.

We didn't walk two steps before he turned to me and planted his lips on my forehead, and it took everything in me to keep it together. It appeared that I was finally melting through that entitled king's exterior.

And I couldn't *wait* to see what came from it.

***

When we finally reached our accommodations, I was tired as a human could be, but before I could reach my door, Aranzeiros stopped me, ensuring that I never made it to my room.

"Wait...it would honor me if instead of sleeping in separate rooms, I join you in your room or you join me in mine. Even if it is just to sleep. It pains me that I have not been able to hold you since the night we first made love," he admitted before I shut my room door.

"Who would I be to turn down a king?" Pushing him back into his room, shutting the door behind me.

Positioning him on the bed, I dressed down to nothing but my bra and panties, prompting him to slip out of his clothes with little effort. In a room full of darkness, he ran his hands along my hipbone and back as I ran my fingers through his luscious strands.

I breathed him in before leaning down to kiss him, a kiss we both now welcomed, as he whispered, "My light," pulling me on top of him, ensuring neither of us was about to get any sleep.

CHAPTER TWENTY-ONE

Aranzeiros

There was no better start to the morning than losing yourself balls deep in what's yours. "My, my. That was ambitious for morning sex." Paige laughed, trying but miserably failing to escape my possessive mouth.

"We've had far too much time to make up for. And trust me, I plan to make up for every...single...second," I assured her, planting kisses with every pause.

"Okay, okay, I missed you. But despite how amazing you are, my body requires breaks," she said with a gentle shove.

"If it were up to me, our time would be without recess." I adjusted on my side, resting my head in my hands.

"I'm sure if you could fuck me all day, we would never leave this room."

"It wouldn't just be sex for me. But yes, my ambitious skills would make it a challenge for you to walk. What truly I crave is your submission, not just your body. But I'm grateful for any piece of you that you trust me with."

"Why do you want me to submit to you so badly?" she asked, smiling as I tipped her chin to meet my gaze.

"It's not just that I want you to submit. I want you to embrace the idea of me dominating you."

"I hear that, and it sounds scary." Those weren't the words a newlywed king longed to hear.

"Have I not been gentle enough for you?"

"Baby, you have," she interrupted, with a tender caress to my shoulder. "And I'll be honest, some of your appeal is that you're dangerous. But when I hear dominance and submission, I think..."

"Think what?" I queried.

"That'll it'll be a *kind* of scary that we can't come back from. It's taken long enough to get where we are now," she added with a shy bite to her lip. Perhaps I should have found contentment in our reaching a breakthrough, but there was so much she didn't know about what I could make her feel.

"What do you think about that?"

"I think it tells me we've known each other for less than a month, and it shows." I reached in, my mouth meeting hers in a devouring kiss.

"I understand you do not fully trust me to unlock that side of you. But my dominance can be painless. It can be gentle. It can be dangerous, but most of all, it can reveal to you my true self. If you think I'm obsessed with you now, words wouldn't describe how much our relationship would flourish. You have no idea what it's like to be with you. You drive me fucking mad and dominating you would give you semblance of what you do to me."

"How does it feel for you?" she wondered.

"Like I'm neck deep in water. High enough to feel safe, but knowing one step in the wrong direction could change the stakes. Sometimes you make me feel safe. Sometimes I feel like I'm in danger," I admitted, the color draining from her warm brown skin. She was blissfully unaware that we were both involved in a union that scared us.

"You would be special. I have never asked this of a long-term partner because all the willing pussy in the world would never amount to the submission of a queen." Lowering her gaze from mine, a quick change of subject told me everything I needed to know.

"I think we should get up soon." She stumbled out of the bed struggling to stand.

"Believe it or not, we have next to nothing on the schedule, so if we just keep each other hostage and fuck for the next twelve hours, no one would come looking for us. I promise."

"Aranzeiros, I don't think I can handle being stuck in a room with you for twelve hours," she offhandedly joked, draping a robe over her naked body.

"All right, six hours. Last offer. I can even throw in a half-hour grace period in between to give your inner thighs a rest."

"Aranzeiros, no!" she teased.

"You're no fun," I huffed.

"Oh, but you know what *does* sound like fun?" She brought her hands to her mouth to mask her excitement. "How about instead of letting the kitchen serve us, we prepare a meal of all the forged goods we found, ourselves? I haven't had a Human Realm-style stew in a while." I stared at her blankly, and soon her discomfort with my silence had her snapping her neck at me.

"*What?*"

"I'm just waiting for you to get to the fun part."

"Come on," she said, with a slap to my chest with a pillow.

"You're telling me that even on your hunting trips, you've never had the honor of preparing what you caught?"

"That's what we have staff for," I huffed. "I've rarely ever stepped my foot inside a kitchen, let alone *cook*." I spit the last word out like a curse.

"That changes today," she demanded.

"I hope you're not asking of me, what I think you're asking of me." She pouted, joining me back on the bed.

"I want to do something that reminds me of home."

"Trust me, you wouldn't be caught dead in the palace's kitchen, either."

"I meant..." She hesitated to finish. "My human home." It would be a lie to deny that her answer made me uneasy. I thought Paige was happy in Esterbrooke, especially given that her life here was so much easier. When she spoke of life before me, it was riddled with poverty and the need to be in a constant state of being productive. Who knew she felt nostalgic for a world she felt unseen in?

"And that is something you miss? From your old life, I mean?" I asked, sitting up.

"When I was back at the palace, outside of hiring people, there was really nothing for me to do. I don't love to cook, but I do take pride in the fact that I have a few good recipes in my back pocket. I guess I've always thought I'd be a stay-at-home parent with the right man. Or if I had to, being someone who worked to alleviate the stress of my partner."

"And you *like* to be responsible for those things?" I asked, trying to understand.

"*No*," she countered. "But sometimes you do things for people because you *care* about them, not because you enjoy doing them."

Slipping into a modest tunic and peasant slacks, I searched for the belt that had somehow made it halfway across the room in our wrestle to the bed.

"If that should please you, I will disregard my comfort in an effort to honor your wishes. If you would like, I shall have them reserve a time to clear out the kitchen...to *cook*." My jaw tightened, as I struggled with the words.

"You don't have to," she suggested, sensing my reluctance.

"But it would...make you happy," I said through gritted teeth. "And I want nothing more...than to see my queen happy."

***

"So, this is so your clothes don't get dirty."

Paige tied the strings of an apron at my back. I was a king. In a pantry apron. Ivaran was right, love sought to humble me. I had arranged with the resort staff a block of time that didn't set them behind on their work for the chance to honor a promise for my queen. We were going to cook. Something I immediately regretted the second we set foot in the resort's north-wing kitchen.

"Thank you for letting me do this." She beamed, with a skip in her step as she familiarized herself with the kitchen. "Ever since I was young, I always rushed to clean, prep, and cook the food I foraged. I guess I haven't really outgrown that." She squealed when she located last night's findings.

Despite my lack of enthusiasm, when it was time to make myself useful to her, I cut up all her roots, fungi bulbs, and tubers, including a few items she had scavenged in the nearby pantry.

"You okay over there?" she asked, and I sensed that my silence had spoken volumes.

"Outside of the fact that I feel ridiculous, I'm just peachy."

"So, being self-sufficient is ridiculous to you?"

"No, taking part in missions that aren't a strength for me makes me feel ridiculous."

"I told you that you didn't have to." Her voice lined with sympathy.

"Nonsense. I love spending time with you, and I've learned that you value quality time. Sometimes I wish I could spend every waking moment with you, if you can believe that," I admitted, popping a cubed root in my mouth as a reward for all my labor.

"The task is far from ideal." I laughed. "But I want you to trust me. And you're never going to if I can't show you I can be different for you," I said, fighting back a shudder of humiliation.

I didn't get embarrassed, and I was rarely made a fool of, but it all seemed worth it just to keep the kisses on my cheek coming.

"I've never asked, but what started your flair for foraging? It is not often I encounter a human as resourceful as you are."

"Do you really want to know?" She softened. Preparing her bone stock was far from simple, especially considering she was unfamiliar with our hunted game. She was, however, determined to devise a savory stew, perhaps even more than discussing her past.

"Paige, I wish to know all there is to know. Even the things you deem unimportant."

"Well, part of it is heritage," she proudly stated." The other reason is that I didn't have the best of parents."

"See, you don't discuss your parents much."

"That's because there's not much to talk about," she deflected. It appeared as though her parents were a challenging topic of discussion, so imagine my surprise when she elaborated.

"I think my parents were too young when they had me. My father resented that he had to be responsible for me, and my mother *hated* having a daughter. From the moment I was born, something destined me for tough love." I cringed at her admittance of her parents abandoning her for days on end. Oftentimes she'd starve, and her only way of feeding herself was hunting rabbits or foraging.

"I think because they never physically abused me, I felt lucky. A girl I went to school with had a mean drunk for a mother. We all tried to pretend we never saw the bruises. Child services never did much in the small town where I grew up in. Most people kept their business to themselves."

The room went silent, finding a commonality in how the damage of generational curses did a number on you. In her brief life, she had struggled with abandonment, and I fear I hadn't been doing the best job to remedy that.

"That explains your fear of being alone."

"I'm not afraid of being alone. I've just always done better on my own."

"Well." I hesitated. "That changes today."

***

Once Paige prepared a proper base, she guided me on the steps that went into putting all the ingredients together.

"So, this is cooking?" I hovered over her as she rigorously stirred the pot.

"It's nothing fancy, but yes." She laughed, finding humor in my suffering. Being so close, it was a wonder I wasn't mauling her. She smelled divine. Like she was at peace.

"Still, it could have gone a lot quicker if we had used magic." I stepped toward the counter, leaving with a kiss on her cheek.

"What do you mean?" she asked, turning on her heels, eyes wide and curious. Leaning against the countertop, with a flick of my wrist, I peeled the skin off a root with just one magical command.

"So you've known how to do that the whole time and just let us waste an hour cutting and prepping." She splayed her arms along the counter.

"To be fair, you never asked," I defended.

"How are you doing that?" she wondered in fascination.

"Most things have shadows. All I'm doing is bending them to my will," I said, dropping the root in the pot.

"Well, it's not first nature for me to use magic. I don't know how to turn it on and off like you can. Sorry if I do things the human way," she huffed.

"No, the apology lies with me," I said with a cross of my arms.

"Outside of basic things, I'm afraid I won't be much help. I have next to no experience bending light, let alone trying to teach a human to do it."

"You showed me before."

"That is untrue. I only advised you to search within yourself to draw it out. And even that was a gamble, considering how often a human's body tends to reject it."

"Will that happen to me if I continue to try?" she asked, clutching her hand to her chest, suddenly fearful.

"You might not like my answer."

"Well, I don't want to use it if something bad will happen to me."

"In theory, if a human were to successfully bond with the magic, coming from a host that's benevolent, it should do them no harm. But truthfully, I've only known cases where humans abuse magic. So it ends up changing them. Which is the exact opposite for us. There probably isn't an Esterbrookian who wasn't born with, at the very least, some comprehension of magic. I don't even know how to explain it because I've never had to," I explained, unsure if that had answered her question.

"I don't know if I want it anymore."

"I'm not sure that's your decision. But I wonder..." I searched her face, her impatience growing. "I wonder if the reason it hasn't rejected you is that you *don't* want it."

Despite all the benefits she inherited from our union, Paige was still irritably humble. People who were hungry for power were predictable. With her, I could never be sure of her true ambitions.

"It does have one advantage," she chimed, a cherub-like grin on her face.

"And what is that?"

"That I can kiss you and it doesn't feel like you're taking me over." I stood, closing the distance between us.

"Is that so?" I asked as Paige stepped backward, her back pressing into the counter.

"I mean, it's still overwhelming, but it feels like the magic in me is settling."

"Or..." I interjected, pressing my body into hers, as she had nowhere else to go.

"Perhaps together we create something dangerous." A blend of her scent and my impulses drove me to meet her lips in a ravenous kiss.

"We always end up here," I said, muffled between kisses.

"That's because you always *put* us here." She giggled, stroking my beard as I nuzzled her neck.

"It's because you're so beautiful. And I want you. Fucking need you. Like nothing I've ever needed." I pressed my lips onto her, nibbling and biting to feed my hunger.

But alas, Paige had stronger willpower. When I lifted her onto the counter, she was quick to put an end to things all things carnal.

"When you get started, you are *relentless*," she laughed with a playful shove.

"I can't help it. You bring out the hunter in me."

"And so what? I'm the prey?"

"You're a good catch. That is what you are," I teased.

"We've wasted enough time. Let's see how the stew came out." In a frantic investigation, Paige searched the cabinets for clean bowls at a chance to try our end result.

Since Paige lacked knowledge of Esterbrookian spices and neither of us was ever sure of the correct measurements, I had low expectations regarding the first taste.

"It may not be perfect, but hopefully it's edible." She held up a spoon to my mouth, eager for me to take the first plunge. It was... an acquired taste. There was no way to know for certain that this was her preferred end result but to spare her feelings, I masked my genuine sentiments until she sampled it herself.

"It's..." she started, forcing a gulp down with a nod of her head. "*Bitter*. And not in a good way."

"I half assumed that most human meals were something you learned to love in your developing years. I didn't want to disappoint you." She attempted another spoonful, deciding this time to spit it out instead of forcing it down. In a fit of laughter, she fell to the floor. Finding her hysterics contagious, I met her level as my stomach throbbed in pain from my nonstop chuckles.

"Gosh, where did I go wrong?"

"A fool leading a fool can only go in one direction," I chastised.

"And you didn't react or anything," she said, wiping a singular tear from her eye.

"What can I say? Being the first son of a king has helped me develop an unreadable poker face."

"Next time, I think I'll leave the cooking to the cooks."

"Finally, *something* we can agree on," I said, helping her up as I encouraged us to tidy up so we could sit down for a proper break-fast. We may not have had any official plans on our schedules, but if I could give Paige one day without expectations, I was going to. Not because I had something to prove, but because I was finally learning about the things that made her happy. And that made *me* happy.

CHAPTER TWENTY-TWO

Aranzeiros

Following Ivaran's advice, I spent most of my morning cultivating the loveliest flowers I could find. Knowing that with how worn out she'd been, I did not expect her to rise for another hour. Since I wasn't aware of where or what containers to place them in, I expected a cup should suffice.

Just as I had planned to enter, the door opened, an alluringly sleepy Paige standing at its threshold. "I was just about to look for you." She warmly smiled, securing that her robe stayed put.

"For you." Handing her the cup, puzzled why the gesture caused the confusion lines now riddled across her features.

She accepted them in a delayed moment, having me wonder if I'd picked the wrong ones. "If you prefer a different kind—"

"No, no, no, Aranzeiros," she interrupted, trying to reassure me. "This is sweet. I was just confused. They're normally in vases, not cups."

Perhaps I should have clarified what Ivaran meant at his claim that humans enjoyed their flowers in water. The concept alone seemed strange, but I was finally connecting with Paige, and I'd just wanted to surprise her with something humans liked.

"Looks like my brother Ivaran and I are going to require a little *talk*," I said through gritted teeth.

"No, it's fine Aranzeiros. I was a little thrown off, but I love them. Thank you." She stood on the tips of her toes to kiss my cheek, before carefully placing her bouquet toward the window so they'd get proper light.

"I have another surprise." Insisting she changed into something comfortable. Since Paige's arrival, I had treated Esterbrooke like her cage. Esterbrooke was a free realm, a place like no place in the Human Realm. If I wanted her to see it as anything other than a prison, I had to show it to her, without the use of tours, guides, politics, guards, or detail watching over us.

"Why are we sneaking out the back?" Paige laughed, unsure of what to expect.

"When you're as used to escaping the public as much as Lianthore and I were as juveniles, you know the ways out of anywhere, without all eyes watching." Walking backward so that I could face her when I spoke.

"Will we need a carriage to get there?" She beamed, amused at this side of me.

"It will require a generous walk, but when we get there, I have taken care of the transportation," I assured.

"I think I'd prefer a *safe* carriage ride," she retorted.

"Where's your sense of adventure, Paige?" As I grabbed her wrist, leading her as far as her legs would go before I offered to carry her.

"What's so special about where you want to take me?" Tightening her embrace around my neck.

"That I am taking you everywhere and nowhere. You've seen so little since Esterbrooke became your home. It is filled with too much wonder for you to be seeing it through just the eyes of palace balconies and political trips."

"Okay." She rolled her eyes, defeated. "If you insist."

"I promise you, Paige. Hence, this day forth, you will experience not a day without adventure."

"Gosh, you're so extra." She giggled.

"Extra? *Extra what?*" Unaware of such a colloquial.

"You're just so...excessive. And theatrical. Sometimes it sounds like I'm watching a historical drama when I listen to you speak." She smiled, lying her head on my shoulder. "But I like it." Nuzzling her face in the crook of my neck, modestly bashful.

"Perhaps I should be *extra* more often. Especially given that it encourages moments like this." It took less than an hour to reach the boat meant to be our means of travel once we reached the shoreline.

Having prepared early, the rowboat hosted a few things Paige might need for an all-day trip. "I have prepared to take you on a tour of my own. Meaning, no protocol, no press, no pretending. I will not be Aranzeiros the King, or the son of Tarron Faeborne. I will simply be just Aranzeiros." I lowered her in, toward the bow of the boat.

Pushing the boat off the shore, I slipped in just in time for it to fully take off. "Would it be more romantic if I did things the fae way or the human way?" Deciding whether to use magic or physical labor.

"*Or* I could just help you," Paige offered.

"Nonsense. This is my gift to you. What type of husband would I be if I expected this kind of labor from you?" Opting to give a go at rowing on my own, but should the water grow unforgiving, rely on my magic for the rest of the way. The task was surely making use of the centuries-long training I'd undergone, activating my upper back and core in a way that made me grateful this was something normally carried out by servants.

"Do you like traveling by water?" Paige hugged herself, as I suggested she take the throw in the sack to warm herself.

"It is not my preferred method of travel, but my brother Vamir's ancestral land, Lelepali'i is beautiful. On both land and sea, that appears as if it stretches on forever. His region of Ester-brooke has lost much of its land over the years. We do our best, but it grows challenging to preserve what Esterbrooke once was."

"And by preserve, you mean away from humans?" Paige asked boldly.

"Yes. I did not want to speak about such things on our trip, but I realize I've never shared why our human/fae alliance is important." She scooted up closer, eager to have a more extensive explanation.

"The one thing humans can't make more of, is land. That is why they need us, our land. Because the way they exhaust resources goes far beyond their basic need. We do need humans. But because it is all they want, we must give in to their demands."

I did not satisfy Paige with that answer. She wanted reasons, backstory, and details even I may not be able to confirm. With our means and numbers, she wondered what was so important that made the peace between fae and humans come to place.

"The reason it filled me with so much anguish over your recent gift of magic was that some time ago, there'd been a human who learned how to *conquer* magic. It was an era known as the Dark Days. And it wasn't just for fae, even humans were forced to face this enemy. Warriors, soldiers, and fighters, both human and fae, worked to defeat this threat. But they couldn't kill them. They didn't know how. All they could do was lock them in a human-made prison, far away from any Fae Realm portals, planes, anywhere they could draw magic from."

"This person is still alive?" Paige hugged her body close, curious yet reluctant to have an answer.

"As far as we're informed by our sources, yes. I admit it happened so long ago, even *I* am not sure this person exists. As members of the royal family, my brothers, even our extended family, are not permitted to even *confirm* this said prison. Our magic would be too tempting for them to draw from. Tarron saw that no Faeborne, Steelborne, Bloodborne or Paleforce would ever endanger themselves. So, we must take the word of humans, that this sorcerer remains in their mundane prison."

It doesn't happen overnight; once land is colonized by humans, over time it strips it of its magic. Sometimes it takes years, sometimes decades. But should this sorcerer ever escape free, it would certainly leave them at a disadvantage, having to scrap to find a place to draw from. They might still regain their full power, but we'd be prepared on both sides before that event came to place.

"They were known as the Arcane sorcerer. But you will find no history book to confirm this. Only those who fought during the Dark Days can recall such events, but many of us have been told both realms became a world without dawn."

Paige was finally understanding my initial reaction to her harnessing magic. Deep down in my soul, if any human could inherit magic without corruption, it had to be Paige.

"So that's why you weren't fond of humans?" Paige asked as it seemed time to let my magic do the rest of the rowing.

"No. I've been alive for a long time and all humans have ever shown me is never-ending war. Deception. Greed. But knowing you? I'm glad to be proven wrong."

***

"Where would you like to land?" Kissing the crook of her neck, pointing to several islands nearby.

"Maybe...the middle one?" she chimed, excited to be asked.

"Another time," I dismissed.

"You said I could pick!" she said, lightly smacking my chest.

"That leads to Pavemark Island, a settlement of Menehune fae, displaced from their homeland of Lelepali'i. I don't believe I've prepared you for fae that small. They're hospitable but quite irritable. It's not a no, just a maybe-when-we-have-more-time situation," I emphasized, using air quotes.

"Then that one," Paige suggested east.

"East it is," I flirted, allowing my magic to steer the oars. We reached a small dock, and I was grateful to have a place to anchor the boat. Paige folded up the blanket, securing it back into the duffle bag she found it in. Helping her out of the boat, she nearly tripped, which was good for me, because it forced her into my embrace.

"You must be careful, my light."

"Your light?" Amusement stretched across her features.

"Could you be anything else to me?" Her smile caught fire because now I was smiling too. She didn't answer in words, only a tender peck on the mouth.

"Where are we?"

"We are on Meadow's Grove Island. A population of fifty or fewer, so there are a lot less creatures to encounter. Private, but not closed off to us, of course. I've not been here for some time, so unless things have changed, I advise we respect the land, so as not to offend its inhabitants."

By respect, not doing things humans would do, which was destroy. With Paige, I knew I didn't have to worry about such things, but it couldn't hurt to remind her. "This place is pretty." Referring to the long grass seeded with wildflowers.

"I can think of something prettier," I flirted, smirking in her direction as her hand slipped into mine.

"What was your first impression of me?" she asked, wearing a bashful smile, as we basked in the sights of autumn leaves twirling and drifting to the ground.

"The idea of you? Or actually meeting you?"

"Both."

"I was convinced there was nothing in the world that could ever have any power over me. I had planned to arrange my claiming that day, convinced I could marry any human." Not intentionally trying to fuel her insecurity, but wanting to be honest.

"But then you called to me. Not on your own, no. Your scent was so overwhelming, I almost didn't *want* to find you. But then I saw you. And it was like looking at a human for the first time." Remembering not only the lust but the warmth I felt as well.

"Then I met you. For all that joy you gave me just by being near you, you just seemed..."

"I seemed what?" she asked impatiently.

"Unhappy. Perhaps even overwhelmed." As she later joked, that was she was content. Her life consisted of living check-to-check, skyrocketing bills, and not even enough space to feel like a true home. That explained most of it.

"Might I trouble you for your first impression of me?"

"Aranzeiros, I thought you were an asshole. But I had literally just seen you on the TV, and I was annoyingly naïve to think I could attract someone so important. But what really hit me was that *second impression*." As she felt the need to emphasize the word second.

"By then, I thought you were a serial killer, a rapist, a human trafficker—"

"Okay, okay, but get to the good part where I changed your mind?" Gesturing my hand to hurry her along.

"*Boy*, there is too much world-building for me to start skipping to the good part," she continued on, describing the conflicting feelings that led to our wedding night.

"And then that's when you were a captive to my charm?" Interrupting, my patience wearing thin.

"No. That night I was just horny and curious." She placed her hand on my hip, taunting me.

"I'm sure there's an 'Aranzeiros completely changed my mind' in that story somewhere," I muttered, prompting her to laugh at my expense. "I'm confused. When *did* your impression change of me?"

"When you took me to the forest to forage. It was the first time you did something for me that didn't seem selfish. It was the first time you've really talked to me where I felt like you actually heard me."

"I *do* hear you." Stopping her, forcing her to face me. "I'm just...stubborn." Struggling to spit the last word out.

"And arrogant. And impulsive—"

"Nothing makes me more impulsive than when I'm with you." Pulling her by the waist to be closer. "It is as if every rule, every law, everything I'd ever felt about humans, I want to unlearn, for you." I leaned in to kiss her, not the least bit slighted that she lightly pushed me away.

"Calm down, babe. You're getting a little excited and we haven't even had time to do something fun here," she said through stretched arms, wearing a wanderlust smile.

"What did you have in mind?"

"We passed a lake recently." She used her chin to gesture the direction in which she spoke. "And I feel like I've experienced so much in my time with you, but so much of it is excessive. Not that I don't appreciate it," she defended.

"But we do things that you're used to doing. I want to do something bad, but simple."

"I'm not sure I understand what you mean." Hoping she might enlighten me.

"I want to do something that could really get you in trouble in the Human Realm if you get caught," she teased, suddenly piquing my interest.

"I'm listening."

"Have you ever skinny-dipped where you weren't supposed to?" she flirted, arching an eyebrow.

"Skinny dip? I am not familiar with that term."

"It's when you take off all of your clothes..."

"Okay, I'm enjoying the sound of this," I interrupted, rubbing both my palms together.

"And you swim," she adorably downplayed.

Confused, I asked for clarity. "Just swim?"

"Just swim," she clarified.

"Since it's not something anyone just risks, there's kind of like a bond with whoever you do it with," she stressed, through squinted eyes. "Most people aren't brave enough to try it in their lifetimes."

"And are you? Brave enough?" I challenged.

"I'm bravest when I'm with you," she stressed through longing eyes and arms stretched out across the back of my neck. "I know with you, nothing bad could ever happen to me."

After that, it took little convincing, as we backtracked to the lake, using the throw she used to warm herself as a place setting for our dry clothes.

"And this is fun where you're from?" Anxiously helping ease her blouse over her head.

"Most of the fun is the *idea* of getting caught." She slipped her legs out of her trousers, trying not to fall. She was half undressed before I realized I hadn't reached to remove any of my own clothes.

Even during our most intimate moments, she'd never seen the back of me, just the naked part that pleased her. "What are you waiting for?" She beamed. "Do you need help?"

We were finally entering a stage of our relationship where there was no looking back. If I didn't trust her not to pity me now, our fondness would never grow. Without further hesitation, I lifted my shirt from my head. I tried to maintain a neutral expression as she came over to help me.

There was some hesitation. She was studying my back, and I was grateful I could not gauge her initial reaction. She reached from behind me to loosen my belt, her beautiful brown hands contrasting against my alabaster skin. I felt her lips meet my back, in soft pillowy tickles, that made the hair on my chest rise.

As I removed the rest of my clothes, she took me by the wrist, leading me into the water, as we waded toward the middle, until we were satisfied with our placement.

Pulling me close to her, she secured her arms around my shoulders, leaning into part her lips to mine. Never had a kiss been so sweet, so perfect. It pained me to recall times when this hadn't been normal for us. Sipping and savoring her warmth, it was all an Elf could hope for.

And she'd been right. This was fun. Basking in her presence made the world melt away. Nothing mattered as her tongue explored my mouth, taking in my warmth, as her naked breasts pebbled and trembled against my skin.

It took all my strength to pull away, for just a moment to peer into those forest-like eyes filled with infatuation and trust. "I think I thought you would bore me." Another reason I'd been reluctant to connect with a human.

"But now, you're all I look forward to."

***

After such an intimate swim, it wasn't even a question that by the time we got out of the water; I was going to be inside of her, one way or another. We took our time, grateful to have packed a hand towel so that we both might dry off without obstacle.

Kissing was becoming my new favorite pastime. The immense joy that came with getting to know her mouth was *almost* as good as making love. Her lips showed tenderness and compassion, as contrasted by my salacious want.

"Baby," she cooed, a fracturing whisper at the act of my teeth nibbling her right breast, drowning in one last kiss to the mouth, before snaking down to kiss her stomach.

Her stomach was soft, but that's what I liked about it. It wasn't my desire to wish her body to be like mine. I liked that her curves contrasted my hard lines, and if I could, I would admire her body for hours on end, to hell with responsibility and kingly obligations.

By the time I reached her luscious thighs, I could already

smell the arousal emitting from her sex. When her folds dripped like this, it made that first thrust especially rewarding, as her thighs began to tremble at the heat of my mouth coming into contact with her.

Like her mouth, I hungrily consumed her folds, drowning in the succulent juices that brought out a frenzy in me.

"Careful," she warned, in a regrettable whisper. "I'm already close."

Which only encouraged me to increase my intensity, slipping two fingers past her walls. She held back a shriek, her thighs caving in on my face, trying to hold on to whatever control she could.

Her breasts heaved in rhythm with her racing heart, as she was so blinded with pleasure, it was no use fighting it, as she pressed my face deeper into her sweet little cherry.

"Fuck, Aranzeiros. I'm gonna come," she spoke through a hushed tone, my fingers expertly massaging her G-spot.

Normally, when I ate her pussy, I did it without the use of my hands. But as I delicately assaulted her petal, an unfamiliar honey gushed around my working fingers. Her walls contracted, rendering her mindless, as her body writhed and twisted in insatiable disarray.

I was sure her body had never reacted to me in that way before, especially given how wet my fingers were after I withdrew.

"Aranzeiros, I don't think I can wait any longer. Give me some of that Elven dick," she cried, inciting me to rush to get on top of her, squaring my hips above hers, as my cock found its favorite new home.

"Mmm..." she moaned a whimper, accepting my painstakingly slick thrust.

"You don't have to whisper, my love. I want to hear you *scream* your pleasure," I encouraged, weakened by her feminine cries echoing the grove.

"You like it when I'm all the way inside you?" Stretching the walls with a few deep and delicate thrusts.

"Baby, I love it when you're all the way inside me." Her voice broke against the gentle pounding, longing to reach her end until there was nowhere left to go.

"Is that pussy getting used to me?" I taunted, withdrawing some of my length, only to watch her become undone as I plunged it back in. "Because my cock sure is getting used to you."

In a greedy display of affection, Paige pulled my face down to hers, locking me in a dangerously addictive kiss. With her legs locking me in place, my ravenous hips ground and thrust, until there was nothing left between us but cum, sweat, and exhaustion.

"You're so good to me." Combing my wet hair between her fingers.

"And the best is yet to come." I mustered some strength, knowing that if I didn't reach for my pants, I was just going to find another reason to be inside of her again. Luckily, she had the same idea, as half her clothes were already on.

Having misplaced my belt, a teasing "Looking for this?" led me to turn to her, her every intention to withhold the leather strap.

"Come on, Paige." I playfully reached out, as she withdrew her hand the moment she regarded my outstretched hand.

"What do you say?" she taunted.

"*Now!*" I jovially demanded.

"Is that any way to speak to your queen?"

"You know? I could *make* you give it to me." Reaching behind her, still unable to retrieve the belt.

"And how would you do that?" she flirted, not even trying to fight my climbing on top of her and kissing her on the lips.

"*Well*, first I'd spread your legs..."

"Mmm hmm?" Her interest suddenly piqued.

"Then I'd slap my cock against your breast." Kiss. "Your

cheek." Kiss. "Anywhere I could punish you for being such a bad—"

"Um, excuse me?" a voice in a rhotic lilt surprised us, causing Paige to scream in a rush to get the rest of her clothes on. For the first time since the skinny dip, I secured my belt, coming to a stand to apologize and greet our guest.

"Oh, no," she shooed away, repositioning her knapsack full of game. "I passed through earlier and when I...ahem, heard her call your name, I thought what an opportunity to invite the king and queen for a meal." Knowing I couldn't refuse.

Paige was beyond mortified, which I didn't understand, especially given the fact she'd waited *after* we'd had our fill of each other before approaching. Which was equally confusing, considering the thrill of skinny dipping was to be caught. I would have to ask her how that works at a later time.

"I'm, like, really sorry. This is such a bad first impression of me—" Paige's poor attempt at apologizing, was easily dismissed by our Dwarven host.

"From the sound of it, looks like you two were shaking up this little island. Word travels slowly around here, so I'll take it personally if this wasn't the time that you conceived." She winked.

"I just didn't want to be disrespectful." Paige blushed.

"Forgive my queen, for she is still learning our customs and etiquette."

"'Tis no problem to me." Her affectionate grin set the tone for the meal to come.

"Feel free to get in some more of that heir-making action to give me time to prepare my game. I take a bit of time, what with my limp and all, to reach my home from my hunting site."

"Take your time," I interjected. "Just tell us where to find you."

"On the cul-de-sac deep into the grove, where the evergreens grow prodigious. You can't miss it."

I met her presence in a bow. "We don't intend to," I welcomed, watching our host beam and strut away, talking to herself about how she hadn't had such grand company in decades. Without proper warning, weighted fabric struck my shoulder three times before I moved out of the way.

"Hey!"

"You said there'd be no one else for miles," she accused, humiliated from the exchange.

"To be fair, I said you did not have to *whisper*. It's you that implied that it meant there'd be no one for miles."

She put her hands on her hips like that was supposed to intimidate me. "So, what was that all about?"

"What was *what* all about?"

"Aranzeiros, I've never seen you bow to anyone. And now we're suddenly invited for dinner?"

"This is good. This will be great practice to show you how I engage with the company of Dwarves. All that you've learned, you must unlearn it when engaging Dwarves."

Knowing she'd need a detailed explanation, I proceeded to prepare her on how to address and behave in the company of one of the most valuable fae in Esterbrooke.

"I haven't had time to explain that Dwarves are a proud people. They handle much of the mining, as well as weapon and architectural engineering in all Esterbrooke." I'd actually been trained by a Dwarf named Heighgard Stonehedge, which prepared me for the weapons dealer role I maintained in the Human Realm.

"They know how invaluable they are, so even as a king, I would never expect a bow from someone Dwarven. While it wouldn't be expected of me, I do it as a sign of respect for their contributions we all enjoy."

Having sparked Paige's curiosity, I educated her on the two things you should avoid at all costs. "One, never turn down a Dwarf's invitation. I don't care if you're tired or not interested. Refusing an invitation is seen as an egregious gaffe."

Holding up a second finger, I continued on. "Two, never offer them help. They have their own way of doing things, you'll offend them if you insinuate otherwise. Take in mind, these are skilled warriors. Trust me when I say they can handle themselves." She nodded, showing me she understood.

At her suggestion, we waited for the appropriate time before honoring her invitation to her planned feast. "Another thing. You will be hard-pressed to meet a Dwarf who hasn't given their service in war efforts. So, don't be surprised if they have a lot of stories to tell. And one should acknowledge their good deeds or prowess. It's another sign of appreciation that you acknowledge that. Names are also important, so if you don't remember a name, don't guess."

"This is so much information for one dinner." She warmed me by lacing her fingers through my open hand.

"You'll do grand. This I have no doubt of."

One couldn't miss the modest cottage in the middle of a show of overgrown trees. Even if we had gotten lost, the active chimney would have surely guided our paths.

In this regard, our exchange should seem familiar to Paige, especially given her explaining how common it was to cook for neighbors during their challenging times. I, on the other hand, had never had a meal in a home that hadn't belonged to my family.

I had to humble myself if there were no less than four-course meals and endless options to choose from. But Paige had that effect on me, and strangely enough, her attraction grew for me when I challenged my normal.

"Hello?" Paige sing-songed, knocking on the autumn-leaved colored door, surprised when a small door opened below us.

"Glad to see you made it in one piece. You must forgive the door. We don't get a lot of Elven or human guests—"

"Nonsense, this is just fine." It bothered neither of us to crouch a few inches as we made it inside.

Hearthy décor ornamented the walls, including an emblem

over the fireplace, to commemorate a Dwarf's service, as I'd be sure to bring that up when the opportunity arose, especially once I learned our hostess' name.

"Whatever you're cooking smells good," Paige complimented, applying what I had shared to make a good impression. "You'll have to share the recipe. Since living in Esterbrooke, I haven't gained a strong grasp on cooking yet."

"Oh, nonsense," she shooed away. "That type of labor isn't fit for a queen." I shot an all-knowing look in Paige's direction. How many creatures had to tell her that?

"But should you like the stew, I would be more than happy to leave you with the recipe so you can pass it down to your staff. It warms my heart when folks love my galbunni stew," she boasted.

There was a healthy fire going and pillows to mark our assumed seating arrangement, as I led Paige toward the fireplace, resting my head on her lap to get comfortable. "You must forgive our rudeness, but upon taking you up on your hospitality, I don't believe I got your name.

"Lorluna Orecloak, Your Highness. But you can just call me Lorluna. My husband, Rubirlan, should be joining us shortly. He's just been so busy with the mine and all, that he never readies himself for much else except for breakfast, lunch, dinner, and supper."

Paige made a face that could only suggest she'd been surprised that anyone could eat so often, so it'd been a good thing she read my non-verbal not to bring attention to it.

It didn't take long before a burly, blue-and-white-bearded Dwarf burst straight through the back door, face covered in earth, as he managed several pick axes, secured by the straps on his hip, back, and ribs.

Not expecting company, he boastfully sang to himself, an act that amused Paige, as her attempts at muffling her laughter had been a colossal failure.

The moment the male Dwarf threw down all his work axes on

the kitchen floor, a belligerent Lorluna was quick to put him in his place.

"By the goddess, could you bring your bloody axes around to the shed, like I told you to? You're not one hundred and twenty-two anymore. I shouldn't have to remind you to pick up after yourself."

As he dismissed her nagging with a wave of his hand. "I've got guests, if you don't mind. You're making me look bad enough—"

"Guests?" he interrupted. "Let me find out you're feeding those irksome little—" It only took him three steps into the gathering room to realize we weren't some common vagabonds that Lorluna had felt obligated to feed.

"Egad, wench. You didn't tell me the King and Queen of Esterbrooke were in our living room." He scrambled to tidy the mess he'd made, backtracking to the outdoor shed.

Lorluna yelled from the backdoor, "I shouldn't have to tell you the king and queen are here just to get a competent housemate out of you!"

It wasn't long before Lorluna gave us an update that dinner was nearly prepared. She was just waiting on her husband to clean himself up.

When he finally did return, gone was a face full of dirt, only to be replaced by a scruffy yet well-groomed appearance. Instead of waiting for him to reach me, I meet him at half the distance, taking a knee to give him a proper greeting of endearment.

"Rubirlan Wraithbow, at your service, Your Highness."

"Wraithbow, you say? Tis a powerful name." Despite not being able to recall the name, indulging him, I furrowed my brow, attempting to fake recollection to appear as a proper guest.

He returned my gesture of placing my right hand on his left shoulder with his left performing the same with mine. Our hands snaked until we were grasping forearms, we shared the emotional greeting typically shared amongst warriors.

"It is my humble honor to have you in our home."

"The honor is mine." I lightly bowed. "I see by those axes over your fireplace that you have had many adventures.

"As a Wraithbow, it's been an honor to serve your father. As my mother served before me, and her father before her."

"I must hear of your many exploits."

"Not before dinner is served," Lorluna interjected. "If you let him go on, he'll be talking until suppertime."

As Lorluna presented her serving tray, which she brought to the middle of the fireplace. No stew could be served without healthy servings of bread and scones, as they were still hot from coming out fresh from the oven. Our host offered us sweet wine and fruit-infused water, on the chance we weren't in the mood for spirits.

I'd probably never had a meal this intimate, as the robust flavor of the game complimented the perfectly seasoned broth in such a way. No wonder they ate four times a day, as Lorluna's skills with a cauldron were unmatched.

"Cooking must be one of your many talents." Trying to compliment with a full mouth to show my enthusiasm. "Your stew is one step away from goddess-like."

"It goes wonderful with the bread." Paige beamed with wide eyes. "Seriously, if there's any chance I can have this when we're back home, I would be eternally grateful."

Now that our bellies were full, I challenged Rubirlan to finish his story. Once again, making myself comfortable across my wife's lap, I lazed about, hearkening to his tales of serving during my father's reign.

Much of the efforts of the highlands had been the reason the tide had turned in our favor. "Mark my words, the Arcane Sorceror 'twas no myth. My sincerest apologies to our recent queen, I mean no harsh words. But, while humans have always brought about dark days, they had never been like that."

As a fae who hadn't been born yet, I'd only ever been taught about the Dark Days as purely academic. Tarron rarely discussed them, whilst Aranzales reveled in the fact that she could manipulate its outcome to justify her harsh feelings toward humans.

"I still have night terrors about those times. If the Arcane Sorceror could have covered both realms in an abyss, they would have done so, unchallenged. No one group leveled the playing field, but Aranzales the White? Had it not been for her, all our efforts would have been in vain. No one could have done what she did. It's a heavy burden to be the bearer of light."

"Isn't she fae? Couldn't her body handle it?" Paige stroked the crown of my hair, as I suspect she was curious since it was now her burden.

"With exceptions for you, King Aranzeiros, no natural-born Elf is born with the power of light or dark, at least not anymore. If you intend on preserving the ability, you have to pass it down through a relic, like the necklace you wear on your neck." His words prompted her to caress the stone.

"They used to be crafted for specific creatures until even other fae abused both light and dark. It's interesting that you were just born with the ability." As *he* even educated me, that darkness and light cancel each other out, which might be why my presence always rattled Aranzales.

Light was strongest in a world without darkness. If anything, she treated me as if I were her biggest rival.

"Queen Aranzales, goddess rest her soul, had been known to be bitter. She made a lot of sacrifices for the crown, so it'd be my guess that her conflicting nature was at odds with wielding the light."

Paige seemed just relieved someone knew more about it than the limited information I could provide. "What if you're human?"

"Dearie, the only reason that pendant's not ripping you apart is because light is the only known element that won't corrupt a human."

"Oh, stop scaring the poor girl. You've got her just as pale as a unicorn, telling her magic's going to rip her apart." Lorluna smacked her life partner on the shoulder.

I came to a stand, helping my queen to her feet. "Thank you for your service, and the meal was lovely." Directing between the two of our humble hosts. "I'm afraid my wife and I must return."

"The pleasure really was ours. Like I told you earlier, we don't get a lot of fancy guests. 'Tis a privilege to know the King of Esterbrooke doesn't think too lowly on our humble island. Know that any son of Faeborne is welcome for a warm meal and a good story." Lorluna's warm smile rivaling the fireplace.

We bid them farewell, and as promised, Lorluna left us with some recipe cards we would pass over once we were back in Regalhelm.

The walk back to the boat was quiet, but I welcomed the silence, so long as my Paige still held me in high regard. "Paige, are you all right?"

"I'm just thinking." As I wrapped my arms around her, noticing her scent shift to something more pleasant.

"I think I feel better about the necklace, knowing no one's really born with the ability." As she wasn't shy about her relief that wielding it didn't have the same effect as other elements.

"I just wished we knew more about it. Nothing would ease my reluctance more than having more information."

I loosened my embrace, backpedaling so I could face her while we spoke. "One thing I can offer you are my grandmother's dying words. They may not help—"

"What did she say?" Her tone was soft but impatient.

"On her deathbed, she claimed she'd made a mistake. That the past could only be healed if my future bride bore that necklace. Back then, I hadn't realized it was a source of power for her, but even when I refused it, she told me this..."

Your future queen may have to bear the weight of what it's like to fight true rage. I could have prevented such events, but in my arrogance, I couldn't see past my resentment. It is why I am so weak today. Because I am living with the consequence of winning a battle. One day, your queen may have to help you win a war.

CHAPTER TWENTY-THREE

Paige

My eyes blinked open, the sunlight peeking in through the curtains made it impossible to sleep in. As I sprawled out along the mattress, a pang of disappointment coursed through me at the sudden discovery that I'd woken up in an empty bed. Aranzeiros and I were different in *so* many ways.

Everything from upbringing, species, worldviews, and even tastes and interests. But the one detail that stood out from the rest was how much of a morning person he was. How he would find the energy to productively function after a rigorous night of lovemaking was a mystery to me.

Those were all the mornings I'd wake up a stumbling mess, exhausted and just a little achy. Mind you, it was always a *good* ache, but just once I would have loved to just stay in bed all day without rushing off to something on a schedule.

Or maybe I just needed a large glass of coffee.

The service at the resort closely mirrored the palace, with adjustable dining times, since on tour, the king and I opted for a lot of late breakfasts. The floating ladies-in-waiting had been extremely accommodating, making our time here another home away from home. I would be sure to send a few thank-you gifts when we made it back to the capital.

Rolling over, the stiff wrinkling of paper underneath me jolted me upright. It appeared that my husband left me with a few words after all. It was in his neat calligraphy-style handwriting, and although I was alone, I fluffed out my hair and dusted the crust out of my eyes to read it.

> *To my shining light.*
> *You always look so heavenly when you sleep, I couldn't bear to wake you. While it would have pleased me to lay with you all day and spend it recreating last night's festivities, I am set to have brunch with an old acquaintance from our hunting event. Just know there isn't a moment during our separation where you are not haunting my thoughts.*
> *A*

Welp, guess that was my cue to get up. Not even one step off the bed, the weighted doors flew open, filling the room with bustling servants who were happy to get me dressed and escort me to breakfast. I wanted to meet up with Aranzeiros but was a bit on the hungry side.

Knowing him, he probably had breakfast already, and besides, what sort of company would I be with a grumpy attitude and a rumbling stomach? Once I got some food in my belly, the search for my out-and-about husband would begin.

***

I took it upon myself to get one last tour of our lavish destination. I could count on one hand how many high-end hotels I'd ever stayed in, and even this made those look like seedy motels. Accepting that this was my life now, I only had Aranzeiros to thank. The more time I spent with him, the more I wondered what it was like to be truly his, the way he wanted me.

If anyone had earned that part of me, it was him, but what would that mean for us? Would I look at him differently? I'd already decided to see this relationship through, no matter how much of an outsider I felt. I still questioned if there was anything left to explore once I took that plunge.

He said he could never grow tired of me, but isn't that what most men said to get you to succumb to their taboo desires? I wanted to know what it felt like to fully belong to someone. Heart, body, mind, and soul. But only if I knew everything that took place to become his. It was why I was still debating it.

A familiar laugh in the distance led me to a far room on the south wing of the resort, the door open far enough to see my husband inside with the Lord he claimed he had a relation to. Just when I'd planned to join them, the mention of me stopped me dead in my tracks.

They would never speak freely if I interrupted, and this was a chance for me to learn what my husband really thought of me. Lord Zorrien adjusted his pool stick, making it an impressive three-ball shot with only one try, as he met Aranzeiros with a smug, satisfied grin.

"I must admit, My King. That human wife of yours is stunning. It's been some time since someone in our family took on a human lover. The ancestors would have been pleased." His accent was commanding and direct, like men from West Africa, but his tone and diction were regal. Surely a result of spending most of his life in the Fae Realm, never spending time with many humans.

"You know, I remember being a child when they banned our traditional practice. You should stay keen on who might disagree with your decision. When I served as a member of the Council, fae were honest about the desire to keep things separate, but we have entered a new era. One where fae such as myself take a back seat and let our sons take the lead. Even so, not everyone will speak the truth. Not when there's a human queen who sits on the throne."

They went on and on about subjects that didn't quite make sense to me. Foreign names, faulty alliances, and even a brief but tense discussion about Lord Zorrien wanting to restore the tainted legacy in his region's reputation. A pang of relief washed over me when they went back to talking about me. There were questions that pertained to my preparation to rule.

"I wonder, does your queen possess the necessary skills beyond the kissing of babes and waving to admiring subjects? Politics is a cutthroat game, and while she does present as charming, no amount of charm prepares one for the viciousness of both court and council. It is half the reason neither of my sons have served or wed. But my eldest, he is like you. Entitled, but ambitious. With bringing back tradition, I expect that to soon change." A brief pause in the conversation convinced me they had stopped speaking, until finally a pool stick out of my line of vision, made a two-ball shot, and with one brief lean, I made it out to be Aranzeiros.

"I agree with you. I am uncertain if my wife has the tenacity the former queen had. She's sweet, she's soft, and she's kind. Three things my grandmother was not. But the way the public responded to her with adoration and curiosity. Someone who can get the public to love her will always serve as a more useful tool. No one wants to challenge someone who is universally loved. As my father Tarron always used to say, to be loved is to also be feared. And my queen, she is a fast learner. I'm quite certain she'll make me proud in her first council meeting."

By now, I had heard enough discussions about how I'd measure up as a leader when I was trying to enjoy the freedom I'd have before the actual work began. In my room, I'd just be me, but upon returning to the Capitol, I'd be Her Royal Highness. I wanted to celebrate just being Paige for as long as I could.

Scattering back to the VIP chambers, I was met with the floating ladies-in-waiting, wondering how they can serve me next. I let them give me some flat twists before sending them on their way with the rest of the day off.

Before, I was lucky to have the energy for even something as simple as two-strand twists, but the Fae Realm was hiding some of the best hairstylists and experts in Black hair.

"There you are." Aranzeiros' voice startled me, as I admired the creature's handiwork in the room's vanity.

"Oh, hey." I turned to face him. "Sorry for sleeping in but you know me. I don't do so well with mornings."

"I know. That's why I had explicit instructions not to bother you until you were fully awake. But as you know, the workers here are eager to serve the Faeborne queen. I do hope they respected your wishes."

"They did," I replied, failing to mention that it only took one step out of bed for them to begin their hourly duties.

"And how was your morning?" he asked, strolling over to the suite's walk-in closet to rid himself of his suit jacket. Opting to leave out overhearing what felt like a private conversation, I started with what I had for breakfast.

"It was nice. The kitchen made me this weird minced game with stir-fried vegetables smothered in this creamy sauce. There are things I love about my food in the Human Realm, but there are things I *love* about the food here. If shit like this existed there, I'm sure some of these creatures would make a killing." But then again, maybe some of them already were.

"So, breakfast, styling? Nothing else?" he asked, taking a spot on the end of the bed.

"No," I lied. This Elf didn't need to know *everything*.

"So, how much did you hear? You know, the time you spent

snooping around to listen in on my meeting with Lord Zorrien."
Gulp. There goes the thought of me being unseen.

"Paige, you should know your scents sweetens when you're
being nosy. Why didn't you just announce yourself?" he asked,
forcing me to release a stifled growl.

"Ugh! Of all the things I have to get used to you, being able to
smell me all the time is my least fucking favorite," I shot back,
leaning into the questions popping into my head after overhearing
their exchange.

"Well, since you already know, I hope you don't mind any
questions that I have. Other than the obvious, what do people
expect of me?"

"You're asking the wrong question."

"Then what is the *right* question?" He got up and made his
way to the back of my chair to rest his hands on my bare
shoulders.

"It does not matter what those *expect* of you. The goal is to
give the public the impression you control the perception of yourself. Everything we do behind the Veil contributes to said perception. Many will want to build alliances with you because a king in
love is hard to come to an understanding with. Many will believe
the best way to get to *me* will be through you. Because of this,
others will respect your opinion in no time." I rolled my eyes,
desperate to shift the conversation about something that had
nothing to do with the council or court.

"This feels like a back-home conversation. While we're in our
last days here, would it be too much trouble to switch gears to
something that's been on my mind all morning?"

"It is mind-boggling how you don't just start with what you
have to say instead of entertaining third-act theatrics."

"Fine," I huffed out of frustration. "I think I'm..." I started,
the sharp cock of his left brow sapping away all my confidence.

"You think you're *what*?"

"I think I'm ready to be yours." His eyes narrowed and his face twisted into a conflicted grimace.

"I do not understand. How was that notable? You already *are* mine. It took you half the morning to tell me something I already know?" He asked, dimwittedly, clearly confused by my confession.

I stood, inching him toward the bed as I made myself comfortable in his lap. Fiddling with the collar of his dress shirt, I met his gaze with what I hoped was a seductive glare.

"I mean, I'm ready to be yours in the way you want me. Completely." At that, his nearly black eyes widened, a satisfied smirk creeping up the right side of his mouth.

"Really?"

"But I have rules. It has to be when we're back home and I have to agree to everything you wish to do. Is that allowed?" I asked, unsure of how all this worked.

"Paige, I wouldn't dream of doing anything you don't like. I promise nothing happens without your say."

***

With our long carriage ride home, Aranzeiros dedicated going over checklists, inquiring about boundaries, and asking me what felt like a thousand and one questions about terms I'd never heard before, like hard limits and safe words.

"Hard limits are essentially acts you've strictly taken off the table. A boundary you know won't spark any level of curiosity or enjoyment," he explained.

"A safe word, on the other hand, is a designated word that allows me, in a much more explicit way than no, to cease my actions and check in on you to make sure you still feel safe." He made a rare display of speaking with his hands this time.

Because this was so new for me and all my past partners had been vanilla, it took half a dozen clarifications that in play, sometimes a *no* could mean yes. Aranzeiros would have some pheromonal advantage, being able to sense my fear even if my words said otherwise, but he insisted that a safe word was my chance to have agency.

"For something this intimate, I take your consent seriously. Having reservations is normal and won't upset me if there are things you don't enjoy. Any information you can provide prior to play helps me know what might please you. What acts I can use as punishment."

"Punishment?" I interrupted, suddenly nervous.

"It is not as scary as I'm making it sound. Not all acts of punishment *feel* like punishment." Which was why he stressed how important it was beforehand to be honest so he didn't cross any of my boundaries.

I didn't know where to start when it came to eliminating acts, so I deemed it best to discover what he liked to see if some of our desires lined up.

"I know I'll require a much more toned-down version of what you're used to."

"You don't even know what I'm used to," he argued back, his lips forming into a small smirk.

"Well, what do *you* like to do?"

"I don't think that's the right question." A primal, glassy stare replaced his smile. "My answer would change based on my experiences because none of them are with you."

"Okay, smartass. Then what are things you fantasize about doing with me?" Aranzeiros straightened his posture to meet my eyes, his expression an unreadable seriousness.

"I have a strong desire to restrict your movement. Given how many times you've chosen to run, I have always wondered what your body would look bound. Does that sound scary to you?" He took the silent shake of my head for my answer.

"Degradation ranks high on my list, so I may say things that in polite conversation, I would never refer to you as. But in domspace, it gives me a rush. Some light spanking, perhaps even some edging. It feels more intense when you don't give in the first time. My four climax rule might be hard to honor when we're in that space." On one hand, I adored how Aranzeiros was so committed to my pleasure, but on the other, that sounded like a pleasant change of pace.

"My queen, when you are with me, you are in responsible hands. We have all day to ease your fears about it. I will not ignore your discomfort, but it pleases me you are open to sharing this with me. It is not lost on me how lucky I am."

He leaned in and kissed me, and not long after, we found ourselves spread out horizontally on the seat.

"Aranzeiros, be serious," I said, trying to play push him away.

"I have no self-control when it comes to you," he joked. "And while we're still on the subject, what are your concerns about walking around nude?"

I hadn't meant to laugh so hard but he had to admit, nothing about my time being here hinted at that being a green flag. I still fought the reflex to cover my ass when my attendants came in every morning to bathe and dress me.

"That might be a hard limit. Or maybe it's a soft limit. Being naked is something I can forget about during sex, but if I could help it, I'd rather be clothed than be naked."

"Your body is beautiful, Paige," he said, almost offended that it appeared I disagreed with him.

"You *would* say that. But seriously, I can be naked for a little while, but maybe as a first time I can wear lingerie until I'm comfortable."

"*Lingerie*," he said, emphasizing it like a foreign word. "Lingerie isn't as common or as popular amongst fae the way it is for humans, but if it will make you more comfortable, I'll be in touch with your seamstress to procure the perfect look.

***

By the time we got back to the palace, sadly, it was business as usual. Aranzeiros and I had used the entire ride getting me to open up about things I wouldn't do, surprising no one that it was a long list. Despite that, there were still a lot of acts to choose from, even if some things made me squeamish.

I feared my lack of adventure would appear boring, but it appeared as though he just appreciated my compromise. It was nice to be in a familiar place, but I was going to miss the time I spent with Aranzeiros doing things on a whim and getting to know there was more to my husband than duty, titles, and obligations. The royal tour showed me that despite how flawed he was, there was a gentle creature inside, willing to try.

Now I had to get used to being separated for hours at a time, stealing glances when we could and hoping the day would fly by fast enough just for a moment to bask in each other's company.

By dinnertime, I was a mess of information I was certain I wouldn't remember and had been so distracted I barely noticed that I sat in silence while I ate.

No sign of servants, no sign of court, and no sign of my dutiful husband. Even my attendants had made themselves scarce, and on my way to my bedroom, I didn't pass anyone in the halls. How strange.

As I entered my quarters, my questions were answered in plain sight and I rushed to my bed to find all the things I asked for in rows of neat piles. Attached to one of three lingerie sets was a note matching my husband's fancy handwriting.

To my dearest queen,

If you made it this far you've learned that I've made arrangements for the night to ensure your comfort. No one will make your acquaintance as you stumble through the halls. Which I find a shame, *as a beauty like yours is meant to be shared. In my excitement, I commissioned three choices I thought might flatter you.*

While it's the queen's choice, I do fancy you most in black. Under the black set, you'll find your first set of instructions for the night. Please follow every step. If you skip one, I'll know.

Your King,
AranZeiros

I tore open the small envelope and pulled out what looked like a small note card with my first assignment.

Change into the set of your choice and make your way to the queen's drawing room. There, you will find another set of instructions.

Laying the note down on the bed, I examined each set he had made for me. The first was a forest green floral lace set with a playful cutout at its center front. It was the simplest of the three, and I loved the color but before I made my choice, I unfolded the next one.

This one was a bodysuit-inspired teddy, a seductive combination of delicate lace and sheer mesh. It was a royal shade of purple, with crystal-studded garters and curve-accentuating lining. The color alone had made it a beautiful choice, but as I examined the back, the thong bottom offered no coverage.

I wasn't really a thong kind of girl, so it was clear I'd be passing on that one. The last one was his preferred. A black lacy three-piece set that included thigh-high stockings. The top was a sheer lace cami that would end at the top of my stomach, and the bottom was a matching garter skirt that stopped at mid-thigh.

The decorative bows and lace accents gave it both a romantic and sultry vibe, and the panties underneath were my favorite kind of cut. I should have known he'd make the one he preferred, the one he knew I'd choose.

I eased out of my dress and slipped into the racy number, admiring myself in the mirror as I marked my attire complete. No, I didn't have the perfect body, but I had learned to love what my body had gone through. It had endured hardships. It had carried me through the worse. It had long to be pleasured. And now it was on its way to be ravished.

To say I had a spring in my step would have been an understatement. I sashayed to the drawing room, a place I rarely frequented since I had no real eye for art. The paintings on the walls were otherwise beautiful, and the furniture was imported. However, the only thing to catch my eye was the note taped to the lone art station. Peeling it off, I tore open the envelope and read his next words.

You are doing well, my love. If you made it here, you'll be pleased to learn I procured another gift. In the drawer, you'll find a collar I had designed for you. Place it around your neck and proceed to your dressing room.

Doing as he asked, I pulled the drawer's handle, and just like he said, there was a collar in its place. It was bigger than I expected. More of a corset for your neck than any collar I'd ever seen. Its rich embroidery was gold against a simple soft black with a matching satin ribbon that fastened it in the back.

As I made my way to the dressing room, the collar had resulted in a sudden change of posture. I walked taller and more confident, eager to discover what my king had in store for me. Entering the dressing room, they had moved all the room mirrors to the center of the room, forming a circle, and inside that circle was a chair. I slipped through the open space to find the next note taped to one of the mirrors, but this time, I used my fingernail to open it.

That's my perfect little whore. If you're wondering why the mirrors are arranged in the room's center, it is because I wanted you to see what I see when I am balls deep inside of you.

Here you shall be the center of attention as you prepare yourself to be mine. Being my plaything means readying my pussy at my command. In front of the mirror, you are to touch yourself and do not stop until my pussy is dripping in juices. I want it wet and tasty before we are to reunite. Bring yourself to the brink but under no circumstances are you allowed to come.

Tonight, you may not climax unless I use my cock or tongue. When my pussy has had its fill, seek the hidden passageway behind the landscape painting. Take the first right you encounter and follow the path all the way down. If fortune favors you, you may just find another surprise.

I sat down on the chair in the middle of the mirrors. Never having touched myself without prior inspiration, I questioned if I'd even be able to complete his task. I was definitely more of a vibrator kind of girl, my second choice being streams of running water. When I touched myself, it took so long to get there on my own, but then I thought about him ordering me to, and a flood of inspiration took hold of my motivation.

It was hard watching yourself come undone, and in a few minutes time, I'd gotten far enough to slip up and surrender to my climax.

But then I heard his voice in my head, of what he might reward me with if I obeyed his command, and just as quickly as I started, I stopped, standing to my feet and in search of the secret passageway.

It was clean and well-lit, with arches of hanging fire every ten feet. When I reached the door he spoke of, I hesitated before pushing it open, wondering if I was ready for his next instruction. But eagerness had overruled fear, and with a gentle push, the door creaked open. I gasped at the sight of Aranzeiros, his throne moved from its regular station to face me at the entryway. There he sat, poised and majestic, wearing just a pair of fitted trousers that hugged his thick muscular thighs.

"Well done," he said, his bold eyes raking me. "Let's start with the king's next instruction. I want you on your knees and I want you to crawl to me. Do not keep me waiting."

Following his orders, I lowered to the ground and crawled to meet him in his chair. With a trace of his fingers, he lifted my chin, stroking my cheek with gentle tenderness.

"There is no better sight to me than you on your knees. It is the position you were born to be in, my love." He leaned in and traced my lips with his fingers, before easing his fingers into my mouth and toward my throat. Fighting a gag reflex, he took a fist of my hair and forced my head back, next reaching in for a sloppy kiss. With slow dragging kisses, his nose grazed my earlobe, bringing my untapped senses to life.

"Now be a good little girl and take my big fat cock in your mouth." He instructed me to unzip his pants, his massive hard cock springing to life against my lips. I was always amazed of his thickness, the way it stretched my pussy was the way it stretched my mouth. I strained all my facial muscles just to take him all, but I couldn't even manage the very base.

"Mmm, that's right, you greedy whore. Take my cock into your mouth like a good little slut," he said as he forced me up and down his shaft. I watched his face as I sucked him, giving me no indication of whether I was doing it right or wrong.

All I could gauge was the way his chest muscles and abs tensed up; otherwise, he had mastered not displaying any weakness. He closed his eyes, finally giving in to the sensation that was my mouth, and just as I expected him to release his seed, by my hair he forced me back, leaving me thirsty for him.

"I see what you're trying to do, but no, not yet. I don't want to waste a drop of my cum unless I'm deep inside my pussy. On your feet," he ordered, my face still wet from his cock in my mouth. Starting from my toes, his eyes grazed my entire body with one demanding stare. He was hard to read now, if you could appear unamused and filled with need at the same time.

"Lose your clothes, starting from the top. The stockings remain," he barked, and just as he asked, my hands rushed to my bra clasp. "Slower," he instructed, his eyes wanton and savoring, forcing me to move slower than I'd ever moved for a task this simple.

He stood to his feet, circling my body. Slowly and seductively, his eyes slid down as he took me by surprise in a gentle embrace from behind. Grazing my shoulders, he ran his fingers down the length of my stomach, graduating to a stroke of my curls. Feeling his hand so close to my sex, I prayed for him to go lower just for a chance for him to feel how wet I was.

"I want to stress to you my rules for tonight. One, obey my every word. Tonight, you are mine. Your body belongs to me. In the instance you feel overstimulated and drained of life, you are to still see to it that you accommodate your king. Secondly, I don't care how good something feels. Your climaxes tonight are allowed *only* if you come on my dick or tongue. Is that understood?" I nodded, the prolonged anticipation almost unbearable.

"Next, unless you use your safe word, do not beg me to stop. You will be used at my disposal, willing and ready to be at your king's pleasure. Hungry cock whores don't receive intermissions. They get fucked as their king demands it. This time a nod will not do. Voice to me that you understand." I took a light shaky breath, both fear and exhilaration snaking down my limbs.

"Yes, I understand."

"And why?"

"Because my king demands it."

"Good girl." He started, pushing my hair off to the side to plant kisses on my neck.

"All pleasure and punishment are to be shown gratitude with a thank you, My King. Tonight, you are not Paige. You are my insatiable, greedy attention-seeking queen. I'm going to do what I please to *my* body. If it is your king's desire to drown you in my cum, I will. If your king sees it fit to take his time, he will do so without protest. He will spend a good deal breaking his queen with the promise to build her back up. Am I making myself clear?"

"Yes." He fisted my hair, the pain sending a shrill of pleasure to my sex.

"Yes, *what*?"

"Yes, My King."

"That's better." From his pants pocket, he pulled out a chain, which he then attached to the front of my collar. "Does my queen like her collar?" Fighting back a smile, I confirmed with a whispered, "Yes, My King." And with the chain, he led me back to his chambers my body bare and for his consumption.

"See how easy this is? Your legs are *mine*. Your breasts are *mine*. Your lips? *Mine*. Nothing proves that more than you parading the halls bearing it all at my command. There are times I pass my queen in the hallway thinking about all the ways I wish to neglect my duties and pull her into a room and take her. Your wardrobe while beautiful, leaves me questioning what my queen wears underneath. Tonight, I do not have to wonder." I sensed he opted for the long way to his quarters to further heighten my fear of the possibility of someone seeing me like this.

The fear crept up my limbs like electricity coursing through cords, but I tried to keep my calm because...I *liked* the rush his hold had over me. He could get me to do anything, and this was certainly proof. When we finally reached his bedroom, he failed to close the door behind him, nervousness slipping back to grip me.

"You're not going to shut the door, My King?" He wrapped the chain around his palm drawing me in closer.

"Do you question my actions?"

"No, My King. I just fear someone might walk in."

"Then *let* them. All they'll see is a cock-starved whore who lives to serve her king," he said with a caress to my face, my heart pounded but somehow the idea excited me.

Especially when he spoke to me like that.

I'd never been a fan of dirty talk or even being called out of my name, but truthfully, I yearned to be his insatiable queen. A filthy little whore who lived for his cock.

Anything that left those lips in that voice made me weak in the knees at the promise of more. In the king's chambers, there was a wall mirror that overlooked his bed on the left side, and like my quarters, his apartment was massive. Gothic, mysterious, and reminiscent of him.

"Get on the bed for me," he demanded. Loosening the chain's collar around his hand, he led me to the bed and eased me down. With a wave of his hand, I slid over to the middle of his bed, as he bound my ankles and wrists to the frame of his canopy.

"Do not be scared, my queen. I only wish to limit your movements and keep you safe. I'm hungry, and I wish to sate my appetite until I've had my fill." With that, he jammed his fingers between my legs with no fight from me.

"I can see that you're already wet for me. I could smell that you want me to taste you." In and out he worked his fingers inside of me, rubbing my clit in sinful circles with his opposite hand.

"Look how nasty and wet you are. You like being your king's filthy little plaything, don't you?"

The skillful stroke of his hands was enough to make me go mad. It was bad enough I had to touch myself earlier with no release. What he didn't realize was just how good it felt just to watch him finger fuck my pussy.

His pale fingers penetrating my wet folds had felt better than any dick before him, and I was afraid that the longer he went on like this, I'd be breaking his basic rules.

"My King, please. I thank you for your pleasure but *holy fuck*, I'm about to come," I said through crazed gritted teeth. A sinister smile crept at the side of his mouth.

"It's so pretty when it's wet and ready for me," he said, adding a light kiss to my hood. To be brought to the edge twice in one night was absolute torture that I finally exhaled a sigh of relief when he bent down to taste me. I could feel the lustful magnetism that made this Elf so damn sure of himself.

His shadows had taken on the form of dark ropes that kept my quivering body in place; licking and sucking, kneading and teasing. Before long, the involuntary tremors of my suppressed arousal rained down like violent storms, drenching his face in wetness as he licked me until he decided me clean.

Before I could process another thought, he traveled up my body, a growl escaping his lips as his tongue caressed my sensitive, erect nipples. Having no control over my actions was absolute torture. I didn't realize how much I relied on touch with nowhere to run.

"Thank you for making me come, My King."

"I plan to untie you. Turn to the mirror and spread your legs."

The restraints loosened against my skin, as he scooted away from me to allow me space to do as he asked.

On my knees, I stood up facing the mirror, barely recognizing how desperate I looked for his touch. He lurked up behind me, his hands gently grazing my shoulders as he leaned in to kiss my neck. In a quick change of pace, his groping became more animalistic.

Scratching at my hips, claiming my breasts as the sharp sting of his other hand slapped my ass. I was nearly out of breath, all while being forced to watch as he ransacked me, claiming my body as his.

"Look how fucking beautiful the queen comes undone for her king. Bend over, so I can sink my cock in my pussy." With a fist of my hair, he forced me over, my entrance welcoming him into my body in one forceful thrust. The first stroke was always the most shocking, slow to start, but electrifying as his speed picked up.

"I love it when my cock just slides right in," he said, with a sexy bite to his lip as he gained a delicious rhythm, meeting my backside in another slap. I attempted to lower down to make it easier for him to work, but with a yank of my collar's chain, I was forced upright.

"*No*, I want you to watch as I fuck you. If you try to look away, I'll see to it to deny you of *any* release. You may be the most powerful woman in Esterbrooke but you still submit to me. It should please you to witness my enjoyment. Do you like being my little cock whore?" I tried to nod but the grip of his chain kept my neck in proper placement. I suppose that was the purpose of it resembling a corset.

"I do, My King. I do love being your little cock whore." In an effort to take him deeper, I arched my back as he loosened his grip on the chain for a chance to secure my wrists.

With driving thrusts, he pounded into me. Not gentle, not caring, no signs of remorse. I was his plaything with no purpose but to serve him. My mind had emptied any thoughts other than what it meant to be his. To wear his brand seared into my consciousness. To feel owned.

Hard rough strokes rocked my body as compliments left his lips for how well I took him. Tears of pleasure streamed down my face as I watched myself get fucked into sinful submission. It was an out-of-body experience, seeing yourself far gone in a state of lust. The excitement of being walked in on.

The thrill of not even recognizing yourself and the sensation of how it felt for my king to take me this roughly was enough to send a rocket of pleasure surging through me. In one big explosion, I came so hard that I could barely sit up long enough to let him just fuck me. This time he had no complaints as he used this opportunity to grind my face into the mattress and pound into me with aggressive strokes.

"I can feel your arrival all over my cock. Such a good girl. I wish to reward my queen by coming inside her." With a blunt fierceness, he pistoned in and out of me, going on for what seemed like forever until he came with a hoarse cry, as hot blasts of malehood coated the inside of my pulsing walls. His sweat-lined body leaned in to kiss my back, as he tilted my chin to meet my mouth in a kiss.

"Oh fuck, you're so fucking perfect." He pulled my face in for another kiss. "Are you all right, my light?" Lost for words, I offered a nod, and sensing that I needed something a tad softer we sat in bed kissing, his fingers unfastening the collar around my now sore neck.

***

He took his time washing me, handling every part of my body with gentle care and attention. It was strange to believe he could be so rough with me one minute and so soft the next.

All I knew was that I liked the gentle aftermath of an act I'd found to be intense. It made me feel loved and well cared for. It made me feel like *his*.

"Your silence is troubling. Tell me how it is you feel." I bit my lip wondering how to describe it in words but did my best, if only to prove that his soothing touch wasn't putting me to sleep.

"I don't know, maybe a little dirty, but more in a good way. The nicknames threw me off at first because rarely does someone call you a whore without being insulting. But as I leaned more into it, it helped me enter a different space. A space where I wasn't myself and where I could enjoy being degraded. It was different, but oddly enough, I loved it." He kissed me on the forehead as he helped me secure my thick hair in a high bun.

"It is unfortunate no one has ever proposed to dominate you before. Building someone back up again is a cherished experience."

"Oh, I've been broken. Probably too many times to count. But never have I been built back up again."

"I'm glad," he admitted as I met him with an irritated stare. *"What?"*

"I don't think I would like you if you had *always* been whole. Some of us are better broken." It pained me to admit it but I had to agree. All of our shared pains and scars helped us reach a stage where we could finally heal together. We had overcome the roadblocks that stood in our way of becoming our healthiest. Here, nothing could hurt us.

"All right, I think you're clean enough. Let's get you standing so I can dry you off." Rising to my feet, he started at my leg as the feel of his teeth on my rear end made me jump, a scream escaping my laughing lips.

"Boy."

"What? I rather like your arse. You don't know how much restraint it took for me not to use you there, too. I think I'll do that next time."

"Next time? *Umm*...not without this human's reservations," I shot back. His brows shot up, patting me dry on the bottom half of my legs and feet.

"I presume that's a hard limit for you?"

"No, but it's not something you can do without me being in pain. From what I hear it takes foreplay and patience. That, and a lot of lube." He worked the towel up my stomach lingering longer as he fondled my breasts.

"I take it you've never done it before."

"Aranzeiros, I'm from a conservative state and lived in a small town. I've never done half the stuff I've done with you."

Being with someone who made you feel safe to be adventurous was a gesture of love I never knew I needed. If I could help it, I never wanted to stop feeling protected.

"One final question for you. And do please be honest with me. Do you like it? Being mine?" A shy smile formed on my face, one that I was proud to say I didn't hide.

"I do."

CHAPTER TWENTY-FOUR

Paige

Being a Faeborne was a wild ride. I'd been queen three weeks and already had to accept that shifting through two hundred daily letters of fan mail was part of the job. I picked at random which ones I'd send personal replies to, but even this I'd choose over busting my ass just to live check to check.

The affairs I dreaded most were anytime I had to play hostess to dignitaries, who would have otherwise not given me an audience had I not been Queen of Esterbrooke.

Most times, all they sought to do was gossip, and while I loved my share of scandals, it was hard to know who to trust, since these creatures even spoke ill of ones they called dear friends.

For every emotionally draining day, I always had my husband to look forward to. Be it in the form of flowers in a cup or midday cuddles, we were beginning to have what felt like a genuine relationship. The day stretched into the night as I relaxed into a warm state of bliss at being reunited with him once more.

After waking from a brief nap, I sprawled out on his king-sized mattress coming to terms that my Elven beloved could spend hours on end just watching me sleep. It didn't suck to have such a beautiful and powerful male obsessed with you, but just once I would have loved to open my eyes without his glittering dark eyes studying me.

"I rarely ever get a chance to wake up with you," he said, extending a pale finger across my cheek. "There is a beauty in your stillness. Imprinting that image of you is what gets me through half my day." I fought the sudden itch to smile; it was too damn early to be blushing this hard.

"Well, let's hope I don't have your chambers all smelling like me to where you can't concentrate," I teased.

"Trust me, I will always find a way to concentrate. Do you wish to test that theory?" he growled, closing the distance between us to crush his lips against mine. His hand snaked between my legs and before I could protest, my hips moved in sync with the motions.

"Mmm, let's not get ahead of ourselves, baby," I murmured between kisses.

"Nonsense. There's always time to relieve stress," he cooed, our mouths in an entanglement of shared desire. "Today will be your first council meeting and you won't have the privilege of anonymity amongst your birth world's spokespeople—"

"You have to be kidding me! That's *today*?" I interrupted, his eyes rolling to the side as I hopped out of bed.

"Paige, this is something we discussed weeks ago. Does your assistant fail to keep you up to date with your schedule?" I smacked my forehead as I paced back and forth.

"Yesterday I dismissed her early because of some meetings that ran late and I didn't want her behind on other things I needed to be done. Not to mention I was busy getting my back blown out when you met me early for lunch." His face furrowed in confusion.

"How does one blow one's back out? The expressions you use are so peculiar."

"Gosh, you're so cute when you don't understand me," I said, leaning back on the bed to kiss him on the nose. "But beside the point, I don't think I'm ready for a council meeting."

"Well, I need you to be ready," he expressed with a stern stare. "Believe it or not, your presence will set the precedent for how my brothers' future wives will be treated by the council. Trust me, Paige. I would not be so adamant on the subject if I didn't think you were," he said with a kiss on the tops of my fingers.

"They're always hard at first, but you're blossoming. Show others that this is your calling." It filled me with pride knowing Aranzeiros believed in me, perhaps more than I even believed in myself. I would have to be in a room deciding things that didn't just affect me, but others like me. What if for my first decision, I made the wrong call?

"Thank you for thinking me capable, but if you really want to take my mind off it, I'm going to need more than your fingers rubbing away my stress." He half smiled, forcing my thighs open with his knees.

"I thought you'd never ask."

***

The wondrous sights of a new place weren't even enough to distract me from my unsteady nerves. Pulling out my small notebook, I scanned the pages of the information Aranzeiros provided that gave me insight into all his brothers' heritages, abilities, temperaments, and behaviors.

"Can we go over it again?" I asked. Unable to decipher my scribbles the closer we wandered into the city of Nobledane.

"For Goddess' sake, what is there to recap? I've already gone over it with you twice." Aranzeiros snapped. He rubbed his palm along his face like he was tired of this conversation.

"So, then you won't mind going over it a third time?" I asserted. Aranzeiros sighed, probably rethinking kidnapping a mate as inquisitive as me.

"Lianthore is the best at handling the room. He has experience with both fae and humans. He has the tendency to paraphrase the ideas that are met with friction in his own words and be met with praise. The humans trust him a little more because he knows how to speak their language, and that's good because often proposals just need to be introduced in a different way."

He'd mentioned before that Lianthore had a lot of responsibilities being the unofficial liaison for the family, which was why I didn't see him much during the royal tour. But he did send me a load of wedding gifts, including treats and desserts I'd never had the chance to try before.

I made a note next to his description that said "best gift giver ever" before scribbling descriptor tags of how many colors I saw when I glanced into his dancing crimson eyes.

"Okay, let's go over Zaos," I said, seeing his name next on my list.

"He's my brother who always has the most to say; even when he's in agreement with you. As a pastime, he'll disagree with you just to spark a different perspective. He challenges *everyone*. Some may find him headstrong, but truthfully, he is just passionate about his opinions. Try not to get offended if he interrupts you or constantly challenges your words. He will get beside himself because that is in his nature, especially given that you're also human. He's much harder on the human half, queen or not."

Just great! Now I had to worry about looking stupid in front of my own family.

"With all things considered, his interests usually align with the family. And it is a good thing if he's not soft on you. It means he respects you. I suppose next on your list is Ivaran?"

Ironically, outside of his brutish appearance, I remembered little about Ivaran. Of all his brothers he was the one who came around the least and who Aranzeiros only mentioned when it was need-to-know information.

"Ivaran hates for meetings to go long, so he almost always

votes in the majority. You won't have to worry about him, so long as his temper is under control."

"What's that supposed to mean?" An attempt to be nosy.

"Ivaran's Elven appearance is misleading. He presents as gentle, but under extreme stress or anger, he can shift into his Demyn form. He was born with something in the Fae Realm we call the Berserker gene, and that is not something you want to be around unless all six of us are there to contain him. Mostly, these meetings just annoy him."

"What about your youngest brothers?"

"Let's just say when it's time to vote seriously, they're typically on code."

Sadly for me, Aranzeiros didn't elaborate more on the triplets, so I had to trust that with my few encounters with them, they'd be nothing but sweet on me.

With what felt like hours, the carriage stopped in front of what looked like a century-year-old stronghold, something you'd only see in a video game. Its size was nearly as big as Regalhelm, but looked more like a place of worship than a luxurious palace.

The door opened on my side, but under Aranzeiros' advisement, I waited inside until he exited on his side and met me to help me on mine. Without taking more than a few steps, I slammed into a frame so hard and wide, my body felt made of fragile glass.

More surprised than frightened, I looked up and met the gaze of my husband's larger, younger brother. At our wedding, I'd mistaken him for close to 7'0" but seeing him today, I was sure in my estimate of a minimum of 6'8".

His wolf-like stare was like a mood ring, shifting from champagne gold to greenish hazel depending on what kind of mood he was in. Today his eyes were calm, but there was always a sadness to them that took away from his fearsome exterior.

"Sister." He spoke low and caring.

"It's nice to see you again, Ivaran," I replied, admiring the intricate design of his chain-mail armor. He was always dressed like he was ready for battle, carrying two swords crossed in a baldric on his back.

"Ah, you've arrived." Lianthore stormed the front building doors wearing his signature style of Italian-esque suits. Did I miss the memo that we could wear human attire?

"Has your wife been informed on how we planned to—?"

"Informed of what?" Aranzeiros interrupted. "Please fill in the blanks as I am lost."

"Perhaps Zaos lacked the time to fill you in. Ivaran and I have decided to escort the queen to a private hall to ensure she is not harmed on her way to the meeting. Earlier, I received an anonymous threat on the queen's life, so I planted a decoy to measure the danger."

A male fae with pointed ears who didn't look as ethereal as an Elf, approached. His skin melted, conforming to a shape that matched my likeness. A veil covered his face, and if I had to take a guess, he was a shapeshifter.

"When we are sure it's safe, you'll be seated with your husband —" Lianthore started before I interrupted.

"But what about my debut?"

"Paige, darling, there won't be a debut if any harm comes to you," Aranzeiros countered with a caress to the back of my hands. "So long as you're with Lianthore, nothing will start without you."

"And him?" I jutted my chin, gesturing toward Ivaran.

"Well, with Ivaran, no one will think twice about approaching you. Both my brothers have shifter blood. It means their skin is a lot thicker to take a bullet through the chest."

A bullet to the chest? For a damn meeting? I wanted to question why anyone would be so bold, but this was neither the time nor the place. The two had led me to a backdoor that headed to a hallway of rooms and back outside to a hidden drawbridge. After we crossed, they worked together on both sides to close the passageway, where we then wandered in what felt like a keep.

"We apologize for the delay and inconvenience this has caused, Paige. May I call you Paige?" His crimson-eyed brother asked.

"I don't see why not. I mean, what else would you call me?"

"I haven't made as much time to spend with you as my other brothers have, but in time, I hope sister will suffice." He smiled a sinister yet warm smile. Or perhaps I'd only accused it of being sinister because he was the one who reminded me the most of Aranzeiros. They both had the same English-adjacent accent, a clear indication they were raised together.

"To spare you the details of a somewhat strenuous morning, we had reason to believe that someone did not want you to make this council meeting. Now it could just be a petty threat, but since the death of our father, we take even the lightest of pranks seriously," Lianthore explained as he led us to the door that would be our current refuge. The hideout was the size of a show-room, only it was littered with bookcases and strange contraptions.

"I'm still not sure what I should be doing or how long this will take." Ivaran looked to his brother as he took a firm stance by the door.

"Humans always feel the need to be doing something. Relax, My Queen. Council meetings can take as little as a few minutes to several hours. Today will be no different," Lianthore said with a quick scope around the room.

"Well, if we're gonna be here for hours, can we at least not do so in silence?" Because there was absolutely no way I could handle the two of them staring at me without being on the other end of conversation.

"What would you like to discuss?" Lianthore took the lead, and if you didn't specifically direct something toward Ivaran, he didn't speak at all.

"I don't know," I shrugged, letting the questions come to me as soon as they popped into my head. "Aranzeiros never discusses your childhood together. What was it like growing up as siblings?" I asked, hoping that wasn't too invasive.

"As he's likely mentioned, he and I grew up at Regalhelm together. Not having prior knowledge of our other brothers, our father brought them into our lives in stages." He went on to explain that Tarron hadn't always taken the time to claim each son, all for different reasons than the last.

"I can assure you our childhoods were quite boring," Lianthore dismissed. "What's more interesting is when we made our marks in the human world."

It shocked me to learn that Aranzeiros, for all his wealth and privilege, was actually an innovative engineer. I found it hard imagining him drawing up blueprints and building *anything*; the Elf could barely put his own coat on by himself.

Apparently, he had created the first drafts to what we humans now referred to as the revolver, and this was when he was an adolescent. I had to wonder what else he did on in the Human Realm that I didn't know about.

"What do you guys do in a human world?"

"I'd like to say I'm an unofficial brand ambassador, the face, if you will. I consult my brothers about which business ventures will get the most out of their talents and ensure they represent the family in a positive light."

In a brief conversation, I learned he ran all of their damage control and had built most of their strongest political connections. All while being a prince, a duke, a publicist, and spokescreature, all in one. I turned to Ivaran expecting the same enthusiasm, but with one blank stare and shrug to his shoulders, his admittance silenced the room.

"I kill people. Or rather I hunt them. It is under a client's discretion on what I do with the targets once they are...*obtained*," he said with an expressionless face.

"Wow. *Okay*, onto a lighter note." I looked around the room at the collection of odd puzzles and games that were likely brought here to waste time. My eyes caught wind of a human game or two that could be a less awkward way to pass the time.

"Anyone up for a game of Uno?"

***

It took twenty minutes into the second game for everyone to get a feel for the overall rules of how the game was played. There was a general understanding that the person with the first empty hand called themselves the winner, but depending on how and who you played with, Uno had the potential to destroy relationships and draw out sibling rivalries.

The first game was an easy win for me, as most of it had been spent teaching them how to play. But something should have told me the two were competitive. What did the ginger one say to me? *Everything* is a competition with them. There was no doubt in my mind that Lianthore's feeble "allow me to learn by doing" had been an act that I fell for by the fourth play.

We should have discussed some box rules first because Lianthore had every intention of annihilating us once he stumbled on the quickest way to Uno out and call the game. Luckily, Ivaran didn't take losing lightly, so when he drew a custom card he'd been saving for a desperate occasion, I thought for sure that would crumble Lianthore's winning streak.

"Custom card, draw seven. The color is green," Ivaran sneered, confident that he had finally bested his older brother.

"So the color is green, brother?" Lianthore smiled through a calm arrogance.

"That's what I just said," Ivaran flared, with a bang to the table.

"I wanted to ensure I heard you correctly...*as* I reverse back to me," Liam challenged, slapping down a green reverse card.

"Ivaran, draw six." He held up a yellow card, forcing his

brother to draw more cards. Ivaran looked at his hand, snarling, and Lianthore saw this as his chance to ruin him.

"Aww, don't tell you ran out of yellows, baby brother?" he taunted. "I suppose that's reverse back to me." With an expert show of skills, Lianthore forfeited our turns and then had the audacity to make me draw four.

By the end of his spectacle, he had just two cards left, and we had no less than sixteen between the both of us. When he called for reds, Ivaran and I had just about every color *but* red.

"So no reds? *Brilliant.* This is the time where I say Uno, and Uno out," he boasted as he threw down his last cards.

"How about we go again?" Ivaran growled, as he pushed the table halfway across the room and lunged toward a standing Lianthore.

Stepping between them to alleviate the tension, my soul almost left my body, thinking I could be an effective mediator between two rumored beasts.

"I think we should keep it at four, boys. Especially if you want this family to stay together." Before I got the chance to suggest a less stressful game, their younger brother Tavnis interrupted with claims that no threat had been initiated with the decoy.

It was now safe to join everyone in the conference room. Ivaran was still clutching the deck in his hand, squeezing so hard that they weren't even fit to play with anymore.

"*Fine.* But we will finish this again. One day in the future," he huffed as he took my hand and led me back to the entrance. Despite his big, scary frame, he wasn't a drag to be around. So long as you accepted that he wasn't a talker.

On the way back to the main building, Tavnis gave us a rundown on how my body double fared, awaiting Lianthore and Ivaran's absence. The human side of the Council was torn between panic and indifference at the presence of my decoy. The fae half had questioned my political experience, but that was to be expected.

The walk to the conference room was positively ordinary, but the biggest challenge was bending the truth as if I had just gone to the bathroom to powder my nose.

Amidst walking through the circus, I had to pretend that all the faces weren't new to me. Until now, I had mostly really only met fae who resembled humans. Elves, dwarves, gnomes, or any mixture of the three.

Taking in the council members, I had to restrain my need to stare at the female who had fluttering wings and the married Lord and Lady who could pass for a troll and a griffin, respectively. No wonder the human way of classifying race seemed so arbitrary to them.

Speaking of humans, they were full and plenty on their side of the council. I hoped they hadn't seen me as a victim of some sort, but with the lack of small talk, I had to assume they were irritated that the meeting was taking so long or sizing me up now that I was maskless. Aranzeiros made my clueless wandering easier by guiding me to my seat, sparking little suspicion. Once Lianthore entered the room, the meeting commenced surprising me that he spent the first few moments welcoming me as both a new council member and a member of their family.

"Now that we've gotten frivolous matters out of the way," a middle-aged white councilman spoke, clearly annoyed by the time it took to formally introduce me.

"Can we begin with *actual* council concerns?" From first glance, he certainly wasn't an intimidating man, but you could tell that having decades of holding power made him feel like the knower of all things, and the only reason he hadn't interrupted Lianthore was that he knew better when it came to that family. Let's see if that respect bled over to me.

"There's nothing that holds greater importance to the council than welcoming a new member. I understand your realm leaders lack a certain decorum but don't get comfortable," Aranzeiros interjected, his first nature to defend me.

Soon into the discussion, Lianthore went over stats, reminding everyone what they had achieved since the last meeting I hadn't been a part of. It was very much like the times I spent an hour of my day entertaining guests, not having a clue of what was going on. The conversation had taken a dark turn when the last matter he warned should be handled with empathy and nuance.

Lianthore started, presenting a series of slides he prepared on a projector. One was a burned property with "Get off our land" written in spray paint visible amongst the burning flames.

Another photo was of a clear hate crime. A sequence of crime scene photos displaying some poor fae's ears being sliced clean off. The rest of the images were too disturbing to bring up in polite conversations. One of the leading Councilman shrugged, almost as if it wasn't his problem.

"What are we looking at?" Councilman Hamilton questioned.

"What is it that my eyes see, that yours do not?" Zaos broke in, pointing at the images before us. "No sympathy, no shame, not even pity for innocent lives lost."

"Aren't all fae almighty and strong? I hardly see how one Elf who lost a fight constitutes as council concerns."

"It is when the rate of attacks has risen in record numbers. While it is true we are formidable creatures, that does not mean we should overlook their deaths for wanting to assimilate into a new home. Perhaps if it were just a few incidents, we could blame it on a few rotten apples, as you say. But fae businesses in areas with a high fae population are the main ones being targeted. This is no coincidence," Lianthore finished, my mind wandering over the idea of fae having weaknesses. What were they vulnerable to? I'm not sure I even asked.

"With my Intel, I have reason to believe the rising attacks against earthbound fae are because humans are being educated on how to expose us. Which brings the question of where these *people* are sharing this information and how quickly is it traveling?" Lianthore questioned the room with his suspicions.

"I do not need Intel to see what is clearly in front of my eyes. It could be one group, or it could be many groups; what we are facing is homegrown terror. Humans can dress it up and wrap it in a fancy bow, but you cannot convince me that once *more* find out about our existence, the very world we know and love will surely fall," Zaos finished, and for the first time all morning, I was compelled to speak.

"I have some insight on that, but I should probably start out by saying it's going to sound like I'm disagreeing with you," I started, my heart stuttering in my chest when Zaos cut his wild stare at me. Perhaps he hadn't meant to, but he always had this frightening glare that looked like he was minutes from putting his hand around your throat. The deep scar on his face only added to that fact.

"Go on." He gestured to me with his hand.

"In the Human Realm, there was a time people who shared my racial background, chose to pass for something else. Much like you all do with the Veil." I used air quotes for racial background considering all the fae members considered humans, no matter the skin color, all the same race.

"If you could pass for another *race*, there were often privileges and safety that often went with it. If you were found out about or had kids that came out looking like me, some would even murder you for deceiving them, so I get why fae choose to hide from humans. We don't all have good intentions, but history has taught me that you can only survive so long in the dark before your truth comes to light."

"And what would you suggest, my opinionated little bird?" Zaos remarked, testing my conviction.

"Maybe, not hide forever." My voice was small as his cruel blue eyes assessed me. "Would it be so bad to be out in the open? All fae are not going to be universally loved by humans, but that doesn't mean they'll be universally hated, either. Radicalization breeds from fear festering from what we don't understand. Lots of fae already have an investment in the Human Realm. We can only fight fear with community and understanding.

"And why should I expose myself to more humans? Why should we trust anything any human has to say? Once we are public, we welcome more threats and more chances for *our* history to repeat itself," Zaos argued, his electric blue eyes darkening to a deep ocean blue.

"With all due respect, Prince Zaos, the only threat that should concern you is when it's your turn to take a wife. Trust me, your fated mate will be the *only* person you can't handle threatening your life, not some imaginary mob of humans with pitchforks and torches." As someone who had gone through the draining experience of becoming a Faeborne bride, I couldn't imagine how much easier I would have had it, had they had educated me on Elven customs and the way they claimed partners.

If I had had some understanding, it would have been less scary and just maybe, I would have had a smoother transition adjusting to foreign traditions.

The way Zaos' nostrils flared, I expected him to jump across the table and slit my throat. Instead, he burst out laughing, slapping the table as if I said the funniest thing in the world.

"Sister, you are right! The stories the king tells of his conquest. I don't wish that on any fae. Is it true you ran no less than three times? You would think this idiot would have learned his lesson and got creative with his confinement." He laughed, pointing to his eldest brother, who didn't seem amused.

A fae council member countered a good argument, one that Zaos agreed with. That if the Human Realm knew they existed, would it be the end of their proud ways?

"Esterbrooke is a realm that fulfills all its basic needs. No one goes hungry. In all the major capitals creatures have housing, but the same cannot be said about the Human Realm. Every time you give them help, within a few hundred years, they figure out a way to squander our aid. I fear that if Esterbrooke was made public, then we'd just be like any other place. Once they know what we have, it won't be long before we're fighting over our resources, constantly at war. Not to mention when humans wear out their welcome, they do what they always do. And that is, attempt to conquer and destroy the very land they seek support from," Zaos added.

"Look, I'm not denying any of that, but we have to bridge the gap sometime. Pretty soon, all of you will have human wives. Humans are going to make their way here, anyway. What about when you have kids, won't they be half-human? Why not make this a better world for them to all live in? A world where we can put aside our differences. Where we're all equal. A world where we won't regret the decisions we made today out of phobias. It doesn't have to be tomorrow, it just has to be considered."

The room was silent, fear crawling its way into my consciousness until Aranzeiros broke the uncomfortable calm. "I agree with my queen. I too dread the idea of losing our way with the onslaught of humans knowing of our existence. But for centuries, nothing about our world has changed. Convenience is what we chose over progress. My father's choices did not make us better, but weaker. We were once a proud race. Why should we live under falsehoods and secrecy? I long for the day humans celebrate our rites and traditions and in return, we shall learn and celebrate theirs. We are in this together. My wife and I couldn't be any more proof of that. As my queen has mentioned, our heirs will be Halfling, and they'll have to navigate what it means to be both human and Fae."

The more I got everyone talking about it, the more people warmed up to the idea. At least four members were in flat out in opposition, but should we have a preparation period, many were open to the idea.

When it came to calling for a vote for if the world of Fae

would mesh with the world of man, every Faeborne male agreed and voted with me. There even had been enough votes on the human side to make the decision unanimous.

One day in the near future, the Human Realm would learn about the Fae Realm. Now we'd have to decide on a date. Those things took time, and I imagined by the direction of this meeting, it would take months, if not years, to come to a decision.

But that hadn't mattered to me. It was the fact that something I said was deemed important and others had listened. I'd have to pinch my arm to convince myself I wasn't dreaming.

As the meeting concluded and we made our way back to the Citadel's entrance, Zaos stopped me at the top of the staircase. "I want to thank you for challenging me, little bird. Sometimes I see things in such a way, it is difficult to view it through fresh eyes."

"Thank you for supporting me. But I have to ask, *little bird?*" I was learning that all of his brothers were kind in their own way, but he was the only one who'd given me a nickname, and judging by the rundowns my husband was constantly giving me so that I didn't mix his brothers up, Zaos was not the one to be on his bad side. And yet, he'd been nothing but sweet to me.

"Yes, little bird. The queen you're supposed to be is finally coming out of her cage," he said with a round of applause.

Ivaran's hulky build approached me, laying a gentle pat on my shoulders.

"Despite your choice in a husband, you are in the makings of becoming a fine queen," Ivaran smiled warmly. It was a challenge to crane my neck to look at him, but all their compliments made me feel embraced by his family.

"Going somewhere, brother?" Lianthore challenged Ivaran. "Thought I might interest you in a little rematch?" He smiled, tapping his palm with the box of Uno cards, and Ivaran's vicious snarl returned.

"Unfortunately, I am unable. If I wasn't behind on my torture schedule, I would gladly go another round. Paige, do not let my older brother's self-importance bleed over your already arrogant husband," he said, with a point at Aranzeiros.

"When we meet again, you will give me a more in-depth lesson on this...*Uno*." As majestic wings sprouted from his back and spread like shields that went on for miles, his eyes shifting to an angsty gold that was so frightening, it was beastly. Okay, so maybe miles is an embellishment, but how else did you describe a wingspan that massive when you've rarely encountered a creature who *had* wings? The beating of wings flapped violently against the air as, without even a goodbye, he made his departure.

"Okay, why didn't anyone tell me he could do that?" It seemed like needed to know information.

"My light, with Ivaran, it's best to learn about him in stages. He is not quick to share. Not even with his brothers."

CHAPTER TWENTY-FIVE

Paige

Today had been the first real day it sunk in that I was the queen of a kingdom. Sitting in a meeting with twenty-odd some people making decisions about our two worlds finally made all this shit real. Lying in bed, the king's powerful arms comforted me and with a run of his fingers, he raked my curls, easing my anxiety from today's events.

"Mmm," he murmured, planting a kiss on my forehead.

"You look troubled, my love. Trouble is not something I like to bring to bed unless it's in the form of constraints," he joked, which only worsened my anxiety considering it was completely off-subject.

"I don't know. Sitting in that room making decisions for people and fae I don't even know. Maybe I'm having second thoughts about integrating. I mean, if you wanted to do it, the Fae Realm would have done it already. Are you sure you support me in going public?" He adjusted on his side, forcing me to sit up from the comforting spot on his hard chest.

"My darling Paige. I do not wish to lie to you. Even I am unsure if I'm completely in favor of. There is a long list of benefits, but there are also an even longer list of disadvantages. This was the part of the job my father didn't prepare me for, but as wise as my father was, he like rulers before for him wanted no change. No progression. He was just comfortable doing things the way they've always been done. I promised myself I would be different. The world knowing what we are, who we are, could be the dawn of a new era."

Damn, he was just born for this. He made things sound so simple, and easy. And here I was suggesting things like I've been living here my whole life. Seeing all those hate crimes against fae, what if things got worst once we integrated? All these wrongdoings were rising with just a *small* population aware of fae. I would hate to be the reason someone buried their child.

"I know, but," I started, a finger pressing to my lips to silence me.

"That's enough with the buts. As a queen, learn how to follow through with your decisions. Yes, you will change your mind but it's best when you feel strongly about something to just own it. No uncertainties," he said, as I wrestled with the sheets in frustration.

"Ugh, I guess I have to get better at that. You and your brothers look so comfortable holding power, which is wild because any time I'm around them it's nothing but fun and games until I'm spilling soda out my nose." His left brow cocked, his mouth twisting into a mask of confusion.

"You spill soda out of your nose?" I rolled my eyes. Just once, I'd *love* it if he would just break down the expression. But then again, he did look rather cute deciphering my words.

"My King, it's just an expression. It means something is funny, like *really* funny."

"But you understand my confusion, do you not?" With a palm to his face, I pushed him back, sending his head into a pillow. With a raging need to avenge, he pulled me on top of him before flipping me over on my back with almost no effort.

"You will pay for that with punishing thrusts and kisses to the neck," he flirted, but I wasn't done having this conversation. When he reached for the ribbon to loosen my chemise, I grabbed his hand, holding it there as another look of confusion danced across his Elven features.

"I just want to be good at this, baby. I want you to be proud of me," I said, as he rolled off me and dusted a loose curl that fell into my eyes.

"Paige, every time you challenge me, I am proud of you. There would be no fun in this union if you were one hundred percent obedient and agreed with me on everything. That is a dictatorship, not a marriage. So it takes a powerful queen to find the courage to challenge her husband. Besides, it was touching to hear you speak of the future. Paving a different path for our children. As you said during your debut, the future heirs of Esterbrooke will be half of you, something that made my support of your proposal easier. I want our children to know that side of them. Heritage, lineage, race, be it fae or human. All these things are important to both of us. What kind of father would I be if I denied our children that?" I stared at him, speechless. The Elf went from hating humans to embracing that our kids would be half. All because he dared to love one.

"I didn't know that mattered to you. Not judging, but you always lead with your Elven heritage and customs. Sometimes I have to remind myself that both your parents aren't Elven."

In Esterbrooke, Elves were the dominating class. I didn't have to visit every corner of the realm to see that, but my king usually spared the details of what it was like to be half Dark Star Nymph. His mother, like all his predecessors, was always a sensitive subject.

"King Tarron's choice was to raise me as an Elf. I present as Elven so I understand how it can appear that I know nothing about what it's like to be a Dark Star Nymph." With a flick of his fingers, he conjured a pulsing black shadow, its energy floating and breathing like a living entity.

"Every time I channel the darkness," he started, the shadow shifting into a myriad of different shapes at his control. "Every time I bend the shadows, I can feel her presence inside me. It's the only way I've ever felt connected to her. My wish is that our children don't need to inherit abilities to feel bonded to us. And even after we're gone, I want them to be proud of everything they are."

His honest words had made me not only proud to pass on his genes but grateful our kids would have the parents we never had. The only thing that bothered me, was that I would pass first, and then there would be decades, perhaps even centuries, where our kids would be without a mother.

"There's this question I've been meaning to ask for a while. I know you're three hundred, or whatever. So obviously, you're granted the time I won't have. Does being here in the Fae Realm affect my age cycle? I don't know how to explain it, but ever since I got here, I feel different. Changed. Does that mean something is happening to me?" Uncertainty replaced his otherwise smothering look.

"Paige, my light, even I am not immortal. Every time you take me inside of you, you become further bound to the realm of the fae. Giving birth will only affect your life cycle more, as a fae born child bonds its life force with yours. You'll be more than human, but not quite fae. I assure you, you will probably outlive me." He smiled, a loving warmth spreading to his eyes.

I loved it when he talked like this. About us. About the future. I was happy to learn we'd have more than a human lifespan to spend together. In such a short time, he had become my every-thing, my entire world. I only wanted time to be on our side.

My thoughts spiraled at the thought of having gifted and magical children. Would they shock me when I breastfed them? Would I have to have a demanding exercise regimen just to be able to catch up with them? *Chile*, the things I had to ask myself now were just wild. Five months ago, I was not wondering if I'd be raising the damn Incredibles.

"Have you ever known Halflings to develop magic or gifts like yours?"

"You are rather inquisitive tonight. Why all these questions?" he asked, running his large, icy hands along the length of my thigh.

When he touched me like that, things escalated from zero to a hundred, but I was staying firm. To hell that he was looking at me with those devilishly charming black eyes and that smart smirk that drove me mad. There was still so much to know.

"Especially when I'd rather be between your legs and making you feel *amazing*," he teased as I pushed his hand away to make my message loud and clear.

"*Goddess*, you win. Clearly, you want me to indulge you," he said with a roll of his eyes.

"All fae have a connection to magic, be them native or foreign. But if I recall the stats, very few develop abilities if they're not raised on this mystic land. How would they? No one is nurturing their talents. Most Halflings have about a forty percent chance of inheriting the ability to exude magic. The forty percent that do, are fortunate. All the power, without any of the drawbacks." Did he just say drawbacks?

"What's the drawback to being supernatural?" I asked, in a sarcastic, almost jovial tone. A tense silence enveloped the room as the amusement died from his eyes.

"There are many drawbacks to being fae," he voiced with an eerie calmness. Perhaps he didn't trust me with that, which was unfortunate because I trusted him with everything. My happiness, my life, my heart, and my submission. What more did I have to do for him to give himself to me completely?

"Aranzeiros, I would never bring harm to you, or anyone, for that matter. It just stings because you have me completely. Sometimes I sense you don't trust me, or you think I'd use it against you if I knew all your vulnerabilities."

"Iron," he interrupted, my eyes narrowing and my body stiffening with shock. "Iron is the one thing that can harm fae. There had been iron shards left behind in a deemed accident that killed my father. You asked what makes us different from a Halfling, someone both fae and human? It is the fact that they do not share the same affliction that stole my father's life. I apologize if this conversation has taken an unexpected turn." He grimaced, but I was relieved.

He had trusted me, trusted me with information that was wise to keep to one's self. He brushed another stray curl out of my face, inching closer to trace the soft hair on my arms.

"Why the sudden interest in what makes me vulnerable? Planning your escape route?" he asked in a morbid, almost deprecating tone.

"The fact that you can ask that proves that you know *nothing* about the opposite sex. Baby, I couldn't quit you if I tried. I lose sleep over the fact that I didn't meet you younger. Do you know how much I've thought about the possibility of you taking another bride if I die before you?" He sat up taking my face into his hands, his dark gaze surveying my face.

"I would die before I took another wife. No one, and I mean *no one* could ever replace the joy, the love, and the infinite need I have for you. If anything should take you away from me, I would die with you. Because a world without you, is a world without love."

Tears welled up in my eyes as I swallowed hard and bit back sobs. Tears of joy. Aranzeiros never failed to let me know how special I was and how empty my relationships were before him, both romantic and familial.

I loved the way he loved me and loved being with someone who showed me what true devotion looked like. Before I knew it, hot tears rained down my cheeks, as he consoled me, wondering what he could do to stop the tears, even if they were tears of joy.

"There's actually something that would cheer me up. Everything here, everything with you is perfect. But there are some things I can't help but miss about my old home. When I first moved to New York, I learned there was this whole other world out there. I'd just love to spend a few days out there, weeks if we can. I know we have responsibilities and obligations but it would mean the world to me if I got to see my old home one last time." With a curt nod, he leaned in and kissed my lips, savoring every second.

"You are my queen, if a trip back home is what you *truly* desire, you shall have it. I meant it when I said I would give you the world, and I am an Elf of my word," he said, brushing my thick hair back as he leaned in to recapture my lips to his. This time, he was much more demanding, and made it far easier to lose myself with. When he pulled away, my lips spread into a challenging grin.

"Even if I plan to run?" I teased, laying another light kiss on his lips.

"Silly human, when will you learn there is no running for me? I will always find you and punish you like the cock whore that you are." I laughed.

"More *incentive* for me to run."

CHAPTER TWENTY-SIX

Paige

Just when I'd spent an hour organizing all the clothes I was bringing with me, a pesky tall Elf made himself comfortable on my neatly folded pile, his right brow cocking in a state of confusion.

"Are you packing?" he asked in his posh calmness, tossing a scarf aside that was caught underneath his elbow.

"Yes, Aranzeiros, I'm packing. That's what normal people do when they're about to go on a short trip. They pack." His upper lip curled up as he shook his head.

"How many times must I remind you? You have a montage of chambermaids that are more than happy to assist you with trip preparation. I had planned to retrieve you so that we may have a quick walk around the palace and unveil a belated wedding gift. But here you are..." He lifted a small plastic bag home to a half dozen of my travel-size toiletries.

"In your room... *packing*." The last word left his lips like a swear. Sure, it was nice to get the queen treatment most times, but there was a joy that came when you readied yourself for a long getaway. A sense of freedom of not knowing what you'll do or see once you got there. That's what it felt like to move from my hometown, and to maintain just some bit of normalcy. Packing was just one small way I did that.

"You know, babe, there's nothing wrong with packing your own clothes sometimes," I said, as I pushed his head backward in the space between his brows. "Besides where I'm from, it's not lady-like to let someone handle all of your racy get-ups and naughty sex toys."

I'd been thinking about the whole anal sex idea since our kinky king play, and while it was terrifying stepping outside my comfort zone, I was also equally curious.

He'd be happy to learn my chambermaids did help me with one thing. A necessary trip to the Human Realm to grab a few generous bottles of lube and ass plugs to get me comfortable with the idea of anal sex. There was always something about vacations that put you in a space to try something new. I just hoped that I wouldn't chicken out at the last minute.

"Sex toys, you say? Perhaps I shall take a look to determine what sort of trip you believe this will be," he said, as he leaned up and rummaged through my suitcase, only to be met with a death slap to the hand. Nosy ass.

"No, this is one of those things you're going to have to wait to see." His onyx eyes widened, his lips curving into something between a smile and a smirk.

"You would dare deny your king?"

"When he's being a nuisance, yes," I said, folding the last shirt and pair of jeans as I laid it on top, before zipping it up and anchoring it to the floor.

He pulled me by the waist, securing me between his legs, and eased in for a patient kiss. From the days leading up to his promise, things had been relatively perfect. *He* was perfect. Deepening the kiss, my fingers traced the points of his foreign-shaped ears. If someone asked me a month ago if I could ever be a big ears kind of gal, I would have laughed, and told you no. But now? I thought it was cute; a sort of odd quirk that grows on you.

"Well, you certainly look the part of promenading on a fall afternoon."

I pulled on his collar, admiring him in his designer custom-fit peacoat, darker gray slacks, and light brown dress shoes. A long scarf draped along his neck and chest in a rich shade of green tartan.

"This feels like an odd choice for you," I said, taking each side of the scarf, as I wrapped it around my hands.

"It is, but every once in a while, I find myself desperate for a splash of color, and this scarf? Well, my brother made it for me." I put my guess on Theoden since he was always rocking his tartan like a badge of honor.

Tapping his pointed ears, I teased him about how it was a wonder how I could miss something like that. The Veil, something I hadn't completely understood yet, was the reason why fae could float back and forth unnoticed between realms. When we first met, all I saw was a man. The deeper we found ourselves in Esterbrooke, the more his true self was revealed to me. How can something be powerful enough to shield you from a neighboring realm?

"What powers the Veil?" I asked, only for him to shrug it off as if it was common knowledge.

"Just magic, I suppose."

"Just magic?" I questioned. "It must be some powerful magic if it protects you from people seeing what you are." He brushed loose curls away from my face, his expression indifferent.

"Not just that, portals, too. Only those who are looking know where to find them. There are some you can't fool, and that is usually those with fae ancestry. But if you have no knowledge of our world, often they refuse to believe what they're seeing. You'll probably view your world with new eyes since you accepted the magic inside of you," he admitted, which had me wondering if New York City had its own Diagon Alley.

I raked my fingers through his soft, long strands, his dark, sparkling gaze observing me in wonder. It was hard to believe that I once feared him. Now it was becoming a punishment to even be away from him.

"I can't wait to show you all the little nooks and crannies of the city. I know you're all fancy-schmancy, but we're not leaving until you experience the real New York and not just the one you see from your five-star hotel rooms." He jerked me closer, his large hands nestling firmly against my backside.

"But we will be staying in one of those five-star hotels, correct?" Rolling my eyes, I backed away, putting my hands on my hips.

"You, My King, are an absolute snob. You're lucky you're so handsome," I said, tapping a finger on the tip of his nose.

"Well, I'm entertaining your earthly vices. The least you can promise are accommodations with a skyline view, and room service that mirrors the palace."

***

Portal travel had rivaled the speed of any subway in the city. What would have taken a four-hour car ride in the Human Realm, took just a forty-minute carriage ride once we hit the Bucham access point.

My husband was right. Nothing about my world looked the same to me. My sight had awakened to hidden portals, well-kept refuges, and fae, so much damn fae. Once you had a glimpse of another world, it was amazing how many people you encountered that were part or full fae.

There had been those I encountered in the past, taken aback by their beauty, and envious of the way people flocked to them.

All this time, they could have just been fae amongst humans, having that unfair advantage of etherealness.

Today's agenda was to venture around Prospect Park, where they hosted a smorgasbord of food vendors and, as luck would have it, live entertainment from a legion of local bands. In my small town, you'd be lucky if you had anything more to choose from than diners, ribs spots, and the occasional pizza restaurant, but even *that* wasn't holding a torch to New York-style pizza. I used to come here every Saturday, hopping from truck to truck to discover something new.

"Okay, so preface, you haven't eaten good New York food unless you had a chance to try street food," I said, our arms interlocked, as he turned to give me his signature narrowed eyes.

"Okay, before you can make that look, expand your horizons and try something. There's literally every culture of food you can choose from, and we're not leaving until you've tried at least three. *Although*, I do think you'll want more. A lot of these vendors are just *that* good."

From the moment I discovered this place, I made it my mission to try a new truck every visit. So far, I was at a dozen, and that hadn't even put a dent in all the tasty places to choose from.

"I have to say, I don't think I've ever seen anyone this happy to try the food before," he chastised.

"Oh, just *try* to act excited to be here with me." He laughed, but it was a rude laugh. One that warned me something cheeky was approaching.

"You mean lie?"

"No, I mean pretend to take another interest in something your queen enjoys. Like the way I do when I'm doing all that new-to-me royal stuff. To anyone, and I mean *anyone* else, this would be fun. Don't you like having fun?"

"We've already established that you and I have our own definitions of what's considered *fun*. My brand of fun involves your bouncing bosom as you ride me at high speed," he joked.

I rolled my eyes, but secretly loved when he said things like that. No one had ever desired me the way my husband did, so it was nice being seen as not just a woman, but a sexual creature.

Making our way through the thick crowd of people, I motioned him over to a specialty ice cream stand, the first and only kind I indulged in when I moved to New York City.

"Oh, let's get some ice cream! Do you want it in a cup or a cone?" His dark eyebrows squeezed together, signaling his confusion.

"A cone?"

"A waffle cone," I elaborated. "It's pretty much just sugar, flour, butter, milk, and eggs molded into a cone that has the look of a waffle. Have you never tried ice cream in a cone before?"

"I'll do you one better. I've never had ice cream before," he said, with a casual laugh. With all his wealth, privilege, resources, and power, the fact that he had never had ice cream was a shame in itself.

Here I was thinking I had so much to learn from him. Turns out he had plenty to learn from me. I turned to the smiling merchant behind the coolers that separated us, as a flash of familiarity reached her eyes.

"Haven't seen you in a while. Thought maybe you got kidnapped or something," she joked. *If only she knew.*

"You know what? I recently got married and have been away for a bit. But it's great being back. You're never going to believe this," I said, with a fan of my hand.

"But my husband here has never had ice cream. What is the *one* flavor that can turn a non-believer into a returning customer?" Her hazel eyes widened before pointing to a picture of their coveted bestseller.

"That would be our Ursula, the sea witch. It's made with our custom blend of ube ice cream, homemade gummy tentacles and topped off with a golden shortbread seashell cookie." Ugh, that sounded *amazing*, but I didn't know when we'd come back here again, so I got my go-to and opted for the crowd favorite for the hubby.

Mine was the Cookie Monster. A bright blue ice cream with rich vanilla flavor topped with bite-sized chocolate chip cookies. With skilled quickness, she handed me mine, while a second counterperson worked on his.

The first bite was always the best. Creamy, satisfying, and rich with every morsel. When the counter person handed Aranzeiros his cone, his dark eyes studied it in brief wonder.

"I feel as though this is one of those human things that will continue to baffle me. A purple frozen treat." I shrugged, devouring another bite of my bright blue ice cream.

"Well, Ursula, the sea witch is purple."

"Clearly, I see that," he said, once again examining his cone.

"No, I mean she's a character. A sea witch."

"*You have sea witches in the Human Realm?*" Times like this, I felt like slapping my forehead. I had already adjusted to his other-worldliness, but I hadn't prepared myself with how difficult it'd be explaining him to others.

"Could I trouble you for a spoon?" he asked the vendor, forcing me to step in and explain his weird behavior.

"*No*, you may not have a spoon," I scolded, as I turned to the counter lady, who by now was faking a smile.

"I have to apologize for my husband. You see, he's from one of those aristocratic families from the British Isles who don't eat *anything* without the right fork and spoon," I said, pulling his free hand away from the stand to let the people behind us place their orders.

"What? Do I just bite into it?" he asked, making me grimace.

"That would be the plan before it melts, baby." Bringing the cone to his lips, he took a hefty portion into his mouth, his left eye squinting as if he was undecided. He made a little *hmph* sound, the flavor beginning to sink in, as he released a gluttonous moan.

"It is so decadent. Rich in cream, and starchy like a root of some sort."

He took another hungry bite, a gummy-shaped tentacle disappearing between his sexy lips. Before I knew it, he was wolfing the remainder of it, leaving nothing but that paper behind with the vendor's logo.

"That is something our staff should learn how to make. Perhaps when we go public, I shall see if they're open to a position at the palace." This time, I *did* press my palm to my forehead. He was so used to having everything he wanted at his convenience, but some things were better in small doses.

"No, Aranzeiros, *no*! Things like this, I don't want twenty-four-seven access to. You enjoy them because they're *not* an everyday thing. That's what makes it special." He pulled me in for a hug, his long arms wrapping possessively around my waist.

"Now that is a lie. I can indulge in you every day and never grow tired." He leaned in for a kiss, our lips a blend of sugar and sweetness. I held up the remainder of my cone to his mouth as he took a hefty bite of mine, as well as half the cone that made it stable.

"Look what you did! Now I have to slurp it out. That's the last time I let you try anything of mine again." After I finished my ice cream, we walked around debating which stands we'd try.

My sights were set on this NOLA-inspired truck I'd never tried since their line was always long and curving. We had time and decided that today was worth the wait. He instead opted for a vegetarian truck because they were one of the few vendors giving out utensils. We sat on the grass and enjoyed some live music as the afternoon escaped us. At the strike of seven, we both agreed it was time to head back to our hotel room and turn in.

"I feel like we should take the subway home. I mean, that's what real New Yorkers do." Under his breath, he laughed.

"Well, it's a good thing we're not real New Yorkers. Is it not enough for us to have a wonderful day together? Why tarnish it by exposing ourselves to filthy means of public transportation? Besides, our driver is nearby and my only wish is that my queen is well rested."

Not him trying to make it seem like it was for my benefit! Not wanting to argue, I accepted his offer, but there was no way we were going this whole trip without riding on one. One way or another, I was getting him on a subway, even if I had the streak naked to do it.

CHAPTER TWENTY-SEVEN

Paige

I was going to have to find a muzzle for this Elf. With the night I planned, I was more than in the mood to spend the whole night fucking, but shower time was supposed to be for just that, *showering*.

Especially since these hotel showers were a fourth of the size we had at the Regalhelm. With my husband taking up nearly half of the water, whatever remained for me was in the form of his restless hands on my body.

"Okay, it's not like I'm not loving the attention, but we need to switch places so that I can actually feel clean," I complained and without protests, Aranzeiros lifted me and turned me to face the water.

Soap in his hands, he caressed my shoulders, easing down in circular motions until he reached my breasts. He *always* lingered on my breasts.

"I don't see why you're so obsessed with being clean. I'm only going to spend the night making you a mess again," he confessed, with a kiss to my earlobe.

"I don't see wearing this, either," he remarked in regard to my shower cap. "I've never seen you wear one at home." He didn't understand that at home I didn't mind getting my hair wet, because there, I always had attendants ready to help me to untangle it and prepare me for the next day. I wasn't getting my hair wet for *anyone*. Not even my dutiful King.

"If I don't, my hair will transform into one giant frizz ball. Something you know all too well," I flirted. He bent down to scrub my thighs and legs, being gentle with my delicate privates. He always insisted on washing me, and I let him because of how much care he put into it. He stood to his full height and reached for a bottle of my favorite face wash, squirting a good amount in his hand as he gingerly lathered my face.

"You know, I rather like your hair," he started, his eyes reduced to a squint. "Am I mistaken that you've referred to it once as *poofy?*" he asked, the last word dragging.

I nodded, and he adjusted the shower cap higher to make sure he got my entire face. "But it feels like a slur and as you know, there isn't a thing I would change about you, especially not your beautiful hair."

As we finished washing up, we made our way back to the bed in a kissing frenzy that left both our towels in the middle of the floor. Forgetting I had my shower cap on, I inched away from him, guiding him to the mattress in one gentle push.

"My goddess, you're a tease tonight," he said, licking his lips, as he reached for my wrist, unsuccessfully.

"I swear I'm not being a tease. I just wanted to separate my hair. You know, since you love it so much," I mimicked.

"While you wait for me, why don't you check out what goodies I packed by your elbow?" I stood in front of the mirror, unraveling the eight twists I put in my hair to reflect my signature style.

"Is this for what I think it is?" he asked as I met him back on the bed, his big cock already growing to a steel-like hardness. He held a bottle of lube in his hand, squirting a decent amount that he massaged between his fingers.

"If what you think it's for is what we discussed might happen with the right stuff," I said with a confidence I didn't have. "Featuring a different hole?" singsonging the rest in a teasing manner.

From all the horror stories I heard of it hurting, there was still that hesitation. But I trusted that Aranzeiros would never hurt me, and I wanted to be his in every single way.

"Are you certain you want to? I know it would be your first time. I thought I might have time well in advance to prepare for it, and I wanted to make it special," he said, his dark eyes growing full and wide with the innocence of a puppy.

Every day with him was growing to be more and more special to me. I didn't need a bed full of roses or custom-brewed champagne. I just needed him.

"Baby, the truth is, everything I experience with you is going to be a first for me. Not every moment will be planned out like a royal event. There are going to be times when I just want you, even if I'm nervous about it. You've lived such a long life, so preparing and planning is just your every day. Even if I never make your lists of firsts. Sexually, mentally, physically, and emotionally. I want to know I am enough."

He pulled me onto his lap, his thick length pressing up against my stomach, as his fingers gathered the hair at the nape of my neck. His lips, soft and gentle, met mine in a patient kiss.

"You were the first to consume my thoughts. The first woman to ever imprison my beating heart," he said, reaching in for another small kiss.

"And you are the first I've ever declared my love to. There is no need to harbor insecurities about whether you are experienced enough. Whether you are regal enough, or whether you are enough. You are...enough."

In an instant, he had me on my back, pushing all the contents of the bag aside as he took my hardened nipple into his mouth.

He coaxed me onto my side, bracing myself for the unexpected pain of his cock entering me; instead, he took his time tracing his masculine hands down the side of my body, taunting me with gentle to rough kisses.

"Your body is absolute perfection. Your curves are nothing short of a masterpiece. I know you didn't think that I would go straight into it without giving you what you need first—what I need. I want you a fucking mess before I go anywhere near your arse, and only then will I give you what you seek of me," he said in a soft whisper that sent haunting chills up my spine.

Parting my legs, he teased and worked my folds in a pool of my wetness, stroking me until I was backing into his crotch, begging him to fuck me. Anytime this Elf touched me, I felt desperate and needy, craving any pleasure he allowed me to have. His problems, my problems, nothing else mattered in the moment our bodies aligned. Be it kissing, sucking, fucking, or touching, desire was our only concern in these moments.

"Your cunt is so fucking wet for me, Paige. Why are you so wet, My Queen?" he asked, his lips searing a path down my neck to my shoulders in kisses.

His soft lips rendered my mind senseless, his fingers working my pussy with true mastery as my breath quickened, a signal of my incoming arrival.

"Not so fast. My little cock whore. That's not the way we're allowed to come, don't you remember?" he said, continuing to stroke me. Continuing to tease me.

"Answer me when I ask you a question," he demanded, forcing my chin to meet his mouth in a deep, ravenous exchange of lips.

"Why are you so wet, My Queen?" Failing to stop, like he wanted me to disobey him on purpose.

"Because my king demands it," I said, through a strained, howling moan. "I am to never hold back in my king's presence. I am to be accommodating to my king as he sees fit. And I am to be wet and ready at my king's pleasure," I recited his playtime rules.

By now, he was using his whole hand to use me, switching between stroking and coaxing thrusts inside my pussy. If he didn't want me to come, it was too late. I was already on my way.

"Oh fuck, baby. I'm gonna come," I announced, as I rose to meet his fingers in a war of uncontrolled passion. My breath came in long, shivering moans as the force of the first orgasm ripped through me, his arousal-coated fingers meeting my mouth with an order to lick them clean. I didn't mind; he taught me how to love my taste, and to never be ashamed of how wet he made me.

"You know what that tastes like" his voice dropped to a whisper.

"A filthy whore who likes being a toy for her king?" he taunted, sticking his fingers deep enough to touch the back of my throat, forcing me to cough and tears to well from my eyes.

"What do you think? Do you reckon I should just see for myself?" he challenged, my clit still throbbing from the last orgasm. I could handle it. I just needed more time.

"My King, if I could just have a few more minutes to come down," I started, but there was no denying him, not when carnal mischief was at play.

"My Queen, we've spoken of this. Hungry cock whores don't receive intermissions. The gracious side of me was going to give you the option, on your back, or on all fours. But since you stand to question me, it will be King's choice. On all fours!"

With a tuck of my lip, I submitted, propping myself up on my knees and elbows, as my backside was met with a hard slap.

"Good girl," he praised, a lost sense awakening as the craving to be his plaything resonated deep inside me. His palms glided over my behind, the soft caress of his hands proof that he knew how to handle me.

Wap. Another sting to my ass had me flinching and curling my toes. A third had me drenched, and willing all over again. Relief set in when I felt his tongue devouring every drop of my pleasure, sucking and nuzzling his entire face between my legs from behind.

"You taste so much better when you're wet, my love. *So much fucking better*," he confessed between licks, swirls, and flicks to my swollen nub.

Determined strokes ran up and down my pussy, stripping me of any sanity. In a shocking turn of events, he ran his tongue along my back hole, coating it in slickness that was followed by a finger.

Away he went as his tongue traveled back to my clit, back to letting me ride his face, back to me trembling by way of his enthusiastic mouth lapping me up, until once again, I was a puddled mess, this time over his face and tongue.

Nestling up behind me, he took my thick hair into his fists, sweeping it off my neck as he brushed his lips across my shoulders. His kisses were tender, eager, and often overpowering. I shivered from the heat of his male power and his lips were soaring me to new heights. Be it filthy words, or savage kisses, I was enslaved to his power over me.

"Are you ready for more, My Queen?" he asked in a low growl, the joy of anticipation leaving my lips in a simple pant.

"Yes, My King." In a smooth, gentle motion, he eased me onto my back and reached for the lubricant we pushed to the edge of the bed.

His eyes raking boldly over me, he ran a generous mound of liquid along his length, leaving no area unsaturated. Squirting another dollop across his fingertips, he met my puckered ass, massaging, caressing, and even testing a finger inside me to determine if he needed more. Thankfully, he did not.

With a careful, relaxed thrust, I gasped, his invading thickness inching inside me.

"Uhhhh," he groaned, as he took my feet into his hands, and guided himself further into my tight depths.

"Fuck, Paige. You were right. It feels so much better this way. So smooth, so tight. Please tell me this isn't too much for you."

Personally, I wasn't sure what I was feeling. On one hand, I was shocked when he was able to work his way all the way inside. With regular sex, there was room to breathe, room to move, and time to distinguish between pleasure and pain. But with his cock easing further up, there was nowhere to run. I was at his mercy.

"You're so deep inside me, baby. I don't know what to feel."

"Talk to me, Paige. I don't want to hurt you."

"Maybe it would help if you kiss me," I cooed, as he lowered his mouth to mine, and I succumbed to the forceful domination of his lips.

His mouth was a surge of energy, a much-needed breath of fresh air after days of being stuck inside. As his dark gaze stared longingly into mine, I tasted his pleasure, I sensed his vulnerability and I yearned for his love. His love that was only reserved for me.

"Touch yourself," he ordered, raising his mouth from mine. His onyx eyes sent a deep blaze through my senses. "I want to see you touch yourself while I fuck your tight arse," he demanded, and with a sense of urgency, I followed his command.

With each passing second, what felt like pain was finally seething into pleasure. I was stretched, filled by his pulsating faehood, as I rubbed my pussy to uncomfortable wetness. His dick in my ass in combination with reckless stimulation, I couldn't believe it. I was actually about to come again.

"You look so filthy with my cock up your arse. A filthy, dirty whore that loves getting fucked," he taunted, which only made me wetter, and more desperate to give in to my own release.

Taking my feet into his hands, he spread my legs wide, bringing my ankles to his lips to kiss, and graduating to my sucking my sensitive toes. A sharp gasp escaped my lips as the sensation grew, and I was ashamed to say I had reached my limit.

"Oh fuck, Aranzeiros, please! I can't take it," I laughed, a devilish smile forming on his face at his torture.

"What's wrong? My little cock slut can take my cock in her

arse, but not her toes in my mouth? Perhaps we need to work on that," he teased, planting one last kiss on the soul of my foot.

"Too...much...sensation...at...once," I whimpered. "I just want to come," I said, pleading, to which he then proceeded to grip my thighs and lift my bum to drive deeper inside me. I felt every ridge, every vein, and every curve of his maleness to the point where I wanted to explode.

"Don't hold back. I want you to come hard while I fuck your tight, little arse. Can you do that for me, My Queen?" Hearing his desperate moans for me was my last line of defense in a useless battle for self-control.

With one final plunge, my orgasm raced through me, rivaling the force and speed of a shooting star. As I eyed him through tear-tipped lashes, he exhaled a breathy moan, his eyes shut as his body quivered in pure ecstasy.

Slowly his mouth descended to meet mine, his kisses pushing all else from my wandering mind. He was going to be the death of me. Judging by his next words, I wasn't alone.

"It's not about want anymore. You, Paige, are my one true weakness. It runs deeper than love. I need you, like lungs breathe air."

We sat there still, mouths meshing with an intensity that had me feeling as if he'd suggest another round. Relief set in as he eased out of me, offering to clean me up with a warm washcloth and a clean towel.

After that little session, I could have slept all night. He finished up, helping me twist my hair into twists, and even offered to help me tie on my scarf. After three unsuccessful tries, the fourth we settled for a simple pineapple, as he comforted me with a gentle caress on my cheek.

"It is all right if you don't yet share this sentiment. I know for you it takes time, but for me, a creature burdened with no free will, I always want you to know how I feel about you."

"I do love you," I admitted, a heavy weight lifting for thinking I could ever not love him.

He leaned in to kiss my forehead, the sudden ringing from his cell phone fading to a whisper as I surrendered to exhaustion. By the second ring, he answered, going back and forth with what sounded like an urgent matter.

"Can't it wait until the morning?" he insisted. "Fine, I'll be there as soon as I can. But this had better be more than just a briefing."

He disconnected the phone call, getting up as he stormed to the room's closet. In the short time, I must have nodded off, because when he returned, he was fully dressed and on his way out.

"Mmm, baby, are you going somewhere?" His gentle hand slid across my bare shoulders, leaving a kiss in its place as he stood up for a final time.

"Yes, my light. There's just something I have to handle for work. I promise to return before you even miss me."

"But Aranzeiros," I yawned, losing the battle to stay awake, as he slipped out without another word.

CHAPTER TWENTY-EIGHT

Aranzeiros

Since I'd become king, there had been no organization my brother Lianthore couldn't infiltrate, always managing to make a few connections with higher-level agents to feed us information. That's where the League came in.

Much like the FBI or CIA, The League was a branch of intelligence compromised solely by the selected few who'd been entrusted with the knowledge of the Fae Realm.

When I received a call in the middle of the night, it disrupted my comfortable cuddle time with Paige, as Lianthore summoned me for an impromptu briefing.

With what happened to my father, my brothers and I struck a deal with the League. We were to be informed of any high-level threats in exchange for lobbying for their interests to the human council. I wouldn't call them my allies, but its leader and Lianthore went back far beyond my time stepping foot into the Human Realm.

If he trusted them, I had little reason not to trust them, too. The League stayed neutral; they weren't more for one side or the other but it didn't hurt to have the biggest pockets, as, with the right price tag, there was no limit to what they could dig up.

It must have been important. It was my first-holiday excursion, and I was missing valuable time with my wife. This better be worth it.

Upon entering the high-security building, both my detail and I headed down the corridor, as we reached an elevator that led us ten floors below the surface. This far down, outside technology was a challenge to hijack, making it the perfect stronghold to store classified information shared through the alliance of humans and fae.

Under my advisement, my detail safeguarded the doors, assuring no one without clearance could enter. With the presence of Lianthore's lead contact in attendance, I began to worry that this wouldn't be a routine gathering.

"Brother." Lianthore gained his footing to greet me, wearing a grimace that weighed down his features, making him appear especially draconian. "Thank you for coming. It pains me to have to bring such bad news while you are enjoying your trip."

As I gathered my brother into an embrace, assuring him no apology was necessary, he insisted I would need to be sitting for this, as I followed him to the far end of the conference table, second closest to the nearby projector.

Melting into the recline of the office chair, without delay, Lianthore slid a stack of documents in my direction. Upon further inspection, flipping through its contents, the information meant little to me. "You will have to forgive me, Brother. Tell me what I'm looking at."

As Lianthore came to a stand, he operated the remote control, and all the information from the folder came into view on the projector. "Across many regions, there have been surges of violent attacks against those of fae ancestry."

He clicked through images, and I feared that if this became a more frequent thing, fae losses and suffering would become desensitized to me. "Part fae, half-fae. Maybe even those who are unaware of their lineage. But what's especially concerning, are the pure fae casualties. We have all been made aware of the isolated attacks from our last briefing at the council meeting. Decades ago, you'd be surprised if you could find five natural-born fae who wanted to build roots in the Human Realm, and now there are close to seven hundred thousand spread across regions."

There could have been many reasons a native of Esterbrooke would want to relocate to the Human Realm. Some now sought out fated mates, but for many, it was simply for a different way of life. With our considerably long lifespans, a fae could grow wealth in a way they may not be able to in the Fae Realm.

"So, it is concerning that through my contact with an agent, I learned that just in this year, the year our father's life was taken, there have been an estimated one-thousand and seven confirmed deaths."

"*Confirmed?*" I goaded, too impatient to let him finish.

"That's not even the half of it. Over two-thousand pure-blood fae have been permanently injured."

I shook my head in disbelief. "Why am I only hearing of this now?"

Whatever took place during this time, I would be responsible for. Pure-blood fae and halflings dying? What a disconcerting way to start my reign. And to think, we hadn't even gone public yet. Our planned assimilation was years, likely decades in the making. If that many fae can be *intentionally* slain, it means many already know that we're here.

"This is where things get more complicated." Lianthore shifted to the next collection of slides. It was of a man in the US military. Highly decorated. This shouldn't have caused any real alarm, but for a human, there was something cynically chilling about his blank, cold blue eyes. Other than that, there was nothing remarkable about him.

"Presenting Jack Hodgins, aka the Giant Slayer. He served in the United States Marines from the years 2001-2013. During his time, he'd been recruited as a covert Black Ops operative funded by an off-the-grid corporation, separate from the government. With the help of one of my contacts, I was able to acquire that this rogue group's main objective was to take out *specific* targets."

As Lianthore flipped through a series of photos, it got more disturbing. They weren't just *anyone*. They were prominent figures in the Human Realm. Philanthropists, inventors, politicians, and entertainers. On a normal day, that shouldn't ring the alarm, but the thing they shared in common was that they were all pure-blood fae.

Dwarves, Elves, Demyns, Selkies. All hidden in plain sight by the Veil, now all eternally resting. Any one of them could have been my brothers. Any one of them could have been me. This discovery couldn't get any worse.

"Why did they call him the Giant Slayer?" I asked, assessing his less-than-impressive build and average height. The man couldn't have been over five-foot-nine. What kind of person gets a name like that?

"It was given to him from his military days. They say he was known for taking on men twice his size without even breaking a sweat. He's broken bones with a single punch. You tell *me* what sort of human is capable of such."

"So, we're dealing with a halfling?" I retorted, piecing it together, but by a fine thread. Why would a halfling invoke war on its own kind? Despite their significant human ancestry, they're often welcome in the Fae Realm without question.

Lianthore pointed his clicker in my direction. The irises of his eyes blazed, like they were on fire. "That is not even the worst part," he continued.

"Three confirmed lump sums of $126,000, $74,000 and a final $50,000 were deposited in Hodgin's bank account spread across days after our father's death. Humans always say to follow the money, so that's what I did." As he clicked through to the next picture, my heart began to thrum wildly, enraged with the picture staring back at me.

My body surged upright in a painstakingly slow stand, and it was times like this, I wished I'd inherited Ivaran's brute strength.

"The trail almost goes cold, but seeking Ivaran's professional guidance, I was able to trace it back to an offshore company, with subsidiaries belonging to a Mr. Benjamin Bourdelon."

Nothing could describe the ire radiating from every pore of my skin. This man was my father's *friend*. This man had shaken my hand, and offered his condolences. And for what? To have played some wicked, twisted part in our father's death?

"How many other council members know about this?" I demanded through a clenched jaw.

"That, I am not sure of. It could be none of them. It could be all of them. But what I do know is that many of them have too many stakes in the Council. Many would not risk war considering how formidable Esterbrooke's Royal Guard is."

My knuckles burned, begging to be let loose. After our father's murder, I thought nothing could ever make me so despondent, so indignant, that my one-track mind could only focus on something reckless.

"*We* could take him. You and me. Off the books. Low profile. Even the others wouldn't have to know." My voice a roughening whisper.

This was more of Ivaran's and Zaos' expertise, yes. No one could be as creative as a torture expert and natural-born predator. But sometimes they were *too* passionate. There was no doubt Councilman Bourdelon deserved to suffer, but even in their discretion, they might fall short of making it look accidental.

"In time, we'll need to send a message, Brother." Lianthore balled his fist into a ball of fire, in an effort to stop my agitated pacing. "But as much as it pains me, that time is not now. Bourdelon doesn't *know* we know. We may require that advantage just to get close. But the Giant Slayer? We don't know enough about his skill set, but we do know he has the intel necessary to kill fae."

He also reminded me that while he was part human and could die exponentially easier than most fae, with his human makeup, he lacked the invulnerability to iron. All it would take was one misstep and our united front would be weakened and left to our brothers less prepared.

Lianthore was right. I had to think rationally. One of the things I *could* do was make sure Paige was safe before I did anything too brash. To her dismay, our trip to the Human Realm may have to be cut early.

"Get Ivaran, Zaos, and the triplets down here without delay. Catch them up to speed so we can come up with something more calculated for our next course of action. One way or another, there'll be a bullet reserved for Councilman Bourdelon, and I don't even want to think of what we'll do to the one they call *Jack Hodgins*."

Lianthore placed his hand on my shoulder, wearing a scowl of knitted brows and eyes that could catch the entire room on fire if he chose not to blink.

"This is where I would have to dishonor you, My King. For a bullet would be far too merciful. For the death of our father, I wish nothing more than to see him singed and screaming, until nothing else remains of him but menial soot and ash."

CHAPTER TWENTY-NINE

Paige

"You can just slide them over there," I instructed the fae royal guards, carrying my bags into the hotel room. After an afternoon of shopping at Aranzeiros' request, I would have rather done it with him, but being by myself gave me a chance to get him some surprises of my own.

I probably would've had to buy everything I tried on at the lingerie boutique I stopped in. He wouldn't have been able to handle watching me try everything on without ripping it all off.

I surprised myself the other day, learning anal play was pretty fun with a trusting partner, so my trip couldn't have been complete without hitting up a sex toy shop. It was about to be Christmas in this hotel room. Not that Aranzeiros celebrated Christmas.

You'd think that I'd be used to navigating so many rooms by now, but it seemed like the presidential suite took forever to find him. Pacing back and forth in a room he'd been using as a study, he conversed in a language I associated was him talking to one of his brothers.

Once he saw me, he was quick to disconnect the call, wearing the weight of the world on his features. "Paige," he addressed me in a tone that suggested he was both tired and not in the best mood.

"How was your afternoon of treating yourself?" Rubbing away the stress lines on his forehead.

"It was good." I shrugged, advancing closer to him. "I almost forgot what it was like to shop until you drop. Not that I've *ever* known what it's like to do that."

Being in a palace meant they provided every necessity or basic need for me without ever having to leave the palace grounds. Human tasks were tiring, but I *almost* forgot what it felt like not to have everything ready when I asked.

"I got you something too," I flirted, taken aback by him barely paying attention. "Maybe I can show it to you later?"

"Hmm...that's nice." He spoke blankly, like he hadn't even heard me.

"And I got mugged. Got into a car accident and survived a bank robbing all in one afternoon," I joked, testing his attention span.

"You'll have to tell me all about it later." His lifeless tone raised my alarm. By this time in our relationship, I usually had his undivided attention. Not that I needed it twenty-four hours of the day, but it wasn't like Aranzeiros to not pay attention to me at *all*.

"Baby, is there something wrong?" I followed him out of the study, his demeanor becoming visibly more frustrated that I was pressing the subject.

"I just have a lot on my mind, Paige. You need not concern your day with my burdens," he dismissed before I jumped out in front of him so he couldn't avoid me.

"Did it have to do with who you were on the phone with—"

"Paige, I am dealing with fae business, and that is all I intend to share." He gently nudged me out of the way.

I was his wife. Human or not, Esterbrooke was my home now. If it was something concerning fae, surely it was my business, too.

"Am I not the Queen of Esterbrooke?" I shrugged, sarcasm laced in my tone. "By extension, how is fae business not my business?"

"It is not your business when I say it is not your business." He spoke through a clenched jaw, but he was always expecting me to challenge him, so I couldn't see this being any different.

"Well, as your *queen*, I'm asserting my right to respectfully disagree—"

Aranzeiros grabbed me by both sides, aggressively shaking me to his wit's end. "I am your husband, your King, your keeper. When I ask something of you, I expect you to do it," he interrupted in a state of controlled rage.

"When I tell you to stop asking questions, I expect you to listen," he continued, grabbing my chin to face him.

Something was off. It was like Aranzeiros had become a ticking time bomb and I suddenly became the recipient of his frustration. "Tell me you understand." He spoke bitterly and coldly, and he wouldn't let go until I nodded yes.

"Gosh, what is your problem? You're scaring me." Trying to hide how shaken up I was. All I could do to ease my turmoil was put enough distance between us so we didn't have to deal with one another.

I disappeared into the master bedroom, so emotionally withdrawn, I almost forgot to take off my shoes. What was with Aranzeiros? It was like we were falling back into our old routine again, and not the good one.

Whatever he must've gotten up in the middle of the night for, must've put him in this horrible mood, because I know I sure as hell didn't.

When I'd woken up, wondering how long he'd be, I didn't have a reason to believe his suggestion to spend my morning shopping was just to distract me from what he was hiding.

Soothing each of my shoulders with a light rub, the door opened, and it was as if he'd had every intention of ignoring our last exchange. "Would you like for me to make love to you?" He asked, instead of offering an apology.

"I'm not really in the mood." Sex couldn't be the answer to *every* problem. "Maybe you should tend to your fae business." I rolled my eyes, visibly annoyed that he barely noticed and agreed with me.

He insisted we amend our trip, as something was keeping his attention, and as soon as he could arrange it, I'd be back at Regal-helm so he can work.

Ugh, he was being a real asshole right now. It almost made me relieved to hear our hotel room door close, insinuating he's stepped out.

Now that it was over, it felt like I'd been holding my breath the whole time. The heat behind my eyes released the tears I'd been holding back and for the life of me, I didn't know how to stop.

CHAPTER THIRTY

Paige

The tear-soaked pillow had been the reason I couldn't get sleep. I just kept playing that last conversation with Aranzeiros in my head.

Aranzeiros made me feel a lot of things. Bad things. Good things. *Amazing* things. But I wasn't used to being made to feel smaller because of him. Or, at least not in a way that made me doubt myself.

Encouraging myself to shower had been the only time my head wasn't in a complete slump, but once I no longer had the relief of the kneading warmth, I was back to feeling like an imposter.

Something must have been wrong. There had to be. Few things could garner that type of anger out of him, but he couldn't even trust me enough to tell me. He would have rather lashed out than share what had been bothering him.

I feel like I gave *every* piece of myself and it still felt like there was a piece of him that would always be a mystery to me.

Deciding that I couldn't be locked in here all day, I threw on some leisure wear and concluded that I needed time to myself.

Without Aranzeiros, without all the detail. Just the city and me. Only then could I come back with a clear head.

My first instinct was to be angry. But I knew my king and I were different. I could come back yelling and screaming, but what I'd really like to do is voice how that conversation made me feel before it festered into resentment.

Using my influence to discourage the guards outside our hotel room door to follow me, I thought I was free until I made it to the hotel entrance.

Vestan, Aranzeiros' faithful coachman and earth-bound driver, stopped me before I could hit the pavement.

"May I offer you a ride, Your Majesty?" Vestan's stern eyes peered through like I didn't have an option.

"Actually, I was thinking that I could experience New York. The *human* way. You know? Actually, walk."

"I must insist. I have strict instructions from the King, not to let you out of my sight. But I know that you're human. And Queen now, so I can't tell you that you can't go. But wherever you go, I go." As he refused to clear a path for me unless I took him up on his offer.

"Fine," I huffed, defeated. Even though I would've loved to experience the subway sporting a thirty-day unlimited Metro card, I'd have the benefit of not worrying about not finding a seat when my feet hurt as I succumbed to the ride.

Allowing him to open my door for me, I tried to see the bright side of not having to navigate through public transportation. At least I was safe. All I knew was that Vestan better be prepared to take me *anywhere* I wanted, because all the good stuff was in the boroughs.

***

Esterbrookian food was divine, but nothing hit like a good old-fashioned plate of jerk chicken. It reminded me of my former landlord. You could always count on the fragrant smell of curry goat or jerk chicken on a Sunday evening after she returned home from church.

I wasn't trying to rush with my food, but I was honestly a little embarrassed that Vestan had recklessly double-parked in front of the restaurant, as it didn't appear to register to him how much of a dick move that was. I guess that diplomatic immunity kept you impetuous.

Deciding to take the rest of my food to go, at the thought of Ms. Robins, I had a crazy idea. I felt like I'd railroaded her by disappearing on her, especially with all the back rent I owed. Now that I had access to endless funds, it felt like the right thing to do to pay her back before our trip ended. Living in New York, I'm sure that money would help.

Once I convinced Vestan to take me to the bank, I hung tight, as we made a detour to Queens and I was reminded why public transportation had been so much more convenient. Traffic in New York was the pits. If I actually had some place important to be, I would be fuming.

It took nearly two hours to reach the former apartment building I used to call home and from the looks of things, not much had changed. As Vestan opened my door, I insisted I would be right back, so there was no reason for him to hover over me.

Personally, if she was upset at the fact I ghosted her, I didn't want anyone to witness that exchange. She was nice, but anyone's mood changed when it concerned money.

It took until walking up the stairs to the stone complex to remember that I'd need to be buzzed in, but luckily for me, a resident was just leaving and had no problem holding the door.

A layer of nostalgia rushed over me at the squeaking floorboards I used to try to avoid every time I came home from a long day. Once I was in front of her door, I decided that it'd be better to just slip the money underneath the threshold to avoid any awkwardness.

A stranger was coming out of my old apartment, and just as he was pushing his keys into his pocket, a flash of recognition stretched across his face. "Paige?"

The sound of my name leaving an unknown person made me nervous at first, but when he caught me up to speed, I easily recognized him as a regular at my time at Lou's Diner.

"I'm sorry I didn't recognize you, it's just I saw so many faces—"

"No need to apologize. That's the cost of hospitality. Everyone recognizes you, but you don't recognize them." He interrupted, but wasn't lacking in charm.

"Jack, was it?" pointing a finger as his face came back to me.

"Surprised you remember!"

"How are you? I know what small talk we shared couldn't count for actual friendship, but how's everything? Good, I hope." As my Midwestern nice conditioning forced me to keep the conversation going.

"Everything's good, considering. I got a couple of jobs going, and once they're done I'm relocating," he said, almost in a bragging manner.

"Oh, what do you do?" I brought my right hand to grasp my forearm, trying to appear interested when I really should have been getting back.

"Get this." He formed his hands into a pinching gesture, and I had to fight not to react to what he said. "I kill fae."

With only a second to react, I laughed, trying to make light that I assumed he was joking. "What do you mean, like, little flying fairies?"

"No, I mean like fae like your husband."

"Boy, you play too much." Trying to diffuse my now looming disposition, appearing as unphased by his words as possible, so I could make my first move to get the *hell* out of there.

"I have to go. I have detail and a driver downstairs waiting for me."

"I don't think you do." He violently grabbed my arm, and an unexpected flash of light burned his hand away, as I took my opening and ran down those stairs like the wind.

The hallway doors flung open, and I could hear his accompanying steps, but I forced myself not to look back, in fear it would slow my adrenaline-infused sprint.

"I'll admit, your little magic trick threw me off," he shouted in the distance.

"But fool me once, shame on me," he taunted, and I swear, he appeared right in front of me, right before my very eyes. I jumped back, hoping I could summon *something* to save myself, but in my attempt, nothing would come. Only, it didn't feel like previous times. This time, it felt intentional.

The image in front of me faded, as strong arms restrained me from behind. At first, I thought I'd been hallucinating, as scenes faded in and out, and my memories of being plucked from *Lou's Diner* that fateful day bled through my peripheral.

Trying to fight back, I kicked and screamed, only to be taunted with, "Fool me twice, shame on you." As I processed a cloth being brought to my mouth before everything went dark.

CHAPTER THIRTY-ONE

Aranzeiros

Allowing what felt like never-ending grief to fester, the idea of vengeance consumed me. Before tonight, I could never put a face to Tarron's murderer. Now I had a figurehead. Now I had a name. The thought of retributive justice had never tasted so appetizing, as I—*we*, were made to be the fool for the last time.

How many times had I looked Councilman Bourdelon in the eye, shook his hand, and considered his counsel? How many times had Tarron had this man in our home? Enjoying our hospitality, all while possibly having a stake in the death of someone who called him a friend.

How could I ever trust the Council and expect them to uphold the standard of a just and fair truce?

Councilman Bourdelon would not live to see another council meeting, that was for sure. But what pains me the most is that Tarron had not even been killed by a regular human. Learning that his murderer has part fae made us fear that even the fae side of the Council could have members that are against our interests.

I needed air. By no means did I plan to sit with this anguish, sitting down and sulking. In a time like this, I could really use some king play, but I feared that in my anger, even that would not be able to take my mind off of our new knowledge.

A vigorous walk was the first line of action I took, hoping that it might channel my rage someplace else. I'd recuperated some of my voice of reason, considering all the ways we could retaliate. They were going to pay for their crimes, but with their wealth or their lives, I've yet to decide.

This, *Giant* Slayer. He might have been part fae, but he was part human too. I was married to a human. In all her foreign strangeness, she understood humans better than me. Perhaps it would behoove me to seek her guidance, as I silently swore, remembering how I'd last spoken to her.

Even in our most challenging times, I'd never seen the light leave her brown eyes the way they did in that exchange. I was ashamed. I'd been doing so well. Maybe I just wanted her out of the city. Regalhelm was the safest place for her and I wanted her to have nothing to do with this newly learned threat. I didn't plan on losing the only person worth protecting in my life, but first, I'd have to humble myself and offer my most sincere apology.

Glancing down at my watch, I was grateful it was still early enough to bear something to accompany my expression of regret. Knowing how much she adored food from her own realm, since we were cutting our time here short, I could surprise her with cuisine she might fancy. Apologies with food helped, did they not?

Down the conjunction of Fifth Avenue and Fifty-Ninth, I flagged down an adolescent male riding his bike, as he wrestled with his earphones to hear what I was asking of him.

"Look, man. I don't know where to buy drugs and before you ask, I live in this neighborhood," he offered defensively, forcing me to think back to past conversations with Paige about skin color. It wasn't my intention to profile him, so I assured him I just needed his help.

"Well, it's a good thing I don't need any, kid. I personally don't care where you live, I'm not even from here." The Veil masking my highborn accent for a New York one.

Lifting his fist to his mouth, the sudden realization that he'd seen me before lit up his face. "Oh snap! Wait, you're one of them. Damn, I already forgot the name." With a snap of his finger, the recollection surfaced.

"Faeborne brothers. Bruh, y'all richer than Michael Bloomberg. You know I gotta get a selfie right quick," he boasted with enthusiasm, taking out his phone before I could turn his snapshot down. I still wasn't quite sure I understood a human's obsession with taking pictures with people they found notable.

"What did you need?" Knowing there'd been a reason for me stopping him.

"I'm looking for a fantastic rib spot. Do you know any around here?"

His left eye squinted, leaving a comical grimace on his strong yet youthful face. "Nah fam. You're gonna have to go to Brooklyn for that. I assume you're talking about soul food, right?"

"Is there any other kind?" I shot back.

"There's a spot called Royal House BBQ. MLK Boulevard. They'll hook you up," he replied. "But be sure to go there before nine, because their kitchen closes at nine-thirty."

I still had a few good hours. Just enough time to flag a cab and be back before it got too dark out.

"Thanks, pal. I appreciate it," I said, and he replied to me with a nod.

"Be careful, though. That's a rough part of Bed Stuy. Would hate to hear you got robbed or something."

"Thanks for looking out kid, but I think I'll be all right." Not wasting a second to flag down a taxi.

"Where to?"

"Bedford Stuyvesant, please."

"That's across town. It wouldn't be worth it for me unless I charged you extra," he replied in his heavy London accent.

Pulling out my wallet, a montage of credit cards and cash fell out, and I held it up so he see could it in his rearview mirror. "Not a problem. I'll even tip ya."

That had been the right motivation because before I knew it, he was cranking up the engine and starting up the meter to make haste.

***

"My Queen, you will not believe what I have for you," I shouted, closing the hotel room door with my foot. Lying my wallet on the nightstand, I got comfortable on the bed, basking in the scent that was sure to calm her mood.

It was no secret that I had my preference for fine dining, but like Paige, her gluttonous choice of food had grown on me. "I placed an entire food order by myself. You would have been so proud. I spoke with the patrons who owned it, as you're always telling me I have to improve my interactions with humans."

The exchange reminded me that I made an interesting gaffe at my lack of knowledge of her place of birth. "That reminds me, one merchant was from Kansas City. And I thought, how lovely. So is my wife. Only to have him explain that Kansas and Kansas City, Missouri were completely different places. That would never happen in Esterbrooke. Once a place is named, its name does not carry to another region. Do you not find that confusing?"

It was only now that I realized she wasn't replying, likely as punishment for our exchange from earlier. Coming to a stand, I made my way toward the bathroom, knocking at the door to garner her focus.

"Paige, can you come out here, please?" Concluding that my words had done damage. It would take time to undo. "I wanted to apologize. Properly. Please come out so I can do so?"

Nothing else followed, as I only had myself to blame for her standoffishness. It destroyed my peace knowing I'd caused her pain, and not in a good way. Knocking one last time, her silence flared my anxiety, forcing me to turn the knob of the door. It was unlocked.

"Paige?" I called out, finding the room abandoned. I took a deep inhale, knowing that my emotions of distress caused me to be out of tune with her scent.

I smelled...nothing. I could not *sense* her. *Smell* her. Most of all? I could not *feel* her. Fear plummeted to the pit of my stomach. What did that mean? *What did that mean?*

In an instant, I sprinted to the foyer that led to the penthouse elevators where the Royal security stood guard.

Usually, I addressed them by their respective titles, but with my suffocating agitation, their names and rank escaped me.

"Why is Queen Paige not in her room? Did she go somewhere?" They looked between each other, their broad builds and stern features carrying the weight of unease on their faces.

"The Queen requested to step out for a moment, as you have. In her attempt to travel alone, your driver would not allow her such without an escort. Rest assured, she is in safe hands."

Even as I heard the words, they didn't grant me peace. From their accounts, she should've been back by now.

Paige was a lot of things, but I'd never known her to hold a grudge. Even when she despised me, she found it in her heart to love me. Just to be sure, I stepped away so I could quietly contact Vestan, relieved he'd picked up on the second ring.

"Oh, thank the goddess you picked up. You almost had me worried for a moment. I request my queen's presence as soon as possible, so wherever you are, return her immediately," careful that my tone didn't sound distraught.

"I was wondering when you'd call." Sweat pooled against my forehead hearing a voice that wasn't familiar on the other end.

The accent was distinct, maybe not enough to know by region, but enough to know it hailed from the southern United States.

"Who is this?" Doing my best to keep him on the phone.

"That doesn't matter right now." His voice was low and menacing but strangely charming. "But I think you should look into getting a new driver. Help like that is too hard to find, and just know that he fought *valiantly* in protecting his queen. It should bring you great sorrow to know his efforts were in vain—"

"Look, you little piece of shit, if you hurt my fucking wife—" I interrupted, thrown off guard when he did the same.

"Hurt her? Why would I want to hurt her? Not when she makes the path to you so effortless."

"What is it you want?" Slamming my fist on the vanity, fighting my flaring nostrils. My hopes was that he didn't notice my tone growing significantly weaker at the thought that something happened to Paige.

He laughed, almost in a mocking tone, before he answered. "You can't give me what I want. Not now anyway. But I predict very soon. In the meantime, your queen will just have to keep me company."

"I will fucking kill you!" I spat through clenched teeth. "If there's even a scratch on my Paige, you won't even be able to *predict* the Armageddon your realm will face—"

"Take your best shot. I actually can't wait to have a go at the next King of Esterbrooke. If anything, it'll earn me a new name to go by. *King* Slayer." Before I could say another word, the line went dead, and all I could do was fall to the floor in torment.

This was the one who killed fae, whom Lianthore dubbed the Giant Slayer. He had my wife. I'd never felt so powerless as I attempted and failed at dialing the number once more. It took me six failed attempts before I dialed the next number.

"Brother?" Lianthore's voice was the only thing that could calm me at this moment.

"I promise, I would not have called you this late if it weren't urgent. I think he has her—"

"Wait, who has her?" he impatiently interrupted.

"Paige! The Giant Slayer. I need the others." Aware that I spoke in fragments but was unable to articulate myself.

Gathering my wits, I composed myself, knowing I needed to speak clearly if anything was to be done about my queen. "Gather the others. I am summoning their presence. *Now*. And it is not optional. Consider this a King's order!"

CHAPTER THIRTY-TWO

Aranzeiros

The rush of air behind me, indicating someone must have rushed inside, forced me to gather myself and wipe the stray tears streaming down my face. No one could see me in this state; not even my queen.

Imagine my relief to see it was the only being alive that I had ever *allowed* to witness me weep, my brother Lianthore. The one I could always depend on to arrive first at the scene of a crisis. I couldn't let the others see me like this. I wouldn't. Not with the immense guilt I carried that it was my fault Paige left.

"I came as soon as I could," Lianthore said, as I stood to my feet to greet him, surprised that he knew I would need the calming effect of an embrace. It felt so strange; there was once a time, when I would hold him and rock his newborn frame to sleep to comfort him. Now I was the one in need of such comfort.

"It's my fault," I said, fighting back tears, comforted by his warmth. At Lianthore's command, the silent, typically motionless Royal security left the hotel room altogether, giving us a chance to speak alone.

Truthfully, I didn't want to do any talking. All I wanted was to find Paige and ensure that she was safe. Things between us had improved over the last few weeks.

"Can you explain what happened to me? Humans are fickle. This could merely be a time when she needed time to clear her head. Humans do that from time to time," Lianthore said, taking a seat at the table, prompting me to join him in the chair next to his.

My mouth attempted words, but all I could manage was a deep sigh in its place. "We were having a wonderful time. One of the best I could think of, given how short we've been wed. Then the briefing happened," I huffed.

"That ruined everything." I reached out and squeezed Lianthore's shoulder, unaware of how our father's death still affected me. "For months, I'd let the death of our father go. Content that we may never find his killer. But then to get one step closer to finding a lead. Learning a name. Putting a face to my rage," I spoke through ground teeth.

"I fear I may have spoken to her in a way that was unbecoming of a good husband. In that anger, I may have driven her into the arms of danger."

Lianthore's lips pressed into a hard line. "Perhaps it is too early to surrender to pessimism, but I must know, have you exhausted all straightforward efforts? I am sure I do not yet know about the coveted scent a fated mate gives off, but I imagine you would not have called if her scent was easily traceable. Has her trail gone completely cold to you?"

If there was one thing I knew, it was Paige's scent. Through that alone, in a normal situation, I could sense her from miles away. But this felt different; it was as if she had vanished from thin air.

"Yes, and that isn't even all that troubles me. He called me. The Giant Slayer. He's the one who has her. Lianthore, I beg of you, I need to find her. It is as if I can't breathe without knowing she's safe," I pleaded, grabbing fistfuls of my hair and pinching the space between my eyes to dispel what anxiety I could with the minuscule gesture.

"I've been trying so hard to make my marriage work. But you know me, I get beside myself when things are in a state where I feel helpless. Paige has had such a hard life and there are often situations I do not wish to burden her with," thinking of all the times when ignoring her wishes was the one thing that kept her safe.

"When I am with her, she is my peace. All this power, all these decisions. All this anti-fae nonsense. I just didn't want her to have to deal with it for as long as I could," I ended with disappointment in my tone.

Lianthore appeared unmoved by that declaration, as a shrug was all he could manage in his otherwise stoic reply. "Paige knew the life she was inheriting from becoming your wife. She is strong, Brother. If it is her choice to be the kind of queen that rides alongside you on the battlefield, then she doesn't just need your protection, she needs your support. We may not have many examples of what a supportive partner looks like. Father taught us many things, but to be a good husband was not one of them."

Even though I still harbored some resentment over my father's death, I now had a sense of understanding. Especially given that he had never taken on another wife. The prospect of losing someone was far too much to bear.

Lianthore, one of the few that could humble me, insisted there was no wrong way to go about marriage unless you keep making the same mistake multiple times. "Being a good husband to a human? That is something we will have to discover on our own. Even though we would've forced your hand regardless, I'm not ashamed to admit you give me hope. Sometimes, I wonder who could love us. We come so damaged, broken beyond repair, and incredibly stubborn. Yet, here you are. Proving that we can have more than what life has promised us."

He was right. Paige shouldn't have fallen in love with me, but she did. I prayed my remaining brothers, who were still *capable* of finding a fated mate, would find the joy that I had.

"But brother, you have to start trusting that the queen can handle the crown. That includes everything that comes with it," Lianthore contested.

As much as it pained me to be in the seat of a mentee, especially to a creature I'd mentored, he was right. I couldn't pick and choose what parts of the lifestyle she was ready for. Instead of voicing the words and hoping them to be true, I had to put into practice that I believed she was my equal.

"For now, we must be patient. There is nothing more important than finding the Queen and ensuring her safety. The realm depends on it," Lianthore followed up.

The thought wasn't lost on me that while only a few knew of our existence, the humans that did, could be spreading lies about the Fae Realm, causing panic to those that already feared the unknown.

The moment we located Paige, we were going to *have* to reveal ourselves. With that came exposing our vulnerabilities, as well as our strengths. But could we *handle* them knowing our weaknesses?

The door opened once more, and the rest of my brothers poured in to provide their support, skill, or presence to keep me centered. As they filled up the room, I was humbled by the fact that while I had no chance of finding her on my own, I wouldn't be alone. My brothers were all the things I could never be and for that reason, I knew that with their help, there wasn't anything or anyone who could hide from me.

CHAPTER THIRTY-THREE

Aranzeiros

The briefing room swelled with swarms of our some of our highest-level government contacts. Back and forth, they provided intel, proposals of strategy, and resources that might find my missing wife.

For an intelligence agency that implied that there was very little they did not know concerning both the Human and the Fae Realm, their results didn't come close to meeting the expectation of finding just *one* human.

They'd been able to track her to a restaurant and a shabby apartment building, but after that, her trace went cold. I wouldn't have needed them if her scent hadn't completely disappeared from me. My range wasn't far, but I could at least tell when we were in the same fifty-mile radius.

Had it not been for my brothers, I would have been tearing down the city. Humans were not my strong point, so if I wanted to find one, I needed their help.

"Your Highness, I think the problem is, most of these old buildings in the city don't have it in their budgets to pay for constant surveillance footage. We'd be better off asking the residents of the building. The surveillance camera at the bodega across the street proves that she went into the building, but we never saw her come out." A blonde, tanned-skin agent in a grey suit, pointed to the timestamps of captured images of Paige's last whereabouts. "She could even still be in the building."

This terrorist wasted no time killing my trusted driver, Vestan. I wanted to mourn him, but I didn't even have time to. He deserved it, as he'd served in our court for centuries. But since he was already gone, I had to worry about Paige.

"Please tell me this is an attempt at jest. This is New York. Better yet, the center of the madness. No one witnesses anything around here and if they did, they certainly wouldn't divulge any details to humans in law enforcement." It was the reason I'd always been the fondest of New York in the Human Realm. Even if I slipped up and allowed myself to be seen, who would talk?

"This is no insult to you, Agent..." I was examining her badge to find the proper way to address her. "But Agent Carstairs, this can't be your best efforts. I hardly find a few screenshots with timestamps useful. I'm losing my confidence that your resources are even capable."

Frustrated, one of the leading agents let out an exasperated sigh, coming to a stand as he leaned toward my side of the table. "This isn't me implying the worst, but is there a possibility that she could have just run? We're all familiar with your customs. I'd prefer to explore alternatives to kidnapping before I send a team out on a duck hunt."

Maybe I hadn't been making myself clear. I was positive that we briefed him the same as everyone else. And I was more than sure that my temperament had remained respectful until this point.

Forking my fingers through my slicked black strands, I took another deep breath to calm myself before I stalked over to him. He certainly wasn't a weak man. By his uniform, one could tell he'd been well-decorated for his service. He'd seen war and the losses that resulted from it.

So, when my right hand took hold of his puny, defenseless, feeble little neck, hoisting him inches above me, nothing stood between me and throwing him through that skyscraper window.

"If you *ever* imply that my wife—"

"Easy, easy, brother," Tavnis intervened, convincing me I didn't need to kill him to show how easily replaceable the agent's presence was.

Dropping him to the floor, he wheezed and gasped, fighting to replace his air, as I turned two seats away from me and pointed in Zaos' direction. "Zaos, show these imbeciles how useless they are."

Zaos let out a rich, arrogant laugh, pushing out of his seat so that he could advance to the head of the table, where all the room could see. The leading agent, finally able to catch his breath, eyed us with resentment, ignorant as to why one of *us* was worth one thousand of them.

"What will he do that we cannot do?"

"It is simple, really," Zaos started, in a condescending tone. "If I did not wish to see your failures or physical distress, I could have suggested my expertise before my brother's hand so cozily made a home on your neck."

Zaos didn't rely on advancements in technology, both through humans or fae. "Since you refuse to do it your way, I volunteer my ability, as my gift of sight greatly outweighs anything your useless military has to offer. I just ask for a mirror. As you can see, you confiscated my belongings upon entry. Surely someone can supply me with something as mundane as a mirror?" as he pointed to Agent Carstairs, not the least bit ashamed that her hand trembled the entirety it took to pass him the mirror.

"Will that do?" she asked.

"This is sufficient." He smiled devilishly, outstretching the mirror to the space in front of him before his fingers sparked with wieldable bolts of electricity. The entire room watched as the lightning traveled from his fingertips to the pupils of his eyes, replacing his once-normal gaze with shaded clouds of blue.

During this stage, he entered a state of hypnosis, a type of gateway that allowed him to improve his reach. There wasn't a tracker alive who could mimic this ability, making him renowned in both the Fae and Human Realm.

I could never be sure of what he saw, but the way he'd move suggested it was like being in the place he could see, while never having to leave his spot.

"What is he doing?" another agent asked. He was dark-skinned, in a hue that favored our father, or Paige. I made out the surname Monroe, visible from his badge.

Ivaran pulled his chair further away from the table, normally quiet but at this moment most prepared to speak. "He has a rare ability that allows him to communicate with reflections. Bodies of water. Glass. Anything that can return an image back to him. Mirrors, he finds to be simplest. Eyes are the hardest, as they require his target to be facing whom he connects to."

Zaos' ability certainly made Ivaran's job easier, but I wondered what mental toll it took to have so many images in your head. His skill was so useful, it was why he'd never been required to learn everything of a highborn Royal.

We watched Zaos reach a catatonic state, shifting through anything that could have captured Paige's likeness. My heart was heavy, considering every possibility that tragedy was right on our doorsteps. War would rage if my fears came true. Gone would be the Earth/Esterbrooke Accords, and to hell with the treaty. I would be done with humans. Even if it cost us this so-called *peace*.

Zaos' head tilted at the promise of a likely prospect. "Where are you, little bird?" The sound of his distinctive term of endearment forcing me out of my chair.

"What of Paige—"

"*Do not touch him, you idiot!*" Ivaran roared, blocking me with his brute strength to avoid touching Zaos. "In his current state, he will view you as a threat. And then *he* gets upset, then *I* get upset, and the last thing you want to be is caged in a room with two uncontrollable Faebornes. Have patience, brother. Let Zaos work."

Following Ivaran's recommendation, like my other brothers, we took a sizeable distance from Zaos, watching him hold his hands out in front as if he were attempting to touch his surroundings. "No..." he mumbled under his breath, but less of a warning and more of a verbalization one expressed when eliminating something.

"*There you are!*" His victory became short-lived, as he cried out, caving down to the table in wrenching pain. "Something...is wrong..." he could barely get out as Ivaran stopped me once again from even approaching Zaos.

"What is happening? You said it'd be fine if I did not come into contact with him?" I argued with Ivaran as he continued to use his strength against me each time I tried to erase the distance.

"I am...I am being blocked?" Zaos spoke in a gritted tooth scowl, holding each side of his head in hopes it would bring relief. "I can see her, but...this has never happened to me before."

Fueling all of our confusion, Zaos fought against his mind, his mental torment forcing electricity to violently flow through him, sending the object across the table to fuel his relief.

The force of his bolt shattered the glass into a million little pieces. While I'd been elated to see his pain subside, with his reckless action, the connection was lost.

"Is it safe now?" Consulting Ivaran, taking his loosened grip on me as confirmation. Zaos' eyes appeared normal, but tired, as if he'd just been tortured.

"She is alive," he said, catching his breath. Finally, some good news.

"Get him some water," I yelled to any guard who would listen. "And get him some aquavit. He looks like he's going to need it." I approached, careful to make sure reaching out to him would cause no further pain.

"Are you okay to speak?" Reaching out to touch his shoulder, handing him both the water and expeditiously obtained spirits.

"Aranzeiros." Zaos reached for the aquavit, ignoring the water. "I must warn you. While alive, the force that surrounds the queen will be dangerous. Whoever they are, they are strong. Even as Paige's location was within reach, it was like they altered, or erased my mind from memorizing its coordinates," he shamefully admitted.

"You've done well." My brotherly instinct kicked in to reassure him. "You saw she was alive. That's all that matters. I hate to be a bother, but was there anything distinctive to where she was being held? Anything that could help me do the rest? You've already done so well."

"It was a place devoid of light. Like it was abandoned. And for quite some time. I remember rundown tracks. Underground, maybe? My apologies, brother. I wish I could have dug further, but whoever was on the other end *knew* I was looking."

"You have done more than any human could have done. You've eased much of my pessimism," I championed. I just needed to use the breadcrumbs he'd given me to aid in my search. Turning to Agent Monroe, I asked for his professional opinion.

"What in your world can you associate with being both devoid of light and near rundown tracks?"

"Only thing I could think of is a subway tunnel. There's gotta be at least a dozen closed platforms," he suggested.

"Wait, I remember something," Zaos interrupted. "Roosevelt. These images appeared, but I do not know what they mean."

"That's gotta be FDR's Station. It was rumored to be built for former President Franklin Delano Roosevelt whenever he traveled to New York. It sits right under Grand Central, on track 61, so it shouldn't be hard to find," Agent Carstairs rushed to answer, praying that her suggestion had been useful.

"That's brilliant!" I said through gritted teeth. I could almost kiss everyone in the room. "Give me the location's coordinates—"

"But Your Highness, it will be dark down there, maybe even damn near impossible to see," Agent Monroe interrupted.

"*Good!*" I punched my left fist into my other palm, allowing the tentacles of darkness to engulf my frame.

"Because I don't *need* the light to see. He better hopes I find Paige in one piece," fighting against the hostility in my tone. "Otherwise, I will make this animal fear *everything* that hides in the dark."

CHAPTER THIRTY-FOUR

Paige

I must have done something wrong in a past life because I couldn't fathom being abducted *twice* in a single year. A past me must have done something to deserve this. As my body was finally fighting off the effects of the chlorophyll, unlike my first experience dealing with this, this time had been *far* from luxurious.

By the time I opened my eyes, both my hands had fallen asleep from being constrained behind me, around a pole of some sort. Not exactly the welcoming recovery bed with a thousand-thread sheet count I'd had in Esterbrooke.

As my eyes adjusted, my vision accounted for more of my environment. I was in a subway car for sure, rusted and old, explaining its look of abandonment.

I had to laugh to myself at the irony of wanting to get Aranzeiros on a subway. I did not doubt that he'd exhaust every effort to find me, though, for my first chance at getting him on a subway. This was *far* from what I had in mind.

My eyes adjusted long enough to notice someone a few feet away with their back to me tinkering, with something decorated all alongside the walls of the train. And it was my instinct to pretend I was still asleep to avoid any unpleasant conversation. Only my captive had other things in mind.

"I know that you're awake." Words that sounded strangely familiar to my last captor, as he spoke calmly, nearly monotone. Like he intended to make me think he felt nothing.

"People. Humans, especially. Have a distinctive thought process, from the time that they are awake to the time that they're asleep. When people dream, they are free from burden, of. Or things that can *actually* hurt them. But when they are conscious, their focus is on imposing threats."

"So, is that what you are? A threat? Are you planning to kill me?" Attempting to sound bold to hide the helplessness that spread through my core.

"I don't want to," he spoke, eerily calm. "There have been some human casualties in my line of duty. But I find humans aren't much of a challenge. I'd rather use my skills on those much more deserving. Our *real* enemy."

"Our *real* enemy?" I repeated, playing dumb. As he finally turned to me, I nearly jumped out of my skin at the sight of his eerie blue eyes.

"The fae. I know you know them. One of them forced you into marriage with them, didn't they?" As he stalked his well-muscled frame further away from his project, in an intimidating gait.

"It's okay. You are amongst friends. I was forced with the burden of being able to do nothing as I watched him carry you into that carriage."

"Wait, you were there?" I asked through squinted eyes.

"To this day, it still brings me great shame that I did nothing to help you. Had I not had orders, I could have saved you a lifetime of pain." He spoke sympathetically, that I almost felt bad when I snatched my head away when he caressed my hair.

"Don't fucking touch me!" I spat, out of fear more than anger.

When he obeyed, I didn't know what to make of him.

It was clear we had conflicting interests. He wanted to kill fae, and I wanted to survive this shit so I could go home and fuck the shit out of my husband. As a woman, I'd never been good at using my femininity to best men, but he'd been strangely empathetic when he admitted how powerless he'd felt during my abduction. Maybe I could use that? At least long enough for help to come.

"I don't know why this keeps happening to me." Hoping my tears sounded convincing. "I'm *finally* away from him. But now I have to worry about you. I'm just tired of being around people who always want to hurt me."

He broke his emotionless gaze to stand to his feet. "Understandable. As someone who is mostly human, hurting you wouldn't benefit me. But it hurts *him*. And he is my *true* target—"

"Wait, mostly human?" I interrupted, making sure my ears hadn't betrayed me. "Are you a halfling?"

"That's what I *should* be considered. But I have little intention of identifying with the dirty blood I inherited from my mother. She cursed me. To see *everything*," he spat, showing the first fit of anger since our conversation.

"The fae blood robbed of both my ignorance and innocence. I would have been institutionalized had I not become...*useful*," he admitted, as the images he'd seen as a child, others could not. I didn't have the sight, but even I wouldn't have wished that on myself.

"Everything changed for me when I learned I could do things. Invaluable things. Things no human should be able to do.

"So, you could kill Aranzeiros for me, then?" Trying to appeal to his human side, as I feigned my fragility. I must not have been as convincing as I thought because he sat there, expressionless, nonchalantly twirling a useless widget in his hand.

"You know, one of the interesting things about *one* of my abilities is that it's easy to tell when someone's lying." Images flooded the subway car. Very *intimate* images. Of Aranzeiros and me.

Fucking. *Everywhere*. I wasn't even sure I wanted him to know me like that.

"Now, does *that* look like a woman that wants to kill her husband?"

"I had to survive," I interrupted, still trying to uphold the lie that Aranzeiros meant nothing to me.

Fortunately for me, he didn't fault me. "I don't even blame *you*. Humans do what they must in a world where they're no longer superior. My own mother chose to abandon me. So, she was human enough to serve her own self-interests. Even the man who raised me, against his interests, has to work with fae to maintain...*order*. Whatever that is?"

"I'm confused. So, you've always known about fae?"

"Incorrect. I was raised to *believe* they didn't exist. My uncle was trying to protect me, or whatever it was he thought he was doing. Once I got old enough, he brought me into his inner circle, something that started as a few dozen people, but has now become a movement."

If his uncle has worked with humans, that means someone in the Faeborne line must have known him. It was times like this that I wished I'd strengthened my efforts to get closer to Lianthore. If anyone would know him, I'm sure he would.

"But, like many cowardly humans, that man will always pick the better hand." He dusted off a book, positioning it close enough where my eyes couldn't betray me, despite such low light.

"Since I don't see you having much of a future, I want to entrust you with something. Something I don't get to share with many people."

Upon having a closer look, it was a photo album. It was old by how worn the pictures looked, but it was then that I forced myself not to react to a group photo I assumed was a family portrait.

Two adult white men, one I assumed to be a grandfather, maybe the other a brother or husband? But what made me lose my shit was the woman in the picture. Her warm, calm smile looked so familiar that I could swear I'd met this person if only a decade or two older.

Corra?

It was Corra, the Halfling in Aranzeiros' court. The brides-maid at my wedding. She was holding a baby, whom I assumed to be my captor. If only he had displayed his Halfling abilities, she could have proudly brought him with her. Who knows? It may have ceased to make the monster he'd become.

Grateful that I had shown no emotion, he pressed his finger up to who he'd *actually* planned to show me. Now that I concentrated, I'd also seen him before, give or take a decade or two.

"Your uncle is Councilman Bourdelon?" This time, unable to hide my emotion.

"So, you *do* know my uncle? I assume you've had the displeasure," he spat, suggesting they weren't on good terms.

"I'd learned a long time ago that even useful people have expiration dates." He closed the book and walked toward the middle of the car, holding his arms out with pride.

"Which has led me to my new family," he bragged, an eerily affectionate pride beaming from his tone.

"To have finally found my tribe. Others who wish to destroy the fae but don't kiss their fucking feet while doing so. That is the nature of Arcane. Before now, there has never been a known way to kill fae. That is, until the death of King Tarron." He turned to me, and even in the low light, appeared like a nightmare.

"I admit the first one is always the messiest. Tarron took some *trial and error*," he lowly boasted, as a sharp tinge in my gut made me want to cave. What if I had to be burdened with telling Aranzeiros and his brothers? Could they already know?

"I've been chosen for something. And you're going to give it to me." Something so familiar to what Aranzeiros had said so long ago, that I was convinced they were the same person.

"And what is that?" I asked, shaken and unsure.

"An audience with His Majesty." He faux bowed. "Because you are his property, and I have no doubt that there is nothing he won't risk attaining his property."

Across the room, I learned that all that fiddling he'd been doing had to do with a timer. I don't think I needed an explanation of what he had planned.

"But first." He used a rusted pole to poke a hole through the emergency exit on top of the train car. It must have been the only safe exit out of the train car.

"You're going to experience a deep sleep. So deep, you may not even wake up from it."

CHAPTER THIRTY-FIVE

Aranzeiros

Nightfall. Shade. Dusk. Twilight.

They were among the many things that not only felt like a second skin but my very essence as I traveled through. The current need made it effortless.

My ability to travel through the darkness felt like both a love language to myself and a love letter to my maternal side. When it spoke, I understood it. Even when it was physically draining, it was when I was at my most powerful.

I drew from the darkness, and in return, darkness drew from me. While I was a conduit for such destruction, a power that could bathe the world in ruin, there was never a time I wasn't in control. But that was before Paige.

I had restrained myself from devastating the Human Realm with darkness the moment I learned my father hadn't died by accident. But I would not be so diplomatic with Paige.

Vague sounds brought me out of my resting space. While I was never asleep when I traveled, with long distances, I was never truly awake. Only the point of disembarkment's sounds brought me out of my stupor.

Zaos' tracking ability spoke of a rundown subway, but the surrounding smells didn't remind me of the unpleasant scents that I associated with public travel. Unraveling out of the shadow, I couldn't help thinking how unwise it had been for someone to think that bringing Paige to some place gloomy would be a challenge for me.

I was literally *birthed* from the darkness. When an abandoned subway tunnel came into view, instead of waiting until I was right in front, I simply materialized inside the car, drawing from the shadows.

It wasn't long before my senses became heightened. She was here. She had to be. I could smell her scent so vividly. My mouth watered at just the thought of getting to see her again.

Fading into the car, when I did finally find my love, my heart pounded faster than it ever had. Whoever had brought her here, tied her to a pole, her mouth bound.

In the time it took to close our distance, I was infuriated. Anger poured through every nerve in my body, knowing the woman I had spent weeks spoiling, catering to and pampering had been subject to a peasant's treatment. For that alone, this person would dearly pay.

"Paige. My love." Grateful that my voice had been the anchor to bring her out of her unconsciousness.

I'd been hoping for better, but it didn't surprise me that through her body language did not share my sentiment. Eyes widening, she struggled to sit up, squinting and fidgeting against her restraints.

My heart sank when she recoiled from my attempt to touch her face. "You're still angry. I half-expected you to be." My failed attempts at getting her to look my way bruised my ego, but the smell of fear felt like too much to bear.

"Paige, I need you to listen to me. Whatever you wish to do after this is your choice," I said, bending a knee to her.

"I apologize for how I spoke to you earlier. I *meant* those things, but I don't think I've told you why. That was my fault. Since the day I met you, all I've ever wanted was a combination of keeping you safe and your undying devotion. Though being with you has challenged me. In more ways than I can admit. But most of all, it has shown how little I've had to consult others before. It scares me to know when I learn of something dangerous, there is a desire to tell you. Even over my brothers. I fear, like now, that may put you in danger someday."

Paige had been a stubborn little thing. The whole time during my revelation, all she could do was nervously look around the subway car and unsuccessfully fight against her restraints.

Hopefully, what I said was getting through to her. "You are my equal. I have to treat you like one, given that we both make it out of here and you still want to be with me."

Her eyes narrowed with both anger and annoyance. That would have to be a problem for another day. For now, I had to get us out of here.

Reaching behind her, I relieved her of the restraints bounding her body to the pillar, but given her history, I thought it best to keep her wrists bound so that she wouldn't fight me helping her.

Scooping her up into my arms, she didn't disappoint by constantly hitting her bound wrists against my chest. "I have apologized, Paige. What more can I say to you? I don't want to fight you. Or at least not right now, while my battery is half empty. Finding you exerted much of the energy required to bend it with fluency. So we'll have to do it the human way."

With that, her thrashing became more ambitious, as if she were hell-bent on me *not* helping her, which wasn't going to happen. Each step closer to the door made her that much more aggressive, making me all the more irritated.

"I'm doing this for your own good, Paige." She fought harder against me approaching the car door.

"If I take this goddess-forsaken cloth off your mouth, will you stop—"

As reaching for her mouth and the rusted-shut door, everything felt like slow motion. Three things were happening at once and with my arrogance, I hadn't even considered all the outcomes.

My desire to find Paige superseded any logic or common sense. So with each word poured from her mouth, it wasn't until then that I considered how *nothing* could ever be this easy.

"*Don't...*"

A chain reaction activated from the moment I opened the door.

"*Open...*"

The sudden smell of fire, a smell I'd grown familiar with, from the moment I could mentor Lianthore. If only I'd taken my *own* advice and listened. Paige's guidance could have avoided this entire thing.

"*The...*"

Ripping off my cape, pushing Paige inside and forcing my shadow to swallow her, I forced her some place safe, away from the fire.

"*Door!*"

Her voice echoed into the shadow, as an ounce of relief washed over me to make me forget the blankets of fire devouring the space.

CHAPTER THIRTY-SIX

Aranzeiros

The pain was crippling. Beads of sweat poured down my face and into my eyes, making everything a blur. It weighed my limbs down, making it hard to move, but even harder to want them to. In a gasping fit, I examined the lower part of my leg, the primary source of the pain.

Blood spilled from the open skin, red and taunting, as I forced myself upright to investigate the other damage. My fingertips burned with the presence of iron. Having never encountered it for myself, in attempts to pick out the visible pieces myself, the broken scream and searing pain that followed humbled me.

I wouldn't be able to take it out myself. I'm sure he intended just as much. Pump me up with iron; make me just as feeble as a human. Perhaps in his attempt, he hadn't tried to kill me, but leveling the playing field seemed to match up with what he'd said over the phone.

He wanted us to come face-to-face. This was his plan all along. If it weren't happening to me, I would have beamed, "*Well played*."

Every ounce of my blood felt like I had set it on fire, only fire was manageable. For fae, iron was not. Rising to what would have to count as a standing position, I blinked in and out, maybe three times before my vision became clear. Limping through the rubble, I stumbled against the remnants of the explosion.

My ears rang, the spicy smell of steel, smoke, and ash coating my nostrils. Even in small doses, iron had the power to heighten my sense of pain, while in attempts to dull everything else. Allowing the tunnel walls to be my balance, I staggered, making out the echoing screams in the distance.

If I planned to survive, I had to get above the surface. I had to find Paige and see if my tactic had worked in the limited time that I'd had. I traveled through shadow and darkness just fine, but I didn't have time to if I wanted to ensure she survived.

She couldn't have been pushed far, maybe a level or two above at best. By the time I shuffled through most of the rubble, nothing but flailing, panicked humans came into view, as the explosion had reached the lower level of New York's biggest station.

The evacuating humans made it even more challenging to manage the noise and chaos, as had I been at my full strength, I wouldn't have hesitated to push either of them out of the way. Not wanting to drain myself of energy, I fought against the pain, reaching the station's upper level.

Despite reaching a sizable distance, I found my palms catching my thighs, just at a chance to could catch my breath. That's when it happened.

Quiet. What once was a hall facing the 43rd Street and Vanderbilt Avenue exits swarmed with patrons, was now chillingly empty. I'd maintained enough affluence in the Human Realm to know New York never slept. And I also *knew* an illusion when I saw one.

My brother Theoden was brilliant with them. So much so, it had always been an inside joke never to fall asleep near him, otherwise, he would influence your dreams and keep you imprisoned there, at a chance for a longer laugh.

But I knew I wasn't dreaming, especially once the quiet halls bled with life.

"*You pathetic, weak, vile excuse for my son's legacy—*" An unmistakable voice forced my focus behind me. Like mist carried off by the wind, the image of colorless hair, dusky skin, and ethereal beauty faded, but solidified in the time it took for her words to carry.

Aranzales.

If this wasn't an illusion, it had to be my memory. Projected back at me to weaken me. Casted shadows faded in and out, feeding from me, clawing at the echoes I buried deep.

"*Your father does not see it, too blind in his ambitions. But mark my words, you will fill the world with darkness. Anything you touch turns to darkness.*" Her centuries-old rhetoric I had long since buried, coming to the surface.

The light pit. Aranzales struck me with masses of divine energy, all the while forcing me not to summon a power of my own.

"*Don't you dare summon that vile black art. If you retaliate, do so without that filthy sorcery you call magic.*" As my childhood self feared the consequence of letting the power that flowed within me be my anchor.

"*I live to torture you. Because your existence tortures me.*" Her voice soaked with every ounce of hatred she held for me, as the scars on my back ached thinking of the day she gave them to me.

"*Mother!*" a voice echoed, and I was sure my ears deceived me. It wasn't until his image bled through that I was frozen, if only for a moment at one last image of my father.

"*Look at what your ridiculous training has done. What are you waiting for? Heal him.*" My father's demands went unanswered as he consoled his eldest son, withering in pain from the result of her cruel treatment.

"*Aranzeiros is to be king one day.*" Her tone dismissive yet strangely charming. "*Someday he will have to know genuine pain, and you berate me over something so benign. You are not in pain, are you, Aranzeiros?"*

Projections of me dressing my wounds determined to show everyone I wasn't weak, replaced the image of my predecessors, marking the moment I became strong. That I couldn't be broken more than I already had.

"How dare you try to use *my* memories against me?" I screamed, beating against my chest, rage inflicting every part of me.

"I am the son of Tarron Faeborne. You can not *best* me with memories. Is that the best you've got?"

In an instant, my hubris got the best of me, the mist bleeding into the one time with Tarron I'd rather forget. Banging my head, trying to ward off the sound, it was like the voices grew louder, at an unbearable pitch, forcing me to listen.

"Sometimes, I fear your grandmother was right," Tarron challenged me as an adolescent. *"Lianthore, at the very least, is loyal. Zaos is resourceful. Ivaran is powerful. But what are you? Hedonistic and unpre- pared."* He paced, berating me with his silent judgment.

"It's not as if I have a choice in the matter. I am to become king, regardless of if I wish it to be——"

"This is why you are a disappointment," he interrupted. *"You will be my legacy, and I fear you will have nothing to show for it. It pains me to admit that at times, I wish you were half-human. At least then you'd be useful, instead of a poor, entitled excuse for a firstborn son."*

His words changed me. Even now, the memory brought me to my knees, as that marked the time my hatred for humans had heightened. He would have rather had a *human* son. That conver- sation scarred me more than any physical scars Aranzales could have marked me with.

I'd wanted his approval *so* bad. Against my desires, I joined my brothers' efforts in the Human Realm, hoping that my contribu- tions helped the humans kill each other since he *loved* them so much.

I'd never faced my resentment toward him, but at this moment, I realized what my grief had been suppressing.

Sometimes, I didn't *feel* like Tarron's son. I felt like his weapon.

As the heat of tears welled behind my ducts, I reminded myself that everything that made me great, I had to learn on my own. Everything I had worth having, I had to take. If I had been a disappointment, it was because I was set up for disappointment.

I had to find my own strength and approval because while I was part of their legacy, I defined my own story.

Rising to my feet, I pushed through the pain, emotionally spent from these childish games.

"Why don't you get out of my head and show yourself? You wanted an audience. Well, you've got one," I spoke through gritted teeth, as the corridor melted back into the halls of Grand Central.

It was whom I expected. The Giant Slayer. Though in person, he looked a lot less intimidating than in photos shared in briefings, and *definitely* hadn't looked like a man who could take down Tarron Faeborne.

"Now you know how *I* feel." His voice filled with torment, though I could hardly find time to care. "Do you know how hard it is to see things no one else can see?"

"You'll have to forgive me. I didn't send for you to help resolve your childhood trauma. I asked you here to kill you." As my instinct to draw whatever energy I had saved, failed to bend to my whim.

"Uh-uh. Maybe that would have worked with a *regular* human. But right now, you're dealing with me." He stalked closer, knowing that my magic was rendered useless.

Thankfully, I had over two hundred and fifty years of tactical, combat, and dare I say, even dear old grandmother's twisted training at my disposal. There wasn't a doubt in my mind that I could fight; the real problem lay in how long I'd last.

With the weight of the iron holding me down, the wrong play could give him the advantage in an instant.

If I wanted to destroy him, I had to know him. I had to be careful with my first move on the board because he'd been careful in making his.

"I learned a long time ago, due to my mother's tainted blood, that life was going to be hard. I can't recall all the crimes against humanity I've had to witness, all because I'd been cursed with the sight. It was almost a relief to know I wasn't going insane." For a Giant Slayer, he talked *a lot*. I'd almost sacrifice myself just to relieve myself of having to listen to his *moaning*.

"Everything changed when I learned I'd inherited abilities. Something *she* hadn't even done. Abilities to project. Abilities to deceive. Abilities to strip."

Looking back at what Zaos had said in his search for Paige, he claimed something had been blocking him. He must have had a negating power of some sort, not excluding his ability to alter one's perception with their memories.

For all I knew, this Halfling's power could be infinite. It was best to keep him talking until I could find the perfect opening.

"So, I bided my time. Used this world's military and my uncle's connections to learn all that I could. And learn I did. You'd be surprised by how...*humble* your kind gets when they're begging you not to kill them."

There was something about the look in his eye that seemed strangely familiar. Maybe it was a reflection of myself staring back at me. Something had caused the catalyst to his hatred for fae like something had caused mine for humans. Though, even in our similarities, I couldn't find an ounce of empathy.

"Is that what you expect? For me to beg?" I asked, pouting my lip, mocking him.

"In a good ten minutes, you won't have the energy to fight me—"

A resurgence of adrenaline coursed through me, convinced

that throwing the first punch would shut him up. The strike left him staggering, a look of surprise on his face, that he could be bested by an injured Elf.

"If we only have ten minutes." Bringing my fingers in a beckoning gesture. "Then we'd better get on with it."

With quickness, he rose to his feet, circling me in attempts to land a punch that despite my injury, I gave him no chance to land. My veins burned from the iron, but my rage fueled me to make this far from easy for him.

With every kick, punch, pound, or parry, we danced the dance of all-out war. One thing was clear; one of us would be dead before this was over. Even for all my arrogance, it was likely to be me.

The Halfling landed a lucky blow, sending me reeling backward, and forced me to my knees. As I blinked, my sight lost its sharpness, so I didn't anticipate him lifting me off the ground. At his mercy, I was obliged to stare him in his cold blue eyes, as I struggled to breathe with his hand around my neck.

Driven to act quickly, I triggered my forearm dagger into my hand, plunging it into his arm, as he dropped me in an effort to pull it out. Gasping, I struggled to put distance between us, crawling in the other direction, planting a false sense of hope that I could get away.

By now, the pain had reached my torso and whatever remained of my stomach came out in violent, throat-burning bile. A sharp pull at my injured leg forced a scream against my will, as he pulled me toward him, his fists raining down like a violent storm. As I choked on the blood, being beaten into bloody submission, my mind drifted to what I thought would be my last thought.

Paige.

"I'm sorry," I said in blood bursting from my mouth, but not to him. My regret was for her. That if I died now, I couldn't protect her anymore. What fate would she succumb to, if I'm not there to ensure her safety?

I braced myself for the final punch, the one I was sure would finally finish me, as a blinding stream of divine light drove my assailant back. My ears rang and I couldn't be sure I'd actually *heard* that accompanying scream. I couldn't move, not in my state, as my one good eye could barely make out the angelic outline that stood before me.

Was she an angel of death? Could she be collecting my soul to join my ancestors? I'd never know, because before I could make out who it was, my functions ceased, succumbing to the terminal venom.

CHAPTER THIRTY-SEVEN

Paige

Everything was happening so fast. One minute I was unconscious, the next I was trying to maneuver my way out of a MAC's Cosmetics. Aranzeiros hadn't given me any warning when he pushed me into a void of darkness. It took navigating the Lexington Passage and getting past the main concourse—which was *way* easier before half of it caved in—before I found Aranzeiros.

He'd taken a horrible beating and I hoped that he was still alive, as my fear of losing him summoned the light. His face looked beyond recognition, as the strongest creature I knew looked so vulnerable in his defeat.

"Baby." I cradled his face, fighting but failing at holding back tears. I couldn't just stand here, waiting to find out if he was dead. I knew I couldn't carry him, but whatever strength I could muster, I dragged him by his shirt, backtracking to the pharmacy I knew I'd passed on the way here.

Chaos invited opportunity, as with the explosion, came the evacuation of the building. *Something* had to help him in here. It'd been a long time since I needed a first aid kit, and there was no better place than a pharmacy to find what I needed.

Grabbing some saline solution, antibiotic ointment, and gauze, I was two seconds away from turning a corner in search of a needle and thread, when a woman wearing a pharmacy jacket met me with a baseball bat, screaming "We don't have any more money."

"I'm not trying to steal from you, I just need help. Someone is dying and I just need to clean his injuries." Her face softened, seeming surprised by my genuineness. Slowly, her grip on the bat relaxed, as she agreed to help an unconscious Aranzeiros.

It took almost the entire bottle of saline to wipe all the blood off of his face, as the pharmacist jumped back, bringing her palm to her mouth in recognition. "That's Aranzeiros Faeborne." Leaning in closer to confirm.

"It is." I had to stop myself from sharing with a stranger why he wasn't healing.

"How did he get like this?" Her tone cautious and strangely suspicious.

"He was fighting someone. That's how he received the bruises. His other injuries came from his contact with the explosive."

Curious, the woman reached out to investigate the wound, but before she came into contact, she violently snatched her hand back, standing to her feet to create as much distance as possible.

"You're not going to help me?" Confused by her sudden change of heart.

"I can't," she screamed, her tone dialing from a two to a ten.

"Aren't you a pharmacist? Surely you could—"

"I said, I *can't*!" revealing her Esterbrookian brogue.

"You're a fae?" A sense of relief washed over me. She would know better than me how to help him. "I promise I have no intentions of exposing you! I just don't know how to help him."

"If humans find out that I'm fae, they'll never support my business again," she cried out, hugging herself to calm her nerves.

"I swear." Not being to hold back the tears falling. "I mean you no harm, I just want to help him but I don't know what's wrong. I'm just learning about all of this fae-related stuff and I just don't know how to help him. Please, I know it's a big ask, but can you help me, help him?" Blinking away my tears.

She crossed her arms in front, pacing nervously at a respectable distance. "It's likely the iron. It's probably been too long since it's been lodged into his skin. I reckon he won't be much help until it's all out. But I'm fae, I can't even hold my hand above it without feeling pain."

The bomb. No wonder Jack had been so adamant about Aranzeiros finding me. He wanted him to activate the explosive, knowing iron was the *only* thing on earth that could kill him. Fae at their smallest had twice, maybe even three times the strength of a human. It was the only way the fight could have been fair.

"So, all I have to do is pull it out, and he'll live?" I asked, hopeful.

"If it's not too late." She eyed me, worriedly.

"Could you get me some tweezers, maybe even some alcohol?" Ignoring how demanding I sounded barking out orders.

"I can bring you some tweezers, but half the stuff in here barely works. I get a fae or two every couple of months, so some Fae Realm remedies might ease his pain."

She disappeared into the back room, as I prayed it wasn't too late, cradling his face to mine. When she returned, she came back with herbs, roots, and medicine, Esterbrooke-style, as she planned to guide me on how to use them.

"This is important. You've got to dip the tweezers in the anti-septic *every* time you pull one out. I'm told iron lingers, and every time you dip the tweezers back into his skin, if not clean, just forces it back into his bloodstream," she offered, as I intended to remove as much of it as I could see.

"Wish I could help you more." She skipped her foot in shame. "I'm just terrified of the effects of the iron—"

"No, you're being a big help." Sniffling, fighting back the pessimism. "When he comes to, he won't forget your act of kindness. What did you say your name was again?"

"I didn't. But it's Evarique. I don't think I caught who he was to you?" she asked as a question.

"He's my husband," I affectionately said, trying not to sound offended that she didn't recognize me.

"You're the Shadow King's wife?" She lowered to a bow, as in the moment, I argued that it wasn't necessary.

"Do you not possess the power of light?" To answer her question, I pushed down my collar to reveal the necklace.

"Sometimes," I said, embarrassed.

"Why didn't *you* just heal him?" she asked confused.

My ability to harness it had always been a work in progress. It only came when I didn't ask it to, and even then, it was infrequent. "I've never tried it with injuries this severe."

"Well, I come from a family of healers, and I've never seen anything work like light magic."

"I think I just don't like to rely on it. Considering I'm human."

"I understand your concerns, but light magic isn't like other magic. It's not widely known that it doesn't affect humans in the way other magic can twist them. The only caveat is, his magic opposes yours, and with injuries this bad, he'll likely drain you. He won't mean to, but that's the nature of his power."

"I'll just have to take that risk," I conceded, as I forced myself to pull whatever inner strength I had to manifest the light. Until I stopped denying I was connected to it, it was never going to feel like mine.

He had creatures that would miss him—hell, *I* would miss him. This couldn't be his last moment. It just couldn't. Pushing through my hypothetical grief, soothing blankets of light brushed out of my hands and over Aranzeiros' wounds.

For as offensive as the light normally felt, the healing aspect of it came naturally. Running my palm along his face, the tortured bludgeons and bruises faded, as his beautiful face had been restored to its former beauty.

"It's working," I cried, a sense of pride that it was not coming at any physical cost to me. That was, until Aranzeiros' eyes shot open. I'd grown accustomed to such dark eyes, but somehow in his wounded state, he'd lost the whites in them, as nothing but blocks of black stared up at me.

"Aranzeiros, baby. It's me." He grabbed me, unaware he was draining me to restore his strength, as his natural brawn and darkness made it impossible for me to move.

"Please, Aranzeiros," I pleaded, unable to speak beyond a whisper. "Be gentle for me."

Aranzeiros' scowl warped into a bewildered expression, as he grit his teeth against the turmoil, the whites of his eyes reappearing as he finally came to.

"Paige. My love." He caught my head before it hit the floor. "Did I hurt you?" Lightly grazing a kiss on my forehead.

"I've been better," my weak attempt at a joke.

"You're one of the *bravest* humans I've ever met."

"And you're one of the most bullheaded fae *I've* ever met. You should have taken my bound off earlier, we could've avoided all this."

"And yet you came back for me." He eyed me down through an affectionate gaze.

"You can't get rid of me that easily," I dryly joked.

Aranzeiros looked around the establishment as if for the first time, confused as to the bowing pharmacist stood just a few feet away. "Who are you?"

"She was the one that helped me, help you," I weakly confessed, as he clocked her for a Water Lily Nymph faster than I could have ever done without his gift of seeing past the Veil in the Human Realm.

"Your patronage will not go overlooked. You will be paid

handsomely for aiding your king and queen," he spoke, nuzzling his beard against my face.

"I'd say taking down a Halfling hell-bent on killing us seems like payment enough." She jovially shrugged.

He kissed my forehead. "If I could give you back your strength, I would. But I can't heal like you," heI admitted guiltily.

Strangely, my energy was already returning, though not as quickly as I would've liked it to. "The problem isn't whether you can heal. The problem is, when he comes back out to face you, will you be ready for him?"

"His power is unique, that much I am not ashamed to admit. But he is no match for me, so long as he doesn't have iron on him. I can't use my magic. Whatever he does, prevents me from doing so, but he won't have the advantage like last time, of that I am sure."

It took some catching up to learn Aranzeiros had already been aware of Jack having a familial stake with Councilman Bourdelon, but he was lost for words learning that not only was it his uncle, but that Corra, a woman in his court had been his biological mother.

"I'm not saying I feel sorry for him, but he's got a lifetime of rage that rivals even yours," I admitted, feeling a ping of displaced sympathy.

"And a chance to cause even more devastation. Paige, he needs to die."

"Aranzeiros, you can't kill everyone just because they're inconvenient—"

"He killed my father, Paige. I will experience only restless nights until nothing left remains of him. Not his name, not his pain, I will rip him limb from limb, because that's the pain that *I* feel." He ended his passionate rant, and it pained me to see how much this tortured him.

They shared the same pain and couldn't even see it.

Sensing he was scaring me, he brought his voice to a calm. "What, Paige?"

I grabbed both sides of his face, hoping that my touch soothed him. "I know that you're in pain. But it's not going to bring him back." I smiled warmly.

Aranzeiros' once scowl was now replaced by an Elf in tears. "What would you do, my love?"

"It doesn't matter what I would do. This is personal for you."

He took my hands in his, pushing his passionate anger away for harmony. "But I promised that I would listen to you more. And trust your counsel."

"Let me talk to him."

"That I *can not* do—"

"Aranzeiros, this is something I'm better at than you. He's a tortured soul. I have experience humbling tortured souls." He squeezed my hand, not wanting to let me go. "You don't have a human side, so you don't know how to cater to one. He wouldn't have even put me in that situation if he thought that it wouldn't hurt you."

"Which is why I don't trust you to face him on your own," he said, his twilight eyes welled with tears.

"If it doesn't work my way, you'll just do what you do best. What you already intended to do." Plus, I had a plan. It was a risk to test it, but I didn't want Aranzeiros to know just in case it didn't work.

"You show me all the wonderful things that fae can do. Let me show you what a human can do."

Aranzeiros stood to his feet, both reluctant but confident I would not fail him. But should things turn in the other direction, he had my approval that if he felt my life was in danger, he'd handle things *his* way.

"I trust my queen knows what she's doing, but should a ringlet on your head fall out of place...well, you know the rest," he conceded, as I was about to leave the pharmacy when we totally forgot about Evarique.

"I know I said taking care of that psychopath was payment enough," interrupting our moment. "But scoping out all the damage here, I would gladly take a check. Assuming that it's still on the table, My King," she smiled, in a graceful bow.

CHAPTER THIRTY-EIGHT

Paige

It took several minutes of hyping myself up to go out there and attempt to reason with a madman. I had a theory worth testing, and should it come to that, I wanted to see how it panned out. As I made my way out of the 42nd Street exit, the background bled, and the crackling autumn New York strip in a matter of seconds warped into a landscape of pure white.

Testing my theory, I tried to bring forth a spark from my ill-prepared magic, and to my shock, a remnant of it came. It meant he couldn't use both his powers at the same time, something that might prove useful if I could keep him distracted.

He was altering my perception, but this time it was different. It *felt* real. From the snow banks covering the forests of my little town of Fort Scott, Kansas, to the piercing bite of the cold.

Kansas wasn't known for its harsh winters like other Midwestern states, but this had been a state record, as a light cough caught my attention, turning around to witness that little brown girl ill-prepared for a snowstorm, trying to survive in a makeshift tent.

He was showing me my worst day.

A day that I almost died. If a park ranger hadn't taken pity on me when he did, I would have lost a toe to frostbite. It was hard to believe I'd only been six years old then. It seemed like a lifetime ago, that in my parents' many gambling binges, due to all the money they owed, were forced to lie low and abandon me for days, sometimes even weeks, at a time.

I was too young to know I couldn't survive a storm that severe, but my desire to find food outweighed my judgment.

The one time social services were inclined to intervene, my sad excuses for parents knew they couldn't collect as much cash assistance if they no longer had custody of me.

So, they convinced anyone that mattered, that I was just some troubled kid that ran away, leaving me to be the blame for nearly freezing half to death during a snowstorm.

Peering down at that version of myself, I felt sorry for her. She lost her voice at that moment. No one protecting, nurturing, or loving her, and most of all, no one able to speak for her. Not even herself.

What made things worse was that moment wasn't even the end of her decades-long abuse. In time, she became nobody. But she wasn't nobody, not anymore. And she had a voice. One she that knew could change *something*.

"Is that your ploy?" I asked calmly, to what looked like no one at first. As the memory faded, a muscular, dark figure stood out amidst the 42nd Street exit.

"Show me my worst memories to exploit my weak points."

"I think we both know you don't have many weak spots," he taunted.

"That's because I was already dead by then. A living corpse whose only aim was to cower and survive." Noticing the burn marks left on his arm. I must have got him good.

"Which is all you'll ever do if we're forced to co-exist with fae. You don't see it because you're different now. You've become something else. Something that shouldn't even exist."

"So, by extension, you shouldn't exist, considering you're half of what you hate."

"I don't hate *anyone*." He stretched his arms out, emboldened enough to take a few steps toward me.

"I just think fae…are always going to choose themselves. And when humans are no longer useful to them, we'll see how they *really* feel about us." A jab I almost immediately associated with his mother. I wanted to share how much she missed him, that he hadn't been forgotten, and that she regretted her mistake.

But the fact that I wasn't dead yet proved I was finally getting through to him. And I didn't want to shift the conversation when I was doing so well.

"Maybe you're right. Maybe this world will eventually destroy us. But from where I stand, *humans* have always tried to destroy me. Humans have silenced me. Humans fight every day to take my power away. But I'm not like selfish humans. Even though you've committed crimes, lives you can't bring back, I still feel like you can be saved. It's why *I* came to talk to you and not Aranzeiros. I don't want anyone to die—"

As before I could finish, five fingers violently wrapped around my neck, making every scrap of oxygen feel like a gift.

"The fact that you see me eradicating those filthy, savage worthless pieces of shit as anything *other* than an act of war shows you have that fairy's cum so far down your throat, you can't tell whether those are your words, or his."

"Please," I pleaded. "I'm trying to help you." As I struggled, beating against his wrists and forearms. His once sympathetic gaze morphed into something twisted and violent, that I was almost relieved that when he let go, it was because Aranzeiros had intervened.

I fell to the ground, coughing and struggling to restore the depleted oxygen, grateful that it hadn't taken long for Aranzeiros to keep his word.

Accompanying screams came with the start of a struggle

Aranzeiros intended to finish, as he made use of a makeshift blade made with the sharp edges of a broken bottle end, driving it repeatedly through the skin of Jack's arm, until he forced him back, with his own tactical training.

"We did it your way, now it's time to do it mine." Aranzeiros enraged, fully prepared to give his assailant the fight he so desperately asked for. Without the hindrance from the iron, Aranzeiros' skilled hands thrust out like blades of death.

The halfling was strong, stronger than any human I'd seen, but I fear he'd be no match for such a kill-happy monarch.

Watching two blockheads kill each other wasn't exactly the thrilling prospect people made it out to be in movies. I was *dreading* this being a potential subject of a future council meeting, and because this was going to have dire consequences no matter what, I had to stop them before either of them committed any *more* damage than their dick-measuring contest had already done.

But I wasn't exactly equipped to break up a fight. Was I?

Neither of them would listen to reason, no matter how many times I'd tried, and since Jack's attention was otherwise distracted, what better chance than to test what I could really do if I stopped fearing magic?

Normally, it only came out during times of fear or distress, but I had never *needed* it before now. I'd never allowed myself to fully bond to it, because of my self-doubt, but if I had any chance at stopping them, I'd never need a better reason to accept that the power was mine to claim.

Add in a bit of my silent rage for being put in so many compromising situations, that was my anchor to bring forth the magic that ill-fittingly chose me.

With that thought, a spark ignited, stretching everywhere my nerves could reach. Hundreds of voices whispered, the singings of every forbearer that owned the necklace speaking to me at once.

Some voices were misleading. Others were reluctant to trust.

But I honed in the last voice, who through effervescent passion, convinced me I was who a Faeborne chose. It was *my* power and that nothing should stop me from embracing and owning it.

The light bonded to me in wrenching, agonizing anguish, as I feared it was ripping me apart, like past warnings. Once the pain came to a calm, it plagued me with nausea and the feeling of energy peeling through all of my nerves, creating a symbiotic relationship with its host.

My palms hit the pavement to gather myself, but when I lifted my hand, light poured through effortlessly, as I brought forth a violent storm, hoping to create a wedge between them.

But despite my efforts, I'd been a second too late. Through my tortuous acceptance of my gift, in their struggle, Aranzeiros had slit Jack's throat, as Jack's instinct to put pressure on the wound served next to no relief.

"I didn't think that you'd *actually* kill him."

"What was there left to do, then let him choke on his own blood, like an animal?" Aranzeiros claimed, defensively crossing his arms across his chest.

"I just think you would heal if you got to receive *real* justice—"

"You mean your human justice?" He spat like it was a gut-wrenching swear. "That is not how we do things in Esterbrooke."

"Well, right now we're not *in* Esterbrooke. You could go to actual prison for killing a human being," I argued, catering to the fact I needed him, and I couldn't bear us being apart again.

Aranzeiros' gaze never softened, as he regarded me with intense anger and annoyance. "He's lucky that I love you," Aranzeiros managed, through a gritted-teeth scowl.

"*Heal him.*" Waving his hands away in a dismissive gesture, as I closed the distance between Jack and me, pressing my palm against his gashing wound.

I'd yet to master anything, but if light could restore Aranzeiros from his former state, surely it could heal a Halfling.

"You're going to be okay," I murmured to myself, fighting against the searing pain, unlike any time I'd tried to heal before.

He must have been on the brink of death. It almost felt like a wasted effort. "Paige, what's happening?" Aranzeiros shouted, desperate to understand the reasoning behind my screams.

"It hurts...so much death." I found myself not being able to articulate the words.

Even in his state, he was trying to project more memories onto me, but it felt different this time. It was more like his own memories. His life flashed before both of our eyes. He was beyond tormented, as it forced me to slush between his trauma, and the trauma that he caused. Even with all the innocent lives he took, I still felt sorry for him. But I had to keep him alive because he deserved to pay for what he had done.

The pendant on my neck heated with anticipation, so much I thought that by the time I was done, there'd be a hole in its place. As Aranzeiros tried to rip my hand from Jack's wound, coming into contact with my skin, the pendant burst into tiny little pieces, physically exhausting me to the point of collapse.

"Am I dying?"

Aranzeiros picked my head up, resting it on his lap. "I don't think so. But magic is expensive—" as he stopped mid-sentence, mouth agape, eyes filled with doubt and uncertainty.

It wasn't until he toothed his fingers through a ringlet of my hair, that I realized why he'd been lost for words.

My hair. It had turned completely white.

"It can't be..." he said to himself, astonishment stretched across his features.

"What happened to me?"

"I don't know." He eyed me curiously. "But I don't think you'll need that necklace anymore—"

As a distant cough forced Aranzeiros to his feet, he grabbed Jack by his torn collar, snarling at him. "The only reason you breathe life is because of the mercy of my wife."

"And the only reason I didn't kill you is that you showed me what you are. I've always known, but now the world will know what threats humans now face. I could have killed you, but I've done my research on you. As extensively as I'd learned about you and your brothers, my mission had always been clear. Force you out of hiding," he charmingly spat.

"And that of Councilman Bourdelon?" Aranzeiros anxiously shook him.

"That weak, inconsistent sack of unbalanced power? He's not who leads me. He's just a small piece on the chessboard. Movements like this require politicians just as much as soldiers." Planting the idea in our heads that this was only the beginning.

"Humans don't have *time* like you do. But unlike you, we're patient." He smiled back as Aranzeiros loosened his grip.

"It's a good thing my wife healed you." Aranzeiros circled as darkness shaped like daggers formed in each of his hands.

Before I could stop him, he lodged his magic-infused blades, one through his ear, the other through his neck.

"Because then, I get the pleasure of killing you *all* over again!" His voice matching his malice, so filled with vengeance, he could see nothing else.

"You wanted to expose me for what I am," he yelled, the darkness pouring through every open wound, filling his body with an inky, malevolent shadow. Black Ichor bled through his nose, eyes, ears, and even his fingernails in swift, vicious streams, as Aranzeiros adopted a bone chilling persona.

"Well, let me *tell* you what I am. I am a Faeborne. And *no one* makes a fool of a Faeborne," Aranzeiros roared, as his victim murmured two last words, before exploding all over Aranzeiros.

Covered in blood, guts, and mixed in darkness, Aranzeiros looked at me, disappointment washing over his features that he had failed to meet my expectation.

"You were wrong about one thing, Paige. As tortured as he

convinced you to believe. *No one* has a lifetime of rage that can rival mine."

***

As the dust began to settle, it had been the first time since my initial move to New York that the streets weren't scattered with people. Sure, crowds came to see the fuss, but an event like this? An incident like this was the first of its kind.

Aranzeiros showed no shame, even confessing to the arriving law enforcement, as they walked him off in a cop car. They couldn't cuff him. He threatened to break each of their hands if they dare try, but he hadn't seemed weary that any of these events would affect him.

He wasn't used to dealing with consequences. In Esterbrooke, he did what he wanted. I knew deep down, he'd only confessed because he thought he'd disappointed me, but since he'd fulfilled the avenging of his father, I prayed he could finally move on from his death.

I waited in the back of an ambulance until I could get a ride from someone I trusted. For now, I wasn't sure there were many that I could.

"Sister, you called upon me?" Zaos seeped through the side of the vehicle.

"Thank you for answering me." Tightening the security blanket given to me around my shoulders. "I'm ashamed to admit I don't have any of your numbers."

"Nonsense, sister," he interrupted. "This is a delicate matter. I am sure Aranzeiros would not entrust your safety with anyone but his brothers."

Lianthore materialized, from what appeared out of nowhere, though through my apprehension, I'm sure he'd been there the whole time. He did the honors of helping me to my feet, and escorting me to a limo they both followed me into.

"Paige, I know that this day was grueling, but was there *anything* you can remember about tonight? Something that could help us with this rogue group?" Lianthore asked calmly.

I was shaken, but not so much that the events of today escaped me. "Plenty," I assured, despite still struggling against the pain radiating from my neck—hell, my whole body, having been choked and forced to heal a dying man. "Only, I don't think all of it would interest you as much as what his last words were."

"Why would we be concerned with his last words?" Lianthore inquired.

"Because they were '*Arcane Lives*'. That means something to you guys, right?"

Lianthore and Zaos shared a look between each other, and then leaned in closer.

"We're going to need you to recall *everything* that happened since the time he abducted you from that apartment building."

CHAPTER THIRTY-NINE

Aranzeiros

"I know that for the many of you, in this room, the existence of anything *other* than human may be a shock to you." As my footsteps echoed against the polished floor. Members of the public poured in, bursting through the seams to witness the highest profile case New York, maybe even the whole country, had ever seen.

"For some, it may even be a sense of relief. Not all of you have been protected by the Veil. Now you can finally make sense of the things you've seen but were forced to ignore."

My lawyers hadn't advised it, but considering it was my Sixth Amendment right to have some level of control over my defense, I also chose to make my closing argument. The prosecutor probably thought he hit the target; this could be career-making for him should the jury vote in his favor, but I thought it best to appeal to the human side of the jury.

"Some of you will make me your children's Boogeyman. I do not blame you. In many ways, I've been my *own* realm's source of fear. That is why it gives me great pleasure to *humble* every single one of you. Because had it not been for my kind—many of you, if not all of you, would be dead."

Feedback from the microphones from the camera crew was drained out by the reactive gasps in the courtroom. My point was coming; they just had to be patient.

"Before either of you were even cells in your mother's wombs, your kind has been destined for failure. No, I do not blame the common people, and certainly not anyone in this room. I blame your incompetent leaders. Every war your race has ever won is because of us. Every recession, no any monumental event you've ever overcome, could not be done without our efforts. But even if we entertained that you could survive without us, what would you do, should another unchecked lunatic storm this beautiful city?

Your world's leaders are never going to tell you this, but I will. I'm the scary bedtime story that you *know*. The darkness that has been living amongst you in plain sight. *None* of you know what lurks in the shadows. None of you are prepared to fight the things that seem impossible to face.

So, next time when you ask yourselves, should *I* fear the realm of fae? Remember that a human hybrid was willing to bomb Grand Central station to work through his unresolved mommy issues."

*****

The jury requested a short recess, and my pace slowed at the sight of my brothers crouched over or impatiently pacing as we waited for the verdict.

"Well...You weren't subtle." As Ivaran came to a stand, he smiled, a glint of humor in the crow's feet of his eyes.

"But he was honest," Zaos continued. "I hope those simple humans consider that with this so-called *verdict*?"

Lianthore kept his pace, and I know it was due to the fact he'd been cleaning my mess up for weeks. "This is a PR nightmare,

Aranzeiros. I do not think you realize how much damage control this is going to take—"

"What's *really* on trial is our heritage," Vamir interrupted.

"But I'm sure that public execution and closing statement didn't help," Tavnis jovially challenged.

Everyone was tense over the last few months, what with all the court appearances and press conferences. No one had been prepared to come out of the forest this soon. It forced the agreement made by the court and council to expedite an emergency executive order on how to deal with the upcoming storm.

There wouldn't be a news outlet that wasn't following my trial, and I'd pushed my brothers, my subjects, and my wife at the center of it.

"Well, I for one, am *glad* Aranzeiros humbled that courtroom. Humans are too comfortable. They think that they are competent enough to survive on their own. Anything he said was nothing short of the truth," Zaos offered.

"Humans do not want the truth, Zaos. They want ignorance. They want safety!" Lianthore interrupted, frustration in his tone.

"I do not give a fuck about what humans want. Because no matter what you give them, they will always want more. Except for Paige, I love her." Zaos shrugged. "All I know is, Aranzeiros saved their insignificant lives, and *he's* the one on trial. A human better not *ever* cross me!" He managed to huff in a nearly single breath.

"By the way, brother. Nice job on Councilman Bourdelon." Theoden winked.

As if in unison, Ivaran and Zaos shared looks between each other asking "What work?"

If any good came from all of this, it was that Councilman Bourdelon's history was not exactly squeaky clean. Following my arrest, anyone who'd so much as *breathed* in Jack Hodgins' direction was being looked into, and with all the cover-ups that could be traced to Bourdelon, it gave me great peace to learn he'd avoided freedom as well.

He'd barely made it to his cell before he was found dead, an *alleged* suicide. It had not been their most creative job, but it sent the message that anyone who tried to make a fool of us would pay for it in blood.

"The jury has reached a verdict!" We were called back into the courtroom, wearing expressions of glass to hide our collected despondency. Human laws were barely fair for *humans*, so there was a chance I might not win this.

Prison was the least of my worries. At best, I'd probably be doing time at some resort version of prison, made available for the rich and powerful. My only concern had been for Paige.

She'd frequented these courtrooms for the beginning of the trials, but the closer the verdict was set to announce, the more I insisted she stopped coming.

She had disagreed with the *outcome* of how I'd handled things, and less with the reason. She was content so long as it gave me peace, but leading up to the verdict, in a heated argument, I made it clear that any sentence I received, I'd prefer her to be as far away from it.

The last time we even got to share each other's company was seven weeks ago. If I was sentenced, I didn't want her to feel obligated to wait on me.

"All rise for the judge," the bailiff instructed, reintroducing the judge and asking us to be seated once they were settled.

"Has the jury reached a verdict?" the judge asked, prompting the jury foreperson to stand.

"Yes, Your Honor." Handing the clerk the verdict form, as it was then handed to the judge.

The judge read it silently to herself before handing it back for the reading of the verdict. The suspense was abhorrent, as this concept of a speedy trial was not living up to its name.

"The jury finds the defendant, Mr. Aranzeiros Faeborne—"

"That's *King* Aranzeiros Faeborne," I interrupted, aware of how that looked to the crowd.

"I'm sorry?"

"Did I not speak clearly enough? It is not *Mr.* It is *King* Aranzeiros," I corrected, leaving a nasty scowl on the clerk's mouth before the judge finished reading the verdict.

"The jury finds the defendant, *King* Aranzeiros Faeborne...Not guilty."

The lightening sensation in my chest spread. A mixture of outrage and relief roared amongst the seated public, as even with my arrogance, I was preparing for the worst.

I was walking away a free Elf. My only wish was that I had more than just a kingdom to go back to.

***

Tarron had always been charismatic with the human press. As I stood before the courtroom steps, I was an Elf out of hiding. As crowds advanced, in search of the best photo-op, I was beginning to understand why.

Humans weren't as dumb as they looked. I still stood by everything I had said, but unlike others before me, I'd actually received justice. Maybe all humans weren't as bad as I had led myself to believe. Paige had been the starting point for that.

"King Aranzeiros, can we get a comment on your recent verdict?" Several members of the press bombarded me with cameras, holding their microphones in my direction, in hopes that I'd stop.

Luckily, for me, Ivaran could part any crowd, but as a last-minute decision, I decided I'd indulge them. Everyone wanted that first-page scoop.

"All I have to say is that both humans and fae have a long road ahead of us. We will continue to grow and work together, learn from each other, and that journey starts today."

With that, the seven of us reached our limousine at the curb, relieving us of our audience of the overcrowded audience of press, anti-fae groups, and admirers alike.

As we disappeared into our transportation, the vehicle pulled off, a shared mash of alleviating heaves filled the backseat with profuse relief.

"You make my job very hard to do, Brother. I will give you that." Lianthore roared, with a gentle slap to the shoulder. "It is why we drink. To a non-guilty verdict!"

As many of my siblings reached into mini bar in search of bottled ales.

"Human laws are strange, but as long as they work for us, I can't complain. And the best thing is, you can't be tried twice for the same crime!" Zaos shrugged in exasperated joy.

"This is good news, but I do not think we are out of the clear just yet. Aranzeiros has set in motion things we can not undo. Bourdelon is dead. Which was necessary. But I fear whoever takes his place will be more of a—"

"A problem for another day!" Tavnis clinked his bottle to Lianthore's and in our celebrated joy, I was regretful for not asking Paige to come. It felt like we'd been on borrowed time and I couldn't bear the idea of the verdict not falling in my favor. But being in the company of all my brothers, it felt like something she should have been there for, too.

I found comfort in stroking my fingers against the handkerchief in my breast pocket. It smelled of her and gave me the comfort I needed with choosing not to see her for the last two months.

"Look at you." Theoden interrupted my train of thought with his Highland brogue. "A free Elf and you can't even celebrate right."

"I know I have a lot to celebrate," I said, balling my hands into. "I just regret telling Paige not to come."

My brothers, especially Theoden, had been wonderful to Paige in my absence. Since Theoden had gifted her his empathy, he'd committed himself to her counsel, even missing several dates from Tavnis and Vamir's shared tour.

It warmed my heart she felt so comfortable in their presence, as I all but held them hostage for any update on her well-being.

When the limousine came to a halt, each of my brothers, one by one, started vacating the vehicle.

"You might want to get out for this one." Lianthore stuck his head into the back of the limo.

Cautiously exiting the vehicle, we were parked in front of one of New York's grandest parks. Not far from where we stood, a horse and carriage sat idly until the coach creature opened the carriage door.

It was my queen. My light. My Paige.

Hugging each of my brothers, she stopped once she reached me and before I could get any words out she shot me with an, "I'm mad at you."

Wiping the solitary tear that fell from her eye, I looked back to my brothers as they made themselves scarce by ordering the limo to depart. Paige and I silently agreed to start walking, as when we reached a respectable distance, I found the strength to break the silence.

"I'm surprised that you came. Surely, I gave you every reason not to."

"Aranzeiros, that time we participated in the hunting event, what did I tell you?" She brought her hands together in a passionate clasp.

"You demanded daily hugs and kisses. Which I intend to greatly make up to you if you can find it in your heart to forgive me." I moved in closer until I left her no room at all to escape me.

"It's like there's this wall of yours that never fully drops. I didn't even get to celebrate your win with you—"

"So, if I lost, you could see me handcuffed and carried off like

some ordinary convict?" I retorted, instantly regretting the look it
caused in her eyes.

"Paige, I apologize. It was not my intention to steal that
moment from you. I just didn't think I could handle having the
last image I saw as a free Elf be that look you're giving me now.
You are my *everything*. Everything I do, I do because I am a fool."
Letting her out of the cage my arms held her up against the
carriage.

"I do because I am impulsive. I do because I do not share that
longing to be good all the time. But I want to be good. For you.
Would you have wanted your last view of me, tainted by
me *begging* hypocritical humans for my freedom?"

With my finger, I gingerly stroke the side of her face. "Especially when you're so much *better* at it than me."

Paige's lips thinned in irritation, as she writhed and undulated
in clear defeat. "Then you say things like that. I came out of that
carriage with the intention of being so fucking mad at you," she
spat, before aggressively pulling me to her height and devouring
me whole.

"I swear if I wasn't so horny and pregnant, this would have
gone an entirely different way." She mumbled under her kiss, as I
violently pulled away to make sure I heard that right.

"Are you sure?" Her lips stretch into a slow, steady smile of joy.
"I hardly gave my best performance last time."

"Trust me, an hour alone with you was enough. I'm honestly
surprised it hasn't happened sooner."

Lifting her up, I swung her in my arms, leaning in so I could
reclaim her lips once again. "I haven't fucked in seven weeks," I
growled at her.

"Boy, we can't do in the Earth Realm what we can in Esterbrooke!" she said, in reference to Central Park.

"Well, it's a good thing you came in a carriage. Because this
time, I plan to give my *best* performance."

EPILOGUE

Paige

"This is all so much information!" I clicked away at my laptop, organizing the folders I'd shifted through in a way that made me feel organized. Computers and I had never been friends, so much that I'd been relieved that in the Fae Realm, I didn't deal with them much.

But after being brought into the Faeborne fold, after careful consideration, they had chosen me to run their stake in big pharma. The pharmaceutical industry was a mess in the Human Realm. Whether I could handle it or not, wasn't the issue for me. I wanted to have a stake and voice where I could change something.

So, when Lianthore assessed where I could fall, I'd requested this above all other opportunities. Plus, being the CEO of a pharmaceutical company meant my name wasn't as important as the company or brand.

"You've adjusted fine so far. There is no doubt you will excel at this, as you've yet to let me down so far." Aranzeiros stretched on the lounge, opposite my office desk. Everyone insisted that this early on I should hire a manifold of assistants—which I would in time. But I wanted to be as hands-on in the beginning.

The door flung open, forcing both of our awareness to spike. "Impromptu meeting in the conference room. *Now!*" Lianthore announced, before disappearing back into the Faeborne Enterprises hallway.

Aranzeiros quickly rose to his feet, but I had to stop him in his attempt to aid me to rise to my own. "I got it." Refusing his help, pushing through the discomfort that came with standing with a sixth-month baby bump.

"Well, you know how I am when you're like this." He kneeled, caressing and kissing my stomach. "I get to do the fun part and you have to do all the work. Anything I can do to relieve your burden, I will always seek to do." He came to a stand and placed another kiss on my forehead.

"Go on without me. I'm right behind you," I asserted, wanting to make sure I got everything before I reached the room. With that, Aranzeiros headed for the conference room, as I waddled toward the mastrena coffee machine in the crook of my office.

I couldn't believe I was already on baby number two, not long after giving birth to Rayvana, our first daughter. There'd been an immense relief on my part to see I'd birthed my twin in Halfling form. The only thing that caused initial alarm was the pure white hair she inherited from my exposure to light magic.

No one was sure whether that meant she'd be born with my ever-adjusting ability, like her father before her, but I was hoping not *all* my hypothetical offspring would be born with colorless hair. Every time I was tempted to dye it back to my original color, Aranzeiros would assure me it suited me, as it gave the impression to others that I wasn't like other humans anymore.

As I waited for my espresso machine to boot up, in a sizable walk to the fridge, my attention drew to my flower in a cup. That was kind of Aranzeiros' thing now. And I got so used to it, I didn't even fancy them in a vase anymore. I accepted Aranzeiros was *never* going to do things the human way and strangely, I would always adore him for it.

Preparing the non-espresso-based drinks was a cinch since I pre-made them at the start of each week. They'd probably never noticed, but with urgent meetings like the one I was headed to, those unruly brothers were a lot more compliant with caffeine.

Learning their preferences, I made sure each tea, latte, or frap was made to Faeborne-tailored perfection. Once I finished everyone's drink, I maneuvered them on a tray, making my way to the conference room to not keep everybody waiting.

"One sweet tea with lemonade for Tavnis." I beamed, making sure not to stare him in the eye for too long.

"You are too kind." He friskily tipped his cowboy hat in gratitude.

"One caramel iced latte for Zaos."

"Thank you, Sister," he said with tired eyes and fatigue.

"Kona brew. Light, two sugars for Vamir. Scotch with a *shot* of espresso for Theoden."

"You know me so well." Theoden smiled back, as Vamir gulped it down faster than I could hand it to him.

"Frap for Ivaran, and matcha tea for Lianthore."

"Thank you, Paige." As Lianthore placed in front of his seat at the table, Ivaran offered a silent nod for the kind gesture.

That only left Aranzeiros. "Black, one sugar." I laid it down, as he eyed me with adoration, before pulling out my chair in front of Lianthore's, and disposed of the tray.

"So, now that everyone's here." Lianthore stood, circling the room, his voice projecting as he paced. "As you remember from our last council meeting, the seat left by Councilman Bourdelon remains empty. There will be no doubt that when it *is* filled, his replacement could be a red herring, or one to watch. But we still have topics of concern to bring to the next council meeting, especially the arrangements made with the League. I will need to marry soon," he huffed, disappointingly.

Even in the years that passed, Lianthore had yet to discover his fated mate. He'd consulted with Ivaran and Aranzeiros, and still hadn't sensed that signature compulsion that came with wanting to claim a human bride. It looked better on our part, as it appeared as though it wasn't our goal to pack our side as quickly as possible. If anything, it was why the former councilman's seat went so long without being filled.

Lianthore hadn't been as reluctant to marry as Aranzeiros had been, but he was dragging his feet with hopes if he was patient, he'd find that special human.

"But that's not what I came to discuss." He handled an overhead projector, sifting through images of anti-fae protests sweeping through nearly every continent with viable life. Signs, banners, recruitment rallies, hoisted signs reading 'Arcane Lives' or 'Arcane will be our savior'.

As a human, I was used to dealing with this kind of violence, but I'm sure it never failed to amaze my Elven brothers how cruel humans could be toward others different from them. Now that I had Halfling children, I was terrified that this was the world we'd created for them. Aranzeiros' actions had thrust this into motion and while he couldn't undo his past mistakes, he was dedicated to fixing his wrongs with a complete cultural shifting campaign led by Lianthore.

"We are now entering the prelude. Whether it's the Arcane Sorcerer, or an unknown plague, we can not let this forthcoming threat come to pass. All that we *have* depends on it."

EXTENDED EPILOGUE

Lianthore

"Your Royal Highness, we have prepared the green room for you. Your scotch of choice was a little hard to find, so I hope the next best thing seconds as a replacement," a production assistant said, in an attempt to make my time before going on air more accommodating.

"I knew one might be hard to find in the Human Realm. So long as it's top shelf, it will do." The mousy assistant clutched her clipboard close to her chest, her gaze downward to avoid my stare.

Since coming out of the forest, I received that a lot now, my eyes a swirling performance of dancing crimson. Some were amazed, others were conflicted, but since the discovery of my dual Elven and Dragon heritage, the humans had given me a nickname. By most mainstream media, they had deemed me the Dragon Prince.

"If you just step this way, we'll mic you up and get you ready before you head out there. I'm Thanh, and I'll be the one taking care of any requests to make your time comfortable," she stammered, as I took one full look over her gamine appearance.

She was certainly attractive. Small, bottle auburn hair, and curvaceous for her height and build. I was better at determining human heritages than most of my brothers, and while her accent placed her native to the UK, her background was likely Vietnamese.

"What did you say your name was again?" I asked, positive that she mentioned it but too focused on her curves to recall.

"Thanh, Your Highness," she stuttered again.

"Thanh, in an hours' time, I want you to meet me in that greenroom and wait for me." Her face broke.

"Why did I do something wrong?"

"Yes, and no. No, you're not in trouble and yes, you distracted me with your beauty. In short, I plan to fuck you and I've determined by your apprehension that a human like you has never been fucked properly. Do not worry about your superiors, they're already aware of my demands to bed someone while I'm here. Consider yourself lucky that I chose you."

"Okay," she stammered, pushing her glasses further up her nose to look me in the eye. She did have beautiful eyes. I bet she'd look even more lovely with my cum streaking her face.

Tonight, I'd be going up against another scheduled guest, someone I wasn't looking forward to meeting since discovering her organization had fueled more hatred of us fae.

Zunaira Choudhry, founder of H.A.U.N.T[2], otherwise known as Humans Against Unearthly Nightmares That Terrify, was a bored housewife with a podcast that blossomed into the nation's largest public hate group. I'd spent my morning watching her musings and learning her talking points.

She commanded her audience in one of two ways; giving people something to fear and passing her beliefs as a brand of pseudo-education. I was used to dealing with humans like her. I made a promise to my brothers that I would keep my composure.

The time had come to collect me, and I was later mic'd up and brought to the broadcast room, then led to the round table where we'd have our discussion. The woman across from me looked much different in real life, or perhaps on her little podcast, she put more effort in appearing everyday relatable.

Her dusky brown skin and long dark hair were the makings of a beautiful human, but her views on fae turned what could be a stunning face into a grotesque waste of exquisite features. Silence fell over the table as we took our cues and the cameras began rolling.

The show's host sat at the head of the table, opening the show by introducing his guests. Zunaira didn't waste any time spouting her biased opinions, falsified statistics, and outlandish conspiracy theories. I, however, was only here for the facts.

"My thing is, if fae occupation is so *vital*, why did you stay hidden for so long in the first place? By the way you all tell it, you've all been sitting back idly, helping from the sidelines, but this Human Realm has faced a lot of disasters. Where were all of you then?"

My lips took on an unpleasant twist. I'd mastered the human smile, devoid of any humor, and it took everything inside of me not the burst into flames. I had had a bit of a temper; from what I was told, it was an unfortunate trait inherited from the line of dragons. But I'd had no choice but to learn how to channel my rage. I still struggled at times, but it'd become something more useful, *in most cases*.

"Very good question, Zunaira. You'll have to ask your own leaders why? Now, I admit I've been around a whole two-hundred-and-seventy more years than you , so it *appears* as though I have more insight. But truthfully, we never intended to hide. We just sought to limit our contact with the Human Realm because once you help a starving man, he always comes back for more."

Her brown eyes narrowed as she adjusted in her chair and played with her pen. Clearly, someone was jaded that this conversation wasn't going her way.

"Humans don't have any access to the so-called '*Esterbrooke*'. But Fae Realm citizens can come and go as they please?"

"Please do not spread falsehoods," I protested.

"Your privileged class, your one-percenters, your legislators have *all* always had access. In fact, laws are being put into place as we speak to open our borders for citizenship. But like most leaders, they only inform you of surface-level problems. Gas prices, the lowering of taxes, and many of you don't even have the capacity to research what's happening in your own country. The preference comes to those with significant fae ancestry first, but the plan is to wave—"

"So basically, only *special* humans."

"I ask that you not interrupt me. I have been respectful and courteous in allowing you to speak, and might I remind you that you're in the presence of a prince," I shot back, pulling back the ever-growing rage.

"Perhaps that means nothing to you, but I accepted this invitation with the impression that one might actually take part in a civil conversation. I have no constituency, seek to hold no office in the world of humans, and have no social media presence to appease. I am not here to boost ratings. I am here to be the representative for the fae in a debate about *fae*, but if the discussion continues to go in this direction, I will make my departure and let you argue with yourself." She shifted in her chair, discomfort and embarrassment streaking her cheeks red.

"Well, why should we have to abide by your laws? I'm not Elven, or fairy. Or whatever it is you like to call yourselves. Why should we respect your customs?" she shot back with a wave of confidence.

"We are not fairies. We are fae. And to call out your hypocrisy, humans live by constitutions that are outdated for their times. Are we not allowed to honor our ancestors with practices that should have never been banned in the first place? If you chose to learn and understand us, you would come to understand that no hardship ever comes to the partner. Through love and perseverance, the two share a bond. Maybe you're projecting because here, in the Human Realm, abductions always lead to trafficking, rape, murder, and perhaps even worse. If you were ever so lucky to be someone's fated mate, perhaps then you would *see* my world, through a new set of eyes."

With a toss of hair over her shoulders, an argument followed, only proving the fact that her only talking points were her false versions of the truth. No actual facts, solely opinions.

"We don't even know if you're hosting weapons of mass destruction. How are we supposed to feel confident and safe, when any of us could be snatched up from everything we know with your prehistoric mating rituals?"

"Why don't you tell me? Since you pride yourself on being the *expert* on all things Esterbrookian and fae. If by weapons of mass destruction, you mean magic? By all means, you're welcome to shadow under a mage and learn all the magic basics, but humans, you are not meant for these gifts. It is why every human who's ever attempted it, has met a regretful end. Any weapons forged by my brother's company were constructed for humans, purchased by humans, and have only been used for you to slaughter other humans. We have no weapons of mass destruction, *unless* you'd like to count good looks and charm."

"Nice try, but that doesn't work on me. I like my men *human*," she argued, using the rest of her precious time to reiterate her stance on the war on humans. Behind us, the monitors displayed footage of the overwhelming rise of anti-fae hate groups, including the one we had high on our radar.

Arcane.

"If you examine our history, we have always existed in your world. You didn't have anything to concern yourself with it then, and there's nothing to concern yourself with now. We, however, have suffered violence, have suffered prejudice, and the politicians who were aware of our world have worked *endlessly* with attempts to conquer our lands. We're not always going to see common ground, but my brother, my family, and my race are doing everything in our power to restore human trust. This symbiotic relationship we have, can not, and *will not* work until you all realize you need us, as much as we need you.

***

There was nothing about a stressful day that couldn't be solved with my cock buried deep inside a human female. I had worn that production assistant out, her pleas and cries still fresh in my mind. The real shocker was finding my sparring match opponent in my limo, begging for a chance with His Highness. She may have liked her men human, but she sure loved her cock big, hard and *Elven*. What could conclude a fighting match like that, then a little hate fuck and sweet degradation.

As I made it back to my hotel, something about the air had changed.

The sight, the taste, the colors, the textures. I took a deep breath, the heat of my blood sending my heart into a thundering stampede.

My eyes, these Dragon eyes, blinked in and out of consciousness, the aroma in the air leading to some unknown path. I took another deep breath, my thoughts in a blank daze, the compulsion pulling me deeper.

In an effort to find its source, I'd fought through every royal guard on the way up to my penthouse suite, stopping on floor after floor until the influence became more prominent.

It was like a drug, an impulsive need that coiled through my veins, directing me—NO, *forcing* me to respond to its cry.

I considered myself an Elf of discipline. Someone who had mastered the patience and willpower of a human Buddhist monk. So why did I find myself consumed with this goddess-forsaken curse?

There were two floors left, mine and the floor below it, my intuition guiding me to what was behind door number two. It was as if my animalistic instincts heightened, the inferno that fueled me, leading me straight to a double-door suite.

I considered trying the handle, but impatience got the best of me. Before I could stop myself, my foot went crashing into it, the door flying off the hinges to a pile on the floor in front of me.

It was a...*woman*. She stood over a corpse, her face hidden from me under a mask. It mattered not that she had likely just killed this man. My only concern was her siren's call that summoned my dragon.

"You're coming with me!" I snarled, not cautious at all about how crazed I likely sounded, reaching for her forearm. Her long svelte leg kicked out, drove into my midsection, and sent me back reeling. From her trench coat, she pulled out a pistol, rattling off three shots toward me in rapid order.

"You just *shot* me," I growled, ripping my shirt away to reveal what damage had been done. The advantage of having shifter blood was that man-made bullets had little to no effect on me. My brother had dominated the weapons industry. Do you think he'd designed something that would make it easiest to kill us? It would leave a mark for sure, but it hadn't pierced through my scale-strong skin.

I lunged at her, dodging with swiftness when she swung a well-concealed hand blade from the holster of her garter. She moved with an unmatched quickness, an attempt to back me in a corner, but with rivaled skill, I landed a kick to her midsection, the devastating blow sending her sprawling into the ground.

She staggered to stand, and in her moment of weakness, by the neck I lifted her off of her feet, my powerful grasp cruelly caressing her throat. As I got a glimpse of her stare, raw hurt glittered in her captivating dark eyes.

Her skin was a rich shade of dark satin, her hair pulled back into a long braid, reached her back in a never-ending curtain. I breathed her in and found myself lost in her seductive scent; her hold on me being my greatest distraction.

As a last resort, her manicured talons dug into my arms, and with whatever energy she had left, she kneed me in the groin, my lack of focus hurling me down, grunting.

Desperate, she pierced her stiletto heel deep into my shoulder, a sudden paralysis affecting my will to stand.

"What did you do to me?" I growled through gritted teeth. In a rush to the balcony with the help of a hook blade, my fated mate attempted to zip-line her way to the building across.

Struggling to walk, with my last attempt to secure my treasure, I mustered up enough strength to yank the cord, breaking her connection, and sending her crashing back into the lower floor window.

To which one, I couldn't be sure of.

I grabbed my shoulder blade to examine the injury, my sight flickering in and out with the help of a fast-acting sedation. I had to get up. I had to fight it, but the more energy I exerted, the faster I submitted to its slumbering effects.

Perhaps this was an ill-timed setback, but this was not the end.

In due course, I was going to make her...*mine*.

The End

Thanks so much for reading Owned! If you loved reading it as much as I loved writing it, by clicking <u>here</u> you can share your thoughts about the story!

Next up is Lianthore's story. Be sure to buy Book two of the Faeborne Brides, <u>Purchased</u>, A Rapunzel retelling.

Sign up for our mailing list to get updates on book three, which will be Zaos' story, <u>Captured</u>, a Beauty and the Beast retelling.

JOIN ME EVERYWHERE!

So many fears went into writing this book. I told myself who would want to read this? And honestly, the imposter syndrome was what caused me to delay the book twice! You never know what people are going to connect to, and while this was my first book to receive *hundreds* of preorders in its first few months, I'm still terrified to have it out in the world.

I'm a naturally sensitive person, and I'm not very social, so these characters have been my beacon of joy for *months*! I hit some lows no less than three times this year, and some days, I didn't even get out of bed. But these characters helped me get through a lot of the grief I was experiencing, losing so many great people in my life the past year.

That's why it would mean the world to me if you could spare just a few minutes writing a review. This is planned to be a six-book series featuring seven Elven brothers, who you've had the chance to meet in Owned.

KU reads, one-click buys, and reviews would help move this series forward. Every brother and Faeborne bride's book share themes that I hope resonates with everyone! Whether you feel invisible, unappreciated or even underrepresented, I want readers to find solace when they read my books. If you have time, you can do so by clicking this <u>link</u>.

Don't forget to join me on social media! If you haven't already, check out where to find me through this <u>link</u>. I would love to connect more with my readers! I'm also in the midst of starting a <u>Patreon</u>. I want to share *exclusive* deleted scenes, progress as I write, NSFW artwork and just my daily and weekly musings. I would love the support once I get started!

I also want to write extended, *extended* epilogues! You won't need them for the main story, but if you love the characters(which I know you will)you'll get the chance to see more of them!

PURCHASED, BOOK TWO IN THE FAEBORNE BRIDES SERIES

Kidnapped as a child and raised in the Tower, my entire life has been dedicated to becoming the deadliest, and most seductive assassin. In the words of my mistress, *What man could turn down such ravishing beauty?*

My skills come with a price--my freedom. Which my mistress promises to me if I complete one last job.

Seduce the Dragon Prince.

I've taken down powerful men before, but they all pale in comparison to the rumored last dragon. Lianthore Faeborne saw me coming a mile away and with wealth and privilege on his side, my mistress wanted a hefty price tag for him to walk away with me.

According to him, I'm his fated mate, but he doesn't even know that I'm still on the job. I'll pretend to be his fated mate if it'll get him to trust me. With my freedom on the line, I have no choice.

Yet, he's nothing like how I was trained to see him. Even I can't help but get lost in those blazing soft crimson eyes. Getting to know him is trouble; the deeper I fall for him, the harder it'll be to betray the man I love.

Purchased is a Rapunzel retelling and book two in the Faeborne Brides series. Each book focuses on a different brother(and a different retelling)as they come into power once they take a bride. If you like captive romances, forced marriages, arrogant Elven heroes, and feisty Black heroines who can tame any man, with a sprinkle of Dominance and submission, you've come to the right place!

These books should be read in order for full enjoyment as details from previous books are necessary for full comprehension.

Available Now!

CAPTURED, BOOK THREE IN THE FAEBORNE BRIDES SERIES

They call him the Viking...

For as long as I can remember, I've always been my father's greatest disappointment. A truth I've learned to live with but *refuse* to let it break me. I'm so desperate for his approval, I follow his every request, fulfill his every demand, hoping one day he'll value me for the dutiful daughter I've become.

So why am I paying for my father's sins, when he's forced to strike a deal with Zaos Faeborne, the third-born Elven prince of the now, openly famous royal family. Me in exchange for my father's deception. Something tells me, Zaos is used to not taking no for an answer and soon enough, I'm taken as his prisoner.

His sinister demeanor scares me, while his wild blue eyes haunt me enough to keep me up at night. As his fated mate, no matter how much I run, there's no escaping a Faeborne. But I don't even know if I want to...

Captured is a Beauty and the Beast retelling and book three in the Faeborne Brides series. Each book focuses on a different brother(and a different retelling)as they come into power once they take a bride. If you like captive romances, forced marriages, arrogant Elven heroes, and feisty Black heroines who can tame any man, with a sprinkle of Dominance and submission, you've come to the right place!

These books should be read in order for full enjoyment as details from previous books are necessary for full comprehension.

Available for preorder!

ACKNOWLEDGMENTS

To my dearest friend Violet, thanks so much for putting the idea in my head that elves are superior supernatural creatures. XD

Also, I want to thank EVERYONE who preordered this book and showed me love on social media! The support was overwhelming and massive! Who knew people would want to read this??? Every share, every like, every follow, and every review makes my heart warm with excitement to keep writing books like this! We authors are a reclusive bunch, but readers like you make me want to be more outgoing! All of your support means the world!

ABOUT THE AUTHOR

Siren Crow is a proud New Englander but her true calling is far off in another realm or a magical castle. She writes scorching fantasy and paranormal romance that's both darker and otherworldly. Alpha heroes is her specialty and the heroines that love them are her passion.

ALSO BY SIREN CROW

The Faeborne Brides series

These arrogant royals will have their human brides—whether the women are willing or not!

Owned (Available now!)

Purchased (Available now!)

Captured (Available for preorder!)

Claimed (Sign up to our newsletter to find out more!)

Ravished (Sign up to our newsletter to find out more!)

Redeemed (Sign up to our newsletter to find out more!)

Standalones:

Wander This World

Made in the USA
Middletown, DE
10 January 2026